WILD DOG

Serge Joncour

Translated by Jane Aitken & Polly Mackintosh

Gallic Books
London

A Gallic Book

First published in France as *Chien-Loup*
Copyright © Flammarion, 2018

English translation copyright © Gallic Books, 2020

First published in Great Britain in 2020 by Gallic Books,
59 Ebury Street, London, SW1W 0NZ

A CIP record for this book is available from the British Library
ISBN 9781910477793

Typeset in Fournier MT by Gallic Books

Printed in the UK by CPI (CR0 4YY)

2 4 6 8 10 9 7 5 3 1

WILD DOG

Serge Joncour

PART I

July 1914

No one in the village had ever heard sounds like that coming from the hills. Wild, desperate sounds. The first shrieks rang out around midnight, distant at first, but moving closer and closer. Even the old people could not identify the source of the noise. It was as though some frenzied ritual were taking place up there in the woods, a savage brawl that seemed to be making its way towards them. At first the villagers thought it must be foxes or lynxes fighting over captured prey. The feverish sounds of these small, rabid beasts making their kills often disturbed their nights. Or it could have been the distinctive howling of local wolves, which pitched their cries to make the pack sound more fearsome. Previous attempts to keep them at bay by scattering the ground with strychnine had been unsuccessful, so tonight villagers young and old were roused from their beds to bang spoons against their pots and pans in the night air, a tried and tested method of keeping wolves away.

At night, the woods were alive with hidden sounds and rustling movements. Under cover of darkness, animals reclaimed their territory, free from human interference. In the village it was often possible to make out the sounds of unseen beasts hunting, mating or fighting. The night belonged to them, and this night more than any other.

'It almost sounds like—'

'Be quiet!'

As the hellish chorus rounded the hill, the sound became more distinct and the villagers were able to make out barking – savage, broken barking that could not have been a wolf and was too loud to be dogs. Only deer could make that kind of noise. It must have been deer that were heard that evening, high on buckthorn berries or driven wild by fear of an unseen predator. But this was the first time their shrieks had torn through the countryside with such demonic fervour. It was no use rattling their crockery now. There was nothing to be done but remind their children that at night deer are even louder than dogs and their barks are lower, more guttural and more frightening. During the rut, the bucks' calls that seek to ward off their rivals seem also to reveal their own desperation. Something must have truly frightened them, however, to cause them all to cry in unison. No one in Orcières had ever heard so many of them at once. They seemed to be hurtling down towards the houses by the dozen. No one was scared of the deer, of course, but everyone felt troubled by the prospect of whatever it was that had caused them so much terror.

Panic spread quickly through the village that night, perhaps because for weeks now it had been haunted by a larger threat. Since the spring, the newspapers had been full of worrying headlines. This had already led some men to search in their cupboards for their *carnets militaires*, just in case they were needed. The silent fear that they would be called away from home circled ever closer around the sons and fathers of Orcières, as if they were a pack of frightened deer. Even in the furthest depths of the countryside, it was clear that the world was subject to the whims of a handful of royals most of whom were related to one another. Sovereigns pictured sailing or playing tennis in *L'Illustré National* were part of prodigious dynasties that linked the King of England to the Kaiser to the cousin of the Tsar and back again; these family ties were about to be torn apart in spectacular fashion. As the summer wore on, tensions rose. It was already unbearably hot, and fear cast a shadow over everything. Europe was a tinderbox; the armies stood waiting as the commanders squared up to one another, forming pacts, not through kinship but because they were preparing for the worst. Meanwhile, in the village, men and women would stay outside talking for as long as possible before going to bed, savouring the evening air as if this were their last chance to do so.

No one wanted a war here. In any case, war was surely an impossibility, especially in Orcières, hidden away at the furthest edge of the *causse* and several days' journey from the nearest border. But that Friday even the calmest of spirits were troubled. The villagers wondered what was lying in wait for them up there, what predator had sent those deer running down the hill in terrified droves. Every summer they were newly surprised by the piercing cries of fighting bucks locking antlers and circling their rivals, but the barking had usually stopped in the time it took to roll and smoke a cigarette. The terrible sound persisted this time, until everyone in the village felt swirls of fear coil around their hearts and linger on their lips, like the stale end of a cigarette.

No one knew it yet, but on this late July night they were poised on the brink of war. In the little hamlet tucked away amid the hills, it was unthinkable that in just a few hours the sound of alarm bells ringing across the countryside would bring the summer swiftly and abruptly to an end. In a few days' time, the war would start to devour their men by the trainload, and by its end, four terrible years later, it would have destroyed four empires and fifteen million lives. But in the early hours of this summer Saturday, what the villagers were most afraid of was the wave of terrified sound that descended on them from the hills. Groups of deer hurled themselves down into the valley in their dozens before disappearing westwards beneath the moon, which was hidden behind a shroud.

When, at last, it was quiet again, the villagers could hear the trudge of heavy footsteps coming from the woods. They were accompanied by the sound of clinking metal, indicating the approach of someone with an animal. The cloud had shifted and the moon was now shining brightly on the thickets surrounding the village, where something was moving through the undergrowth. Those with more active imaginations wondered if they might see a giant wolf emerging from the shadows, dragging a limp foot caught in a hunter's trap, or even the infamous Champawat Tiger. In fact, it was a hooded, monk-like figure that came into view, accompanied by a weary-looking mule, bowls clinking on the haversack on its back. The adults crossed themselves as the children crouched behind them in fear. No one here had ever seen a pilgrim pass through the village. Walkers heading south from the Auvergne had once crossed the woods on their way to Spain, but it had been a long time since anyone had come through the village to reach Santiago. The appearance of this harbinger of doom should have alerted them to the fact that this night marked the end of an era. That this was their last evening in the old world and that the new day would herald the beginning of four years of suffering. The sight of the wandering stranger should have helped them realise that tomorrow they would wake up to the dawn of a new age which would be rung in with madness, gunfire, fear and, above all, blood.

Spring 2017

The advert promised an oasis of tranquillity, a simple gîte tucked away in the hills. It was hard to make much out from the three available photos, but they seemed to confirm this description. Zooming out on the map, the house was a tiny dot in an ocean of green, surrounded by peaks and valleys in the heart of the Causses du Quercy Natural Regional Park. Lise was convinced she had found a peaceful hideaway. Others might have said the back of beyond. According to the blurb the simple house at the top of a hill had been built in the nineteenth century. The nearest neighbour was ten kilometres away, the nearest town a twenty-five-kilometre drive.

Lise had come across the advert whilst browsing the internet. Most people would have clicked away from the page after reading the description, but in many ways the house provided exactly what she was looking for: nature, sun and isolation.

And it really was isolated. Lise noted with interest that the gîte came with far fewer amenities than the other houses advertised on the website. It seemed to have none of the conveniences of a normal holiday home: no swimming pool, no air conditioning, not even a television. There was also no telephone, which meant no Wi-Fi.

That was what persuaded her that she had found the perfect place. For years she had longed to cut herself off from the world by spending three weeks with no internet or phone, and here was the perfect opportunity to go completely offline.

'Lise, can you imagine us going three weeks without the internet?'

'I could do it.'

'Well, I'm telling you now, I couldn't. Because of my job, I can't be offline.'

'It would be so good for us. And we'd be away from all the noise and pollution, and especially the radiation . . .'

'Lise, please don't start all that again.'

For several years now, Lise had claimed to suffer from the harmful effects of electromagnetic radiation from phones and Wi-Fi. This was the reason she wanted to get away from it all. More than anything she wanted to lead the healthiest existence she could, waking up with the sun and then watching it set in the evening, living in the moment, aiming to do nothing more than walk, meditate and breathe air that was free of noise, waves and particles. Further research online had revealed there was an organic supermarket in the nearest village. The rest could be picked from their surroundings; she could already see herself foraging for berries and roots in the garden. This was what she had been dreaming of: three weeks in the depths of nature, in the wild, cut off from everything.

'Look, Franck, you just don't get that many holiday homes that don't have Wi-Fi or a TV. It's lucky that I happened to come across this one, and it's free for all of August, too!'

'That's exactly what I'm worried about. Don't you think it's strange that no one has commented on the page or left a review? And what are we going to do with a hundred and twenty hectares of forest?'

'Nothing at all. That's the point.'

'Lise, it's not going to be very relaxing – no air conditioning, no TV . . . There probably isn't even a kettle or a toaster.'

'You can't go a few weeks without a kettle and a toaster?'

'No, I can't. I'm a modern man; in the morning I need my kettle and my toaster. And there's no pool! Where did you even find this site? Are you sure it's not dodgy?'

'Franck, you're just scared of it just being the two of us for three weeks, without our friends and their kids and their motorboats, not even neighbours to distract us.'

'If you're looking for rest and relaxation, why don't we go on a cruise, or trek through the desert? I get emails advertising those kinds of things all the time. Trust me, there's plenty of other places in the world you could find your peace and quiet.'

'Because your idea of relaxing is planes and trips, and big groups. Being surrounded by other people, following a schedule, having a plan – that's what you call a holiday?'

'Well, anyway, your website says you need a 4×4 to get to the place. Look, it says there, "4×4 recommended".'

'OK, so we'll rent one!'

'Lise, do you know how much it costs to rent one of those things?'

'Probably less than going on a cruise.'

The warnings about the track leading up to the house were unambiguous, and whilst Franck saw this as yet another reason not to take the house, for Lise it was further confirmation that she had found the perfect place. According to the description, the road leading up to the top of the hill was extremely steep and in poor condition, hence the need for a vehicle with four-wheel drive. To see for herself, Lise tried searching for it on Google Earth. There was no postcode, just the name of the local area, and she had to scroll over acres of emerald screen before she found the right place. This had to be the house; it seemed to be the only one for miles around. She could make out the track in question curving towards it. On-screen it was difficult to gauge how steep it was, a winding pale streak twisting away from the main road that stood out from its surroundings like a line of chalk on a blackboard. When they zoomed out they could see the house was surrounded by hills, trees and scrub, but no other houses. To the east of the house though, a flash of something sparkling caught their eye, a circle of light glittering in a dark patch of shadow. It could have been a ray of sunlight caught on camera or a reflective surface. Franck zoomed in further get a closer look, but all he could see was a white shape.

'What do you reckon?'

He was already feeling oppressed by the prospect of three weeks out in the sticks with nothing but trees and hills for company.

'I reckon there's something fishy about this website.'

'No, that bit of light over there – what do you think it is?'

'I don't know, Lise, probably a mirror or something. Or a pool of water.'

'There you go. You can swim in that then!'

'At least check if there's reception up there.'

'A reception?'

'Phone reception, Lise.'

August 1914

The bell at Orcières-le-Bas no longer chimed, but everyone in the village heard the alarm being raised across the countryside. The hellish toll of church bells frantically ringing tore through the sky from nearby Limogne and Villefranche. It would be some time before the village forgot that terrible sound. Every time the wind blew, people thought they could hear the desperate ringing that had plunged the country into terror on that sunny summer afternoon.

The portentous pilgrim and his mule had spent the night at the doctor's house. Of the thirty or so households in the village, this was the only one that had room for a guest. There were several reasons for this, one being the considerable size of their farmhouse, and another that Doctor Manouvrier and his wife, Joséphine, much to the surprise of the rest of the village, had no children. The pilgrim set off for Santiago with his mule the following day at dawn, unaware that he had woken up in a country at war. To avoid finding himself at the mercy of his fellow men, who might have proved less forgiving than God, the pilgrim would probably have had to turn back at some point. Or perhaps he fell down one of the many sinkholes in the region. No one ever found out what had become of the pilgrim and his mule, and they certainly never reappeared in the village; but everyone remembered that the day they walked into the village was the day that war broke out.

That first day of August was glorious. The harvest looked set to be exceptional and the crops were plentiful; the landscape glowed with rich colour. But, whether they were working in the fields under the sun, or resting in the shade of the walnut trees, everyone in the village felt the same sense of dread. Tucked away in the craggy hills of the *causse*, Orcières was thirty kilometres from the nearest police station, but, as in every other village in France, the sound of bells ringing and a poster hastily put up in the main square were enough to tip their world into a new kind of chaos.

> By decree of the President of the Republic, the mobilisation of the army and navy has now been ordered. All animals, vehicles and other necessary equipment required to support this effort will also be requisitioned.

Spring 2017

'Peace and quiet guaranteed.' Even the heading above the description on the website was depressing. Franck and Lise had never gone away together for more than ten days at a time. Their holidays were mostly spent by the sea, in houses rented with other friends, more often than not surrounded by plenty of other people. They had never chosen to take themselves off to somewhere so remote just the two of them.

'I don't think so. Sorry, Lise.'

'Look, Franck, I don't want to fight about this. After everything I've been through in the last two years, I'm not fighting about this. It's not a big deal. I'll go on my own.'

'It's you that I'm worried about, Lise. What happens if you don't like it after a couple of days? There's literally nothing there, it's in the middle of bloody nowhere. I looked it up on Google Maps and there's nothing nearby, not even a village. Just hills and trees.'

'That's exactly what I'm looking for.'

'Don't you think there's something a bit funny about the website? There's something about it that doesn't feel right.'

Franck had compared the page with a couple of other rental websites and found a few things that worried him. The house had clearly not been up on the website for long, as no one had left a comment or a review. Perhaps even more unusually, it was almost June and the gîte was still free for the whole of August.

'I think that's a good thing!'

For Lise, the fact that the house was still available when everything else was booked up was further proof that it was meant to be. They were meant to rent it. As for the lack of amenities, she had already come up with a plan. If there was no washing machine, she could already see herself washing their sheets in the river and hanging them outside to dry in the fresh air. There was nothing that could have put her off the house – more than anything she wanted to get back to nature, to practise meditation among the trees, to paint something other than city scenes and urban life, and to walk off the beaten track, safe in the knowledge she would not encounter another soul.

The person whose contact details were given on the advert seemed to take a long time to respond to emails, and when they did the messages gave little away. Twice Lise had dialled the 0065 number provided. The voice on the other end spoke neither French nor English, and when someone rang her back it was always at two or three o'clock in the morning and the caller never left a message. But the website was certified; it couldn't have been a scam. In any case, Lise had decided not to let any of this worry her. This would be her approach to life from now on: she would let her instincts guide her.

Franck was also gradually coming round to the idea. He told himself that at least if it went badly, he would be proved right. He wouldn't labour the point, he would simply say, 'You know, I said from the beginning we're not cut out for country living.' He wasn't worried; he knew it wouldn't end up being three weeks there. Work would give him an excuse to make regular trips back up to Paris, and he would have plenty of ways to limit his time there. Unlike Lise, he had no desire to cut himself off from civilisation and not see anybody.

'You know no one would come and visit us there, right?'

'So that's what you're really worried about! You don't think we'll be able to cope for three weeks on our own, just the two of us, do you?'

'No, Lise, I just think that . . . you don't know what it's like, living in the countryside.'

His own feelings aside, he reflected that for Lise this would be a chance to test her intuitions about her health and the new daily regime she was putting herself through. She wanted a month away from absolutely everything that was bad for her. Spending such a long time fearing for your partner's life takes a toll on a relationship. Even if at times you're not sure you still love each other, even if you often have arguments and swear that it's over, when one of you suddenly finds themselves waiting months for diagnoses and test results, then all that love that seemed to have faded is revived; all that love you've stopped showing each other comes back with renewed force. He had lost count of the number of times he had told himself during the six months of her treatment that if he lost Lise, he would lose everything. He didn't make sense without her. He had enormous respect for the courage she had shown all through her illness, for the way she accepted the doctors' appointments and treatments without doubting them, or without appearing to. He admired that in her – her ability to stay calm and relaxed. Since Lise had recovered, he had taken care of her. Without making it obvious, he looked after her, even though he knew that she was more resilient than he was. He understood how her cancer had affected her, her need to get close to nature, how furious she became each time she switched on her computer and discovered dozens of Wi-Fi connections available, how she disliked seeing everyone on their phones in the street, on the Métro or in cafés, because now she could physically feel the electromagnetic radiation. She felt irradiated by the waves from those millions of connections, phone calls and networks which were always there, passing through us, to say nothing of the hotspots and myriad communications on RER trains and in cafés. And on top of that were the warnings about pollution and air quality, the constant reminder that, in the city, even breathing was dangerous. She had grown to hate the scooters and the buses belching black fumes, the coaches which kept their engines running even when they were at a standstill, the lack of consideration that was at the root of everything.

She worried about the ever-increasing traffic or the daily revelations about the pesticides everywhere or the endocrine disruptors found in green beans . . . At least, at the gîte, there would be no farming nearby, no fields, just limestone plateaus.

She wasn't thinking of changing her way of life, but she was absolutely certain that her environment was toxic. It was like a daily assault, and, from what she understood about the gîte, whilst there she would be safe from pollution. She had emailed the owners with a question that probably surprised them. She asked if it was correct that there was no internet, and more importantly, no mobile signal at the house. They took three days to reply, 'No, sorry, no signal at the house,' fearing that was the wrong answer.

August 1914

When war was declared on Saturday, 1 August 1914, people expected human deaths. What they did not foresee was that alongside the tide of humanity sent to die there would also be millions of animals. In cities and in the countryside, horses were requisitioned even before troops had been gathered. Mobilisation posters that had mouldered for years in drawers in town halls were dusted off, pasted on walls and a date inserted in the box provided. Immediately, in response, husbands, fathers and sons filled entire trains taking them to kill those other husbands, fathers and sons who had been designated their enemies. Animals that had done nothing to cause war were caught up in the madness.

All over Europe, animals were enlisted for war. Hundreds of thousands of terrified horses were sent into battle, ridden by light cavalry or dragoons, carrying officers through the battlefields or towing all that was yet to be motorised. Oxen were yoked to cannons on impossible paths. It took three pairs to pull one wagon overloaded with munitions or kit, or heavy artillery weighing tons. They were exposed to the line of fire. All the docile, loyal animals man had domesticated now found themselves engaged in the fury of war and became targets for the enemy.

As soon as hostilities began, everyone was ordered to declare all their animals to the army recruiters. The prospect of war seemed to have unleashed madness. It was a madness that led to kennels and pounds being emptied in order to quickly train up dogs to sniff out mines or gas. Fearsome hounds and cuddly lapdogs alike suddenly found themselves in the heat of combat, detecting bombs. Sometimes they were loaded with explosives and a fuse and sent to blow themselves up in the enemy trenches. Just as the Romans threw flaming pigs at Hannibal's elephants, so, in 1914, men forced sheep onto minefields so that the mines exploded under hooves rather than feet.

Mankind, overnight it seemed, embraced barbarity, rage and death, that universal blight that affects all species. In the space of four years, generations of men were wiped out, along with millions of horses, oxen and mules, and as many dogs, pigeons and donkeys. And that's without counting all the game mown down in the insanity of gunfire, all the wild animals caught unawares by bombardment, all the deer and foxes slaughtered without even having the honour of being hunted, and the hares obliterated in scorched earth. Other animals were poached by shadowy figures desperate for something to eat.

Sheep, cows and goats were requisitioned from farms and dragged off to combat zones for meat. Every day trainloads of trembling animals were taken to the front to feed soldiers exhausted by fear and fighting. Thirty-five thousand cows a day had to be killed to keep the troops going. And even that was barely sufficient for the millions of hungry soldiers who were served soup, cold by the time it reached them, in which there was no sign of meat, only kidney beans, which were starchy but unsatisfying. The cows or sheep which had been sacrificed to assuage the hunger of the troops had been boiled in stock and broken down so much that they were almost useless.

Men who were fit and healthy had left for Gramat or Cahors to cram themselves onto trains for the front, but it was still necessary to get the harvest in before the weather worsened or the crops spoiled, so it had to be managed without them. According to the newspapers, in big cities men were proud to go and fight, so fired up by the idea of killing the Boches that they climbed onto the trains singing. But, in villages, men departed downcast and in tears. The women left behind also had to give up their horses and oxen, and even their mules and donkeys, if they were any use, because until factories were working at full capacity, the war effort needed horsepower. Their precious pigeons reared high up in the dovecotes were all recorded or set free; sometimes gendarmes killed them on their own initiative, for fear that they would be used to help the enemy.

The one thing in Orcières's favour was that it was hidden in the hills, and gendarmes did not normally go there. So the mayor, Fernand, hid the flocks that were grazing up on the summer pasture from the requisition committees. He hid two hundred sheep, keeping them safe, away from prying eyes, in the meadows beyond Mont d'Orcières. And he also, a week later, said nothing about the five lions and three tigers which arrived in his village, eight large wild beasts hidden away behind the yellow and red panels of Pinder's Circus wagons. Eight deadly dangerous animals, roaring and enraged.

August 2017

Franck and Lise had set off that morning. Their aim was to arrive mid-afternoon to pick up the keys at the agreed place and get to the gîte in time to explore the surroundings before nightfall. With a bit of luck, they might even be able to get back down to do some shopping, if they could find a town, and the shops didn't close too early. They were confident that at the height of summer there would be something open after seven o'clock.

Yet, from the very beginning, nothing had gone to plan, starting with the traffic jams on the way out of Paris. It was the first time they had had to leave in peak holiday traffic on a Saturday at the beginning of August, and they got caught up in the big rush. Then at lunchtime there was the endless wait at the service-station restaurant, followed by a problem starting the huge hired Audi 4×4, driven poorly by Franck. It was as complicated as it was cumbersome, but it was all they could find to rent.

After the motorway, there was a main road and then a series of small roads, at which point the satnav was so inaccurate it seemed they would never reach Orcières. Again and again, they would be nearly there, only to get further away once more. The directions the computer voice gave seemed to contradict one another. Franck began to doubt whether the place really existed. From the start he had had a nagging feeling that they were being taken for a ride. He had always thought there was something odd about the advert. The telephone number they had tried to call was in Asia – Singapore, to be precise – and even though it was possible that the owners lived there, there was still the strange fact that they only ever responded via email. Maybe the advert was a hoax, and they had been defrauded of their €1,400 deposit.

No expert in hire cars, Franck finally understood why he couldn't get to Orcières. The vehicle was so big that the rental company had put the satnav in camper-van mode for safety purposes, and because of this it only recommended the larger roads. The narrow or steep ones were never suggested, so they were just circling around their destination.

It was seven o'clock by the time they finally reached the village where they were supposed to be picking up the keys, Orcières-le-Bas. It was more a sparsely populated hamlet with tracks leading to a number of unsignposted farms. There was someone waiting to hand over the keys in one of these, though they could not tell which one, as no names or house numbers were visible at the entrances. It was still so hot – the dashboard read thirty-six degrees – that the shutters on the doors and windows were kept closed. Three times they knocked at doors without success. The fourth time, someone appeared.

'Sorry to disturb you, but do you know where Monsieur or Madame Dauclercq lives?'

The old woman replied coldly, 'The Dauclercqs are the last farm, at the end on the right.'

Franck saw in his rear-view mirror that she was eyeing them suspiciously, probably because of the size of the car and its imposing appearance. They finally found the right farm, La Combe.

This time, Franck drove the 4×4 straight into the yard. He noticed a figure at the back of a shed: this must be Madame Dauclercq. He hooted in a friendly manner, but instead of coming towards them, the elderly farmer headed towards the house. Franck and Lise got out of the car to follow her, but the woman had already come out again with a bunch of keys, holding them in front of her as if to get rid of them, clearly indicating that she had nothing to say to them. Even so, Lise tried asking some questions, to which the woman replied sharply.

'Is the house on the hill up there?'

'No, it's not that hill, it's the one six kilometres further away. At the hairpin bend you take the track on the left and go up.'

'Thank you. It's pretty here.'

'You think so? It's too dry.'

'And for shopping, do you have to go to the village at the bottom of the hill?'

'No, there's nothing there.'

'But there is a shop in the village, isn't there?'

'There isn't a village any more.'

Irritated, Franck shot back, 'Wait, there is a supermarket; I saw it on the internet.'

'If you want shops you have to go down to Limogne or Saint-Martin, but it's quite a drive.'

'Oh really? How far is it?'

'A good half-hour.'

'So not far.'

'Yes, it is far.'

As he was speaking, Franck noticed a surprisingly large kennel near the shed. The kennel must have been at least one and a half metres high, as if it housed some sort of enormous dog, but at the moment it was empty.

They were still standing in front of the woman, who was herself still standing on the doorstep. She had not asked them inside, much less offered them a drink. Franck felt that not only were they bothering her, they were also incurring her sharp disapproval. From this he concluded that the woman had no wish for the gîte to be rented. Quite clearly it wasn't hers and she was only looking after the keys, but deep down, for whatever reason, she didn't like the idea that it would be occupied.

'And where are the owners?'

'Madame Henderson has been in a retirement home for a long time.'

'Henderson? That wasn't the name on the advert.'

'That's their business.'

'It's not a local name?'

'No.'

'I see, and how old is she?'

'Not far off ninety-eight, maybe even a hundred.'

'But then who placed the advert?'

'Her daughter – she's in America or somewhere. That's why we have the keys. Otherwise do you think I'd bother with all this?'

'And Singapore, why is the telephone number for Singapore?'

'How should I know?'

'Sorry, Madame Dauclercq, I just want to make sure I understand. It is you that looks after the gîte?'

'We help out, that's all. My husband mows the fields, and believe me, you have to mow them every month at the moment, otherwise it would be a jungle up there, a jungle, I tell you. I hope you're not expecting a beautiful lawn. You'll see as you go up. Even when we cut it, it grows back straight away.'

Franck gestured to the barn and mischievously replied, 'But I imagine that works out well for you; all the grass you mow for them makes hay for you, right?'

'In a way . . . Let's just say it suits everybody.'

'And has anyone rented the gîte before us?'

'The girl used to come for a bit in the summer, but they live a long way away. And then with children it's impossible. I hope your children are older – or your grandchildren, I don't know . . .'

Lise and Franck never knew what to say in this situation. As if they were at fault for not having children, as if it weren't possible to not have children.

'We don't have children,' said Lise, as casually as possible.

The woman found this strange, as strange as the big black car that had thrown up so much dust when it came into the yard, dust that was still floating in the air.

'Then you'll be fine, but it's tough living up there; there's no telephone, no heating and no pressure in the taps. And I should warn you that there's a big open water tank behind the box trees, but you mustn't drink from it or you'll get cholera.'

'I hope you're joking . . .'

'I'm telling you because that's what everyone used to say. In any case, I wouldn't give that water to my goats.'

'Is it deep?'

'Of course, it's huge! It's only animals that drink there – it attracts them. You'll hear them at night, trust me, and sometimes they fall in. A drowning animal makes a lot of noise . . . Right, well, I have three rows of beans to pick, and I'm behind, what with the heat today . . .'

Lise answered with disconcerting good humour: 'But that's great! You know what, we'll do our shopping with you. Can we get some beans from you?'

The woman was not won over but was tempted by the offer, though she did her best to hide any satisfaction she might have felt. Her bad mood quickly returned, and she told them to come back tomorrow as the beans were yet to be picked. Lise, with an eagerness that was remarkable in the circumstances, asked if she had eggs by any chance. The farmer stared at the Parisian the way you might weigh up an enemy, as if asking, 'Who the hell are you?'

'We'll see tomorrow. I'll save you some, I promise.'

Franck didn't know what to say or do to make his exit. He watched Lise approach the woman to shake her hand. He admired Lise's natural warmth and profound empathy. Although he didn't really know what had kept their relationship going for the more than twenty years they had lived together, what was certain was that he envied her way of always seeing things in the best light and finding the good in the most dislikeable people. She would have found some humanity in even a murderer or a monster.

The Audi again threw up a thick dust as they left the yard. Franck surreptitiously examined the kennel. He could see it now in the rear-view mirror; it went back a long way, as if it were the opening of a passage to hell from where enormous animals emerged, huge dogs with rabid bites.

August 1914

At all significant moments in history there are freethinkers prepared to swim against the tide. The lion tamer was one of them. Wolfgang Hollzenmaier. That was the name written in gold lettering on the circus wagons. Years before the church bells had rung out, he had taken the decision to stay silent. Other than his interior monologue, he would speak only to give orders to his lions and tigers. He had worked with them for the past fifteen years in the biggest and best circuses in Europe and directed them with peremptory commands in German. Even though he was a performer, a lion tamer and German, the mobilisation applied to him too.

In the preceding few years, travelling shows had reached a peak of popularity. Circuses brought joy almost everywhere they set up their big tops, whether on the outskirts of a city or in a remote market town in the country. But the moment war broke out, travelling troupes were forced to disperse and cease performing, becoming bankrupt overnight. The artists and handlers mostly found themselves conscripted, like other civilians, and so did the clowns, jugglers and acrobats, who were pressed into service in the infantry.

Faced with this sudden catastrophe, the lion tamer had only one thought – to save his animals. He didn't want to abandon the big cats in their cages, but nor did he want to release them into the wild, leaving the world to cope with their possible cruelty, adding animal savagery to the chaos of war. He decided to ask the mayor for permission to hide up there on the rocky hill above Orcières. As well as his wild animals, which stayed well hidden, the lion tamer had a large dog of a kind that had never been seen in those parts before. It was a black and tan sheepdog; the mayor told everyone it was called a 'German shepherd'. People thought that the Germans mixing breeds to create dogs that were huge and haughty, muscular and ferocious-looking, was proof of their arrogance.

Animals were requisitioned from everywhere, including the circus. Horses and donkeys were taken first, but also elephants, which were used for earth-moving or to stand in for oxen sent to the front. In Lot-et-Garonne, where Wolfgang was when war was declared, the Pinder Circus's three elephants were recruited to work the fields the very next Tuesday. They were put into extra-long harnesses and replaced the beasts requisitioned by the military authorities.

After a few days there started to be food shortages. Over most of Europe people abandoned their principles and began to kill animals in zoos to ease their hunger. People ate buffaloes and sea lions, camels and llamas; in Prague two giraffes and some kangaroos were eaten. In a world where nothing made sense, news of these things travelled fast, partly because they were shocking, and partly because they provided some distraction.

As the murderous spree continued, some donated their own animals to the war effort. But in border areas when some people refused to slaughter their domestic pigeons, it was decreed that those who did not empty their dovecotes would be liable to the death penalty. A few weeks later, hundreds of huskies were taken from Alsace to the front, to provide support for the mountain infantrymen who were dealing with early snow in the Vosges. In this mad war, it seemed as if the entire animal kingdom were being called up – but there was no place for big cats. The lion tamer understood that the fascination his lions and tigers had always exerted over crowds was very likely to count against them now. They were no longer sought after for their astonishing beauty, but because they would make a very tasty meal.

*

It took only two days for the circus to break up. The big top, the circus ring, the clowns, jugglers, acrobats and horsemen all went, and Wolfgang found himself alone with his beasts. With no trailers or stage, what could he do with his big cats but hide them? He would have to conceal himself as well since he would be classified as a deserter, missing from action. He needed to hide quickly and it would have to be nearby, somewhere in the deserted plains of the *causse*. On the evening of the fifth of August, after two days of heading due east, he turned up in Orcières-le-Bas with his two wagons and two display cars hitched to four horses. He asked to see the mayor.

This was not the first time the lion tamer had been to Orcières-le-Bas. A month earlier, on the advice of the slaughterman, he had come with an empty wagon to collect the bodies of ten ewes that had died of fright during a storm that had roared down from the summit of Mont d'Orcières, the hill with the abandoned house. The lion tamer had immediately realised that no one wanted to set foot on the hill, believing it to be cursed. Now that he needed somewhere to hide, he remembered the unhappy crag and said to himself that it would be the perfect place for him and his lions and tigers.

There was no one to guide him up the impossibly steep track. And when he reached the house, he found it had no lock, only a hermetically sealed thick door. There were a few panes missing from the windows, but he would have the time to repair them. At least on that benighted hill, he would be protected from the rest of the world. It would be the perfect hiding place for the lions and tigers, because, although they feared nothing and had no predators, in this world of war their days were numbered. They could sense that things had changed. They had already noticed that it was harder for their master to feed them. Everything depended on the lion tamer being able to provide food, for if their master could no longer guarantee their sustenance, he would lose all authority over them. Then he would no longer be able to defend or protect his beasts and they would have no choice but to attack and eat him.

But up there, on the rocky summit, he would be able to re-establish the status quo. And more importantly, he would be forgotten; he would have the mountain all to himself, a mountain less sacred than Noah's and less noble, no doubt, but no less exposed to the extreme violence of the elements. He settled there with his animals. A Noah without a wife.

August 2017

The Audi was very powerful, but Franck was hesitant about starting up the hill. He got out of the car to have a look at the slope, wondering if the car would make it up a hillside that was almost vertical and full of potholes. There was no signpost, but this must be the turning. From the road, the track went off to the left just as the farmer had told him, an access road that was even steeper than a parking ramp, ravaged by rain, the ground cracked by the sun. He made sure he was in 4×4 mode. From below, the track looked like a tunnel formed of holm oak and box, dense masses on either side that joined at the top. He noticed rocks showing through in some places, so he would have to be careful not to swerve or stray from the track. That said, he was excited by the prospect of testing the motor; at least now he could unleash the three hundred horsepower that he had been holding back, making sure not to exceed the speed limit. They refastened their seat belts and took off as if they were on a fairground ride.

The ascent quickly proved challenging, especially as it was two kilometres long; two kilometres of stony, potholed track with a forty per cent incline. He struggled to rev the engine enough to pull the weight of the Audi whilst trying not to gain too much speed. The rocky ground gave way beneath the tyres; the car tilted so far at every turn that he feared it would roll over or spin off the side of the road. The sensors were beeping on all sides, the monitoring system going crazy, but still, rather than stopping, Franck kept his foot down, the stones spraying out from under the wheels like a hail of bullets. The track seemed to go on and on. Franck was becoming increasingly tense. He felt as if they had fallen into a trap, realising that there was no chance of turning back and that the higher they climbed, the deeper the ravine to his left became. He felt increasingly panicked by how high up they were, while Lise hung on tightly and told him to carry on, as if she were finding it exciting . . .

This went on for five minutes, five minutes of an arduous ascent, five minutes of driving a car that was far too big while listening to its bodywork screeching. The polished metal had been scratched by branches the whole way up, and in the last few metres the slope had become so steep that Lise and Franck had their backs pressed flat against their seats, as if they were in a plane taking off. Then they were driving through shady pines. They approached the summit through rows of tall conifers. Still pinned against their seats, they could see the sun above the tops of the hills and then, suddenly, they found that they were horizontal once more, as though they had finally landed. From the crest of the hill, the surroundings looked like another world.

The panorama that opened out in front of them left them awestruck. At the end of the shady track the landscape jumped out at them. They had a 360-degree view, bathed in evening sunshine. Even Franck was moved by it. The hill stood like an island in the middle of an ocean of green, and from the top, you could see out over swathes of identical hills that seemed to go on forever. They stayed in the car, gazing at the scenery in total amazement. They felt as if they had entered the highest layer of the stratosphere, rising above the everyday reality of the world. They still could not see the house. The track was bordered by a low drystone wall, and the gîte must be at the end of it. They would just have to keep following the crest above the exposed hillside.

But instead of driving on, they stayed where they were, recovering from their journey and absorbed in the view. The landscape was a wilderness of hills and woods that stretched into infinity. Looking eastwards, Franck imagined seeing the area from above like on

Google Earth; he imagined the *causses*, then the Massif Central, then stepping over the Rhone to the Alps, and Eurasia and the Ural Mountains beyond . . .

'It must be behind the trees over there.'

'What?'

'The house!'

Lise pointed to a grove of various types of tree surrounded by cypresses on their right. There was a eucalyptus in the centre, and next to it an oak tree that was probably a hundred years old. The house must be on the other side of this wooded sanctuary, which offered a solitary patch of shade on the bare hillside. Lise wanted to go for a walk to take in the view, drinking in the fresh air. It was the perfect place for her; she felt so lucky to be there, outside the world. Franck was speechless. He – who would have much preferred to meet friends in Corsica or on a boat, or to spend two weeks in a civilised seaside setting – was struck by the beauty of the place, then immediately overwhelmed by the feeling of absolute isolation emanating from it.

Yet the sun shining on the glossy emerald hills filled him with wonder. Some landscapes are like faces: as soon as you see them, you recognise them. Franck had gone on shoots all around the world for his job, but he had rarely had this feeling that the landscape was welcoming him. It was probably due to tiredness and the desire to rest. They had been on the road for a long time, and they were as exhausted as they were relieved to have made it up the hill after hours of driving in the summer heat. They still had to see the house and find out what it was like. He was expecting a nasty surprise, but at least they would still have this spellbinding view, even if he knew that, for him, the attraction would last no more than a couple of days.

Lise wanted him to take her hand. They had never been alone like this before, never lived in this kind of environment and never been lost in nature, just the two of them. Even when they went to the desert three years ago, they had never left the group, and apart from one night in a tent, they had gone back to the hotel every evening. This time their isolation was much more tangible.

As they marvelled at their surroundings, they became aware of a faint smell of rotting coming from the warm scrub. Franck frowned and looked around him, searching for a dead animal. Just before the grove of trees, he saw a large patch of box. Leaving Lise to her own thoughts, he walked up to the wall of green, and the bad smell got stronger as he approached. The belt of two-metre-high box trees was indeed hiding something: a perfectly rectangular water tank, like a swimming pool more than six metres long, made of very old cement that had turned black with time. He went closer. The sides were barely a metre high, but the basin looked deep, full of stagnant, murky water with green spots floating on the surface. The water level was low, or perhaps the water really was very deep. Franck's eyes struggled to adjust to the gloom. But when he looked closer, he could see the shadowy lake two metres below; thick, dark water covered in an array of tiny flora that had seized their opportunity. There was no dead animal though; the smell was perhaps coming from those rotting spots on the water.

Meanwhile, Lise was slowly turning her face to the sun, making the most of the panoramic scene. When she turned around again, awestruck, she could no longer see Franck and, for a moment, she had the terrible feeling that she had lost him and was utterly alone. She was overwhelmed by a horrible sensation of total distress and abandonment, coupled with infinite contentment. Alone.

August 1914

The lion tamer could make himself at home up there and stay as long as he wanted. The mayor had handed the area over to him. He was not even asked for rent or any other quid pro quo. Perhaps the mayor thought the village would benefit from the illusory protection of the wild animals. Ever since all the healthy men had left for the front the village had been fearful. Fernand had already hidden a flock of ewes in the hills, more than two hundred of them, so why not hide some lions and tigers as well? No one ever went up Mont d'Orcières any more. Certainly no one would have wanted to live in that house, because the land was cursed. Everyone left it well alone.

'If the Hun wants to live up there, let him get on with it,' people said, as you would say about an enemy advancing on a minefield. 'Let him settle in that sorry place; it's the devil's land. He won't last long and nor will his lions . . .'

Mont d'Orcières had once been covered in fertile, exuberant vineyards, but at the end of the nineteenth century they had been devastated by phylloxera, and carbon disulphide and coal tar had been poured over them. The people would have tried anything to eradicate the disease afflicting their glorious vines, and the chemicals had burnt deep into the layers of soil. But the yellow insects had still won. Here, as everywhere, phylloxera had wiped out the vines, proving that even tiny insects can change the face of the world. For the last thirty years the land on Mont d'Orcières had been considered cursed. Not only had it been poisoned with chemicals, but its shadow loomed over the village, contributing to the feeling that it was the harbinger of doom.

At the beginning, the phylloxera infestation had been like a war. A war many thought it would be easy to win. Even though the insects skipped across whole areas, jumping from one vine to another at the least breath of wind, people refused to view it as fatal. Yet even the most optimistic quickly understood that this was a war that had been lost at the outset, a war against a tiny little parasite a few millimetres long, which managed to destroy the vines across the whole of the country. The entire nation lost to the insects. Over the course of a few springs, all French vineyards were decimated by the greedy aphid, a minuscule creature that buried its eggs at the height of summer like mines that would explode the following spring in the form of docile nymphs, which in turn began to suck the sap from the vine stocks, drying them out and killing them from the bottom up.

There had been vines on Mont d'Orcières for two thousand years. The limestone plateau of Quercy was excellent wine country. In the Middle Ages, this was where black wine was produced for the tables of kings, and for export to England. Back then Bordeaux was merely where the wine from all along the Lot river ended up. But after the advent of the sap-sucking insects, and their treatment with naphthalene and carbon disulphide, the vines were reduced to rows of burnt stalks, aligned like fossilised soldiers or Pompeii gladiators.

Nothing would grow on Mont d'Orcières, not even new grafts, because the soil was too chalky. Around Bordeaux, on the other hand, the new grafts took quickly because the ground was soft and well irrigated by the Garonne river. The Orcières winegrower and his wife, exhausted by a succession of harvests ruined by chemicals, tore up what remained of the vines before setting fire to everything and hanging themselves from the big oak tree. They even threw the casks and the wine press into the flames, so that the conflagration took over the whole hillside, devouring the vegetation round about, including the juniper above the rocks. Everything was destroyed except for the house and the handful of trees which gave it shade.

By making a human chain and passing buckets of water up from the reservoir, the villagers had at least been able to save these.

As the land was damned anyway, the German might as well move in there with his big cats. He might survive but no one could prosper up there. Not even lions and tigers and their master. The mayor lent him the house and land for as long as he wanted. At least his being there on the roof of the world with his cages and carriages would mean that they had one strong, able-bodied man in case of emergency. As for the lions and tigers, no one was sure if they should be frightened of them or not. Everyone knew about the Champawat Tiger, shot by an English hunter; the newspapers had reported her killings constantly. In areas where wolves still prowled, the image of that Bengal tiger that had killed four hundred people in India had awakened ancient fears. Other than in newspapers and illustrated books, creatures like that did not exist for the people of the *causse*. They might also have seen pictures of them on circus wagons and posters, but no one wanted to see them in real life. And knowing they were up there was unsettling.

Down in the village, Mayor Fernand had been wise enough to invent a story that would persuade people to accept the German's presence. He told them that this saintly character's conscience had prevented him from joining up because he loved the French and refused to fire on them. He made it known that he was a pacifist, a rebel who refused to follow orders and spill blood. Couderc, the schoolmaster, backed the mayor up in this. They both wanted to reassure the thirty or so remaining inhabitants of the village, especially the women. In any case, even were the Pope or God himself to settle up there, Mont d'Orcières would still be cursed. The great overhanging rock, with its brutal cliff edge rising above the village, was like a frontier between earth and sky. It loomed. And was hated even more in the winter months. From November to April it blocked the sun in the morning, casting the village into shadow until the afternoon.

If that man succeeded in living on the deadly mountain, if he managed to survive on those lands after all that had happened there, it must be because he was the devil incarnate. After he arrived, the lions' roaring and deep terrifying growling carried down to the village on the evening winds, heart-stoppingly brutal, yet silken. The cattle and the few horses left in the village were unsettled by the sound. At each roar, the mayor's old nag or the doctor's unbroken horse whinnied as frantically as if the stables were on fire. The leonine cries frightened the dogs as well. They were so scared by the noise from on high that they did not even bark. The roaring rang out in the evening, but also in the morning, like a daily warning, sending shivers down the spines of the villagers.

Coming on top of missing the men, the crushing exhaustion from doing all the work, the increasing deprivations, and the terrible fear of hearing one fine morning of the death of a son or husband, the cries of the lions were hard to endure. A feeling of doom quickly took hold in the village. If the lion tamer did not sense the curse on the land, no doubt his animals did. Their instinct must have told them they were in a place they should flee, that they should not live there, and that was surely why you could hear them roaring from down below. No doubt the wild cats' only thought was to escape.

August 2017

Even if you listened carefully, you could hear nothing but birdsong and the hum of insects. There was not the faintest noise of any car or neighbour, not even a dog barking in the distance, or the sound of a far-off road or a plane, and not the slightest trace of human activity. It was complete happiness for Lise; for Franck, total anxiety. Once inside the house it was worse. He was oppressed by the silence of the thick walls, and felt literally cut off from the world, a feeling exaggerated by the damp coolness that is the fate of houses that have been shut up for a long time. He might as well have been in an underground cave, or even lost in space. The silence was even more complete inside than out: here, the quiet was troubling. Franck suddenly felt ill at ease, or at least out of his comfort zone, while Lise opened the doors and windows wide, cheerfully bringing life back to the dull interior.

On looking around they saw that the fridge was new. It was the only part of the furnishings on the ground floor that suggested the house was supposed to be rented. Everything else looked ancient, dating probably from the 1950s. Although perfectly clean, the gas cooker, wood-burning stove and bathroom looked as if they came from a second-hand shop or a film. Franck was immediately reminded of the palpable sense of unreality you get on a film set. It was something about the delicate round handle and old-fashioned bolt on the door and especially the section of sky-blue tiles surrounding the sink, a basin carved out of a single piece of stone of a sort that had not been made for centuries. As a producer, he instantly had the same feeling of anachronism that you experience when you visit a set recreating a bygone era, whether the nineteenth century or the 1950s. If the set designer has achieved their effect, you find yourself truly transported in time. As they explored the house, everything that unsettled Franck left Lise spellbound. It all delighted her. She seemed happy; for her it had all the elements of the dream package: quiet, nature, isolation. It was a good thing they were far away from everything.

With the shutters open, the house was bathed in evening light. There was something simple and unpretentious – or, in Franck's eyes, dubious – about the vivid colours of the furnishings, which glowed in the warm light. Looking at the blue shutters and bright-red curtains, he could not tell if the decor was intentional or simply the result of the place's history and successive owners. There was not much by way of equipment: a big table, four chairs, a gas cooker and a wood-burning stove. The basics were there, nothing more. The ground floor was made up of one large room, then a smaller room on the left, and a bathroom at the end. A wooden staircase led upstairs. They opened the shutters up there as well to reveal a huge bedroom, with four windows that looked out in all directions. Lise was delighted. Every time she pushed back the shutters in a room, she would rediscover the sea of hills outside, a view that enchanted her. She was comforted by the authenticity of the stone walls, the solid wood floor and the exposed beams.

Despite his discomfort, Franck was relieved. At least it wasn't a scam. At least they hadn't been taken for a ride. There was a house at the end of the advert. Lise, too, was relieved to find that her phone had no signal. She had been glancing at it ever since they set out on the track and had never had even a hint of signal, unlike on the road before the ascent. In the last few kilometres she had only had one bar, and eventually none; the little fan shape at the top of her screen was empty. But she was careful not to mention it to Franck. It seemed just as natural and wonderful to her as the sun going down in front of them, setting the slightest reflection in the bedroom alight:

every lamp, every window, every mirror or piece of glass sparkled. It felt as though the sun were paying them its respects, greeting the newcomers.

Once they had opened the doors and windows and explored the house, Franck had a sudden premonition. He quickly went downstairs to get his phone from the door of the car and, to his horror, found that it had no signal. Frantically, he started walking up and down to try to find a connection somewhere, holding the phone out in front of him as if it were a remote control that could turn the world on again. He even walked along the crest of the hill and criss-crossed the whole meadow at the top, and still could not get a signal. Wherever he tried, he couldn't even get one bar, and surely that was impossible. So, he set out down the big slope in front of him, hurtling down the beautiful meadow that rolled into a valley in the east, a good five hundred metres from the house. He crossed the whole hillside in his city shoes, catching his feet in the tall grass and going faster and faster.

Lise watched him from the window. She saw him rush down into the long sloping meadow, carried forward by momentum. It looked as if he were trying to walk slowly, but the slope was pulling him down. He kept his eyes on his phone without really looking where he was treading, as if trying to revive a small animal.

He turned around when he got to the foot of the hill, surprised that he had walked so far. The house seemed a long way away, or high up at least. At this time of day, the trough of the valley was in shadow, and it was almost chilly. Another hill covered with holm oaks and box rose up in front of him, a mound of dense, sloping woods that would be almost impossible to get into, unless you fought your way through the tangle of bushes and brambles.

Lise took in the valley from above, with Franck impatiently stamping his feet at the bottom. She looked in admiration at the slope in front of him. It was just as steep as the other one, but the thick vegetation and tightly packed trees made it look impenetrable. From the window, the green mass seemed to rise like a wave, especially with the sun beating down on its summit, lifting it up even further. Lise was in seventh heaven. She had what she wanted: all she could see were hills and trees, turning the house into an island in a bottomless ocean of green. She thought to herself that it must be crawling with animals; wild boar and wolves, foxes and deer. She knew nothing about the wildlife around here, but the idea crossed her mind and made her shiver a little.

Right at the bottom, Franck looked like a figurine. His pink polo shirt and city trousers showed just how out of place he was. She carried on watching him. He was walking all over the place, going left and right and staring at his phone the whole time. At one point he even went into the woods to see if he could get a signal.

'Well?' She had called out by way of encouragement, but he was too far away to hear. She watched him: absorbed in his problem, he was walking with his arms stretched out in front of him, like a diviner searching for water. She was happy to see this. Clearly there was no trace of an electromagnetic wave here, no Wi-Fi or hotspot, not even a telephone line. Nothing. Everything was as she had imagined, and it filled her with a deep joy. However, she knew it was not good news for Franck. Though he did not realise it, he was addicted, and she knew he would be furious – the man who was always on the internet, compulsively checking his emails and notifications, always waiting for news and lapping it up at the table and in bed, even while watching a film. In some ways, it was cruel to see him so disorientated. She knew Franck needed his phone for work and to keep in touch with his business partners. But she was still keen for him to try to live without it not so that he would give up the internet completely, but to gain a bit of perspective at least, and to find the peace he could no longer imagine. While she wanted to get away from harmful waves, she wanted Franck to stop worrying constantly about his job. Producers have no fixed hours, so the job takes over everything, and she wanted to see if he could manage to switch off. Sometimes a job takes up so much of your life that it consumes your very being, bringing its share of satisfaction but also constant stress. It was the first time she had seen him so destabilised, and the first time she had watched him from afar, standing out in the wild.

They had been inseparable for much of their adult lives – in their professional lives too. It is quite something to think that for twenty-five years your life has been bound up with the person you live with, to the point that you are almost fused together. Lise had been filming a lot when they first met, getting one role after another and often travelling to the USA. She had even helped him produce his first feature film out of her own pocket. Franck had only produced short films before meeting Lise, small things that won awards at festivals but made no money. His first two feature films were flops, and again Lise had saved his skin and stopped him from going broke. Maybe that's what being a couple means: needing someone absolutely and relying on them, knowing that depending on the circumstances, one of the couple will need to be doing well when the other isn't, otherwise the relationship would not be balanced.

She knew better than anyone what an ordeal it was to produce a film; she had a huge amount of respect for the work producers did, having to put on a show of strength and reassure others while deep down they were terrified of losing everything. Without her, Franck might not have succeeded in building the career he now had. Had they not met, he might still have been producing short films or adverts, or maybe he would have opened the restaurant he had talked about at the time, the kind of back-up plan you cling to when things aren't going well. Over the years, Lise and Franck's roles had balanced each other. For ten years they had both succeeded in their own careers. They had never worked together but they had always loved and supported one another, until Lise could no longer find roles at her level, and then she lost the desire to act. Acting is a profession that leaves little room for you to be yourself, and once she had reached forty, Lise had no longer wanted to be somebody else, to play a character more or like her, to appear in front of a camera that captured the slightest wrinkle or lack of sparkle. She could no longer stand the feeling of having that eye focused on her, observing everything. Because screen acting always comes back to lying about your age: you play thirty-year-olds at forty, forty-year-olds at fifty, and you lie more and more desperately. Having played one character after another, she no longer knew who she really was, or what she liked, or what kind of life she wanted. What she was really searching for was authenticity, calm and peace. That's why Lise felt completely at home here before she had even seen the whole house or explored its surroundings. At least here she had everything she wanted, for three weeks minimum.

Down at the bottom of the valley, Franck had not lost heart. She was reminded of a man struggling to keep up with the times. Over the past few months, she had realised that he was worried. He was uncomfortable with the direction cinema was taking, the trend for young people to watch films on increasingly small screens. She had known for a year now that he felt that he was making old-fashioned cinema. Things were also going badly with his two new partners, two men in their thirties who didn't talk about film, but about content, and dreamed of one thing only: a co-production with Netflix.

Franck was a stubborn man. He had vanished from her field of vision ten minutes ago. She thought how ironic it would be if he spent his three weeks here just searching for somewhere to get a signal. She walked out onto the perfect little south-facing balcony and decided that this was where she would set up her easel in the morning. When she had started painting again two years ago, she had promised herself that she would have her first exhibition next year, whether she had a gallery or not, and there was no lack of inspiration here. From this viewpoint overlooking the hill, she decided she would do her hour of meditation among the reeds and box beside the water tank as soon as the sun came up. She would relax in the shade of the big lime tree. In the evenings she would paint under the great oak tree. Everywhere she looked, she was happy; everything was full of the promise of activity. Franck finally came back into view. He appeared from the undergrowth at the very bottom of the hill and began to climb back up to the house, no longer looking at his phone. She called out to him again.

'Well?'

He replied with a weary gesture. The slope was clearly steep. It was strange to see Franck in this environment, with his polo shirt and trousers that he had obviously just torn in the brambles. The grass was taller than it looked, and he had to lift his knees up to get through it, as if he was wading through water. He did not look like a man who could cope with this, especially not in his calfskin moccasins. He was out of breath and soaked in sweat.

It was then that Franck heard insects buzzing around him and the frantic chirping of cicadas in the distance, as well as a pounding in his temples. In fact, it was not as silent as all that here. And then his phone rang – at least, he thought he heard it. He hurriedly took it out of his pocket, pulling it out as if it was burning. But nothing, not even one missed call. It was a phantom ring, a kind of mirage. They say this happens to people who are truly addicted. After an hour, he was already getting hallucinations. Lise understood what was happening, and how much it would bother him. The hill was an island where they would be completely alone, isolated, and she had a strong feeling that they could be happy here, making the most of the wholesome ambiance. They could be happy here . . . Or it might be hell.

August 1914

The first problem of the war was the fact that it had started at the height of summer. The sun had ripened the ears of wheat throughout spring, and the crop seemed as promising as ever, but the call-up had started just as they planned to start harvesting. The fields were bursting with grain and there was no one to harvest it. The nation's bounty was in danger of dying unreaped. Millions of francs would simply evaporate from the fields, and across the country there would no grain for bread.

The day after war was declared, the President solemnly called upon the nation's women to stand in for the men so that the harvest could begin. Even though the women would have stepped in anyway, notices were printed and the village police sent to drum up support. The President went as far as to plead with his female citizens in the newspapers:

> Arise, women of France, arise children, arise sons and daughters of the homeland! Take your place in the fields to replace those on the battlefields ... Prepare to show them on their return cultivated land, gathered-in harvests and fields sown with new crops! Arise! To action! To work! Tomorrow there will be glory for all. Long live the Republic! Long live France!

In Orcières-le-Bas, as soon as the husbands, fathers and sons departed, the women took over. As the men were heading in trains to the eastern front where killing was the only way to avoid dying, the women turned the other way, towards life. The men were moved from position to position, mere pawns on the great chessboard of death, while the women kept things alive. On 4 August they started to harvest, cutting and threshing the wheat and then bringing in the straw. They had to pull the ploughs themselves. Before the war, three horses or two oxen had been harnessed to a plough but now they had to make do with a single old ox or nag that could barely shift the plough, so that the women had to use all their force to engage the ploughshare. Because the tools were designed for men, they were always too high or too heavy. As soon as the ploughshare snagged on a stone, the handles of the plough would catch the women in the chest and the earth in the furrows would hit them as if rejecting them. Some women, who had no oxen, hitched themselves to the ploughs like beasts of burden. Working the land was a hundred times harder for the women than it had been for the men, but still they harvested, they threshed, they ploughed and spread the straw out to dry, and on top of that they had to feed the children and look after the old people. Each woman put their own wishes to one side in a world stalked by death. They took it all on. They often worked for fifteen hours straight, did the washing, cooked, sowed and got no sleep. In that village nothing daunted the women. Except the sound of the lions growling and the fear that one day they would meet them face to face.

As weeks passed, the idea of the German and his wild beasts living above them became more and more intolerable. After a month they were very scared, a normal reaction to having lions so close. In the early days of the war, the newspapers reported that the Germans were not to be feared. They fired soft bullets which barely passed through clothing. If *La Dépêche* were to be believed, the Germans were so weak that the French soldiers could defeat them just by marching at them; the Germans would crumple like old sticks. It was the mayor who received the daily newspaper. Because he had a club foot, he was the only one with the time to read. Sometimes people wondered if he rewrote the copy on the orders of the *préfet*.

Whether the Germans could be defeated or not, the war went on and on. It lasted far longer than the fortnight promised at the beginning. After three weeks of combat, people talked of a torrent of gunfire, a hail of bullets, of German machine guns the equivalent of a hundred rifles, an image that terrified the villagers, as if each German soldier had a hundred rifles in his hands . . . The women began to realise that the men would not be coming back soon, and that in addition to taking care of this harvest, they would have to plan for the next one, and prepare for winter.

The sergeants had been right to draft in all the farmers. They knew that the strong countrymen would make formidable infantry battalions. But that left the women – the young wives and mothers and girls – to tend to all the rest of life, the animals, the children, the old people, the worn-out donkeys, the poultry, the rabbits and the meadows. In a world intent on destruction, all life was as fragile as a flickering candle. It was up to the females to be strong. One day, should the war ever end, they would be asked to receive back and console the men.

In Orcières, there was not a single able-bodied man except for the German. And the German, with his army of barbaric roaring lions and tigers, was, like all his compatriots, essentially an enemy. What was even more worrying was that the women did not know how to use the hunting rifles stored at the top of cupboards, and did not even want to touch them. Now that they were in charge, it was up to them to ward off fear and to avert danger.

But the roars of the lions and tigers shattered their evenings. The barbaric noise which burst out like a storm was becoming too much to bear. In the black of night, the growls bore down like another sky on top of them. Some believed they could hear in the noise the pleas of their men, refusing to die. Others saw it as a nightly reminder of the months of anguish and cries to come. The lions and tigers were roaring in hunger, the terrible hunger of enormous beasts weighing two hundred and fifty kilos, an insane hunger. The villagers wondered how the lion tamer would ever be able to satisfy their appetites.

August 2017

He was already bleeding. Franck had gone back down the hill. He wanted to climb the hill opposite this time but was battling with the brambles that stopped him from either going any further or turning back. When he had arrived back at the house, he had changed and immediately wanted to go up into the woods, convinced that he would find a signal there. However, the plants on the slope were prickly and dense, making it impossible to get anywhere. What's more, his decision to wear shorts was proving disastrous, as the holly bushes and brambles tore at his legs, wrapping themselves around him as if trying to ensnare him. He could no longer go back down, nor could he carry on going up. After eight hours on the road, he no longer had the energy to fight, especially not for a tiny bit of signal.

Life is a constant logistical balancing act, and Franck knew that better than anyone. The role of a producer comes down to this – constantly finding solutions, calming fears, meeting demands, settling day-to-day problems and invoices, managing the whims and mistakes of others, being a father figure to directors as well as to actors. To be a producer you must always be strong, or else pretend to be, but he had no desire for this kind of trial in the first few hours of his holiday.

He would never be able to spend an evening without internet access. On shoots in remote areas, crews were willing to make all sorts of concessions – they were prepared to go for weeks without seeing their children, even if they had joint custody, to go without a bistro or casino, comfort or running water, but no actor or technician would ever agree to stay somewhere without a signal. Never.

Anything but that! He groaned out loud, with nothing and nobody to hear him. He was on the verge of crying out. He thought to himself that gone were the days of *Fitzcarraldo* and its boat, lost in the jungle. That was the image that came to him as he found himself trapped in brambles that wound their long stems around him. *Fitzcarraldo*, a film that was emblematic of the madness you need to direct one. He looked at the unassailable slope in front of him, thinking it would be better to abandon it. Then, twenty metres ahead, in the middle of the tangle of leaves and bushy branches, he thought he could see a shape moving, a brown creature running towards the right. He had too much sweat in his eyes to see properly. Yet he heard a sound, the sound of an animal slipping through the bushes, moving away. He did not like this place.

Lise carried on exploring the house. She was getting to know it. The more she explored, the more surprised she was by how perfectly it matched her expectations. She tried out the chairs one by one and tested the unexpectedly new bed. The mattress still had a label on it and the base still had its plastic protector. Obviously nobody had ever slept in it. As for the house, that was no doubt another story. Lise thought about what it must have been originally, wondering who had lived there, and more importantly, who had decided to build it there. It was a strange idea to build a house somewhere so out of the way, and on top of a hill as well.

From above she saw Franck coming out of the woods, looking defeated. He was convinced he had imagined the creature, or else it was a frightened deer or wild boar; the wild scrubland must be full of them.

Lise watched from the window. Franck seemed completely different after an hour here, not just because of his torn polo shirt and messy hair, but also because he looked like a frail adventurer. He had clearly not lost hope of a miracle, that he might suddenly find a signal next to a rock or hill that would bring him back to life. A hundred and fifty years ago when building the house, some sort of water diviner had probably searched in the same way as Franck. Before erecting a house so far away from any river, you had to make sure there was an adequate water supply. Incidentally, where did the water come from today, and was there any in the taps? Lise thought back to the water tank the farmer had told them about. Suddenly she was seized by doubt. She went downstairs to the ground floor and hurried to the kitchen to turn on the tap. Nothing. Lise had forgotten this feeling of total distress, of not having a drop of water when you turned on the tap. Anxiously, she leant under the sink to see where the copper pipe was coming from. She followed it as it ran behind the furniture, then disappeared under the flooring, probably to emerge outside on the other side of the wall. But outside all she could see was a bulky trapdoor. She struggled to lift it as it was covered with a heavy stone, and there she discovered a clump of compressed straw, a dense and putrid mass. With great disgust, she pulled out the blockage of ancient compacted straw that concealed a secret hiding place. She feared she would come across a dead animal or a snake, but at the bottom there was a tap, lying forgotten in the shadows. She turned it with force and heard the magical sound of the water splashing on the stone sink. The other tap a few metres away was running fast; when she went back into the room it was spattering everywhere, but at least it was working. She approached the source of the gushing water and sprayed herself with it, like a nomad in the middle of the desert.

She turned the tap off again and silence reigned once more in the cool room. There are some places that make us uneasy as soon as we set foot in them, and there are others that welcome us, that take us in, as if they have been expecting us.

She touched the walls. Some parts were unplastered and you could see the stone. The thick walls guaranteed coolness, and despite the overpowering heat outside, inside it was a pleasant temperature. It was a place where time stood still. Life went on as it had done in bygone centuries; people were self-sufficient, working on the land, looking after orchards, cattle or goodness knows what else. It was then that she made the connection with the two patterns carved in stone she had noticed on arrival. When she was trying to find the right key, she had spotted two motifs engraved in the wall on either side of the door. Although they had rubbed away you could make out the outline of vine leaves with two bunches of grapes on one side, and a barrel on the other side, suggesting that the house had originally had something to do with wine.

Franck was now climbing back up towards the house, bitter and worn out. Lise watched him from the shade inside, while he was in full sunlight. Two-thirds of the way up the slope he put his hands on his hips, still cluthcing the lifeless phone. The signal bars had completely disappeared. He had even got blood on it, blood that had already dried. But he had to be contactable. He couldn't tell Lise everything. He was reluctant to open up about his recent disputes, but going into partnership with two colleagues twenty-five years his junior was no joke, particularly given that the pair had made their money not in film-making but in video games. Franck was wary of them, of their way of questioning everything, and especially of the meeting they had planned with Netflix in the next few days. Liem and Travis had been worrying him for three months, but he didn't want to admit it, for fear of looking like an old fool. That was why he had to be contactable, to stop them from doing something stupid.

Lise saw him arrive in the doorway, out of breath as if he had been running for hours.

Completely distraught, he said with the little breath he had left: 'Lise, it's awful, there's nothing . . . There's nothing!'

'What do you mean, there's nothing?'

'I don't understand, there's no signal anywhere; I can't even get one bar. Can you believe it, not even one bar?'

'Have you seen how out of breath you are?'

'For goodness' sake, Lise, it's all uphill here. Or rather it's up and down, and on the other side there are brambles and creatures everywhere. This really is the back of beyond.'

Seeing Franck in such a state, Lise was keen not to make things worse. He was still holding his phone in his hand like a poor bleeding animal.

'Did you hurt yourself?'

'It's nothing. But, shit, it's crazy; we're up high and there's no reception anywhere. It's madness!'

Lise came closer and looked at his legs, which were covered in scratches.

'We should think about buying some surgical spirit and dressings, just in case.'

'We're not in the darkest depths of the jungle.'

'But, look, after an hour you're already covered in blood!'

Lise led him to the tap. She could feel that he was hot and seeing the grazes on his legs reminded her of what she had read in the paper about the dangers of ticks and Lyme disease, but she kept quiet for fear that he would panic, city dweller that he was.

'Lise, you don't seem to realise, this is serious.'

'But you can still do lots of things with your phone: take photos, check the time, and you can use it as a torch.'

'Listen to me, Lise. I will not spend three weeks in this godforsaken place; I really can't afford to, I can't!'

Lise burst into hysterical laughter at that.

'It's not funny, for God's sake! It's not funny. I need my phone . . . Believe me, I cannot have a single day without being contactable.'

'Even on holiday?'

'Especially on holiday . . . You obviously don't understand what I'm going through.'

'Did you get the easel out of the car?'

'You're really going to start painting now?'

'No, but it's reassuring to know it's there. A bit like you with your phone.'

'The difference is that my phone is for work.'

Lise let him have the pleasure of this little dig. She left him to calm down, assuring him that he would be bound to find a signal by going towards the cliff, or the other way, towards the west. It crossed her mind to tell him to climb the enormous oak tree that stood a few metres from the house. She kept this to herself, but it put a smile on her face that he could not understand.

For now, the most important thing was that they settle in and take their time to unpack their bags. Once again, Franck noticed his wife's composure; her natural way of doing things slowly, never letting things get to her. For as long as they had been together, she had always reassured him. In a long-term relationship, there are many opportunities to discover the other person's true colours, to challenge them or draw inspiration from them. Franck deeply admired his wife, not least because she always kept her cool and never gave in to panic. And even though she had gone through lots of struggles and disappointments, in his eyes she was still the calmest and most serene person in the universe.

They started getting things out of the car. They had brought bed-linen and enough clothes to last them three weeks. In this heat they would not be wearing much. The problem of dinner soon arose. It was too late to go back down to wherever it was to go shopping; everything would be closed.

'Tell me, are those really hazel trees down there?' Lise asked playfully.

'I don't know, Lise. I don't know anything. You think I'm looking at the trees?'

'You should. Because if they are hazel trees, there might be hazelnuts, or blackberries, and mushrooms. Have you looked to see if there are any?'

'Seriously, Lise, you really want to eat mushrooms with hazelnuts?'

Lise made no reply. Instead, she unpacked two big bags, containing crisps, three packets of warm salad, as well as a bottle of wine and an assortment of drinks she had bought at the service station just in case.

Franck felt lost. In these new surroundings, he was unsure what to do or where to put himself. He followed Lise's instructions to get this or that bag out of the boot, to take this or that upstairs. She was on top of the situation. He watched her; she seemed cool and relaxed, while he had scratches all over his body and was soaked in sweat, with blood on his arms and legs. He listened to her obediently. In the bedroom he gave her a hand making the bed.

'This mattress is brand new. That's odd, don't you think?'

'The important thing is that there is a bed.'

Franck plugged in his charger near the bedside table, but that was not working either. He began to complain, until Lise told him to go and turn the electricity on to calm him down. Franck went downstairs and looked everywhere to find the meter. It was behind a curtain; he set it to 'ON' and the radio immediately started up in the bathroom, an old FM radio playing a Bob Marley song that sounded out of place, but at least he had got something from this house. Disturbed by the sudden burst of noise, he went to the bathroom to switch it off. It was an old black Telefunken with a knob and a big aerial, the same type of radio he had had as a teenager.

Lise wiped down the ancient table outside and they took out the chairs. There was no garden furniture apart from the table. A meadow of wild jagged grass stretched away for two hundred metres, ending in a row of trees and bushes on the edge of a sharp drop down into the valley, above the access road. The sun was going down on the other side of the faraway hills facing them. The track they had come from must be below, hidden by rocks and trees. The remains of the old village should be at the bottom of this hill, the village that Franck had read no longer existed. Only a few ruins were left.

They ate in the extraordinary silence. The birdsong gradually quietened down, merging into the evening calm. A woodpecker tapped away in the trees. There were no other sounds, save the buzzing of insects – late bees or weary flies. Lise already seemed at ease, to have become part of the scenery. Franck was disorientated, on the verge of panic, of leaving, of not being there, of taking refuge in the car, the huge great SUV that was clean and plush, without any insects . . . He wasn't feeling good, but he said nothing. Lise could sense it. He knew she could sense it, but they didn't talk about it. Biting into a crisp made a disproportionately loud noise in the silence, a crunch so loud that Franck feared you could hear it all the way down in the valley.

'I think I could live here.'

Franck made no reply. In that sentence he might merely have heard a city dweller's idealised notions of country living. But he could also hear the disenchantment of an actress who has abandoned all ambition, who has no desire to ever make another film.

The sun sank beyond the hill opposite, setting the woods ablaze with a colour that spread across the entire sky, a sky of velvety red. Lise freshened up in the shower. Then she turned on the old radio on the bathroom shelf. You could turn the knob through the entire FM dial but there was only one frequency, a station that played just music, with no adverts, news or talking. Lise turned the volume down to its lowest setting, thinking this would reassure Franck. When she went outside again, she came up behind him barefoot, and asked simply, 'Feeling better?' He jumped. It was dark now. A sliver of moon illuminated the mysterious outdoors. Inside, near the sink, Lise spotted a switch that must control the bulb outside, and luckily she was proved right. Franck inhaled. Seeing more clearly reassured him. Only, now that they were standing inside a pool of yellow light in which everything was visible, everything else was plunged into darkness and made even more disturbing, a sort of shadow that was infinite and completely impenetrable. Franck went upstairs to get the headlamp from his toiletry bag. He put it on and went back downstairs, the beam of light shining from his forehead.

'Turn that off, Franck. Enjoy the silence, the fresh air. Breathe.'

Eventually their eyes adjusted and they could make out some shape. They could even see the row of trees on the cliff edge. Lise was sitting next to Franck, and he could not help turning his headlamp back on. The twenty-watt LED lamp cast a narrow beam that shone far into the distance; it swept the bottom of the valley, awakening thousands of white moths, some of which threw themselves into the lamp. With the beam pointing downwards, something came into view in the ravine. There was no need to confer; each knew the other had seen it. It had revealed itself to them both at once. On the edge of the woods, they could very clearly see two yellow glimmers, about two hundred metres away, two pupils that reflected the light, two narrow phosphorescent eyes, not too close to the ground. An animal was plainly standing there, watching them.

'What's that?'

Lise feigned a lack of interest, replying that it must be a deer, a doe, maybe even a fox or a cat; there were enough animals around here.

'You have no idea what it is, do you?'

'No, Franck, I don't. But I think it's pretty.'

There was a wide space between the two slanting pupils, giving the animal an intense look. The two fluorescent eyes seemed to be fixed on the house, unmoving, unblinking. Whether the beast was hostile or friendly, it was staring right at them.

'Maybe it's a wolf . . .'

'Are you serious?'

'I'm sure the woods are full of wild animals, I read it on the internet.'

'Don't talk nonsense, Lise.'

'Don't worry. All that matters is that it's pretty, don't you think?'

'Well, maybe. Yes, maybe.'

The dogs were lost without their masters. They couldn't understand why the men were absent for so long. For fear of them wandering the streets and catching rabies, people tied their dogs up most of the time and did not let them stray far from their houses. No more long hikes for them, no more days spent outside following the men across the fields or into the woods hunting. In Orcières, dogs were never allowed inside houses; on the contrary, they usually kept well away. But now they crept timidly towards the door. It was obvious from the way they looked inside that they did not understand why the men never came out any more. They couldn't even smell them now. And it was the same with the deserted stables when they looked there. With the oxen gone to the front and the sheep still up in the summer pasture because no one dared bring them down, the dogs felt as if part of their world had vanished without explanation or consolation. Instead of the words of their masters there was the howling of the big cats. Each time the lions and tigers growled up above, the dogs lowered their heads, afraid. They were so frightened by the noise that they no longer dared look up at the hill.

Since the lion tamer had moved up there, everything had felt wrong. It was he who had brought the storms. Before the arrival of the German and his big cats, the sky had never trembled under the weight of such terrifying clouds, there had never been such crazy storms of hailstones the size of ice cubes. And no one could remember such squalls of rain. From the middle of September onwards thick, heavy rain fell for hours at a time, then suddenly stopped. The clouds vanished to be replaced by sun and clear skies. But the next day the thermometer would go wild and the barometer plummet again. The beginning of summer had seen luminous, cloudless skies, but now they were unrecognisable, violent and roiling, flinging down treacherous hail, leading people to make dire predictions that the weather was broken, that winter would be freezing, that wolves would come out and that the war would never end.

'It's the bombs that are destroying everything. Apparently they're bombing each other all day and all night long. Swarms of bombs, thousands of them, ripping through the sky and throwing the stars off course. Nothing will ever be the same again.'

There were no bombs to be heard in Orcières, only lions and storms. The other explanation for the strange weather was provided by La Bûche. La Bûche was the old blacksmith, a bit deaf from years of pounding metal and a bit addled by too much alcohol. He thought that all the storms were caused by the large metal cages the German had set up for his wild animals. There were three of them, it was said, and one of them was enormous, fifteen metres wide, and taller than the trees. La Bûche claimed that it was the steel that acted like a magnet on the stars . . . And people believed him. Since the lion tamer had brought all those metal bars on his huge wagon and assembled them on top of the mountain, the weather had changed. Some days it was hotter than Africa, but in the space of half an hour it had clouded over and begun to rain freezing stair rods. It wasn't normal rain; it was more like stones thrown down by an icy firmament. Before the Hun, Orcières had never experienced so much anger and water. Down below, children cursed the sky, shaking their fists at the rocky overhang, and old people were too superstitious even to glance at the peak. After the torrential rains the soil was so eroded that silt flowed into the river and land turned to sludge. Ground that was already depleted, because there was no one to work it, now slid from the fields and gardens all the way to the houses.

What made it harder to accept was that it had taken centuries to fertilise the soil here. Entire lives had been spent picking stones out of the ground, stones that had then been used to build walls between plots of land. Chalky soil had become arable land through the villagers' ancestors' toil. Before the vines died, precious Malbec from the area had made up fifty per cent of the Bordeaux market. It had been a rich region but now, again, the land was being ruined, this time by the rains; it was running away, just as the men had been stolen away. Now everything and everyone was deserting the village.

In an effort to quash some of the villagers' more outlandish theories, Mayor Fernand and Couderc, the schoolmaster, reminded everyone that the previous winter, 1913, had been severe too. Long before the arrival of the lion tamer, people had been making dire predictions, swearing that the weather had gone mad. From January to March 1914, conditions had been appalling. Snowstorms had gone on until May. To refresh villagers' memories, the mayor got out last year's newspapers (having kept them to use as kindling), showing photos of tornadoes twisting the Roussillon vines. Almost all those newly replanted vines had been torn from the ground. In *L'Illustré National* he found the very image of the Promenade des Anglais in Nice that had made such an impression. It showed the storm-hit promenade and the shoreline littered with wrecked boats. The Baie des Anges, which they would never see, was on the front pages, battered by the elements, as if after a flood or a hurricane. Couderc reminded everyone that in the winter of 1913 all people could talk about was trains trapped in snow and the route between Marseille and Bordeaux being blocked for days. From November until spring came, the weather dominated the newspapers. Even in Lot and Tarn there hadn't been such cold weather since the time of Napoleon III. This proved that the problematic weather was nothing at all to do with the German.

People tend to forget past catastrophes just as they fail to see new ones developing. Some women, when they saw those photos of frozen fountains and springs, told themselves that the harsh winter of the previous year had been a premonition of things to come. The icy beaches and vines bent under the weight of snow had not lied; they were foreshadowing a tragedy – proof that pessimists are always right. From now on, it would be wise to heed the old people, those who said that the roaring of the wild cats boded ill, and was causing the storms. It was time to listen and to take steps before the mayhem spilled over onto the villagers down below. They were living with a sword of Damocles hanging over them and the fear of it falling was a harder burden to bear than if it had actually dropped.

August 2017

Franck couldn't sleep. At two in the morning he got out of bed and went to stand by the window, oppressed by the darkness outside and the complete absence of any points of reference. As his eyes adjusted, he noticed the outline of the hills in the distance, a faint distinction between sky and land. Apart from that, he could see nothing and no one; there was no light, whichever way he looked. He went out of the house in just his shorts and walked a little. Everything was quiet. And yet he was not calm, for there was a constant hum: a crunch in the distance that he took to be the sound of footsteps, or maybe the rustle of leaves; strange hooting; the brush of wings; it never ended. Every time he turned on his headlamp to point it at the area in question, a swarm of insects flew into his face; tiny moths darted at him from below. He even swallowed one or two of them. But when he turned the light off, he felt anxious again. In the darkness he could sense the presence of thousands of beings around him; he felt he was at the centre of a troubling world, populated only by insects, animals and creatures lurking in the shadows. When night fell, this planet belonged to them, a planet of millions of invisible beings where humans had no place. He had a strong sense that he was not accepted by the wildlife that surrounded him.

At three in the morning he went back to the room. He wanted to turn on the bedside lamp that Lise had dimmed with a scarf and turned off when she went to bed, but didn't dare, for fear of waking her. The room was plunged in darkness, just like the house, like the nearest trees, immersed in shadow like the whole universe. A little earlier, at around midnight, the sliver of moon had still cast some of its light on the landscape so you could see the trees, the hills, the car and the little shed that must once have stored tools. But the moon had since disappeared to the west, and thousands of stars were twinkling in the sky without casting any light below. He remembered that while researching the holiday online, he had come across an expression that he immediately disliked: 'the Black Triangle of Quercy', an area of total darkness with no light pollution at all. He was right in the middle of it.

It was ten past three. His phone was now only good for telling the time and for shining a light in the room. He still didn't want to go to bed. The idea of sleeping with the windows and shutters open filled him with terror. He could feel the presence of the darkness like an ink that would seep into everything. But it was too hot; you had to open everything to get even the slightest draught. He went out onto the little balcony beyond the French windows and felt the silence of thousands of hectares cut off from the world. Then the hum started up again, even louder. He kept watch. In addition to the heat, mosquitoes were buzzing all around him; when one of them came close to his ear he slapped himself and killed it. He went back into the room, taking care not to make the wooden floor creak. He sat in the old armchair so as not to wake Lise. He wanted her to sleep; it reassured him that she was sleeping. Her breathing was slow and peaceful. When she used to travel constantly for shoots and promotional tours, she had got into the habit of wearing an eye mask and earplugs. She was in a deep sleep, completely untroubled by anything. Franck could see her at the other end of the room, in the big bed. How come she wasn't even bothered by the mosquitoes? He shone the light of his smartphone on her; she had pulled the sheet over her face, so the mosquitoes didn't stand a chance. She had fallen asleep like that, happy in the simple setting. All evening Franck had watched her getting on with things. He couldn't believe she was so comfortable in this rural set-up; she seemed to be in her element, though she had never lived in the countryside before.

It was 3.32 a.m. It felt as if they were floating on the dark lake of the ground floor. The downstairs doors were also open to let in the air. Above them was the attic, from where faint creaking sounds came. When they were going to bed, Lise had told him it was the heat making the beams contract, or else a barn owl – indicating that she knew what a barn owl was and wasn't scared of them. Where did she get her composure from? She had fallen asleep to that, swallowed up by the silence of the stars. Before going to bed she had gone for a long walk around the water tank without a light, not even from her phone. It had only been a few hours and she had already stopped automatically reaching for her phone. He picked his up again and turned off airplane mode to see if by any chance there was a signal at night. He stared at the rectangle of light. Then he heard noises outside, noticeably louder than any before.

He got up to look out of the window, gazing in the direction where they had seen the yellow eyes earlier, eyes too far apart to belong to a cat. He couldn't see anything, and yet the noises continued, sounding like footsteps muffled by the grass, heavy footsteps, coming from the very bottom of the valley. Franck refused to be frightened. He was not going to spend three weeks here; he would never be able to stand it for that long; he was not interested in this type of holiday. Tomorrow morning, he would find a town where there were people and shops to buy the papers and, more importantly, a bistro where he could sit and connect to the Wi-Fi . . . That was all he wanted: to find somewhere civilised. Perhaps he would even make up an excuse to go back to Paris, unless a genuine reason forced him to return anyway. Liem and Travis had not taken holiday; they would be sleeping peacefully in an air-conditioned room in Paris, with no creaking or other noises. He was the only one panicking in the darkness in the middle of nowhere. Standing there on high alert, surrounded by strange noises and scared stiff, mirrored what was going on in his professional life. He was a producer whose last two films had been flops; TV networks and banks no longer trusted him, and vultures were circling around him – ambitious young men ready to swoop and buy up his film library, knowing very well that he needed the money . . .

Now there were not merely noises, but actual movements below, countless heavy footsteps thudding in all directions. He didn't turn on his headlamp for fear of showing he was there, but it was clear that all kinds of night creatures were moving around. It had to be animals and not humans, large animals pawing the ground or scratching at the earth. He thought about waking Lise so she could hear it. It was an impressive sound, of wild animals emerging from the woods to fight or gather together. He already knew that when he told her about this tomorrow, she would not believe him. But if he woke her up right now, she might panic and then they would both be frightened, and that would be worse.

He could wait for it to pass, proving himself to be a coward. Or, of course, he could go and see up close. He didn't want to stay here feeling cowardly, the way he had felt when facing Liem and Travis, on the day they had made the killer remark that still made him wince. It was one of those things people say in the heat of the moment, but it had hit home. So he dwelled on what they had said; three months later it still felt like a poison arrow that would never stop spreading its venom, and every time he thought back to that moment he wanted to kill them . . . Especially as he hadn't responded at the time. He had been so shocked that he had not been able to think of a comeback. But he had since imagined a thousand things he could have said, and it drove him crazy thinking about it.

The noises were frenzied now, but more disturbing was a shape just below, a dark mass skirting the walls of the house, some large creature or person crawling on all fours. He went downstairs, annoyed that fear was getting the better of him, that ghosts were trying to unhinge him. As he crossed the kitchen, he had the presence of mind or the dubious impulse to go over to the drawer by the sink, feeling around for a knife, the biggest possible. Strangely, having a knife in his hand did not calm him for long. Grabbing hold of a blade in anticipation of danger creates the illusion of safety only momentarily, because the blade very quickly becomes a nuisance, the thick handle is hard to hold and it means you can't use that hand for anything else. Going out with a knife in your hand is oddly not reassuring. Quite the opposite, it adds to your fear rather than alleviating it.

September 1914

On 3 August 1882 the local Parlement passed a law declaring war on wolves. They were all to be destroyed. Thirty years later, Mayor Fernand still had the bounty dockets in his drawer and was ready to pay one hundred francs to anyone who killed a she-wolf and half that amount for a male or wolf cubs. The bounty hunting had calmed people's terror of wolves in the countryside, but anything could set it off again. Fernand knew his citizens, and he saw that the wild cats were stirring up old fears, reviving memories of rabid wolves that not so long ago had attacked women and children. And although the packs of wolves had supposedly moved on to the Cézallier plateau, towards Cantal, the lions were right there, just a hundred and twenty metres above the village.

Thinking it would calm nerves, the mayor put the big circus poster up on the municipal notice board, so that everyone would get used to seeing the lion tamer all the time, rather than fearing him unseen. There the German was, on the wall of the mairie like a Roman gladiator, a Spartacus armed with a sword and a whip, a Spartacus surrounded by lions and tigers, some trampling on snakes, others standing on giant stools, their mouths wide open and paws raised, lions and tigers ready to eat everything . . . But the most arresting part of the poster was his name written in gold on a red background, Wolfgang Hollzenmaier. That name was truly terrifying. That name, fanned out in large golden letters, was worse than a threat or a declaration of war. It was impossible to pronounce but should anyone try they would risk provoking a storm . . . People turned away as they passed the poster.

Only Joséphine did not tremble at the sight. It reminded her of the evening in Villeneuve in June when she had gone to the circus with her husband, Dr Manouvrier, and seen the gladiator surrounded by lions. She thought he looked fragile, vulnerable in the midst of his massive creatures. She could not persuade herself that he was just a performer executing his act to perfection. No, she saw a man in mortal danger, surrounded by beasts capable of piercing him with one of their claws. Watching this man dicing with death, she had been overwhelmed with feelings, closing her eyes and squeezing her husband's hand, the same husband who was now at the front and from whom she had had no news for more than a month . . . The poster reawakened her emotions, and troubled her.

After three days, Fernand was forced to remove the poster and put it in the barn near his house. As people's anxieties had not diminished, should they denounce the German and his wild animals? *La Dépêche* was full of stories of the fate of Germans who found themselves in France on the outbreak of war. Unable to reach their homeland, they were trapped – 'like rats', people said. And the lion tamer, in spite of his lions and tigers, was one of them; he, too, was trapped like a rat. The Germans and Austro-Hungarians who were in France on 3 August 1914 were men and women who overnight ceased to be foreigners and became enemies. And there were thousands of them spread across the country, placed on house arrest if they were lucky, or beaten up, if they were not. As all the trains had been requisitioned, they could not travel back east. Whether in France to take the waters or sell their wares, to travel or toil, whether they were there for work or there for love, all were stuck there. And if any of them had tried to force their way onto a train carrying soldiers, they would not have survived.

Seeing the hatred foreigners inspired, the police had been forced to take radical action to protect German citizens, even going as far as to house them in police stations or in prison. Overnight, all sorts of stories sprang up about these parasite Huns. One of the most popular told of an elegant German woman in a hat who distributed poisoned fruit jellies to the children. In Lot, newspapers alarmed the population with tales of the 'sweetie lady', who was said to drive around the Figeac area, ready to strike. A German woman, especially in a car, could not be mistaken. So it must be true. At the end of August a child died in Lugagnac. No one knew what he died of, but he had been found on a road, with no visible injuries, and no trace of wolves. There were hundreds of stories like that, proof that Germans were not there by chance, but to sabotage France. So it would be better to denounce the lion tamer to the police. After all, it was the metal cages that attracted lightning and brought storms to the village. To keep that devil above them was to expose them all to terrible dangers.

But they could not bring themselves to denounce him. Partly because he had just bought ten goats and ten ewes from them. They had brought them down from the summer pasture for him and it had been a real godsend to be able to sell them in secret and at a good price. As Fernand said, soon the government would claim more livestock to feed the soldiers, and they would have no choice but to honour the requisition. And the state did not pay in notes, it paid in Treasury bills, which would never be redeemed. At least if the lion tamer stayed, they would be able to sell him animals for food for his wild cats. They had calculated that on the basis of five kilos of meat a day per animal, in two weeks' time the lion tamer would need ten more ewes and ten more goats, and so it would go on.

What was more, the German had given the mayor two horses he no longer needed and was unable to feed, two useful mounts which were not recorded in the army registers. Those horses did not need to be hidden away to avoid requisition. The women had agreed to give them to the Dauclercqs of La Brasse farm, two old women who had very long parcels of land with tobacco plants and three immense fields that ran along the river, but no one to help with tending them.

The other reason for not denouncing the German was that no one wanted to have anything to do with the gendarmes. It was the gendarmes who had come to requisition the men of the village, and perhaps one day they would be back to distribute death notices.

Jean, the retired village policeman, added the clinching argument. According to him, denouncing the German would risk something worse than a storm. It would amount to declaring war on a bunch of wild animals. Old Jean was known to be a purveyor of old wives' tales and was always peddling myths. Yet people believed him. Born in 1850, he had never been to war, but he had received twenty bounties for killing wolves. Old Jean had learnt in childhood how to put crushed glass and aconite into stinking rotting carcasses. He had not waited for the new law to start liberating the area from the wolves that ate the animals and the young shepherds as well.

'It's war that gives wolves the appetite for men . . . Beginning with the Hundred Years' War, then the Wars of Religion and the Napoleonic Wars. It's wars that give wolves the taste for human flesh; as soon as there's a war they know the men aren't there and they prey on the weak left behind. When there's war, they attack, and here we are at war again!'

'But what do wolves have to do with the lion tamer?'

'He talks to them! Animals do what he tells them to do. Believe me, it's far better to have that devil up there on our side than to cause problems for him.'

'You're just saying that because you want to sell him your goats!'

'So what? So do you, but I warn you, picking a fight with a man who can make lions and tigers sit will bring nothing but bad luck.'

In Orcières, superstition reigned supreme and life was governed by popular belief. It was bad luck if you got out of bed on the wrong side, bad luck if you put the bread crossways on the table, bad luck if you broke a glass or saw a black cat or if two knives crossed. And in the evening, it was bad luck if a bird came into your house, if you knocked the salt over or swept after sundown . . . Even when the men had still been there, work in the fields was equally regulated by superstition. For a good harvest you had to burn leaves in the bonfire on St John's Eve, sow seed by the full moon, ring the bells during a storm and not give clover to the cows if there wasn't an 'r' in the day of the week. In this climate it was easy for old Jean to create new superstitions about the lion tamer. The women tried to navigate through all the old sayings, knowing that the more you listened to them, the more pervasive they became until eventually they stopped you doing anything at all.

Fernand and Couderc tried to set the villagers' minds at ease by organising a meeting in the big old farm at the bottom of the village. Everyone had their say. All had tales of grandparents or great-grandparents bitten by rabid wolves, innocents who foamed so badly at the mouth that the parish priest could not even give them extreme unction. The Dauclercqs' cowherd had been eaten by a wolf in the time of Napoleon III, a boy of fourteen of whom only his head and part of his arm were found. His death had made a profound impression on the villagers, not least because the province of Gévaudan, where a man-eating beast had once roamed, was just the other side of the hills; the Lot ran through it. No one wanted to see a return to those days.

'If we turn on him, who's to say he won't set the lions on us? Who's to say he won't round up all the wild animals and get them to attack us? There are hundreds of wild dogs, lynxes, boar and wolves in the hills round here . . .'

August 2017

Franck drew on his anger, the anger of someone who is worn out and feels threatened by everything. Fear can drive you crazy. He had walked a long way from the house and was now standing at the top of the hill, clutching the knife in his hand and ready for a fight; with whom, he did not know. The noises were getting louder and louder, coming from the valley below. He walked towards the sloping meadow, but each step was painful without shoes. The dry grass stabbed the soles of his feet, every little twig and wisp cutting into him. It was like treading on thousands of tiny knives, and it got worse and worse as the slope steepened. He couldn't go any further. It was three hundred metres from here to the hill opposite. Shining a light would have been no use; it would only show the enemy he was there. It infuriated him that he couldn't keep going, if only to scare off the terrible shadowy creatures that panted and pawed the ground. Edgy from tiredness, travelling and sleeplessness, he imagined himself hurtling down and destroying them all.

He had only been renting the house for a few hours, but it felt a bit like it was his. The simple fact that he was staying there had already made it his land, his territory. This was his home, and the commotion below outraged him, particularly as he couldn't understand it. He felt like a fool with the long meat knife in one hand, his phone in the other, and was getting ready to turn back when he saw a black shape about ten metres away from him. He could make out the silhouette of a tall animal keeping watch; it could be a dog – a big dog – or a wolf. He froze at the sight of this beast, which seemed to have come out of nowhere, not to mention the fact that the animal must have seen him long before he had noticed it, might have been following him for hours. And yet the animal did not move, engrossed in the sight and smell of the spectacle below. Franck searched its gaze. When you come face to face with a large dog, the only way to work out its intentions is to read them in its eyes. But in the middle of the dark night, they were like two fluorescent dots, two startling little beacons. Could dogs see in the dark? Yes, probably. The animal had that advantage over him.

Franck felt totally powerless. And the knife, could the dog smell that too? Would it think it was part of him? All Franck knew was that the animal was staring at the foot of the hill; it too had come to watch the night-time scene, but, unlike Franck, it knew what was going on. The most surprising thing was that the dog wasn't bothered by him being there. It hadn't barked or growled. In fact, the dog was his only ally. Despite himself Franck clicked his tongue to establish contact. The dog responded straight away by coming closer, suddenly panting heavily as if it had been holding its breath. Franck watched the huge mass approach. The dog sniffed his calves, and then the knife. Franck immediately dropped it, horrified by the idea that the animal might think it was aimed at it. The dog sniffed vaguely at the knife on the ground. Then it lifted its head and looked over towards the hill. Franck lowered himself to the dog's level; kneeling down, his head was at the same height as the dog's. He wanted to see its expression, and sensed that it wouldn't bite or attack him.

'Who are you, eh? What are you up to over here?'

The dog took no notice of his words. It was still fascinated by the racket going on below. Franck stroked the back of the powerful animal, as if to get the measure of it, or to reassure it. It was a kind of wolf dog; its coat was long, both soft and coarse, and it was thick; the dog had an air of arrogance, the majestic indifference of those who know that they answer to nobody. The animal didn't respond to his touch or show even the slightest sign of recognition. Feeling the need to hold the knife again, Franck slowly picked it up and rose to his feet. The dog took this as a warning. It positioned itself in front of Franck, standing up tall. Franck shone the light from his phone on the dog and its eyes became even more luminescent. He recognised them from earlier in the evening; these were the eyes that had been spying on them from the undergrowth. The dog stared at him as if it was expecting something, straining its neck as if hoping for an instruction. Franck understood this instinctively.

'Tell me, dog, what is it over there, what is it?'

The dog started to yap and move around. It stopped itself from barking by letting out short little yelps, throaty whines that betrayed its nervousness, while squirming in front of Franck as if it were coming to take orders from him.

In a commanding tone that surprised even himself, Franck shouted: 'Go fetch! Go fetch!'

And then the dog froze. It shot Franck an eager look, and he wondered if it was going to jump at his throat and devour him, but instead the dog turned and bolted off with startling urgency. It threw itself headlong into the descent like a galloping horse. Franck couldn't believe it. At the bottom the dog began to bark, barks that rang out in a night that had been suddenly turned upside down. Franck heard stones slipping and rolling underneath the paws of overexcited animals, as if they were fighting one another or the dog; or maybe the dog was trying to eat them all, or indeed the opposite.

Then the commotion became quite different, as if all the animals were dispersing. At one point it became obvious that the dog had something; it wasn't barking any more but growling and howling, as if it were hurt or attacking its prey, a limb, a piece of flesh. The noise was appalling. Franck realised he had been stupid to set the dog off, but why had it listened to him? He looked towards the house to see if Lise had woken up, if she was watching this unfold from the window, but she was obviously still asleep. The dog must have let go or lost its grip; he could hear it barking again. It was on the move, but further away this time. Franck knew it was climbing back up the hill opposite, running through the woods behind a frenzied pack of animals that crushed branches and bushes as they went. The dog was howling loudly and sharply now, as if it wanted to prove that it was pursuing its prey, chasing after it, or even hunting it down to bring back. Franck felt bad for having told the dog to 'go fetch'; perhaps it would really carry out his order.

Barking rose from the hill opposite, becoming further and further away, and it carried on like this for a good five minutes. Then the noise became even more distant, just like the stampede of panicked animals, which had fled to the other side of the infernal hill. It was calm once more, completely quiet. Franck didn't really know what he had just done. In hindsight, he was scared. The shock of coming face to face with a dog in the dark, a dog that was a good metre tall, had left him drained.

He stayed outside looking at the dark contours of the hills for a while and then walked back towards the house and went upstairs. He realised the big knife was no longer in his hand. He must have left it in the grass. He didn't know any more; he didn't understand anything but lacked the energy to go downstairs again. Now he wanted to sleep. He was exhausted. It wasn't as hot in the room any more. He lay down on the big bed and did what Lise had done, pulling the sheet over his head and burrowing underneath it. Every now and then he thought he could hear barking, but very far away. Perhaps the dog would chase the animals all night. Franck listened carefully and then let himself fall back onto the pillow, picturing forests opening up in the darkness in front of him. At last, he could feel the effect of the hundred and twenty hectares of land and the thousands more all around, sensing that he was at the very heart of their endless silence. The windows were still open, but there was no longer any noise from outside. He dozed off in the new-found peace. It was a revelation to feel the bedroom becoming one with the wide-open space, the two merging in the ether. It was just as unsettling and soothing as falling asleep under the stars.

PART II

September 1914

Gendarmes never came to Orcières so when they turned up that Saturday, everyone assumed they had come about the German. But no, they had come to look for two young men from nearby farms who had not joined their regiments. Both were apparently eligible soldiers who should have presented themselves at Cénevières station but hadn't shown up. For good reason in the case of Joseph Chartier – he had died two years ago. All that remained of him was his old parents and a military record in a drawer. As for the other one, the Cabréracs' son, from La Touche farm, he had disappeared the day of the church bells. He was in trouble because during his military service the year before in Aurillac, he had been arrested along with all those who refused to do the famous 'extra year' introduced by the Briand law. They believed, like Jaurès, that the State had no right to steal three years of a man's life. Now, having escaped the call-up, in the eyes of the authorities, he was the thief. He was stealing his liberty, and that made him a criminal.

Gendarmes were part of the military. Why didn't they go to the front themselves instead of chasing conscripts? They should be fighting rather than court-martialling men who could ill afford to leave their land. The arrival of the blue-uniformed gendarmes always signalled trouble. They brought the orders from Paris like the one on 2 August instructing the husbands, sons and fathers to leave. No one slept that night, knowing that the next day the men must depart for war, and there was no knowing when or if they would ever return. It was inhuman. And so they were not about to give the gendarmes the gift of revealing the Boche in their midst.

They did, however, send Le Piqueur up to tell him to clear off. Old Lucien was a well-built man of seventy-five and they called him Le Piqueur because, in his younger days, he had been an expert hunter, flushing out prey with his dogs. And it was as a hunter that he went up one morning to tell the German to make himself scarce. Mont d'Orcières was no place for lions and tigers, nor for metal cages and bare rocks that attracted lightning. Since they had been there, the looming hill, which had always made the villagers fearful, was now driving them mad. In spite of his age and his gammy leg, Le Piqueur climbed the track with his dog, Atlas. Part Pyrenean Shepherd, part Beauceron, Atlas was large and imposing and capable of keeping a bull at bay. Le Piqueur didn't take his hound with him to intimidate the lion tamer, but to give himself courage. You are never on your own with a dog; they will always back you up. Especially this one, a beast capable of holding off two wild boar for an entire morning. A forty-kilo dog who was fast and stood tall, who could jump like a horse. Atlas was often to be seen bounding along narrow paths chasing deer through boxwood and crossing rivers as nimbly as land. He could drive a 120-kilo boar into a corner and keep it there, even if it meant rubbing against its tusks, which could easily gore him. Le Piqueur was linked to his dog by an invisible bond. All the way up the mountain, the dog patrolled in front of him, full of pride to be leading his master, but with no idea of what he was about to hunt. When old Lucien started up the last part of the ascent, which was so steep his shoes slipped on the dry ground, he felt his dog hanging back. By the final few metres Atlas was glued to his side.

As he arrived at the top, Lucien was practically bent double he was so out of breath, and sweat ran into his eyes, making it hard for him to see. Even so, he sensed that the lion tamer was there, standing waiting on the overhanging rock as if he were expecting them. He watched them approach, as impassive as one of his big cats. Atlas lowered his head, so reluctant to go on that he was almost flat, his stomach brushing the stony ground. He uttered little whines that were not like him at all. Lucien had to yank him up by his collar. And still the Hun did not move, enjoying the spectacle of the two of them out of breath and hauling themselves up towards him. He was staring at them with no hint of ferocity, but, like his tigers, he exuded such an air of authority that neither Lucien nor the dog dared look him in the eye. Le Piqueur had never seen his dog frightened before; he was squirming like a worm. He sensed it was because of an obscure power that emanated from the German, a sort of mysterious force which he used to control his lions. The truth was that the poor dog was overcome by the stench of the big cats. His hunting instinct was totally confused by the maddening scents all around him, the odours exhaled by the feline encampment. He did not know what beasts these were, but his instinct told him to keep well away.

Of the two creatures coming towards him, the lion tamer seemed only to notice the dog. He paid no attention to the man with the faded moustache and the steamed-up glasses, an old-timer puffed up with pride at being the one to bring the message from the people down below. Except that, now that he was here, Lucien's anger had evaporated. He couldn't see anything, he could barely breathe, his legs felt as if they were about to give way and he had nothing to say to this circus trainer ringed by his lions' roars. Judging from the noises coming from the large round cage, the felines were agitated and excited by the presence of the newcomers. Lucien was as surprised as his dog by the size of the beasts; they were enormous, of quite another dimension to any of the animals round about. Their mouths were as wide as tree stumps and their bodies as heavy as horses. Even from a distance the reverberation from their growls could be felt. The lions were roaring in hunger, a sound that froze the blood, and, like mountain storms, filled the listener with terror, as though they were a lamb in the mouth of a wolf. Behind the lion tamer, Lucien could make out a slab of rock, flattened like a table, a butcher's block on which he had just cut a carcass – impossible to tell of what – into large chunks. Lucien wiped his glasses with his fingers, and was able to discern red pulsating flesh, gleaming in the sun and attracting flies. That was why the lions were roaring. Le Piqueur had arrived at a bad time, right in the middle of dinner. Yet the lion tamer stood there in front of him, still mute and blocking his view so that Lucien could not tell what species of remains lay on the large sacrificial altar. The enormous hunks of meat the lion tamer had just cut did not come from a sheep, they did not come from a goat, nor a giant ewe, nor from deer. No, what the man had just divided up must come from something very large. There was at least two hundredweight of vermilion flesh. Perhaps a cow, or maybe a fat, well-padded man. The lion tamer went on blocking Le Piqueur's view, and then extended his hand from above. Lucien did not dare shake the huge spade-like hand because it was covered in blood, and because of the way the man was looking at him.

Old Lucien would not say what had happened up there, nor what the German had told him. He wondered if they had actually spoken. But at least he had dared to go up there; he had confronted not only the steep climb but also his own fears. However, he would not divulge what he had seen. Nor did he relate how Atlas had lain down at the feet of the lion tamer, who had given the dog a command in German, no more than two syllables of one scathing word, perhaps one of those he used on his lions. Whatever the word was, the result was clear. Without even knowing the dog's name, the tamer had got Atlas to lie down at his feet, as submissive as a newly hatched chick. Maybe that day the lion tamer had only spoken to the dog. But in any case, Lucien swore he would never go there again, that it wasn't worth the climb. He did not worry everyone by mentioning the sacrificial altar he had seen with the bloody heap of flesh, but he now knew that the German fed his big cats the meat of large mammals, the raw flesh of prey with gleaming muscles that looked human. He thought of the Cabrérac boy, and perhaps others. Men were animals, and animals were meant to eat each other. It was the turbulent cycle of life. He thought it better to keep his suspicions to himself. He didn't want to terrify everyone. But of one thing Lucien was certain – the lion tamer would never find enough ewes or goats to satisfy his lions. To keep them going, he would have to resort to the slaughter of who knew what creatures – and in large quantities. To nourish eight huge, heavy carnivores every day, eight outsize, greedy wild cats, even a hundred sheep would not suffice . . .

August 2017

The bustling atmosphere was doing him good. Franck had only had three hours' sleep before he was woken by the sun. He had felt an inordinate need to see people, to feel life around him. Here, in the centre of Limogne, he found himself amid a nice little crowd. He felt revived, just as he had when he switched on his phone and found there were five miraculous bars! The only slight disappointment was that no one had really tried to contact him; he had only received three calls since yesterday evening, and only one voicemail from an unknown number that he would listen to later. He was saving it as a treat.

Limogne was thirty minutes from Mont d'Orcières along a small road barely wide enough for two vehicles. He had only come across one car on the way, an old van in which he thought he could make out Madame Dauclercq behind the filthy windscreen. As he was driving, he glanced over at the undergrowth, looking for the dog from last night, but maybe it never came out of the hills up there, hiding in the woods like a wolf.

Limogne was a small town. Even so, it had two cafés and two big grocery shops, but no supermarket. He spent a long time driving around the back streets before eventually parking right in the sun. What mattered was to reconnect with civilisation and see some people. The main street was shut because it was market day, Sunday. Earlier, coming into town, he had almost been grateful for the minuscule traffic jam going into the centre; he even delighted in the difficulty of finding a space large enough to park the 4×4. It was doing him the world of good just to be away from the deafening silence of the hills.

When he had left that morning, Lise was still asleep. He closed the curtains as he was getting up so she could carry on sleeping. At nearly nine o'clock she still had her head hidden under the sheet, as if she hadn't moved since yesterday evening. She seemed peaceful. Anyone would think she really was in her element here. He couldn't understand why she was so at home in this bedroom, this bed, this house, why she was completely at ease on the hill open to the winds, right in the middle of nowhere. It made no sense. Yesterday he had told her that he would go shopping early so he would go on his own. He knew Lise had no desire to go into town. She would prefer to spend the morning relaxing in the house, avoiding the crowds. She had written him a shopping list – tea, vegetables, pasta, then salt, sugar, milk and lots of basic things, organic if possible. Once in town he started to wonder if it was really wise to have left her all alone in that isolated house, with the windows and doors wide open. Yesterday they had wedged them open with stones to create as much draught as possible, and he hadn't closed them when he left this morning.

He told himself it would be too difficult to drive back there and up that terrible road to lock everything. That slope was a real ordeal, no matter which direction you were going in. When you set off, everything started beeping and the distance sensors went mad because of the branches and stones. The car was so wide that the bushes and brambles scratched the sides noisily. It was painful to hear, but worse, it was difficult to keep the 4×4 on course without going too close to the edge, because to the right were jutting rocks, and to the left a drop hidden by the undergrowth . . . The Audi was uselessly big, too large for the small roads he had had to take, and even for the roads in Limogne. This was galling because it had been so expensive to rent, and the insurance wouldn't cover all the scratches it already had. Even so, he wouldn't put it on Alpha Productions expenses as an example to the two newbies, even though his own finances were tight at the moment. He shouldn't have rented such an expensive car for three weeks when his last two films had done so badly – two films in a row that had sold fewer than 100,000 tickets. But it was the last four-wheel drive available, apart from a Maserati Levante, which would have been even more expensive. Truth be told, he didn't hate driving the monster; he actually found it exhilarating.

When he had parked, he didn't get out straight away, but sat there for five minutes. He watched the little town come alive around him, comforted by the sight of people coming and going. At the same time, he felt distanced from them, like a complete outsider. He noted the way they looked at him. The car projected an image of affluence and good living, when in fact his self-confidence was at rock bottom. Since the end of March even the smallest expense had worried him. He didn't want to talk about it with Lise or show that he was worried, but he felt just as vulnerable as when he was starting out, with as little financial stability as he'd had at twenty-five. Every new production was a gamble; he always felt as if he were starting again from zero. Taking risks is inherent in the job of a producer, whatever their age and experience, but at more than fifty years old, he no longer had the carefree attitude of someone starting out. He had spent his career soothing anxieties, comforting directors and actors and reassuring partners who took failure badly, who were destroyed by it, beset by the fear they'd never make another film. But having spent so many years supporting others, he no longer had the energy to convince himself.

The car door shut with a smooth, controlled click, like the sound of a silencer on a gun. He stared at the Audi, trying to picture it as his. Not only was the bodywork covered in scratches, but there were dents in the undercarriage that must have come from the flying stones. He had already damaged it. That hill was like an access ramp out of the civilised world and into a savage, lawless one full of ferocious, mysterious animals; a world that was no longer truly human.

He joined the little crowd that was moving towards the square. He was the only one on his own. All the others were in couples, with their families or in groups. It was then that he started to worry, realising that, at this very moment, Lise was completely uncontactable. Thinking of the lifeless phone lying in her handbag, he was suddenly panicked. As he stood at the edge of the noisy market, he even wondered if Lise had actually still been under the sheet earlier. He had not checked properly before leaving, merely glancing at her as he got out of bed, taking care not to wake her. He thought back to the ferocious dog from last night: would it come back? That's if it hadn't come back already. And why was it watching them yesterday? It was clear that it was the same dog down below in the woods, those yellow eyes that had watched them while they ate . . . Franck was suddenly soaked in sweat, prey to a host of idiotic fears. He calmed down, resolving to go and get a coffee; sitting in a bistro would be good for him. Yes, sitting down in a civilised place would restore his equanimity; he only had to get out of the packed market crowd and find somewhere.

He recognised this crippling anxiety and knew where it came from. It wasn't just tiredness and uncertainty about the future, no; the sickening worry came from the complete impossibility of contacting Lise. For twenty-five years they had always been able to reach one another. Since living together, even when one of them went abroad they had always been contactable 24/7. Now, for the first time, that wasn't the case. The fear also came from the house where he felt completely disorientated, and his distress at the thought of a three-week stay there. He realised it wouldn't be as simple as going back to Paris now and then. He had planned to make as many trips as possible for work, but now he could see it was unthinkable. He could never leave Lise all alone up there with no telephone or neighbours, and with that dog roaming around. He was doomed to stay here, unless he could convince her to leave, to abandon the awful solitude. She may have been dreaming of this place for months, but he could easily convince her, even if he had to scare her . . .

He had to calm down. He had to pull himself together. Maybe he could slowly get used to the idea that there was nothing to fear. Of course, there was nothing to fear. Apart from that dog, there was nothing to fear. Apart from those woods and those abandoned hills, there was nothing to fear.

According to some kids, the two bistros in the town were on the other side of the square, so he had to walk all the way through the market. It was a bit of a shock after a night of almost total silence. He walked past the stalls, looking at them as if they came from another world, a colourful pastoral world he wasn't a part of. Lise, a staunch vegetarian, would not have been comfortable with this profusion of artisan charcuterie: many and varied hams, hanging *saucissons* and preserves, stacked jars of pâté and terrines made of all sorts of crushed, cooked and compressed flesh . . . But he also came across stands of nice big vegetables; he couldn't see anything that said it was organic, but what did it matter? There was a sense of bubbling excitement here; it was as if he were inside a huge stomach, an insatiable stomach that would devour anything: meat, vegetables, fruit, charcuterie and fish. Everywhere was bustling; the customers and the vendors all seemed to know one another and every transaction took a long time because they were all talking to each other. There was something gluttonous about it all, a sense of abundance, festivity and perhaps even happiness. Yes, these people all seemed happy, happy that their appetites had brought them together. In the middle of this maelstrom, Franck didn't exist. He felt like a spectator and nothing more. He certainly wasn't part of the celebration, of this feast; it was like he had landed on another planet. And it was getting hotter and hotter. He would rather go inside to do his shopping, into a peaceful air-conditioned shop where you could serve yourself, a normal shop with music, where you didn't have to ask anyone anything. All he wanted was to fill his basket without getting into a conversation with goodness knows who, or being served with goodness knows what.

He asked a lady at random: 'Do you happen to know where I can find a shop?'

'What kind of shop?'

'A food shop!'

The woman must have thought it was a joke, or she assumed he was a foreigner.

'Isn't there enough food all around you?'

He felt stupid, but mainly he felt hampered by the slow-moving crowd; he must have come at the busiest time. It was unfortunate that he, who no longer ate meat, found himself stuck in front of a large red stall, an immense stand right in the middle of the market, a giant altar dedicated to meat. He looked at all the refrigerated carcasses and thick pieces of nauseating flesh that were magnified by the little display cases. And yet the display of death fascinated him, especially as the smell of grilled chicken wafting from the rotisseries rekindled a childhood memory, taking him back to his grandmother's house. She would open the oven and the room would fill with the smell of grilled chicken, a smell to make your mouth water.

There were so many people that the crowd was no longer moving forward. Franck thought he would suffocate, but he didn't dare push. Despite himself he watched the butcher, a big man dressed in a white apron stained with red; he saw him busy at work like a priest performing some religious ceremony. He was spellbound as if watching a horror movie. Good Lord, the butcher was huge, stationed behind his stall with the bright-red awning above his head and a crimson canvas stretched behind him. The sun beating down gave the backdrop a surreal radiance. As well as being big, the butcher was standing on a platform, a bit like the priest at Mass. He looked like a deity in his little sacrificial theatre, but a pagan one; powerful and bloody-minded. You could imagine him stuffed full of all the meat in front of him. He was made of the same flesh as the enormous *côtes de bœuf* he handled and as the sides of beef his assistants grabbed with both hands. As the crowd thinned, Franck could better make out the parts of animals. Al the way along the display were livers and kidneys, and even a calf's head on a square of white marble, a poor, deathly-pale little animal with its eyes closed, a meditative head which had pride of place in the profane hubbub. Next to it were lots of pig's trotters, pigeons and quails lined up like cadavers, rabbits hanging up by their back legs, and heaps of little dead animals, little nothings oblivious to their own death. Good grief, how could people still eat these things?

'And for monsieur?'

'No, I'm just looking.'

'Tourist?'

'No. Well, yes, a tourist if you like, but French . . .'

'Then you are like my meat! Everything here is French. And bred in France!'

'OK. OK.'

Franck was fascinated by the stall, just as he would have been fascinated by any shrine where the dead were glorified before being devoured. Although he wasn't really vegetarian, for ten years he had only eaten meat when there was no other option. Lise had persuaded him long ago. He didn't find it at all shocking that others ate meat, but faced with this mound of it, so exhilaratingly raw, so real and palpable, along with the red-handed butcher surrounded by his enormous knives, it disgusted him. It seemed like a trade from a bygone age. The barking of the dog from last night came back to him. Running after who knows what, on the other side of the hill it had howled for death – not as an abstract notion, but a death it was preparing to deliver by killing the prey it was pursuing. The beast must have spent the whole night running after creatures that were even more cruel than it was, and even hungrier. Franck was sure that the dog had rushed after these animals because of the little click of the tongue he had used to goad it on. To be honest it was he who had provoked the dog.

A stupid brass band passed through the middle of the market that was why he couldn't go forwards or backwards. The butcher's face was the same colour as those pieces of beef; there wasn't the slightest difference. He thought he could see a red tinge to everyone around him, even the kids who were blowing their wind instruments in the terrible brass band. He suddenly felt as if he were paying a visit to another people, lost in a tribe of eager hunters where dogs were man's ally and all other animals were just prey . . . Maybe the stray dog's owner was here amongst all the people surrounding him. Unless it was truly wild.

Franck could feel the butcher still watching him even as he carved the meat. Maybe he was the owner of the house, the one who was replying to emails from a foreign address to avoid paying taxes. Maybe he had recognised him; maybe he knew exactly who he was. In a sudden fit of paranoia, Franck thought that Liem and Travis had perhaps plotted all of this, and Lise was in on it. He was stuck here in this godforsaken place, not realising that he had been the victim of a prank from the very start . . .

He was letting his imagination run away with him. Sensing that the situation was out of his control, he was telling himself that it had all been planned by others to throw him off course. But why would Lise want that, when she had always done everything to reassure him? Liem and Travis, on the other hand, in the full flush of their triumphant thirties, were capable of anything.

In an effort to calm down, Franck got out his phone and listened to his only message, but there was nothing, just silence broken up with distant beeps. He kept the phone to his ear, pretending to speak as he casually weaved his way through the crowd and off to the left. Seen from a distance, the butcher on his platform dominated the scene. Franck could feel him watching him as he boned the shoulder of beef. He was watching him as he cut around the animal's radial bone with practised movements. The butcher watched him leave without even looking at the carcass, as if he were saying: 'The two of us will meet again. We'll meet again.'

September 1914

Lucien would not say what he had seen up there. Instead he told everyone that the lion tamer would definitely need eighty pounds of fresh meat a day to feed his eight massive wild animals. That was the equivalent of one large dog, or a ewe, or two children. But, he said, the German still had goats and ewes left, so he must be feeding them something else . . . The women were immediately fearful for their children. The villagers also worried about the sheep hidden on the other side of the hills, the large secret flock that the requisition committee were not to know about.

When the weather was good, the sheep were left on the summer pasture. From April to October they grazed in the grassy valleys, the land having been left fallow after the destruction of the vines. Le Simple watched over them up there with three dogs. In the evening, he herded them into the shelters and during the day he took them from one clearing to the next, according to what kind of grass he wanted them to eat. The pastures on that side of the hills were fertile, with thousands of hectares which would go to waste if not used. In a sense, the sheep were gardening, and without them, trees would have taken over, and the hills would have been covered with forests. It was comforting to know that the sheep were enjoying those enormous pastures, far away from everything. Le Simple was not afraid of wolves and always slept with two loaded rifles beside him.

Since the lions' roars had started to echo round the hills, an instinctive fear of predators had been reawakened, predators that attacked men as well as livestock. But this did not affect Le Simple, who was the only soul on earth not to know that there was a war. He thought that the bells on 1 August had been a fire alarm, and no one had corrected him; yes, a big fire had indeed broken out somewhere far away. They also did not tell him about the lions for fear he would panic. In the east, downwind, he could not hear them. Le Simple was a child born too late, as the saying went; he wasn't quite right in the head, but he had clear opinions, slow but clear. It was agreed in the village to make him the shepherd, which suited everyone. No one else wanted to live for six months all alone on the high plateau, spending the fine days watching over the sheep. And the nights in abandoned *gariottes*, those drystone huts built during the Second Empire, with ill-fitting doors and no creature comforts. In the winegrowing days, the huts had been used for storing tools, protecting them from the elements, but they hadn't been intended for sleeping in.

Twice a month, someone took Le Simple bread. It was a three-hour walk, but old Lucien declared that from now on it would be wise to go more often, and to count the sheep once a week. Everyone had faith in Le Simple; he was a skilful, hardy shepherd. He knew how to read the sheep and slept close to them on a stone bench, or on the grass, even when there was a hut nearby. He liked to sleep in the open air, and even if he did not get much sleep, it meant that he could keep an eye on the sheep. In between the supply trips Mayor Fernand would go up to check for himself that everything was all right, and also to get away from the village for a bit. Morale was at a low ebb and the women were exhausted, because not only was the work endless, but now the days were getting shorter. As time went on, the feeling of impending doom grew.

It did not help that the women received no news or letters from their menfolk. Buried in the hills, it was impossible to know what was really going on at the front, almost a thousand kilometres away. Couderc, the schoolmaster, was convinced that the newspapers did not tell the truth about the war because they remembered how, in 1870, they had inadvertently provided the Prussians with precious information. With few facts to go on, rumours from England started to circulate that the French army had suffered a rout, a veritable massacre, but no one was talking about it so as not to demoralise the rearguard. Couderc, who received post from many places, had a friend in Exeter. The papers in England were more forthcoming than the ones in Limogne. In France, papers had blank columns, where whole articles had been removed by the censors. However, according to his friend in Devon, thousands and thousands of French soldiers had been killed in a single battle at the end of August, the equivalent of ten towns the size of Cahors in one night – could that be true?

In the village, people felt that Couderc might have kept this to himself. They didn't want to believe it, yet feared it was true because of the complete silence from the soldiers. Either they were all dead or they were paralysed by fear. Since the letter from England, the villagers did not believe the optimism peddled by the French press. They told each other the war was going badly, and every time the lions and tigers roared it felt symbolic and they trembled for the men and for the defenceless ewes over the hills. Like a fateful allegory, the howls and cries coming down the mountain evoked the image of frightened men deep in the Ardennes forest, men unwittingly offering themselves to the mouths of cannons, just as the ewes were vulnerable to the wild cats.

From then on, twice a week, someone checked up on the ewes. Nothing could be done for the men, but at least they could ensure that the ewes were safe. One morning, Fernand yoked up his rickety old cabriolet and went up to the plateau with old Lucien, who wanted to count the animals himself with clean glasses. Old Maurice had also gone twice, on foot, just to prove to them all that at nearly eighty he was not finished yet, that he could still walk all day in the sun like the soldiers under the clouds in the east. Yet Maurice had more reason than most to dislike climbing up to the pastures on the other side of the hill. He used to have vines there and walking on the land brought back memories of the kingdom of abundance it had been before, a treasure trove spilling out litres and litres of fragrant nectar, the hillside covered with opulent vines. Nothing remained of that golden age except the huts and stone rows, derisory vestiges of a vanished El Dorado. Of all the men left in the village, the only one who refused to go up at all was La Bûche. At nearly sixty, he was certainly fit enough to go; in fact he was the strongest of the men left behind, but he would not hear of it. It was obvious that he didn't like the lion tamer. Anyone would have thought that there was an old grievance between them, but as he was not the talkative type, no one wanted to ask him.

Fear continued to take hold. Ever since the villagers had learnt that entire French regiments could bé wiped out in a single night, leaving heaps of bodies equivalent to ten large towns, they felt as if death was all around. Mothers sometimes saw in their children's faces the ghosts of their fathers, but in order not to worry them further the women had to stay strong and not show weakness. Their role was no longer to be gentle. Working the land had given them calloused, thickened hands. Hands that before had been for caresses and affectionate gestures were now hardened for work.

School started again at the end of September. Couderc, although he had recently retired, stood in for the new schoolmaster who had been called up. He taught dictation as instructed by the authorities. According to the demands of the local education officer, he must teach the boys that Germans were barbaric, bloodthirsty monsters, devils . . . even though there was one living above them, a Hercules surrounded by big lions. However, Couderc did not go as far as to make them sing the patriotic songs mandated by the Minister for Public Education, refusing to use the school to produce future soldiers. He despised the new instructions emanating from Paris with their implicit message that the war would never end, and that even when it did, it would be essential to prepare for others, and that whatever happened Europe would erupt in turmoil. All the newspapers glorified the idea of the child hero, reporting hundreds of incidents where boys had taken up arms and gone to the front, and showing girls of twelve pouring water into the mouths of wounded soldiers. The villagers feared that the kids would be influenced by this and take it into their heads to go and kill the Hun and confront his lions.

When the women went to the fields, they didn't want to leave their children on their own because of the lions. And they certainly didn't want them going to play by the river as they had always done. They were worried they would go up the mountain, naïvely offering themselves as prey, because they were dying to see the lions up close ... To discourage them, mothers resorted to old tricks. Once the sun had gone down, old Jean and Maurice hid at the edge of the wood or on the riverbank, and, under cover of darkness, made terrible howling sounds. They made such convincing noises that even the lions must have thought they were real. If the children were not frightened of lions, they were terrified of wolves. Wolves were part of the landscape and they were needed to inspire fear, which was why they would always be there. If one day there was an end to the war, which seemed unimaginable then, there would still have to be wolves, even if it meant bringing them back. Man needs to know he has enemies, something to fear, if only so that people can unite against them.

August 2017

On the terrace, the customers gathered around the tables in the sun. Franck, on the other hand, took refuge at the back of the café. The motley chattering market crowd had disconcerted him, and he had had a strong sense of being unwelcome. He couldn't get that butcher out of his head. The guy had singled him out, and he didn't really know why.

The waiter was busy. He was always on the move but never came inside, his time taken up by the outside tables. Franck had to signal to get his attention. He asked for a double espresso and the Wi-Fi password. For years now, logging on to the internet had become completely automatic. He needed it as much as he needed coffee. He gulped down two double espressos in a row while browsing Facebook and Twitter to try to reconnect with the real world. From his faraway café, he imagined how this person on holiday was feeling, or that person posting photos of a shoot or releasing a trailer. Then he went to film industry websites to see ticket sales for new cinema releases. He looked at the box office for each day in France and across the world. He wasn't worried by the figures as he didn't have a film out at the moment, but he needed to understand the market and know which films audiences were interested in, and to evaluate the success – or failure – of others, as if there were conclusions to be drawn A film release is a cut-throat business. He knew some people had rejoiced when they saw him screw up twice in a row, especially since everyone knows everything nowadays. Everything is counted and added up, day by day, hour by hour, and a film that flops clears the way for its competitors. It's completely brutal, just like unleashing a pack of carnivores on the same piece of land, knowing the amount of prey is finite, and the predators will first have to neutralise one another, or, put simply, kill one another off. There is no room for compassion in the distribution of a film. The only law that counts is the law of the jungle.

Franck felt himself come alive again as he scrolled through the sites which opened relatively easily on his smartphone. Having access to all his data again, he was in his element. He desperately needed the phone that he always kept within reach. Even though the connection wasn't that strong, he browsed avidly for more than half an hour, time passing without him noticing. He felt like a smoker who hasn't had a cigarette for forty-eight hours and grabs the first packet he can find. There was nothing very interesting in the news. The same American blockbusters were dominating the industry as they always did in August: sequels, prequels or spin-offs that were declared successes, a raft of films whose only purpose was to push others out. It had become pointless to release a film in the summer. He let himself be drawn in by clickbait on his news feeds, headlines that directed him to a news story, then to an article or video he wasn't really interested in. On the other hand, there wasn't much in his email inbox. He was relieved not to see the names Liem or Travis, but they must have scheduled the meeting with the guys from Netflix, unless they were doing it on Skype. He would never do a Skype meeting, and certainly not to establish contact for the first time.

Nobody had got back to him about the film he had been trying to get off the ground for three years. It was the story of a woman in the Swiss canton of Aargau who had stood in for a sick priest at Mass, a lay preacher who had also officiated at weddings for several years, bringing worshippers back to the little church. In a religion where women weren't even allowed to be altar servers, the Bishop of Basel was furious, especially as the lay preacher advocated freedom of choice, including in sexual matters. It didn't help that the lay preacher made the parishioners happy and encouraged others to find their vocation. The story was made more interesting because all record of it had mysteriously disappeared from the internet, so the two scriptwriters had had a hell of a job working on it. Certain subjects and people inexplicably vanish from the internet. The problem was that his usual partners weren't interested in the project, and nor were the banks or television channels. They had accused him of wanting to produce a film just so Lise could play the lead role. After all, Lise was the same age as the woman, Rita. The people who thought that were not wrong. Franck was upset that Lise was no longer acting or being offered roles. Lise, on the other hand, said she was relieved not to have to please or convince others any more, especially as, after the age of fifty, an actress only ever plays women who have been cheated on or abandoned, women who are damaged in one way or another. But her no longer working created an imbalance. Sometimes in childless couples, the one who is out of work is considered vulnerable and fragile, in need of protection. Lise was his wife, but she was also a little like his child as well, the child who didn't achieve the career she wanted at the outset and had diminishing chances of success. Even though Lise was perfectly happy meditating, doing yoga and finally taking advantage of her four years at the École des Beaux-Arts to rediscover her first passion, painting, Franck would have done anything to see her acting again. Even if it meant ruffling the feathers of his partners and inventing money that he didn't have, and even though Lise claimed she no longer had any ambition. He was sure that, really, she missed acting, though she wouldn't admit it to herself. Actors are fragile because they are dependent on the desires of others. If they don't want you any more, you don't work any more; if you don't work any more, they don't want you any more. It's a profession that can drive you mad.

The phone in his hand started to ring. It was Liem or Travis, or at any rate, it was the office number. God, he wasn't ready. Sitting here alone at the back of the café, he wasn't prepared for a work call. He muted it, preferring them to leave a message. He placed the phone cautiously on the table, almost scared to touch it. After a little while he picked it up again and listened to the voicemail. He played it twice to make sure he didn't miss anything. He tried to interpret the tone of voice. Liem and Travis had been his partners for only eight months, but they were already behaving in a disconcertingly patronising way. Ever since they had hurled that hurtful remark, something had snapped, in Franck's mind at least. In fact, now he wanted only one thing: to catch them out.

Liem was again talking about that blessed meeting in Paris. The Netflix people had in the end decided to do a tour of Europe in the hope of finding partners. They had offices in Amsterdam and Dublin for tax reasons and had agreed to come to Paris, but only had two dates free. Franck knew perfectly well that Liem and Travis wanted to hand over the library, *his* library of the fifty or so films he had produced over twenty-five years, his war chest in some ways, a demand he would never give in to. By proposing a meeting, were Liem and Travis indicating that, unlike him, they were not on holiday? They were quietly reminding him that they hadn't stopped arranging important meetings just because it was August. They were showing him that at twenty-eight and thirty years old, they hardly even thought about the sacred rite of going on holiday, the obligatory August at the seaside. What's more, they had managed to slip in that, in the American production world, only an idiot would take holiday in August.

Liem and Travis were the kind of ambitious young men who were confident they could regenerate the French production industry, thanks to their considerable experience in digital and video games. They had done part of their studies in the US; Travis had been born there, and both had got their first jobs in digital technology before going into video-game development and editing. They didn't understand how Franck could go away for three weeks; for them, being a producer meant working day and night. He returned the call, and straight away they presented him with yet another brilliant idea, but he immediately put the brakes on it.

'There's no way we're doing that, guys. Or at least I'm not.'

'But, Franck, it's a no-brainer, it's genius!'

'It's completely ruthless!'

'No, it's not; we just have to get hold of all the good directors whose last films bombed and suggest filming a series! It would give them a few months' filming and some financial security. Netflix is offering them unlimited resources; 120 million subscribers counts for a lot . . . But, Franck, we'll need your contacts; you know all the directors!'

The money-grabbing idea disgusted him, but it was worth considering. He had to give his associates some room for manoeuvre.

'OK, so Tuesday 12th?'

'Yes, Liem, I'll be there on Tuesday 12th.'

'Is nine o'clock all right?'

'No problem.'

'And which café?'

'Liem, it would be better if they came to the office so they can see where we work, and it would give us the upper hand.'

'No, Franck, we'll meet them at Starbucks. We'll waste less time.'

'No, definitely not Starbucks.'

'Where then, Café de Flore, or Les Deux Magots, or Café Marly at the Louvre?'

'Anywhere, but not Starbucks.'

He knew that his experience and contacts interested them much more than his cinematic vision. But this was pushing it. All that mattered to them was producing *content* as they called it, diversifying their offer by producing television series and a full-length film every now and then, preferably a comedy. At first, Franck had told himself that working with two young people with a fresh perspective would be good for him, and particularly since they brought new capital to the business. But with each passing day he noticed more and more things that divided them, the differences that could turn into disagreements. He knew nothing about video games, he wasn't interested in them, and he saw only fighting and violence in what Liem and Travis had shown him. The production and design were excellent, but the sole objective of these games was to shoot at as many opponents as possible, taking out enemy soldiers or fantasy animals, just killing all day long.

He dialled Lise's number for peace of mind, only half expecting a response. No ring of course; it went straight to voicemail and he didn't leave a message. Imagining her alone in the house on top of the hill made him think about how vulnerable she was, but also how vulnerable he was – time had caught up with both of them. He imagined her still sleeping, still underneath the white sheet. Lise in an empty house with the windows open, Lise all alone in the middle of the remote hills, left behind by a world that no longer wanted her. He couldn't stop thinking about it. An actress who doesn't act is like a painter who has been forbidden to paint, or a writer prevented from writing. He was haunted by the image of Lise trapped in the isolated house, surrounded by animals that had come from the hill opposite, besieged by the wildlife that had run amok last night, by a pack of hungry carnivores or that strange big dog that would devour anything if prompted with a little click of the tongue.

September 1914

Whenever men depart for war, predators range freely in the countryside. Wolves, foxes, rabid dogs and other feral savage beasts return to plague the farms. By the end of summer, fears were mounting. On top of the anguish of hearing nothing from the front, and exhaustion, deprivation and torrents of hail, there were the ceaseless lion noises that soured the cows' milk and terrified the dogs. 'Death is all around us,' said the mothers.

Couderc tried to provide reassurance – not about the war, but the lions, perhaps. The retired schoolmaster was regarded by everyone as a wise man, an enlightened being, more knowledgeable because of his profession than the mayor or the *préfet*. Couderc had taught three generations to read and write. It was thanks to him that everyone in the village could measure their parcels of land, count their flocks and read the paper or their letters. And it was thanks to him that they were able to write those letters to the front which still went unanswered. Without the schoolteacher, no one here would have been able to communicate with absent family. Just to see the magnificent building in Cahors where Couderc had trained to be a teacher was to understand that a man who had graduated from such a place must be ten times better educated than a parish priest and a thousand times better informed than the ordinary man.

That evening Couderc and Fernand organised a meeting outside the mairie. All the women gathered whilst the old people looked after the children. Couderc and Fernand reiterated that the storms had not been more violent since the German had been living up there on the hill; the German was not responsible for the torrential rain and sudden squalls, any more than he was responsible for declaring war on France. On the contrary, he was the only German in the world they need not fear: not only had he turned his back on his own country, he was also, like them, exclusively devoted to his animals. His priority, like theirs, was his livestock. From now on, no one should be worried about a man who had made the choice to distance himself from his people and concentrate on his animals. Enquiries had been made and it had been established that he had lived with his lions and tigers for years and years. For twenty years he had moved from circus to circus, from show to show across Europe, and also, according to Fernand, in America, and in Monaco. He had been selling dreams and delighting children for decades. That proved that he was an entertainer, an artist and what could be threatening about an artist? 'Circus people are benefactors, magicians . . .' But instead of calming the women's fears, Fernand and Couderc provoked a storm of objections.

'You obviously like him a lot, but you can't deny that he needs far more than a handful of ewes or goats to feed his monstrous beasts, and he hasn't bought any animals from us for two months now!'

Couderc did not reply and, anyway, no one gave him the chance.

'Apparently he went to Limogne to get carcasses from the butcher,' shouted Angèle. 'But the butcher wouldn't help because meat is already rationed for humans, so there's nothing left for wild cats . . .'

'On Tuesday he went to the market in Limogne,' added the Berguelles' daughter. 'He ordered tar from the hardware shop, two drums of oil and blocks of salt – what's he going to do with that?'

'It's true, I saw him on the road on the way back. And there weren't two drums of oil in his cart, there were ten!'

'He's not going to feed his lions oil!'

'Of course not, it's to make flaming torches!'

'What does he want with those?'

'To set fire to us, I tell you!'

'That's it! He's going to grill us and eat us, but before that he's going to eat all our goats and sheep and children . . .'

'Stop seeing evil everywhere,' countered Couderc.

'But, Monsieur, evil is everywhere. It's you who doesn't want to see it, as clever as you are. The books you read are full of goodness but can't you see that the world has gone wrong? Can't you see that madness has taken over? You'd have to be a saint to believe that it's safe to go to sleep with tigers waiting there above us. A saint or a madman . . .'

Couderc took over again and invited the only proper witness to speak, the only man who had been up to see for himself. 'Tell us, Lucien, since you have spoken to him, what does he feed his animals?'

'I've no idea.'

'Don't be frightened, you've already told me he still has sheep.'

'Yes, there are still sheep.'

'How many?'

'I didn't count them. But at least a dozen . . .'

'You see!' said Jeanne angrily. 'He still has all the sheep he bought from us, so what is he feeding to his lions and tigers?'

'Perhaps he does with sheep what Jesus did with loaves of bread?'

At that point, all the believers crossed themselves. Yet even though they wanted to believe in miracles, they did not swallow that one. Once a sheep was eaten, it did not skip back into the meadow the next day, alas. Fernand and Couderc did not know how to reassure the women, except to say to those who were most upset that they should go up and see the German and ask him how he fed his hungry animals.

'I'll go . . . I'll go and ask him.'

Normally, Joséphine never spoke up, never even came to meetings. Joséphine was a dreamy, poetic sort of person. But since the departure of her husband, it wasn't just that there was no doctor in the whole area, but now everyone knew she was all alone with little to occupy her. She should have been the object of envy because she had all her time to herself and a large farmhouse just outside the village. But people felt sorry for her because she had no children. Even if she and her husband had been able to have them, they would probably have been dead by now along with their father, in that famous Battle of the Frontiers, the shadowy butchery of 22 August that had been covered up. The doctor had set off from Rodez with the 16th Army Corps so he must have been caught up in the hell of Morhange. Unlike the others, Joséphine had received five letters in August, but since the beginning of September nothing.

'Don't you believe me? I promise you I will go.'

In a sense Joséphine had nothing left to lose. It would be hard going up there; it would be like glancing into the depths of hell. None of the other women would have risked going: they were all too frightened that it would bring them bad luck. If they went, they might encounter the ghosts of all those loved ones. Not just the winegrowers who had committed suicide, but also all the men who had not been heard of for two months, and who were assumed to be damned and wandering on the accursed mountain. And anyone who worked the land had no desire to see the land up there. It was said to be blue because of the chemicals used on it, or red, according to some versions. In any case the soil was dead – burnt and poisoned. What was more, the mountain was not really of this world, nor was it on the moon, but sort of between worlds, an elsewhere that women did not venture to. Ever since the vines and winegrowers had died, it had been a foreign land and now, with the roaring carnivores, it had become the den of a demon. The women crowded round Joséphine, warning her not to go up Mont d'Orcières. There was only one thing to do and that was to stay well away. To stay well away or else to set fire to it. But even if they set fire to it, who was to say that the flames would not go right up to the top and that flaming torches would not fall on the village. To set fire to the mountain might mean setting fire to all the hills round about and to the village . . . For generations Mont d'Orcières had been bad for everyone, except for those who stayed well away. But Joséphine merely repeated calmly that she would go, that she would go tomorrow.

So it was agreed. She would go.

The other women saw Joséphine as different. She was from Bergerac and had never worked on the land. They saw her offer to go up as something spiritual, a noble sacrifice.

But, also at the meeting, there was someone who was a malicious gossip, and jealous. He saw the offer not as noble but as selfish, and unchaste. The old blacksmith, who also acted as the farrier, was nicknamed La Bûche, or The Log, because of his bull neck, but also because of his blunt character. His name was actually Jules. La Bûche feared that Joséphine, who was impossibly beautiful and a quasi-widow, wanted to go up there not to look at the lions and tigers, but because she was attracted to their master. Jules knew perfectly well that she had not slept with the doctor for years. He looked after their horses and had built them a wrought-iron balustrade, and he had seen that when the doctor returned from work, he barely kissed her on the cheek and addressed her formally. He was absolutely sure that in the five years since the doctor had taken over his father's practice, he had touched the bodies of everyone in the area, but never his wife's. Malicious gossip . . . that was the fox that was always there prowling around the houses, sticking close to the villagers in the certainty of getting a tasty morsel.

August 2017

In the film world more than any other, your survival depends on the scent you give off. When it's the sweet smell of success, the offers and invitations come flooding in. But when an odour of bad luck begins to cling to you, when your films flop and your projects are abandoned, then the telephone stops ringing. In cinema more than in any other business, people like you when they need you; they like you because you are useful. Franck knew that what was true for him as a producer was also true for Lise as an actress. The strange thing about it was that he was more upset than she was. He of all people knew that an actor who no longer acts is like an animal left behind by the pack, a feral dog no one wants. Faced with that there are two options: rebel or retreat. The risk is that you start seeing everyone else as enemies.

Feeling slightly rattled, Franck headed for the next road down. He was following the instructions to the organic shop the waiter at the bistro had given him. Unlike the market, the atmosphere in La Vie Claire was monastic, meditative in fact. It was reassuring to return to the silence and packaging he recognised: white cartons of soya milk, packets of pasta and fresh ravioli. The vegetables here were smaller than in the market, and a little more faded, more tired perhaps. Or sad; that was the feeling that came to him as he sorted through soft aubergines, carrots with dull tops, bulbs of fennel and tomatoes of all different sizes. He knew Lise liked colourful salads, made up of a bit of everything. In her opinion, the most important thing was that vegetables were organic, no matter what they looked like. He also got oil, salt, bread, butter, everything on the list she'd written for him, the very basics for a house with absolutely nothing. All the cupboards were empty; there wasn't even soap or toilet roll. He couldn't believe the house had been rented out to other people before them; they were surely the first. Or else the owners cleared it out every time, taking everything and removing all trace of the previous guests. He thought maybe Madame Dauclercq came on the sly to pick up anything that was left in the cupboards once the holidaymakers had gone. He didn't trust that woman. She seemed strangely annoyed by the rental property, a business that wasn't hers.

He joined the queue. There was only one till, and the electronic scale wasn't working, so the six disgruntled people that had been in the shop when he arrived were now in single file in front of him. He could be here for some time.

In the cool of the air conditioning, a sudden thought crossed his mind: perhaps Madame Dauclercq rented out the house without the owners even knowing; perhaps she was making money behind their backs, which would mean this rental was no more than a sham . . . No, that was impossible. There was the telephone number in Singapore, the bank transfer to an account not in the name Dauclercq, and the emails that always had a response, even if it was three days later. He had trouble imagining that old woman replying to his emails; he doubted she even had the internet. The scam must be somewhere else. Unless there wasn't one. Or maybe it was some sort of cursed house that no one in the area wanted to live in; land that, for one reason or another, nobody would even think of buying, the kind of place where things have happened. Franck knew his imagination could run away with him. It was foolish to believe that producers don't have any; that because they had to see to all the practical details of film-making, that was all they did. Franck knew that wasn't true. Producers are the biggest dreamers of all, the storytellers who have to make it all happen. That was why he had convinced himself that all these people with their big baskets had deliberately pushed in front of him . . . There was no one behind him when he left the shop, not even one customer.

He went around the square to avoid getting caught up in the market again; he especially didn't want to come across the butcher. He caught sight of him from afar. The man fascinated him even from here, a sort of big warlike Buddha or bloodthirsty deity presiding over everything from behind his stall, as if it were at the centre of it all: the market, the village and the surrounding area. The crimson canvas of his great meat display shone through a gap in the crowd. Franck thought back to the way the guy had looked at him. Everybody here was looking at him with the same cold strangeness, the same distance. It was as if they all knew he was the one renting the house at the top of the hill and that he had done a deal with a cursed animal, a dog that, at his instigation, had caused the wild animals of the entire area to scatter. In their eyes, he was perhaps some kind of devil or deranged god, someone who had been put forward unknowingly for some sort of experiment . . . No, he knew perfectly well that he was getting carried away. His anxiety often resulted in paranoid delusions that he managed with the tablets he always kept in his pocket, in his little green pillbox. And yet last night he had definitely seen that dog, or wolf, just as he had definitely heard the pack of excited animals. In that respect, he wasn't going mad.

Franck kept an eye on his phone as he drove back to Mont d'Orcières, watching the number of bars between bends in the road. It had felt as if he was plunging into a lost world since he had left Limogne. The network fell away one bar at a time, severing his lifeline; he was losing all his points of reference and entering another world not confined by telephones, and where not everything is trackable. He got a signal again in places along the byroads; a bar or two would suddenly appear and then disappear, then come back, before vanishing a hundred metres further on. After one bend an 'E' briefly appeared for the last time. After ten kilometres he turned onto the little road to the old village of Orcières, and there his phone became completely useless.

He pulled in at the bottom of the track leading to the gîte, got out of the car and looked at the potholed incline. It was incredibly steep. If you crouched down it looked steeper still, the angle verging on forty per cent, like a ski jump. He couldn't believe he had climbed to the top yesterday and gone back down again this morning. Without a 4×4 there would be no chance of getting up this path, unless you had a tractor. He didn't understand why anyone would have come up with the idea of such a steep access road. At the time, you could probably only have got to the house on foot, or else by horse-drawn cart; or maybe the people who lived up there were completely self-sufficient, and were independent enough not to have to go down to the village.

Opposite the turning to the house, a narrow river ran beside the road. Beyond it, buried under climbing plants and trees, you could make out the low ruins of houses, traces of the old village that had been abandoned or destroyed. But by what? By time, or by flames perhaps, or deadly boredom or even by the marauding beasts in the woods last night. Everything was to be considered a danger here, including the sun that was frantically beating down now, past noon. Franck turned around. He caught a glimpse of the hill rising above him. He couldn't look straight at it because of the sun; he could only make out the shape of the mountain of scrubland and limestone that dominated the valley. More than a hundred metres high, it was like the prow of a giant ship sailing high above the road. The gîte was sitting up there as if on an island, cut off from its surroundings. A short succession of barks came from behind the hill. Franck thought back to the dog from last night, wondering if it was the one from Madame Dauclercq's enormous kennel. It must be; he could see no other explanation for a dog to be roaming around here, unless it didn't have a master and was truly wild. He decided to make sure and got back in the car, turning around instead of going up the track.

Mont d'Orcières receded in his rear-view mirror, then rose like a reef on the horizon until it appeared in its entirety, before vanishing at the first bend to be replaced by other hills, hills that were gentler and less menacing.

September 1914

If she wanted to tempt the devil, let her. Even if she could convince the Hun to tell her how he got enough meat to feed his lions and tigers, that wouldn't mean he was telling the truth.

In the village, people were wary of upsetting Joséphine because two days ago Dr Manouvrier had officially been declared missing, meaning she was almost certainly a widow. No one knew where he was, but there were no witnesses to his death. According to procedure, it was necessary to have two witnesses for a declaration of death, so although the doctor was categorised as 'Deceased' on the document received by the mayor, the box for 'Date and place of death' contained nothing but a terrible question mark. In the absence of a formal declaration, and because the mayor had not received a certificate signed by the public prosecutor of the Republic, Dr Manouvrier could not absolutely be considered dead. He could not be awarded the honour of 'Mort pour la France'. But the fact that a soldier was not considered dead did not necessarily mean that he was alive.

As soon as she saw the document, Joséphine was sure that her husband was no longer living, but perhaps he was not quite dead either. At night, this vertiginous ambiguity drove her mad. Her husband wandered somewhere between life and death, between heaven and limbo, between the memories she had of him and that empty space beside her in the bed. It was dreadful. His body was nowhere, but everywhere.

On the other hand, the document the mayor had received put

things into perspective for all those who had received no news of their father or son. At least they could tell themselves that no news was good news. The worst thing about it was that Joséphine did not pray; she never called on God to reaffirm her soul, never went to Mass, and sought no other solace than the cold comfort of her secular books. That was to say she was utterly alone. Joséphine may have been a beautiful woman with slender white hands, a large house with a grand gate, but as of two days ago no one even thought of envying her – quite the opposite. Instead they avoided her.

No doubt Joséphine knew nothing about lions, but everyone was waiting for her to go up and find out what type of animal flesh the German found to nourish his beasts, when down below they would soon run out of everything. They were waiting for her to honour her promise, which she did the day after the meeting without telling anyone. Right in the middle of the afternoon she saddled her horse, a stallion everyone was afraid of because he was so jittery, but who was as docile as a lamb in her hands. No one saw her start up the steep path and then embark on the impossible climb that went all the way to the top of the mountain. It was mad to set off when the sun was at its strongest. The women were working in the fields and spotted her between the trees. Her graceful silhouette could be glimpsed as she followed the steep twisting track upwards. The women stood up to get a better look at her. They exchanged glances but did not say a word. The higher she climbed the more she was hidden by the trees, until she disappeared from view completely. Then the women felt a little ashamed that they had left the widow to sacrifice herself.

The lion tamer was not a total stranger to Joséphine because she had seen him at the circus with her husband. She had watched him all through his act and had feared for him, which made her feel closer to him. She did not see why he needed to get so close to his beasts. He didn't have to put his head in their mouths or go near their fangs and claws. She had seen his body exposed and toyed with by huge lions, his almost naked muscular body, and she had been so alarmed for him that she dug her nails into her husband's palm. She was the only one worried; everyone else had been indifferent.

She had no idea how she would go about asking him to tell her what he was up to, but she had to let him know that his presence was disturbing the villagers. They were all afraid of the lions. Joséphine was running through all the arguments in her head when, at the last bend before reaching the top, she came face to face with him. There he was by the trees, searching for berries, rooting in the undergrowth with a long stick. She was taken by surprise, but he was not.

Joséphine halted her horse, trying not to let her emotions show. She was hot in the late-summer sun. Here was the Spartacus from the big circus cage, the hero magnified by the circus lights, the man who had caused her to tremble and clutch her husband's hand. It was his face she had seen in the gaping, gigantic, growling mouth of a lion. Never had she gripped her husband's hand so hard, never had she embraced him for so long and here she was face to face with the man who had been responsible for that embrace. He was more impressive than anyone she had ever seen but her eyes betrayed nothing of what she felt. He came towards her without a word and stroked her horse. The horse was astonishingly calm, soothed by the roughened, heavy hand caressing his muzzle. Daring neither to dismount nor to move, Joséphine ventured a couple of banalities about the red berries he had been foraging a moment earlier, how they shouldn't be eaten, nor any other berries on the mountain as they were all poisonous. No doubt the man did not consider this worthy of a response. He appeared only to be interested in the horse, in the beautiful stallion that Joséphine mastered so completely because she had trained him over the years. The horse, who normally bit anyone who came near, was putty in the lion tamer's hands. For once, he was well behaved, as quiet as a lamb.

'You shouldn't ride this horse. He's dangerous.'

Joséphine did not reply. His voice was not the same as when she had seen him in the middle of the ring, barking orders at his fierce animals as drum rolls built the atmosphere of fear. That day she had quivered, as you do when you see a man dice with death, even when you don't care about him.

'If you're going to give the shepherd his provisions, you've come the wrong way; you'll have to go back down a bit and then take the path on the left.'

'No, it's you I've come to see.'

She didn't know what else to say and he didn't ask her anything. There was a long silence. He still stroked the horse. Joséphine felt the breeze caress her ankles, knowing that even the small amount of her body that was on show was enough to enflame a man. She was annoyed at being there, having that effect on the man beside her. He stayed standing downhill from her, at the same level as the horse. He seemed at one with the horse that she could feel warm between her legs, swaying in appreciation of the touch of the man. She felt the slow frisson that passed from the hand of the man to the horse, and from the horse to her back. She was distracted by the thought of her husband. She tried to repress the thought but could not help seeing his long, emaciated doctor's body, an educated body but lacking definition, a body that knew about other bodies, touching them with his science rather than his hands, a body that could cure other bodies, but a body lacking generosity, a body without any real force, a body without body. Her husband's body had left nothing behind, not even a child, nothing except the arid sensation of having slept beside him for years.

She heard the lion tamer without listening to him. He was giving her two or three recommendations about the horse, because it was obvious that he had been rubbed too hard there, on his neck. There was irritation in his sensitive areas. When she washed him she shouldn't use too much soap and especially not round his penis. She must have blushed when she heard that. It was true that she was always washing him. She was embarrassed to think of all the time she spent cleaning and brushing her horse, especially now that no one visited because the doctor wasn't there any more. She now served no purpose in the world, she was useless and worthless . . .

There was more breeze at the top of the mountain and it was making Joséphine light-headed. She felt as if she were floating above the village. From up here all you could see of it was a few roofs between the trees, a long way down, far away, in another world. The man continued to talk about horses, his this time. He had a strong accent but his vocabulary indicated that he had been speaking French for many years. Then she reminded herself he was German like the men who had killed her husband. She was surprised that she found it so difficult to look him in the eye. Of course, there were all the terrible things she had heard about him, but there was also something wild about him and the way his gaze seemed to envelop her. She was thinking this when by accident she caught his eye. He looked at her without any evident emotion yet his gaze pierced her and she felt the full force of it. She tried to hold his gaze but scarcely had the man looked at her than she lowered her eyes, overcome by the power she felt emanating from him.

It was one of the last days of summer and the lion tamer's shirt was plastered to his chest by the heat. The cicadas sounded hysterical, their cry as sharp and precise as a blade. The noise closed around Joséphine like the bars of a cage, a cage in which she felt desperately lost – no one knew she was there, no one would talk about her or believe what had happened to her. She fanned herself by pulling her blouse away from her chest, still sitting upright on her horse. His determination not to look at her aroused her further. It was something new for her, to have her charms, her scent, her natural beauty thrown back in her face. Suddenly she wasn't even sure that she was beautiful, and she didn't dare test this in the face of his indifference. She felt a defiance in him as if it were she who had to tame him. As a widow, she had no right to think of doing that, but it was sweet to have to forbid herself to desire this man.

To everyone in the village, Joséphine was magnificent, the most beautiful woman in the area – even in Figeac, the women were not as beautiful. Yet this man did not even look at her. That sweat she noticed on his neck was like a wave coming to get her, a wave flowing over the long beach of her isolation, a beach she would be happy to offer him, right there, to blot out all sorrow, so that she could drown in the feeling of sin. At least she could negotiate with guilt. She could commit a sin here and leave it here. Whereas the death of a husband – that would stay with her . . .

Down in the village the others must have lit a fire to kill the weeds – you could see the smoke from here; the mayor must have moved on from one preoccupation to another; the children were probably trying to be good by only playing in the enclosed school playground. That was life down below, where time had to be got through, with no joy or excitement, just worry and deaths to come. Whereas here, halfway up this accursed hill, in this mountain kingdom, time stood still and Joséphine had found the respite in a world which was not worried about the war or what time of day it was, nor the death of a doctor. Here everything was natural and wild, with the hot smell of lions mixed with the odour of this man. It was exotic and exciting. She could feel this world calling to her; she would come here as often as possible, and each time she would climb a little higher, until she lost herself in the harmony of the peaks, and let herself be taken by this man here as if under the influence of a wild animal . . .

First her head started to spin, then she lost her seat on the horse, who became agitated. The man did nothing but catch her just before she fell. She was light; he could hardly feel her. Something animal was at play here; he was no longer just a man, she was no longer just a woman; they were two beings drawn together instinctively. He had not held a woman in his arms for a very long time. His most recent experiences of an embrace were from his last circus acts, when his lions lay down on him one by one, crushing him with their weight so that he felt their heavy bodies on top of him and their warmth on his skin. Two years earlier, there had been a woman, in a circus in Koblenz, a horsewoman as well. But since then the only embraces worthy of the name were from his wild cats when he held them bodily, carried them, hugged them, lifted them, especially in that routine where he held Léa in his arms while Théo jumped over them, sometimes coming so close that he felt his big paw catch in his hair, as if the male was doing it on purpose, perhaps as a challenge.

It unsettled him to hold a woman like this, to breathe her in. At once he thought of Léa and Théo, and of the other lionesses and the tigress. He could guess what they would make of the smell of Joséphine. If he got too close to a woman who smelt like jasmine, the wild cats would be jealous. Once, in Provence, an over-perfumed woman had kissed his cheek just before the lights went up on the circus ring, and all through the performance the perfume had upset the animals. At the time he had twenty big cats with him and that day the lions didn't understand why the man who knew how to control them, the master who controlled them, was giving off the jasmine scent of a doe. It was as if a doe were giving them orders, a doe telling them to sit, to get up, to stand on their hind legs and to growl. That day he had had to cut the act short. He was a prisoner of the scent which meant that his lions and tigers no longer obeyed him. He had had to withdraw under the uncomprehending gaze of the public and the mocking faces of the children. The lion tamer had left the ring before the wild cats and had not taken a bow. All because of a scent just like that of the woman he now felt sink into his arms. A woman belongs to another world and to hold a woman close was disorientating. He felt soothed, at peace. It was so long since he had felt that, he thought without anger or unease. He could hardly believe it. He was looking at two small breasts, and what came to him was the unthinking desire to lay his head down on them, just once, as if to breathe her in, before biting more deeply, but he restrained himself whilst dreaming of sinking his teeth into her.

August 2017

Franck drove straight back into the Dauclercqs' yard, surprised at the cloud of dust that rose into the air as he hurtled across the dry ground. A blue Renault 4 and a tractor were parked in front of the shed, a sign that Monsieur Dauclercq was in. Given the time, they were probably having lunch. These old farming types ate at noon on the dot. He had misgivings about disturbing them as he cut the engine, but what did it matter? He slammed the door as he got out of the car. Not only would it show he was here but perhaps it would also wake the dog in the big kennel that was always strangely silent. But nothing happened; nobody came out of the house and the dog didn't appear. Instead of heading for the farm, Franck went over to the kennel to see what kind of hound was hiding inside, certain that the dog from last night would be sleeping there, recovering from its adventure. He had a look but couldn't see anything inside because of the contrast between the sun and the shade, so he got down on all fours to inspect the dark chamber. He found nothing but a dirty old cushion right at the back.

'Looking for something?'

Franck got up, dusting himself down.

'Nothing. No, nothing. I just said I would come and buy some vegetables off your wife.'

'Ah, OK.'

Monsieur Dauclercq came out of the barn and walked slowly towards Franck. He must have been over seventy-five, maybe even eighty. He was wearing a vest, his skin tanned by the sun, and was toned and slender like an athlete. He had a cap on and his neck was like thick, cracked leather. He shook Franck's hand very firmly and Franck felt obliged to grip just as hard. The man had almost hurt him.

'You don't have a dog?'

'I do have a dog. Why?'

'Because I can't see it. Is it never in its kennel?'

'It's too hot. It's in the barn, in the shade.'

'I see.'

Franck nearly asked if he could see the dog to find out if it was the same one as last night. In a way, he would have found that reassuring. Or perhaps it would have made him more worried. He didn't really know any more. All the same, he thought to himself that if that dog was hiding in the barn right now, that meant it was really unfriendly because it must have smelt him even from a distance, even if it was sleeping. The dog should have recognised him just by smell and at least come to greet him.

'What sort of vegetables do you want?'

'Listen, we'll talk about it later; I don't want to disturb you in the middle of your lunch.'

'Well, since you've already done that, come inside and discuss it with my wife.'

Franck found himself in a long dark corridor where it felt cool. Madame Dauclercq emerged from another room and shook his hand, no friendlier than before. She gestured towards a crate on the floor.

'There you go, your beans. And your twelve eggs.'

Franck looked surprised.

'It was beans and eggs that your wife asked for yesterday, wasn't it?'

'Yes, that's right. Perfect.'

Franck paid them what he owed; he didn't have time to do the maths or work out if it was cheaper than at the market, but she only gave him two coins in return for a twenty-euro note. He left hurriedly with his crate, and his eggs wrapped in twos in newspaper.

They hadn't asked him to sit down or offered him a drink, and to be honest, it was better that way. He didn't want to spend any time with them. He put the beans in the boot, feeling almost guilty about all the La Vie Claire bags piled up inside; guilty for having bought so many vegetables from competitors. Franck felt the man's eyes on his back. He had stayed on the doorstep, watching from a distance. Franck paused before getting in the car, turning around and waving goodbye. 'Well, thank you.'

The man didn't say anything but came towards Franck, scratching his head. He gazed at the car, studying it as if it was something extraordinary. In some ways, it was. Then he pointed at the new scratches and marks on its bodywork.

'Tell me, isn't it too big to get up there?'

'Yes, there are some places where there's only just enough room to get through. Mind you, there's three hundred horsepower in that engine.'

Franck thought that would be a conversation starter and the man would follow up with another question. Three hundred horsepower should have impressed him, but, no, he just walked around the car, evidently doubtful, and placed his hand on the bodywork as if it was some livestock he was weighing up. Franck felt obliged to say something.

'How long has the village at the foot of the hill been deserted?'

'Since the war.'

'The war? Which war?'

'The first of course.'

'You're not telling me that the war came to this region in 1914!'

'Not here. But to Orcières, yes.'

At that point, Madame Dauclercq came out of the house with a tea towel and a knife in her hand. Her husband looked at her. She took a moment before saying, calmly: 'Paul. Come and eat.'

Monsieur Dauclercq didn't reply. He looked away from the car and straight at Franck.

'It was carnage, let me tell you, carnage.'

'Oh really? What happened?'

'You know it's animal territory up there; it's not made for man. Do you know that?'

'What do you mean?'

'I'm telling you this so you know. Stay close to the house and don't wander too far into the hills. It's best not to get involved with all that.'

'But why?'

'There are animals . . . Just remember, there are animals.'

Franck registered this without saying anything. Maybe he was being funny, he didn't know. He had a last quick look at the barn, which the dog still hadn't come out of, but he wasn't going to ask any more questions; he would leave it there. He felt the old man was taking a perverse pleasure in playing with him by avoiding his questions or exaggerating, doing everything he could to worry him. He didn't want to give him any further opportunity. He put the key in the ignition and hit the accelerator, making the three hundred horsepower roar. He knew the man would be impressed by that.

As he manoeuvred the 4×4 through the yard, Franck couldn't help calling through the open window: 'Still, it's a big kennel.'

'It needs to be!'

He could see in his rear-view mirror that the Dauclercqs hadn't moved and were still watching him as he left the yard. It was a bit like the panning shot at the end of a Western that settles on the natives, the indigenous people watching the rider thunder away on his horse, a harbinger of the unrest to come. He was a cowboy provoking the Native Americans on their own land. Yet he knew he had everything to fear from these natives, from their curses and from their allies, whose souls had perhaps been reincarnated in all sorts of wild animals.

Franck focused on the brambles that scratched the car as he drove back up the track, physically affected by the long screeching sounds.

He hadn't played any music since the morning; he hadn't touched the car radio since he arrived. Though he was hooked on information and felt an overwhelming need to listen to multiple news bulletins every day, he hadn't even thought of switching it on since the morning. The silence suited him perfectly, as did the noise he was creating. The wheels slipped on the stones in some places, causing them to spray up violently into the air. Inside the car he was shaken about as if he were in a spaceship travelling through the atmosphere, or in a kayak hurtling over rapids . . . Actually, he was enjoying himself. He had to concentrate though, to avoid the big holes in the ground and stay on the track, with the steep hillside on his left lined by trees but overlooking empty space. If he skidded or swerved to the left, he would plunge into the oaks and box trees below, which would not take the weight of the Audi. The trees disappeared completely in places, so even veering off course slightly would mean plummeting off the side.

When he reached the house, everything was as he had left it. All the doors, shutters and windows were still open, and the curtains upstairs were still closed. The building was like a ghost ship with all its sails lowered, travelling alone through the ocean without a soul on board. Franck got out of the car with the pride of someone who has journeyed the entire land for provisions, full of the hunter's sense of satisfaction at returning with a haversack full of game. He called Lise twice. She didn't reply. He opened the boot and the bags were warm; he had to get them all out quickly. He called her again.

'Lise, come and look at what I've got!'

Lise still didn't answer. She couldn't still be asleep; it was gone midday. Franck left the bags there and went back into the house. He couldn't see her, so he went upstairs. She was no longer in bed. The sheet was where it had been that morning with the bedspread discarded on the floor, but she wasn't in the bed. He was afraid of shouting from the window, of making her name ring out through these hills. He was afraid that by calling out 'Lise', he would awaken whatever enemy might be lurking in the hills and trees, watching them. Lise's phone was still on the bedside table. Switched off. He didn't like seeing phones turned off; it seemed like death to him. His imagination ran riot before he could do anything about it. This time it wasn't because of the wild animals he didn't want to believe in but had heard loud and clear last night; this time he was wondering whether Lise had simply left, terrified at waking up alone in the big open house. Maybe when she saw the car wasn't there she had panicked and fled, either distressed or disappointed, or pursued by that dog . . . He was again overcome with crippling anxiety at the thought that if he lost his wife one day, or if she lost him, there would be nothing to show for their life together: no descendants, nothing apart from absence, a silence just like the one all around him. Children help to fill the silence, the emptiness. Humans don't have children to populate the world but to prove they exist. If he lost Lise, he would lose everything, and now he couldn't find her.

October 1914

Fear makes a bad counsellor but is very often the first to show up. That Sunday, after Mass, Couderc found it difficult to conceal his anxiety. Beneath his assured demeanour, he struggled to suppress a terrifying thought. As he stood, perplexed, looking at the empty square, he wondered if the mothers' premonition of doom had been fulfilled. There was not a child in sight. The square in front of the church, usually filled with the bustle and sounds of games of hide-and-seek, now lay under an atrocious pall of silence. The children had all disappeared and there was no laughter or shouting.

Since the outbreak of war there had been a resurgence of religious belief, or, at least, people had begun to attend Mass again. The women brought the old people, who all gathered in the front pews of the little church, apart from Fernand and Couderc, who sat at the back. All the women felt that because God decided when it was time to die, God must have something to do with the war. Perhaps he was the instigator, or the one who would save them from it, but either way, his role was crucial. With the men gone, the women came to church to talk to God about them and to have the little cardboard crosses they had made to send to them blessed. They prayed for the men to come back soon, hoping the authority they prayed to did exist. Since the outbreak of war the parish priest had made the effort to come up to the village with his big golden chalice and his censer sent from Rome, although he didn't have a car or a horse any more. For the last two months, he had made the journey on foot, inspired by the newly canonised Joan of Arc, who featured in all his sermons; he always glorified her army of liberation, saying very definitely, 'God is on our side, not on the side of the Germans, those wicked Protestants, those heretics who desecrate the Virgin and go straight to Damnation when they die. No one dared contradict him. He would then lead them in singing, always hymns that attested to miracles, because even if individually they sang out of tune, all together they made a kind of harmony. Anyway, it felt good to sing to God, who might be able to help them, so good that for an hour or so they forgot about the children, who had stayed outside to play.

Outside the church a succession of prayers and readings could be heard, the word of God echoing around the old stones. But once Mass had finished the only sound was that of a piano being played at the other end of the village. Music flowed from the house of Dr Manouvrier. Since Joséphine had learnt that her husband was lost, she had had no further interest in God; she refused the facile hope offered by censers, and during the service she played particularly loudly. Her harmonies filled the emptiness of the large rooms, and spilled outside. The melody wove in and out of the damp vegetation like a needle sewing. Joséphine's piano was the only music to be heard for miles around. Other than the sickly organ accompanying the prayers and the liturgy, there was never music here, except when someone began to sing as they worked, back in the days when people still felt like singing. The villagers said that Joséphine played on Sunday morning on purpose. Because, like their parents and grandparents before them, they always believed the worst of those who had different ideas from them. Perhaps she played then because that was when she felt most alone. She took advantage of the fact that everyone else was curled up in the arms of Christ, hoping for a miracle from him, or his pardon; perhaps she was being considerate.

So it was with Joséphine's recital in the background that everyone came out of the little church, pleasantly surprised by the warm October weather. The sun had moved across the hill and the plane trees were bathed in that eleven o'clock sunshine that brought the village to life, like colour returning to cheeks. But when the women saw that their children were not there, they grew pale. Normally at the end of Mass, their children fell upon them eagerly. But this Sunday, there was not the slightest sign of life outside the church. Up above, Mont d'Orcières had finished hiding the sun, which glared at them like never before. That morning the sun seemed to be sitting on the summit, aiming at them like a mirror reflecting a huge bright light. They shielded their eyes to look up at it, but they were blinded by the glare and by the sudden feeling of being controlled by the mountain. Even with their hands as a shield, that morning the flaming yellow scorched their eyes. Strangely the lions were calm. It felt eerie not to hear them. All that could be heard was the piano in the distance. Fernand immediately guessed what the mothers were thinking. And once again, he defended the lion tamer, in the name of human decency. The women were quick to panic when it came to their children, and seeing the way the mountain crushed them that day, spitting the sun back at them as if it were the coin of an evil deity, they interpreted that as a warning that a sacrifice was to take place and they immediately assumed that the lions had stolen the flesh of their flesh.

In view of their irrational response, it was important to find answers quickly. Everyone, for once silent, looked to the mayor and the schoolmaster. As for Priest Magnard, the old prelate who accompanied his flock to the church door, as if gently returning skiffs to the sea, he could not conceal his horror at the sight of the empty square. He made things worse when he reminded everyone that, according to the Bible, lions were impure animals, like all quadrupeds which were not shod, and that even Noah had not welcomed them into the Ark because lions, as well as being carnivores that devoured carrion, did not mind eating men, and he spoke of several missionaries, white priests, who had ended up in the jaws of those monsters. The most savage lands had not been evangelised for fear of lions. 'Lions are the enemies of God; they have deprived parts of the colonies of the best of all religions . . .'

The priest knew he must never underplay the concerns of his parishioners. Even if that meant embracing any of their passing fears, it didn't matter; it was important that his flock felt listened to. A priest is a man who is profoundly aware that he is not God, but who must at all times emphasise His omnipotence.

The continuing strains of piano music felt chillingly inappropriate. The men who were left, that is to say those who were unfit for service and the old, agreed on what should be done. They would have to go up the mountain, immediately.

La Bûche went to the wash house down by the river. Sometimes the kids took it into their heads to go and play there, even though none of them knew how to swim. But he returned without any children in tow. There had been no footprints on the riverbank, so they hadn't been there that morning. They couldn't be playing in the fields either, because they would have been visible in the filtered light of the walnut trees, or elsewhere. And in any case they would have heard them. A group of children, excited by Sunday morning games, would make enough noise to be heard wherever they were, even if they were hiding. They would call them; of course they would. But it was terrifying to begin calling the name of your child, especially there, coming out of Mass and walking towards the edge of the village. It would be appalling to be shouting their name whilst looking in ditches. It would be like a horrible roll-call. Joseph, Ange, Marie, Jeanne, Louis, André, Madeleine, Lucienne, Aimée, Reine, Léone . . . For a mother, calling the name of her son or her daughter, calling it loudly across fields, was as heartbreaking as losing them, but in addition it implied they had done something wrong, that they had not watched over their children. And yet they began to walk, calling out towards the mountain. They left the village and began climbing in the shadow of the mountain, towards the east, still calling but more and more faintly as their throats constricted.

August 2017

He was about to cup his hands around his mouth and call out . . .
But the idea of calling 'Lise' over and over, making her name echo
round the hills, seemed excessive and frightening. For the first time,
shouting was the only way of reaching her. And yet he couldn't bring
himself to do it. In the vast echo of the hills her name would ring out
alarmingly. He got back in the car, turned on the ignition and honked
several times in a row, a series of quick blasts. It was incredible, the
way it echoed. Unbeknownst to him, he sent the jays, magpies and
goldfinches into a panic; the deer, wild boar and hares in the woods
stiffened in fright; he terrified the foxes, field mice and all the other
fleeing creatures. He spread fear everywhere his hooting could be
heard, setting off waves of frightened reactions. In giving in to his
fear, he had caused all of nature around him to panic. Yet when he
stopped, the silence became even more complete. He got out of the
car, terrified at how powerless the woods made him feel.

It had become so normal to find somebody as soon as you
wanted them, to reach them straight away by phone call or text.
But here, surrounded by hills that went on forever, he couldn't do
anything. So, he pulled himself together, doing what he would have
done if she had been there with him, telling him to calm down.
He told himself that she must have gone for a walk, that she had
gone for her first hike; yes, that was it, she had wanted to come
here to go walking and take full advantage of its isolation. Unless
she had been frightened when she woke up all alone in the big bed
and opened the curtains to find nothing but green, empty space. He

leant against the car, defeated by his surroundings.

Suddenly he became aware of chirruping sounds rising like a wave from the ground, and adding to his anxiety. It started with one cicada, then another over there, and then hundreds. The clamour enveloped everything in its repetitive hysteria of mingled song springing up from everywhere . . . Perhaps the horn had woken them up, but in any case, they all came together in one cacophony. When he had left that morning, he hadn't noticed the frenetic noises now filling the air; in the morning cicadas don't stir. But now in the sunshine, the waves of sound were like an extra element in the atmosphere, so high-pitched that they rushed into his ears like a stream of water and encircled his brain. Perhaps their song got ten times louder on the stroke of noon; perhaps that was when they were at their most powerful – or else it was just his own fear taking hold of him like a migraine. He tried to get a grip. He repeated to himself what Lise would have said had she been there: 'Franck, calm down, don't worry. Get everything out of the boot and put it in the shade or in the fridge. I'm coming . . .'

If she had been there, she would have told him to calm down. Only he couldn't. Because of the image that kept coming back to him. Last night, the dog had been right there, the huge dog with the shining eyes, standing there alertly, just as he had been, while the terrible racket came from below, listening to the growls of the animals hiding in the half-light at the bottom of the valley. Even now at midday, the valley floor was in shadow, turning the land into folds of dark, humid terrain, from which the hill opposite rose. Its dense, wooded slope went up to the crest in front of him with the hill rolling down on the other side to an area of shadow like this one, a valley at the foot of which another hill rose up, and so on until you reached the Massif Central, and then the Urals. In this landscape, every wooded hill was surrounded by a mysterious gully of shadows, a dip in the land that the sun didn't reach. The noises had found their way out of that dark, damp ravine last night, and now Lise appeared from those very shadows. She emerged from the undergrowth forgotten by the sun, walking calmly, slowly, straight ahead. He couldn't believe it and nearly panicked, fearing that she had been regurgitated by some predator. But she was strolling serenely, with her big hat and a foam mat under her arm, as if she were leaving a yoga or meditation session. He was so pleased to see the beloved figure, so calm and free as always, as opposed to him who was soaked in sweat. He loved Lise for her grace, for the elegance of her every movement. Now when she walked through the tall valley grass, rather than dragging her feet, she lifted her knees high, appearing slender and almost weightless. The sight of her took him back to the day they met in real life, for before he had only ever seen her on-screen. In some ways, she was still the same as she'd been that day, whilst he felt he had changed a lot, weighed down in all sorts of ways.

She signalled to him from below, a happy little wave that he answered by raising his hand, barely moving it. He was annoyed at himself for being scared, but relieved that she was there. Before starting up the long meadow that ran all the way up to the house Lise turned around as if waiting for someone. A dog sprang out of the undergrowth, the famous wolf dog of unknown provenance, which now began to run around her, overjoyed that she was letting it come with her. Franck didn't understand; the animal had obviously been following her since the morning, or else she had found it down there. But it was definitely the same dog that had rushed down the hill in its crazy pursuit through the Black Triangle last night.

Franck was moved to see it again, but he was also worried. Next to Lise, you could see just how enormous it was. Last night he hadn't noticed if it had a collar, even though that's the first thing you look for when you come across a dog in the middle of the countryside, to see if there's a way of identifying it. Only a collar would reveal who the animal belonged to. Lise and the dog were still five hundred metres away. Lise was now finding out just how steep the slope was, and she was only wearing flip-flops. Franck felt a hint of irritation on seeing that; it wasn't sensible to go walking through tall grass and into undergrowth in nothing but a pair of flip-flops. At the same time he was moved by how free she always was, by her ability just to be, possessing a kind of insouciance that never left her, and made her carefree, never anxious. The dog was playing beside her as if they had known each other for ever. Then it positioned itself in front of her, stood up on its hind legs and put its paws on Lise's shoulders, as if it wanted to lick her face. It almost knocked her over. She stumbled, and he heard her laughing. Her laugh, breaking through the manic chirping of the insects, stood out like a beacon of hope. Even so, the dog was strong and lively, and it thrashed around her as she climbed, repeatedly moving away and going back to her. It could have easily knocked her over without meaning to. It leant against her and she pushed it away. The animal thought it was a game. It was already very hot in the midday sun.

Franck walked down to meet her and she waited for him halfway up the hill, getting her breath back.

'You scared me. God, you scared me!'

'Why? I was meditating. In the shade. It's amazing down there, you know. It's like a jungle – you can hear all kinds of noises. It's perfect for reconnecting with yourself.'

'Reconnecting with yourself?'

Sometimes she infuriated him. Though he envied her simplicity and her natural inclination always to look on the bright side, at times she appalled him, since he was so unlike that.

'Have you seen? I found a dog.'

The dog must have known they were talking about it; it looked Franck right in the eye, as if everything was suddenly getting serious. It didn't move. Franck could sense the animal was expecting something from him. It seemed to be awaiting an order or instruction; to find out if it could carry on playing or if it had to start pursuing new prey, like last night. Franck gave an order, as if he were the dog's master.

'Fetch . . . Go and fetch the animal!'

The dog stood attentive but totally confused. It started to bark roughly while staring at Franck, as if it was asking him to say something else, to be more precise.

'Franck, what are you doing? Leave the dog alone.'

'No, Lise, you can see it expects something from me.'

'Come on, what are you talking about? Let's go back up, I'm thirsty. And hungry. You got the water?'

'Damn. I got everything apart from the water . . .'

Lise had started to go back up towards the house, with new purpose in her step.

'Well, if the dog's waiting for you to give it an order, tell it to go and fetch some water.'

'Wait, Lise! I have to tell you about what happened last night.'

Lise answered him without turning around: 'What are you going to tell me now? That you've seen wolves? Bears? Apparently there are lynxes around here – I read it on the internet but I didn't tell you because you'd have made such a big deal of it.'

Franck caught up with her.

'Well, maybe it's that, Lise, lynxes . . . Maybe that's what it was last night. There were strange noises down there – you've no idea. They were incredible; it was awful.'

'You know, you should have been a scriptwriter, not a producer.'

'No, Lise, wait, stop. I swear there were animals down there last night, loads of animals making extraordinary noises; it gave me the creeps, believe me, and without thinking I told the dog to "Go fetch", and it did. It ran after those animals and it must have been chasing them until dawn. I heard it howling far away, barking from the other side of the hills, and then afterwards, nothing.'

'Oh right, because it was already here last night?'

'Yes, it kept me company.'

'You're talking about it like it's a human being!'

'No, it's just that in the pitch dark, it was there.'

'Well, look at you, the one who'd given up on making new friends!'

Franck ran his hand over the dog's back, cautiously touching its neck. Its coat was rough, thick. The dog was looking elsewhere, as if it couldn't feel his hand and couldn't care less for his affection. Franck stroked the top of its head just a little, still not daring to go too far.

'Lise, have you seen . . .?'

'What?'

'It doesn't have a collar!'

'So?'

'So it doesn't belong to anyone . . .'

October 1914

To be the master of an animal is to become its God. Above all you must provide food. Otherwise the animal will turn feral, or die. Food is the reason an animal gives up its liberty. But lions only eat animal flesh – dark-red pulsating flesh, newly wrenched from life. Like all big wild cats, lions and tigers need the meat of other mammals, which are not necessarily slower than them, but weaker or isolated. They kill their prey with brute violence, ripping open the flanks of antelopes or buffaloes, devouring the flesh of their victims and deciding more than God which animals are to live and which to die.

In the wild, this happens naturally, but, for the lion tamer, feeding eight big cats five kilos of fresh meat every day was an impossible challenge. That was why he had decided that on Sundays they would go hungry. He had always made them fast one day a week, on Wednesdays. But since the outbreak of war, he had added another fast day. The lions must be made to feel pangs of hunger. This saved him from the burden of finding fresh meat every day of the week, but also accustomed the big cats to hunger and lack of food, reinforced his power over them and showed them he was still their master. He had to drum into the animals that, without him, they would not eat. Their lives depended on him.

Without knowing anything about calendars, the lions at least knew when it was Wednesday and Sunday. On those two days they paced up and down their cages even more than usual. Whether they were each in their own box, or all together in the big round cage, on Sunday and Wednesday they twitched nervously, maddened by hunger. When they saw a buzzard circling in the sky, or a goat or cat running in the distance, or caught the scent of the flock grazing in the pasture because of the direction of the wind, they would stare into space, obsessing over the thought of the prey that was not being offered to them, and they would roar. In their heads they would howl with rage and devour the prey, killing it with a snap of their jaws. In their dreams they swallowed that goat, cat or buzzard that continued to live in front of them. Then they would lie down on the fresh ground, coldly resigned to submission, to leaving everything up to that man who spoke louder than the blood lust rising in them.

Although all lions think about is eating, they do not think of eating humans, unless they're too old to hunt real prey. Of all kinds of prey that tries to escape, humans run the slowest, so make a conquest that is so ignoble that only old or injured lions lower themselves to attack them. As for eating children, they might do that in a frenzy of savagery, or if they had been hungry for a very long time, or maybe to get their revenge for all those years spent being taunted by children at the circus, children with their unbearable frightened or laughing faces, children who sometimes threw stones at them. In those cases the lions did not react; they pretended not to see them, staring past them through the bars. To lions therefore there was no reason to eat children, unless to make them pay for the silliness of others. Other than that, lions were not the least bit attracted to these fresh-faced creatures, with their unformed scent and salt-less sweat. To gobble up a kid would be to bite into little muscles and swallow blood with no taste. Quite the opposite of the thick meat seasoned with the taste of conquest, of those buffaloes whose flavour was enhanced by the struggle. To a lion, a child was no kind of meal.

And to a pianist a child was no kind of audience. And yet here they all were, sitting on the ground, good as gold, listening to the young woman playing. Some of them – boys, of course – could glimpse Joséphine's fine ankles moving under the lace of her dress. They followed the movement of her feet as she worked the pedals

144

modulating the high and low notes. As for the girls, as well as the music, they were discovering up close the delicate complexion and sweet smile of the pianist, and a feminine ambiance that was much more enticing than muddy farms or mucky stables.

The villagers had never seen the children so calm. Joséphine closed the piano and rose, tall and svelte, with her long musical fingers. She turned to the group of worried mothers looking in through her window. They didn't dare get angry with her and had even forgotten to feel relief.

No one would ever dare reproach Joséphine. She was regarded as the first widow, although they did not speak of this, and so embodied the tragedy they were all hoping to escape. Her misfortune made it seem as if she had been chosen as an offering. A bit like a lightning conductor, her sacrifice protected the others, and it made her sacred. Since the disappearance of her husband, they were wary of her grief and did not want to upset her. There was also the fact that she was associated with medicine, and, whether her husband was dead or not, she was still in a small way representative of that science from which they wished to benefit. When the doctor had been there, it was Joséphine who would greet you if he had not yet returned from his rounds. She would invite you to sit down and could always find some reassuring phrases. Providing comfort like that was part of medicine. Just as she had known how to reassure the village by riding up to see the lion tamer, and then swearing to everyone that the wild animals were firmly controlled and locked up, that there was nothing to fear and the lion tamer could be trusted. According to her, the lion tamer still had two goats and four sheep. She had also told them about the ossuary, beside the water tank, a mass of bones and carcasses jumbled together, which showed that the lion tamer had another source of livestock, big animals with large bodies, wide vertebrae and ribs twice as long as sheep ribs. The important point was the German knew where to get food for his lions, so there was no need to fear for humans.

Elegance and misfortune insulated Joséphine from malicious gossip, but some had noticed that since the day she had been to talk to the German, she could sometimes be seen on her horse in the evening, heading in the direction of the mountain, the suspicion being that she was having a liaison with the odious lord on high, that she had supped with the devil. Without ever saying that they were sleeping together, the villagers assumed that this was one of those unnatural couplings that were formed by superior beings, the sort of pact that it was best to stay well away from.

By the time they got home with their offspring, the mothers had recovered from their anguish, but they remained downcast for the rest of the day. Their heads were still full of all the terrible atrocities they had imagined. They wanted the joy of Sunday to last at least until the evening, when fear would take hold again. Every night as they went to bed, they were invariably seized by the worry that they would never see their husband, brother, fiancé or son ever again, or that the world would ignite and lava made from the dust and earth of the Ardennes would rain down on them. Lava could reach even the most remote places. That Sunday evening they tucked up their children more tightly and closed the doors and windows. Children were a reason to live; you had them so that they could be your friends later, your allies. It was warm for October, too warm to have everything closed, but outside there were noises. Much as they wanted to trust Joséphine, they could not convince themselves. She seemed too close to the evil man: she must be biased. And just as boar and foxes had started coming up to the houses, so, in winter, the wolves would also come and there was no one to hunt them. No village policeman either. The predators would have free rein. Some already claimed to have seen lynxes at night, and then, of course, there was the noise of the lions. There had not been this din when the men were still there – or perhaps no one had paid any attention to it. But fear meant that the least noise caused anxiety. The hooting of white and tawny owls and the howls of fighting cats mingled with the screeches of the foxes.

After the roe deer of August, during the first nights of autumn they heard the terrifying cries of stags crashing into each other, as they fought to the death. Every night fear weighed a bit more heavily on the world, like a glass cloche, a great dome which covered everything. Inside this, everything reverberated in the dark, even the horrible squeaks of bats, and the chirping of birds, keeping the village from sleep. People got up several times a night to take a look outside; more than once they thought they saw someone in the distance. In the dense shadow of the wood, they thought they could make out the pilgrim from the night before war broke out, the monk with his mule who had come from Santiago and was turning back, the bearer of ill-luck from the first night, the pilgrim who had set everything in motion.

August 2017

For lunch, Franck prepared the kind of salad they liked in summer. Tomatoes, basil, rocket, mozzarella and finely sliced courgettes with lots of olive oil. Meanwhile Lise took a long shower. He heard her singing in the little bathroom downstairs, a room so basic it echoed. The pipes and hot water tank made a terrible noise, though he didn't actually know if Lise was using hot water – cold water should be enough in this heat. The dog was outside, standing guard a good two metres away from the house. The door was wide open, and it could easily have come in out of the sun, but it didn't. Franck could feel its eyes on him. It was watching his every move from afar, as if trying to work out what he was doing and what he was making. As a meat-eater, it would not be impressed with the salad. Just for fun, Franck showed the dog the bowl of salad, and it sniffed the air and wagged its tail but stayed where it was.

Perhaps someone had taught it not to go into houses, or perhaps instinctively it didn't feel it should. Franck didn't know. Several times, he patted his thigh and held out a piece of bread to entice it inside, but each time, the dog made a strange movement with its the head, pricked up its ears and whimpered, but didn't move. It hadn't moved since it arrived, even though it was right in the sun. Had it shifted towards the shade on the right, it wouldn't have been able to see what was going on inside the house. At times you could hear the snap of its jaw as it gobbled up one of the wasps buzzing around it. It was a harsh, deep noise, made up of the sound of teeth coming together and the clicking of its thick tongue. Franck couldn't tell if it was really catching the wasps and swallowing them. But he noticed that the dog pricked up its ears every time he raised the knife to slice the tomatoes, mozzarella or bread. Franck even tried picking up the big knife and putting it down several times – the knife he had left outside the previous night – and the dog reacted differently depending on what he did. It paused and tensed when Franck picked the knife up, not moving and barely even panting, but when Franck put it down again, the dog relaxed and went back to its staccato breathing.

'You're hot. Come into the shade. Come here, come on . . .'

The dog cocked its ears, nothing more. Franck filled a big salad bowl with water from the tap and put it outside. The dog sniffed at the surface but didn't drink it, looking at Franck again as if waiting for something, but it clearly wasn't water.

'What do you want, doggy, eh? And what's your name, eh, and why don't you have a collar?'

The dog stared at Franck with a disarmingly disappointed expression, as if it could understand his words but didn't know how to respond.

Lise reappeared in a simple sarong, combing her wet hair.

'So you speak to dogs now?'

'No, I'm trying to work out what it expects from me . . .'

'It must be disappointed.'

'Why do you say that?'

'It's just been watching you cut up tomatoes, vegetables, basil . . . It must be missing meat.'

Franck looked again at the dog, which was still staring at him. Maybe that was what it was waiting for: meat. Franck rolled some bread into a solid ball and tossed it over. The dog stood alert, but when the ball landed near it, it glanced over and didn't even sniff it. Maybe it was only interested in hunting real prey like last night, or wanted at least to honour its master, since dogs pride themselves on obeying orders, in which case this dog probably wasn't as wild as all that. If it belonged to the Dauclercqs down the hill, perhaps they didn't really look after it, or maybe they relied on the animal to stand guard. Yes, that must be it, the dog was an informer and it was there to keep an eye on them. The Dauclercqs were so odd that they would be perfectly capable of sending their dog to spy on them and to make sure everything was as it should be. But it would be unbearable to be monitored by a dog. On the other hand, had it belonged to them, it would have had a collar, if only to attach to the chain that was always trailing outside the kennel.

Lise started laying the table outside. The dog watched her, unmoving. Perhaps it was just delighted that there was so much going on; maybe it was quite simply bored.

'Lise, do you think it's lost?'

'No, because it would be scared.'

'A stray dog then?'

'No, if it was a stray, it would run away.'

Franck looked at her, amazed at how she had an answer for everything and was so calm and self-assured. As he prepared more salad he tried to come up with other explanations. It could be a hunting dog that had escaped from a battue a long time ago, or the dog of a distant neighbour who didn't mind their animal roaming far and wide. Or it could even be a real wolf dog, a hybrid born of the union between a she-wolf and a dog. Especially as the people in this area had deserted their land, the farmers had given up on their farms, the station had gone, the railway tracks were no more than cuttings overgrown with brambles and acacias, and the little villages had been abandoned one by one and the once inhabited areas reclaimed by the wilderness. The parts that were already wild were becoming wilder still. That was what was happening in various places; nature was becoming wild again, because with animals reigning supreme and doing whatever they pleased, pigs and wild boar, dogs and wolves all cross-breeding, it was inevitable . . .

'My God, Franck, what are you doing, we'll never eat all that!'

Absorbed in his game of winding up the dog by playing with the knife, Franck had cut up six big tomatoes and two packets of mozzarella, and then sliced three courgettes before seasoning everything.

For lunch, Lise wanted to move the table into the shade of the big walnut tree on the left. Franck reminded her that you shouldn't sit under a walnut tree: his grandmother always said it was unlucky, as the leaves gave off a poisonous gas. But Lise retorted that that was nonsense, an old wives' tale put about by farm owners to stop their employees taking siestas under the walnut trees. In fact, the shade of the tree was perfect, dense and cool and good for them in every way. For just a moment, they both thought back to their distant backgrounds, grandparents born in the countryside who, luckily for them, had left behind their rural roots for the city. They settled under the tree without further delay, and the dog joined them, though it remained a little way away. Lise was right that it was nice here, and they were happy. All three of them.

They barely ate half of what Franck had prepared. After lunch, Lise rolled out a mat in the shade to take a siesta. Franck stretched out on the grass. It was getting hotter, even underneath the tree, and the air was like a furnace. But there was a slight breeze from time to time, they had got used to the song of the cicadas, which was now just background noise, and the rustling leaves made a swooshing sound. It was a perfect moment. Franck took off his T-shirt and rolled it up under his head like a pillow. Once again, Lise dozed off straight away, and there was something angelic about her beautiful face as she slept. It wasn't the same for Franck. He was bothered by the prickly grass, and by the flies and wasps that only seemed to go for him. The dog was lying down too, less than a metre from Franck, its stomach flat on the ground, in search of whatever coolness it could find. Franck wondered whether it was doing everything he did, if it was imitating him, or if he was imitating the dog. It had drunk from

151

the salad bowl of cold water several times while they were eating, but its tongue was still hanging out and it had been panting for a while, even though it hadn't run anywhere, and the sound of its breathing worried him. Franck looked at the unlikely visitor. As soon as a wasp or fly came near them, the dog tried to gulp it down in one, chasing it in fact. Was it making sure Franck wasn't bothered by the insects out of kindness or was it just an automatic reaction? Whatever it was, the dog kept watching him, doing an even better job than if he had ordered it to stay beside him. What he had learnt from the handlers on various films was that dogs can't stand being alone; they need company. Franck noticed that the dog was attaching itself to him in some way, although he didn't know how to get anything from the dog, nor how to give it an order, or any kind of instruction. He wondered if he could somehow be blamed for keeping the dog, or for having stolen it? Surely not. Anyway, nobody would ever come all the way up here.

Franck finally managed to close his eyes. There was a slight breeze at ground level, and as he was wearing nothing but shorts it bringing welcome relief. At one point, the dog put its head on his calf. He couldn't believe it. It must have been a gesture of friendship from the animal. Franck opened his eyes again and lifted his head a little, as carefully as possible, catching the dog still staring at him. Perhaps it just wanted to get along with him, but the intensity of its gaze was rather disturbing.

It was hot, too hot in fact, but Franck wanted to try playing with it properly; maybe that was what the animal expected. He stood up, walked in front of the house a bit, then decided to go in the direction of the large water tank that was well shaded amidst all that greenery. He didn't need to say a word for the dog to get up and follow him, watchful and alert, ears cocked and no longer affected by the heat. Franck spotted some cones on the tall cypresses, dense, compact balls that fitted nicely in his hand. He picked one off and felt its weight bouncing it in his palm while watching to see how the dog would react. The animal stared him dead in the eye with a piercing gaze, and then, without warning, Franck took aim and threw the projectile as hard and as far as he could towards the slope. He threw it so hard that he hurt his shoulder; the cone flew through the air and rolled on and on, like a tennis ball. The dog paused, glanced at Franck, then at the slope, and suddenly shot off despite the heat of the sun. Taking to the game with surprising alacrity, it threw itself down the hill after the makeshift ball, running so fast it left a cloud of dust in its wake. The ball carried on rolling and had travelled more than a hundred metres by the time the dog reached it. Its nose collided with it, sending the cone flying for a few metres. The dog caught it in one swift movement when it bounced one more time, snaring it firmly between its teeth. Far in the distance, it stopped dead and turned back towards Franck.

'Bring it here . . . Come here!'

As if it had been waiting for this instruction, the dog came running back towards him immediately with the cone in its mouth, even though it must have been exhausted from going up the hill in this heat. But once at his feet, it didn't want to let go of the cone. Franck tried to pull it from its mouth, but the dog was growling and made a sharp movement, freeing itself from his grip with a jerk of its head so violent that Franck nearly lost his balance.

'Whoa, gently. Gently . . . Come on, give it to me. Give me the ball!'

From then on their understanding was at an end. The dog dug its heels in, its expression fierce, its lips drawn back and its teeth clamped down on the ball. Franck couldn't make sense of it. Clearly the part of this animal that was dog wanted to play, but the part that was wolf didn't. The wolf part expected something completely different from fetching a ball. Franck could see it when it growled, its oblique wide-set eyes narrowed, their wild yellow colour electrified by two black pupils, two sharp points that disappeared under its eyelids when it snarled, giving it a sudden air of utter menace. Still facing Franck, the dog began grinding its teeth in a frantic attempt to destroy the cypress cone, as if it wanted to negate the game by shattering it completely. Its mouth was contorted by effort into a strange smile that was more terrifying than playful, especially as it was growling with excitement, fragments of cone falling from its mouth. It was fear, then, that Franck felt, a fear that wasn't just in his head but seemed to be coming from all around him, suspended in the oppressive heat and the pockets of air that rippled just above the ground, lingering in the chirping of insects that was getting louder and louder, and in the growls of the wolf dog that had now started to bark, still looking Franck straight in the eye as if challenging him to take the shattered ball that was clenched in its mouth and that it didn't want to relinquish. It is profoundly frightening when a wolf dog comes towards you snarling, especially when it's tall and strong and you don't know what it's thinking, and it's staring at you with a furious expression, back half lowered. Franck picked up what was left of the mangled ball and the dog watched with a look of incomprehension that bordered on contempt. Then it started barking again, but louder this time, an outburst so intense that it went right through Franck, the animal projecting more than a hundred decibels of fury or warning at Franck while staring at him and moving closer. Franck dropped the remains of the ball on the ground, but the dog just became more and more threatening. It could probably be heard from miles away. Lise came running over, awoken by the racket, but she instinctively kept her distance. To stop it barking, you just had to stop looking at it. Franck realised this and walked towards Lise without so much as a glance at the dog, aware that it was still staring at him.

'Lise, I think it's trying to tell us something.'

'What did you do to it?'

'Nothing, it's the dog. I'm sure it's asking us not to stay. To leave.

It's trying to warn us. That's it, it's trying to tell us that something here doesn't want us.'

'Franck, is that the only excuse you can come up with for going back to Paris?'

'No, Lise, I'm serious.'

October 1914

The mornings were even more disquieting than the nights. Before the war, days would begin peacefully. The sun gently roused the leaves; light and noise built gradually as robins and blackbirds began to sing. Birdsong spoke of blue skies. But now the soundtrack to dawn was provided by wild cats, a much darker theme. Birdsong signalled survival. When birds sing it is to announce themselves, to mark out a territory. Lions do the same, but their raucous growling thunders out like falling rocks. When you're woken by those noises they stay in your head all day and haunt you until sundown with the fear of being eaten.

Three months is enough to form a habit and in the village there was now a little saying, born of people's natural tendency to create proverbs and elevate them to the status of principles: 'If to a lion's roar you wake, all day long you tremble and quake.' Couderc, however, declared himself enchanted by the roars. And in this he was like the children. When they were in bed and heard the lions, they prayed for the noise to continue. To them, the cries of the lions were like the call from a promised land. It was as if the animal magic of the fairy tales and fables they were made to read at school had come to life. Hearing the wild beasts told of a full-size circus or some other tempting world. Fortunately, the hill was too steep and too off-putting for the children to attempt to get near the lions. And like their mothers, they were too exhausted to try to run away. In August they had worked hard to bring in the harvest and the hay, and then moved straight on to ploughing and sowing the new crops, doing it all without the men, at a time when there was no more manure, no oxen and no energy. School had started, but after class the children did not go home to do their homework. They were in the fields until sunset. As well as pulling potatoes, there were walnuts, chestnuts and mushrooms to harvest, all of which required bending low, something the old people could no longer do.

In the autumn, there would also be a thousand other picking tasks to be performed, and the only livestock left were three oxen between ten farms – old, limping creatures the army did not want. Women were not used to handling oxen, and they found them impossible to manage. Children helped their mothers lift the yoke over the horns of the huge beasts, saving the women hours wrestling with the harnesses and becoming exhausted before they set to work. Old heavy oxen required strength to master them and, once harnessed, the women struggled with the mass of uncooperative muscle to get them to work. They had to coerce and shout at them, and control them very tightly, particularly when it came to ploughing between trees and turning at the end of the furrows, when there was not a centimetre to spare. After these intense days of work both women and children slept soundly. Fatigue was a blessing, blurring their thoughts and dampening their fears. In the morning when the howling of the lions drove them from their beds, mothers arose thinking of the thousand things they had to do. The children on the other hand lingered in bed, savouring their dreams of who knew which African country, where they were surrounded by loving felines, without an ounce of malice in them. They imagined exotic bulrushes on the banks of a stream, luxuriant oxbow lakes, a beautiful river, immense and warm, unlike the river down below which you could cross in three steps and was nothing more than a stream edged with purslane.

Then one day irrationality took over. In mid-October the sun sank all of a sudden, as was the case each autumn. But the old people decided that the shadow which lasted until midday was this time the fault of the German. Couderc kept saying that the shadow projected

157

by the rock had been there since Jurassic times, that Mont d'Orcières had always cast one side of the valley into morning shade. But for every ill, someone must be held responsible, and everything was laid at the door of the Hun. He had become the thief of their mornings; he kept the sun for himself, and the closer they got to winter the worse it would become. Until April, he would keep the sun to heat his animals' fur and would not let it go until midday, like a half-empty watering can.

Couderc had read enough books not to give too much credence to those beliefs, and if it is said that travel educates children, reading is even more important because it teaches you to see the world from lots of different points of view. Couderc understood that the animals up above frightened the villagers and he did his utmost to counteract their beliefs and superstitions. People always used to listen to Couderc, but once they realised that he couldn't say whether the war would end soon or go on, they understood that all his knowledge had no power to change things. Their instinct told them that power came from a higher source than man.

The mountain had been damned long before the lion tamer settled there, but obviously the fact that this false Noah had come to live there was no coincidence. It was proof that he was damned too. And the fact was that, since his arrival, everything had gone wrong. And they missed what they had had – plentiful food, farm animals. And most of all they missed the voices of the absent men. Since the German had been there, fatigue and privation combined to poison everything. Even if it was unfair to hold him responsible, they needed a scapegoat. As their troubles mounted and they saw there was nothing they could do about it, the German provided an outlet for their feelings of powerlessness. They genuinely believed he was responsible for the shadow cast over them until midday, and the shadow was a worse punishment than damnation. When they raised their fists, they weren't aiming at the the heavens but at the black summit to curse the Hun. He had chosen that spot, which showed he was the emissary of the curse from the east, and since all war was a conflagration, this Hun and his lions had brought conflagration to their door. He and his beasts had not come by chance; they had come to spread hell.

August 2017

By the end of the second day, they had established a routine. Franck woke up at seven in the morning like the day before. He got up to adjust the blinds to stop the dazzling daylight from flooding the room. The bedroom was bathed in soft light as the sun slipped between the slats of the old wooden shutters, giving the impression of a beautiful summer's morning, soothing and cool. He went back to bed but didn't really fall asleep again and, as on the first day, got up at nine.

When he went downstairs he was appalled to think he had once more slept in a house that was wide open to the four winds, without an alarm or any protection. In the city, he would never have dreamed of going to sleep without even locking the door. And it wasn't certain that there was more to fear at home than here amongst the hills.

Outside all was calm. The cicadas weren't singing yet, but there were a few bursts of birdsong. He could only recognise the characteristic notes of the cuckoo. He could not identify the others, whose musical calls were totally mysterious to him, but the area was surprisingly peaceful despite that, without even the slightest sign of civilisation.

Yesterday evening, he and Lise had gone to bed late. The soft air after midnight had enticed them to stay outside, enjoying the coolness that had finally descended. The air had become a soothing balm that provided some respite from the heat of the day. Franck remained sitting on the chair after one of Lise's fragrant herbal teas, feet up on the table and arms dangling. He stayed like this for a long time as if he were weightless, overwhelmed by feeling of well-being.

The dog hadn't been back since the afternoon. Franck had had to resign himself to the fact that he couldn't play with it, though he had made a second attempt by throwing a large stick, again flinging it far off down the slope. Just like the cone, the dog ran to fetch the piece of wood and brought it back clenched between its jaws, but again it didn't want to give it back. It was keeping the stick for itself, starting to eat it as if it wanted to grind it to shreds. Franck had done his best to get it back, but the dog had started snarling at him, suddenly unrecognisable, as if furious. It was stubbornly ripping apart the stick, bizarrely determined, so Franck turned his back and left it there, partly to show his disapproval and partly because he was frightened of the dog, which had growled aggressively every time he reached out to it. At one point Franck had thought it was going to bite him.

That was why he had left the dog there, next to the water tank. The dog, too, was sulking, continuing to chew the stick, until it was completely destroyed, after which it did not move, offended at having been left behind. An hour later, Franck saw it going slowly down the hill, tail lowered and clearly disappointed. It crossed the entire meadow before going into the woods lower down, no doubt in order to come out again on the other side of the hill, and yet there was no path over there, much less a road, and certainly no houses. It was strange that the dog always went off in that direction, where it was wildest.

Neither he nor Lise had seen it again in the evening. Franck thought back to the luminous mark they had spotted on Google Earth the day she had shown him the advert. From memory, that large light area must be to the east, over there on the other side of the hills. That was where the dog returned to every time.

The only thing that was certain was that the big dog didn't know how to play nicely. Nobody had ever taught it to fetch a ball and bring it back. Franck had never had a dog and didn't really know anything about them, never having spent much time with them – apart from two shoots where he had worked with several dogs and paid them handsomely, though in truth it was their handlers he dealt with rather than them. That was when he had discovered that animals respond to authority, and that you can get anything from a trained animal. He had also discovered how much actors dislike working with animals, because, at the end of every take, the compliments would always go to the animal rather than to the actor.

Though he was far from knowing everything about the behaviour of dogs, Franck had at least understood something about this one: it was particularly stubborn, or selfish. It would fetch what you threw for it, but that was all. It would keep the ball for itself and destroy it. The dog didn't seem to understand that it was a game and there was still fun to be had in throwing the ball again and looking for it again. The dog didn't seem to want to play; it wanted something else. That was why Franck was convinced it was a wolf dog; it thought every game was ridiculous, for the benefit of the human more than the animal. It fetched a ball as diligently as if it were bringing back game, knowing that once it had brought its master the prey, it wouldn't be asked to go and fetch it again. On the contrary, it had to make sure it was really dead. This dog wasn't domesticated and was probably not used to humans; every journey had to be useful and every hunt had one aim: food, not play.

Before nightfall, Franck had walked over towards the water tank, and then a bit further. He tried calling the dog with all sorts of noises, 'Oh-oh', 'Oh-là', 'Eh-ho', before settling on 'Ohé'. To summon a dog in this vast space you needed two syllables that would resonate, not soft ones. He hadn't been afraid to raise his voice and yell as powerfully as he could, 'Ohé, Ohé', but the dog didn't appear. Around midnight, Franck walked all around the house again in the pitch black, even going down to the foot of the hill to have a look in the valley, to see if the dog was hiding out on the edge of the woods, either sulking or watching them like he had done on the first evening. But he didn't find it. He vowed he would ask the Dauclercqs whom the dog belonged to, and if they knew where it came from. He thought back to the huge gleaming thing that the satellite image had revealed, a flash amidst the ocean of green, an apparition where science fiction and fantasy converged. Perhaps this was the den the dog kept going back to, a sort of *igue*, one of those strange karst sinkholes you found near here. Maybe wild animals gathered there, or found themselves trapped in the limestone pit that might even be full of water, a deep lake that all the wildlife flocked towards. Perhaps the dog was the master of the animals that were so noisy at night but by day retreated to this secret world.

October 1914

Feeding wild animals encourages barbarity. For his lions to survive he had to kill. Every day he had to be utterly cruel; he had no choice. But the barbarity came from them. It was their gaping jaws that forced him to his crimes. 'Kill to live' was the unvarying watchword of the animal kingdom and it now fell to Wolfgang to honour this, gradually making him more bestial and more savage than his lions.

The animal kingdom runs on cruelty. Even herbivores, which don't themselves commit crimes, end up in the mouths of carnivores and so, as prey, play their part in the carnage. The lion tamer's animals had been relieved of the existential anguish of hunting, even though it made them bitter not being able to hunt. But the fact remained that his lions and tigers had assigned him the daily task of killing, and he was becoming obsessed by it. Every morning he re-engaged with the instinct of the carnivore, automatically enlisted in the great cycle of life, high-priest of the murderous round. He saw nothing noble in the ritual, nothing beautiful; it was savage and that was all.

To relieve his guilt, he reminded himself of all the cruelty that nature itself caused. Nature was capable of burying all the goats in the Himalayas in a single night, of asphyxiating thousands of sheep with flurries of snow, of burning all of life in the raging savannah fires, decimating fish in sudden floods, burying horses, deer and calves in molten lava . . . Nature was murderous and the animals he killed with his hands to feed his lions and tigers were part of the food chain.

Although they lacked the solemnity of Inca sacrifices or the nobility of sacred offerings, his murders were no less ritualistic. Once the circus was no more, the German took care not to overfeed his animals, but old Théo weighed more than two hundredweight, and the others were all adult now so that meant at least fifty kilos of fresh flesh to find every day. He could not provide this with fish from the river or game, and certainly not from his handful of sheep and goats. He had to get his hands on much more fleshy beasts. But if the worst came to the worst and there was nothing in his traps, he would fall back on one of the sheep or goats. He simply took the goat or sheep round to the other side of the house so that it could not be seen from the cages. Of course the lions could smell their dinner, and they could hear the bleating of the poor little animal, which increased their excitement. For ten seconds the peace of the *causse* was electrified by the death screams of the little animal, then calm was restored. To a lion, the dying of a ewe was pitiful, nothing like the bellows of a buffalo or baby elephant as it fell under its claws, and far removed from the feverish struggle of prey defending itself from death, or the dancing surrender of the antelope, or the earthy running of the warthog before submitting to the lion's teeth.

Each time the lion tamer killed for his lions and tigers he thought back to the spectators he used to have, the parents telling their children that wild cats were lovely, as if they were cuddly toys, when actually you could read in the animals' eyes how ardently they would love to devour everyone. To wipe the smiles off the faces of the rosy-cheeked children, Wolfgang would tell them how, in the wild, male lions ate baby lion cubs, killing them so that they could impregnate the new lioness with their own semen. That was why back then old Théo had been kept separate from the others. Otherwise he would have broken the necks of the young lions that had not been born to him and that were now big enough to defend themselves.

Every day the lion tamer went off into the hills and found a wonderful, endless supply of wild animals. He had learnt how to capture wild boar, deer, and all large game animals, not from the great hunters of Africa, but from his woodcutter ancestors in the forests of Bavaria. Wild boar were the master prize, and the most abundant. He didn't want anyone to know how he snared them, because, in addition to the violence needed to kill prey without a rifle, you would also need savagery to defend the traps against the villagers down below.

As the world was sinking into an epidemic of death, here roe deer and wild boar roamed free and were proliferating. Without hunters, they had no predators, and were recolonising the hills as if they had discovered new lands. In accordance with ancient custom, the lion tamer had rigged up a store of grain at the bottom of an *igue*, a natural pit in the limestone deep in the woods. His trap was a round cage which he had set up there, a tall cage in which he had sunk two wooden containers. As well as putting grain in his trap he also coated the base of the trees around the cage with Norwegian tar, the pine resin that in northern countries was used to waterproof houses. This had led to the discovery that pitch attracted wild boar. As soon as a surface was coated in tar, boar would show up and rub their flanks against it. If the lion tamer found a boar trapped in the cage, with the gate closed, all he had to do was stick it with the spear. He did not kill his prey with a rifle because, first of all, he didn't have one, but secondly, he wouldn't have wanted the noise to attract attention. If there were several animals trapped, he needed his dog to help contain them. The dog instinctively started with the largest to neutralise the greatest danger. Nature is perverse in that way; animals that take flight are always less cunning than animals that hunt.

Once the boar were dead, the lion tamer had to drag them back to the lions using the horse harness. Then, he had to use more than brute force to cut them up while they were still warm; he had to become as savage as the wild cats. By the time the eight felines with the gaping mouths saw him coming with the bloody meat, they had been salivating for hours. He always began by feeding Théo, since he was the most senior, and then the others. He tossed them whole sides of animal, tough and full of bones, so that they would experience some of the barbarity that was the joy of their lives. The big cats plunged their snouts into the scarlet animal parts, biting into them as if devouring the evening sun they had never been able to catch, a red sun tasting of death. As they tore apart the flesh, they were drunk on the odour of the cadaver, their jaws and forelegs covered in blood.

The lion tamer stayed close as they ate. An eating lion does not purr, nor does a tiger. They devour their food with complete concentration, making an arresting picture of pleasure and displaying the kind of carnal greed that he had known himself and that still plagued him if he crossed paths with that woman. He could not stop thinking about her although he tried not to. It was just that since he had held her in his arms, the day she had fainted on her horse, since he had felt her body so light and gentle against his, he had imagined himself holding her again many times, and could not rid himself of his unquenchable desire. Sometimes he saw her passing on her horse on the lower paths, as if she sought to lose herself or perhaps to find herself. Each time he saw her, it was more than desire that he felt, it was a hunger. Yet if she were to come back here, if they got close enough to each other to embrace or even to form a bond, he would be impregnated with her scent, her odour, and the lions would not put up with that. From that point on, he would definitely lose all authority over them, and his wild cats would respect him no more.

August 2017

Franck had forgotten to buy coffee the day before, and it gave him an excuse to go back into town and return to civilisation. He also had to download the thirty scripts he had promised to read on holiday, and print them, if he ever managed to find an internet café or shop where they would do that. He drove down the hill with a bit more confidence this time. The slope was so steep in some places that he was looking down on the dashboard, the weight of his body thrust over the steering wheel. He was starting to get his bearings now, and knew which parts were a bit tricky, like the two very narrow sections bordered by box trees on one side and protruding rocks on the other. And he knew where there were stones that stuck out and scraped the rocker panels, long branches that spilled over onto the path and coarse bushes that caught on the car.

Once down on the tarmacked road, he suddenly let go of all his stress and drove at a low speed. He still didn't want to put on any music, much less listen to the news, and he had no desire to know what was going on in the world. After two days he was already feeling strangely disconnected. In a way Lise had been right; he would never have felt so far away on a cruise or beach. Here, he felt that he had not only left his life behind, but civilisation as well. He would never have believed there were such isolated areas in France, and it probably explained why a handful of unusual individuals had sought refuge in these *causses* at one time or another, from Louis Malle to Romain Gary, André Breton to Nino Ferrer or Léo Ferré. All of them had come here to lose themselves or to escape from the world.

He didn't pass anybody on the road into town, nor did he see any houses round about. Sometimes there were turnings down country lanes or paths of grey asphalt to left or right. If he looked over as he passed, he couldn't see anything: invariably the path plunged into the greenery or round a bend. Just as abruptly, the road ended at the town. After a high cliff and a tight bend you would see the sign for Limogne, and very quickly the first houses appeared. A rather dense suburb led to the town centre, so you went straight from the isolated country road to the little streets of the town.

The simplicity of the town made him feel better. He parked in the shade this time and turned his phone back on. It started to vibrate excitedly in his hand; there was a whole string of emails, notifications, and many calls, mostly from Liem and Travis from their mobiles or from the office. It annoyed him immediately, before he had even found out if they really needed to ring him and if it was with good news or a counterproposal. They had obviously decided to put pressure on him. No doubt their intention was to make him feel guilty, just to highlight the fact that they, unlike him, were still in Paris. They were the ones taking care of things while he was off on a three-week holiday. Liem and Travis were part of the digital generation and worked according to US business practices, up-and-coming young men who were hungry for success and never switched off from their jobs. Franck had known that straight away when he went into partnership with them. They were barely thirty, but they were as hungry as wolves, and it was precisely this aspect that he had liked. But now with two days' perspective, he was sure that these two had more in common with vultures than wolves.

In a moment of depression, he imagined them taking advantage of his absence to try and redefine the terms of their contract. It had only been two days, but already he felt he could see more clearly. After more than twenty-five years in the film industry, he was no fool, and he suspected that, in addition to his company and equipment, it was his feature film experience that Liem and Travis were interested in, as well as his record of achievements and, of course, his much-vaunted library. Forty-eight films to date. A collection of films he owned the rights to, about ten of which were hugely popular, representing the fruits of a quarter of a century's work. A library for a producer is like treasure, it acts as life insurance, especially when some films are regularly shown on TV and across the world. He had two Chabrol and one Resnais, one Jarmusch and two Giannoli in his library, as well as a good twenty others he was proud of and which had been successes. He didn't want to share his treasure, much less give it up. He still wanted to own it, even if he needed the money. Perhaps Liem and Travis were parading about with it, claiming to be co-owners to lure in the people at Netflix; they were of course obsessed with having 'content', and 'creating content' was all they could talk about. Liem and Travis knew very well that, like Amazon, Netflix needed content to fill their schedules, and unlike Franck, who was wary of the tech giants, his partners wanted to get closer to them. They even planned to offer them shares and get them to invest, which would be like inviting the fox into the henhouse thinking it was an ally. At no point did they consider that when you make a deal with someone much bigger than you, you risk getting eaten.

It all became clear to Franck when he went into the café. He again went to sit right at the back; the other customers were on the terrace, where there were no more free tables. He opened his laptop, which connected automatically to the Wi-Fi this time, and immediately spotted the emails from Liem and Travis in his inbox with the little red flag for urgent. They both had the subject: 'Amendments to contract'. At least it was clear. It wasn't even worth reading the emails; Franck already knew what was in them. He ordered a double espresso and resolved not to forget to buy coffee and some five-litre bottles of water at the organic shop, because Madame Dauclercq was probably right about the tap water and Lise didn't feel comfortable drinking it, not even after boiling it.

The real problem was that Liem and Travis didn't work to the same rhythm as him and everything had to happen quickly for them. They had grown up with smartphones in their hands and then trained in the digital economy and video games, working in various countries including the United States. Franck felt the full impact of the difference in age and culture. The simplest thing would be to phone them now to get things straight and explain his point of view. But he couldn't bring himself to. Even here at the back of this big empty room, although he was perfectly calm and undisturbed by anyone, he didn't feel he was in the right frame of mind to make a phone call. Especially not to talk about Netflix and the library. In these surroundings he felt completely off balance. After spending a second night in that house, after only two days in these remote hills, he was so far from his bearings and usual worries that he had lost the words and presence of mind you need to talk business over the phone.

A big 4×4 pulled up opposite the café, on the other side of the road. In the back was a huge metal cage fixed to the bed of the pickup, split into several compartments. Franck could see two big dogs inside, each wearing a bright phosphorescent orange collar that glowed in the dark of their wire mesh prison. Franck suddenly saw himself in their place. That's what Liem and Travis were intending to do to him, catch him and put him in a cage so they could take him wherever they wanted. He quickly read their emails and immediately grasped their game: this time they effectively wanted him to hand the rights to the library over to them, and, in the meantime, they were asking if they could use it as ammunition in negotiations with Netflix and Amazon, because these behemoths didn't frighten them and they had contacts there — a friend of Liem's looked after Europe. He had just taken up a role in the Netherlands of all places, to be in a better position to get round the rules. In exchange, Liem and Travis informed him bluntly that they would give in to his 'whim' as they called it. They would allow him to produce the film he had in development, by which they obviously meant the film he wanted to make for Lise to star in or possibly even to direct. It was meant to seem like a win–win situation, but was left unclear because the enticement did not appear in the amendments to the contract.

In short, they were forcing him to make a deal with the enemy, which to him was like delivering himself up to those behemoths with his hands and feet tied. He was aware that this was increasingly common across the whole industry, as if joining forces with an American platform was enough to guarantee you would benefit from their millions of subscribers. The practice of releasing films in the cinema was seen as old hat. Knowing that every time you had to pray that ticket sales were high enough from the first showing on Wednesday morning, that the weather was favourable that day – not too nice but not rainy either – and all of that for some tens of thousands of spectators. The new generation of producers found that outdated; for them it was the cinema of the past, it was cumbersome and too risky.

Franck had an image of Amazon and Netflix as two predators with an infinite appetite, a thousand times bigger than everyone else, two super-predators that regulated the ecosystem like wolves by first getting rid of the weakest, smallest, most vulnerable prey, before establishing themselves as the absolute masters of the game. Liem and Travis didn't realise that, in this game, everybody would be eaten up, with the big digital platforms pretending they needed the experience of French producers when actually it was just a trick to swallow them up more easily.

The old Land Rover remained parked, motor running, but nobody got out. You couldn't see the driver's face, which was in shadow. Eventually, the left-hand door opened and a man of about thirty got out wearing cargo trousers and an army T-shirt. Another man who was much older and also wearing cargo trousers walked up to him. They shook hands and stood there, smoking fags and talking, leaning against the side of the vehicle, paying no attention to the dogs. Inside their cages, they seemed calm. Without even really deciding to, Franck turned off his computer, crossed the room, went outside and over to the two guys on the pavement opposite. He started talking to them, out of the blue, about the dogs.

'They're beautiful!'

This choice of adjective seemed to surprise them. Or else it was the fact that a stranger, a tourist, was speaking to them. Either way, they took a moment before responding. Then the driver turned to the cages and replied, 'Beautiful? If you say so. More importantly, they're tough . . .'

'Are they hunting dogs?'

'No, that one's a Rhodesian ridgeback and that one's a Hanover hound.'

'So they *are* hunting dogs?'

'No, they're blood-tracking dogs.'

It was clear that the two guys didn't understand what this holidaymaker wanted from them, no more than Franck knew what a blood-tracking dog was. The driver of the 4×4 seemed friendly and polite, but the older one was silent, not hiding his irritation at this tourist, this townie, who had perhaps come looking for stories about hunting or something like that. At least that's what Franck felt, from the suspicious way the older guy was eyeing him. The driver, no doubt flattered that he was being asked about his dogs, walked towards them, keen to impart his handler's knowledge, inspecting them through the bars as he did so to check that all was well. Innocently, Franck had another go.

'And what are blood-tracking dogs?'

'You're not a hunter, are you?'

'No.'

'They're for tracking injured game. You set the dogs to follow a blood trail and they lead you to the injured animal. But they won't find prey to hunt; they're not pointers.'

'Oh, I see. And do you think there are stray dogs in the area? I mean dogs without a collar, dogs that have run away.'

'Now that, I don't know. It would surprise me. You always lose dogs in battues, but you usually find them again, and they always have a collar.'

The older guy seemed increasingly irritated. Franck sensed that he didn't like the mention of hunting and especially of 'battue'. You don't talk about that kind of thing, not with a stranger at any rate. The people from here, or at least the hunters, had no desire to broach such a controversial subject with a townie from God knows where. Franck felt obliged to add something to lighten the atmosphere.

'Following a blood trail must be exciting. And do you do that, as, how can I put it . . . well, as a job?'

'No, it's just that we like animals. There are always hunters who injure game animals but don't kill them, either because they've aimed badly, or because they don't have the right bullets. Rather than let those animals suffer in the wild, we track them down; it's more humane.'

'And what do you do with the injured animals?'

The man looked Franck straight in the eye, baffled by his naïvety, and the older one spat out, 'We kill them.'

A little thrown by this, Franck replied simply, as if he approved, 'Yes, of course.'

He couldn't have said it with enough conviction because the two men didn't really believe him. Nonetheless the owner of the vehicle, out of politeness, said that one day he should come with them, and then he would see what it was like.

'I'd like that. Has the hunting season already started?'

'For us, yes. But only at sundown, and with a clean shot.'

The man wasn't trying to mystify Franck; he just assumed Franck would know what he meant, when in fact he had no idea. Franck suggested they have a coffee but the younger one declined, claiming they had to go before it got too warm. Clearly the dogs were hot. The older man wasn't even looking at him any more. The two men got into the 4×4 and the driver asked Franck, 'Are you on holiday?'

'Yes.'

'Whereabouts?'

'Near Mont d'Orcières.'

The young guy seemed surprised, almost shocked.

'At the top?'

Franck didn't know what to make of this reaction. He didn't dare say exactly where it was, and, besides, the engine started up loudly at this point.

'No, below. Why?'

'No reason. But don't spend too much time up there, it's full of beasts!'

The older one was making no attempt to hide his annoyance now and urged the driver to leave, taking his arm and telling him to drop the subject. The younger man started to manoeuvre, but Franck persisted, holding on to the car door, 'Beasts . . . What do you mean by that?'

'Once you're up there it's a straight line to the Massif Central and the Alps . . . Directly east! So there's everything – wolves, wild boar, lynxes – it's a savannah, and there are some people with strange hunting habits, if you know what I mean . . .'

'No, I don't.'

The older one finally lost his temper and shouted at the driver: 'For God's sake, Julien, let's go!'

'It's the Wild West up there, the real Wild West!'

Franck still had his hands on the frame of the car door when the Land Rover pulled out, leaving him standing there. The exhaust pipe belched out a large black cloud and the pickup drove off, backfiring hoarsely and making an unpleasant raucous noise. The dogs were standing tall in the cage in the back, keeping their balance, with their fluorescent collars and rather unwelcoming expressions.

Franck felt just as lost as a character in the kind of film he might have produced, the naïve wanderer who has just been done over by two cowboys, two locals who had said too much. And now he would have to fear them, to worry about bumping into them or their cronies. In fact, he felt threatened.

Franck turned back to the café. The owner behind the counter, a tall guy with a nose piercing, who hadn't said a word to him until now, caught his eye. Franck sensed disapproval, as if he'd just been speaking with criminals.

'Do you know them?' asked the owner.

'I've just met them . . . Do you?'

'I don't talk to meat men. Haven't you seen the menu?'

Franck glanced at the board hanging above the bar. Apparently, the place was vegetarian – at least, there was no meat on the menu, though they still had pike and trout. Franck was encouraged by this and leant on the counter and asked for a second coffee.

'Another espresso?

'Yes, but a double.'

The owner was tall and blond with a Rasta hairstyle, dreadlocks tied in a bun. When he had chosen this café the day before, Franck had felt uncomfortable with the young man who had greeted him with a cold '*bonjour*'. At first glance, Franck saw a thirty-something in a too-short T-shirt with tattooed arms who was probably some kind of anti-globalisation warrior. His discomfort had meant that Franck had barely said hello, either yesterday or today. To the owner, he must have seemed like a churlish holidaymaker, the customer who deliberately positions himself right at the back to avoid talking to the locals. Franck was not that reclusive and unfriendly, but he felt unsettled in this little town where he was completely out of his comfort zone and everything was unfamiliar and disorientating. That's the terrible thing about being ill at ease, you think everybody can see it and nothing else, and you start resenting them for having figured you out so easily. But the young owner turned out to be friendly. He took the coffees from the machine and put them on the bar, as a way of inviting Franck to chat.

'Look, I need to print a few pages. Where do you think I could do that?'

'That depends. How many are there?'

'I'd say about thirty lots of a hundred pages.'

'Seriously?'

Franck needed to print out scripts the old-fashioned way in order to read and make notes on them. Rémy only had one old inkjet printer in a little nook behind the bar, and more problematically, only half a pack of paper. But he told him about Sören, an illustrator who lived on an isolated old farm ten kilometres from Limogne, and who would be happy to print everything he wanted for him, as long as he offered to pay. Franck gathered that this was the kind of place where people helped each other out and made do. When he explained that he worked in the film industry, that he was a producer, Rémy's eyes lit up. Franck regretted saying this, especially as people could see him driving around here in an Audi Q7, not because he was worried about them noticing him, or thinking he was loaded, but because he was worried that they would come to him with their proposals and make demands of him. They would talk to him about such and such a project or actor who needed a role. But no. Rémy simply noted down the name of the place where Sören lived on a Post-it, adding a little drawing of the route, because it was tricky to find. He even called the illustrator while Franck was there to find out if he could print the scripts. He could. Three euros each, which indicated that they were not trying to rip him off but just to help him out.

Franck asked Rémy what he thought of Mont d'Orcières, whether the place had a particular reputation.

'Orcières? Well, there's nothing there any more.'

'Yes, there's a gîte.'

'The one at the top? They're renting it out? That's a first.'

'You didn't know?'

'No. Nobody ever goes up there, the road's terrible, and there's nothing in that shack – I don't even know if there's water. How did you find it?'

'An internet ad.'

'On the internet? That's crazy; the old woman must be more than a hundred years old.'

'Do you know her?'

'No, she's lived in Spain for years, I've never met her. Anyway, once you're up there there's nothing, not even a river, and the paths aren't well looked after; you couldn't even go dirt biking there when we were kids . . . No, that place is wild. Apart from the dodgy hunting there's nothing there; it's all abandoned.'

While he was listening to him, Franck had a vision of Lise the way he'd left her that morning, naked under just a sheet, windows wide open to the winds, alone and defenceless at the top of the hill that was apparently the haunt of poachers and hunters who went there to settle scores (if he had understood correctly). And then there was the roaming dog as well – what if it decided to turn nasty like it did yesterday, to bite, to attack? He slapped a ten-euro note on the counter, retrieved his computer and bag, and left, saying goodbye to the owner, who was rather surprised to see him suddenly in such a rush.

'Hey! Don't forget the Post-it . . . Or you'll never find it.'

Once outside, he couldn't remember where he had parked the car. As he looked for it he realised he had completely forgotten to call Liem and Travis. He didn't want to think about them now and especially not to talk to them. Perhaps keeping them waiting was the best way of dealing with them.

The Audi was now in direct sunlight, no longer protected by the leafless old plane tree. With its dark bodywork, it was like an oven when he got inside. He was immediately soaked in sweat and turned the air conditioning up high. He was wary of the stories about hunting, of animals that might or might not be wandering around.

But he had sensed that there was something malevolent about this place from the beginning; even the name Mont d'Orcières sounded ferrous and sharp, and talking about it here had reawakened his suspicions. Even the advert was weird, and the fact that you had to communicate with people who were evasive and strangely cold, but now, after Madame Dauclercq's welcome and everything he had been told, it seemed that something really wasn't right.

He kept the air conditioning on full blast as he drove. It was barely midday and the thermometer on the dashboard said it was thirty-one degrees. Again he didn't come across anybody on the way. He reached the beginning of the track that went up to the gîte, but decided to carry on driving until he got to the farm. He wanted to say a few things to the Dauclercqs; he knew the dog was theirs and wanted to know why they had sent it to spy on them. As he was preparing to go into the yard, he realised his mistake. A big dog was standing just in front of the kennel, a big brown dog that was a bit bedraggled and dirty, nothing like the other one. The dog stiffened when it saw the car, pulling its chain taut and barking, so Franck backed up. He wasn't scared, but he now had the answer to his question. The wolf dog up on the hill did not belong to the Dauclercqs. The kennel here was not its kennel. Franck was about to turn around, but Monsieur Dauclercq was already coming towards him. He was coming from the left so must have come out of the shed, where a tractor sat in shadow. Franck had no choice but to stop. Monsieur Dauclercq came up to the car. Franck lowered his window.

'Do you need something?'

'No, thank you. It's just that I missed the track, so I'm turning around.'

'Really? You're a long way from the track . . .'

'It's easy to get lost when you don't know the area.'

The dog had an enormous head and was almost as tall as its kennel. It was observing them from a distance. The most disturbing thing was that its head was so large that it seemed human, and it wore an expression of total hostility.

'What kind of dog is it?'

'A Rhodesian ridgeback, but he's old.'

'They're used for following blood trails, right?'

'They can be; he has a good sense of smell, but ridgebacks were originally for hunting lions.'

Franck looked at him coldly, angry at being taken for an idiot, and in fact he nearly told him that, but he stopped himself.

'In Africa, when dogs are looking after livestock, they may come across lions and cheetahs. They rely on the ridgebacks to drive away wild animals.'

'But what are you doing with a dog like that, what do you need it for? There are no lions around here . . .'

'No, but I used to have livestock.'

Monsieur Dauclercq's expression was hard to read. He might have been joking, or he might have been deadly serious. The sight of the dog's monstrous face was giving Franck terrifying ideas. He imagined himself arriving up there to an empty house like yesterday, with no sign of life, then going up to the bedroom and finding the shutters still closed and Lise's body there on the bed in the warm half-light, torn to pieces.

October 1914

There were suffering bodies everywhere. First and foremost the soldiers who had offered body and soul to their country. Exposed to enemy fire, they were dazed, exhausted, wounded and broken by bombs. A few kilometres behind the men were the bodies of the women, fatigued by fear and deprivation, by having to replace the men in factories or in the fields, or by having to harness themselves to pull the plough, taking the place of animals sent to the front. People's bodies were no longer their own; whether at the front or behind it, people had been forced to make a gift of them to the homeland. France had become a country of missing bodies.

In the autumn, the women understood that, in spite of the reassuring news and the supposed victories, the men would not be back to do the winter farm work. So it would be up to them to cut wood, clean ditches, repair paths potholed by rain and unblock gutters. They mustn't wait for the men or the farms would be swamped with mud and manure. So once again women and old people would have to force themselves beyond their strength to make up for the absence of men, robust men accustomed to carrying loads since the beginning of time.

In this world of exhaustion, only the body of the lion tamer, strong and upright, seemed not to suffer. Joséphine saw him when he came down to the village to collect straw, early in the morning. She thought about him all the time. When she observed how his body was sculpted like a gladiator, she remembered seeing his naked torso at the circus at Villeneuve, as he performed his act. That day, when she sat in the front row, the magnificent body was right there in front of her, lit by spotlights. She had watched him as he moved within his wild animal kingdom, and, at the sight of the semi-nude body in the midst of the lions, the audience had feared that he would be killed at any moment. Afterwards she had seen him dressed as Spartacus on the red-and-gold posters advertising the circus. They were still displayed all over the area. And now that body had held hers. Which meant that on the mornings she saw him in the village, she was careful not to look at him directly, although she was aware of him. In this world of solitary despised bodies and the hideous vision of her husband's body somewhere, it was not possible to look at his body, nor should she be thinking about it. Yet he haunted her. He haunted her, this lion tamer whose body she was astonished by. He haunted her to the point of taking up more of her thoughts than the memory of the body which, for five years, had slept there, right beside her. Now she didn't even know if Dr Manouvrier's body was still whole or if it was in pieces mixed with earth. It was unimaginable to think of him any other way but intact, when, actually, he had probably been blown to pieces by a bomb. The body which for years had lain in the same place in the same bed. For years they had loved each other without touching each other, but he had been there. Every time the lion tamer passed in front of her window, she was furious at the thought of the greedy war which had taken possession of everything, depriving people even of what they didn't have any more. The war took everything from you.

Eight weeks after the doctor had been declared missing, the mayor received more detailed information. One morning he passed this on to Joséphine in the utmost secrecy. He hated having to impart the terrible knowledge and prayed never to have to do it again, although he feared he would. When Joséphine heard him knock on the door at such an early hour and then saw that he was immaculately dressed, she immediately understood what he had come to say. As he struggled to find the right words, she made him coffee. In the report on military operations, it had been noted that Dr Manouvrier had acted heroically. In the official language, he had had the opportunity to 'demonstrate proof of his courage'. But at the end of August – already in August – he had been captured by the Germans as he was treating wounded men on the battlefield who had just been caught in machine-gun fire at the Battle of Morhange-Sarrebourg. In spite of his armband and those of his adjutants, in spite of the ten injured men they had just loaded onto a requisitioned livestock truck, in spite of the evidence of their status, they had been taken prisoner and escorted to a presbytery that had been converted into a hospital by the Germans.

In the makeshift hospital, the Germans neglected French prisoners. They kept the tincture of iodine and the dressings for their own wounded, and also the meat and the potatoes. All they left for the French was milk and water, and morphine so that they would not howl and disturb the Germans. But the front line was getting nearer. Although the flag of the Geneva Convention flew from the roof of the hospital, a hundred-kilo shell landed in the courtyard, followed by a second one, and then others. Yellow smoke spread through the hospital, stopping dead the wave of cries and noise, ending the wails of the wounded, the shouts and the shattering glass. They had all been scattered; their bodies did not lie under a cross, not even one of those wooden crosses on which names were written in lead pencil, becoming unreadable after the second shower of rain, and erased after the third. Joséphine imagined all the scattered bodies like bits of carcass flung into graves which would also be blown up or trampled over by passing troops. What would be left of her husband now? Surely nothing, apart from his communion chain which he had left for her when he departed and which she wore.

The mayor passed on the information about her husband, but he was silent about the savagery that surpassed that of wild beasts. He did not tell her of the horror he had been made aware of. He did not tell her that in this war, in a single day, bodies fell by the thousand and that for fear of outbreaks of disease the corpses were thrown in batches into pits and then covered with quicklime and shoved quickly into tombs that were destroyed the very next day by bombardments. The men were returned to the soil and mixed in like fertiliser. He did not tell her that sometimes the dead were not buried, but left out on the parapets as protection against enemy bullets instead of sandbags. And when the position was lost, the trench was used as a communal grave by the opposing army, who tossed in all the bodies of their enemies. They wanted to forget about the bodies and move on to more killing without wasting time. Bodies were worth nothing.

Once the mayor had left, Joséphine was overcome with grief, for there was no hope now. But she was relieved to finally know the truth. Not knowing had added to the cruelty of his absence and she was comforted by the knowledge that right to the end her husband had sacrificed his life to save others. When he had still been with her, Anthelme had lived for his work as if it were a calling. Even when the world was still at peace he had given so much of himself that after he had made his evening visits he returned home exhausted. A country doctor lives all the time in the pain of others; listening, sympathising and travelling all over the place on bad roads whatever the weather. The roads around Orcières were terrible and every day Anthelme spent hours in the saddle, devoting himself to his work to such an extent that, once home, all he wanted to do was rest in silence. A country doctor gives so much of himself during the day that in the evening there is nothing left to give. And the wife of a country doctor must deal with the waiting patients, encourage them to talk, listen to their troubles and hear about their recoveries, and finds herself dreaming of bodies that are not sick, of bodies that are not exhausted by the troubles of others. The wife of a doctor, when she knows her husband has been dead for weeks, finds herself all alone in a house deserted by all bodies, healthy as well as sick, a house that had been for some a place of hope and healing and for others a place of distress, but now from one day to the next, a house that nobody came to. It was only La Bûche who visited her, always finding a pretext to check the roof, or shoe a horse. She felt dirtied by his constant presence and started to fear him.

From now on she would be nothing but a wife in mourning, a soul in pain, a woman with neither flesh nor blood. Yet at the height of transgression or of sin, in the tunnel of war, with winter coming, she felt like a body that was waiting, a body seeking revenge, a body more full of desire than ever before.

August 2017

They had been walking for fifteen minutes and Franck was already drenched in sweat. Lise wanted to go deep into the woods, to explore beyond the first hill. She planned to do a few sketches or watercolours as well as having a picnic, so if they found the light-filled *igue* that had been referred to, she could draw it instead of taking photos. Franck was carrying both the picnic and her art materials, and the walk quickly became hard work. But he didn't mind testing himself to see how fit he was. He was also driven by the thought of finding out where the dog came from in the mornings and went in the evenings – somewhere beyond the hill, perhaps from an *igue* filled with water rather than light.

Lise was already imagining herself beside a small, isolated, deep lake, though it might turn out to be a hot spring with clouds of invigorating sulphurous steam, a treasure hidden away from the rest of the world. As far as she could tell, they had to cross the first hill to get there, then the second one, and walk across the highest crest with its panoramic view. She was sure that the horizon would open out and they would be able to see the Montagne Noire in the south, and maybe even all the way to the Pyrenees if there were no clouds. She had a dreamy, almost poetic way of forgetting about distance, and Franck had come on the walk to keep her fancies alive. He didn't like the idea of going into woods that were so dense, steep and wild, completely untouched by humans. He was anxious first of all about getting lost, and then about getting bitten by a tick or a snake. He didn't want to show that he was scared, or that he was dreading how the dog would react when they arrived on its territory, in its hunting ground. Franck hadn't told Lise what he had just learnt about the remote hills: that they were full of all sorts of animals, as well as all sorts of hunters and poachers.

Lise was an optimist; she didn't worry about anything, and he acknowledged it again with admiration rather than bitterness. She was always open and seemed unafraid of anything. She had been leading the way since they set off and was so relaxed that she was whistling, even though it was a hell of a climb. They had to weave through trees instead of following the path, which disappeared in some places. As well as the picnic Franck was carrying, they had brought three litres of water with them. They had everything they needed. As they climbed up the wooded slope, the path petered out, swallowed up by bushes and brambles.

'D'you know how to make sure you don't get lost when you're walking in the woods?'

'No, Lise, I don't.'

'You have to keep the sun on your right-hand side.'

She told him to keep his bearings that way. As if she were suddenly a hiking expert.

'It's the same on the way back; you just need to keep it on your left. It's easy.'

Franck thought she must have found this piece of advice in some guidebook when she was getting ready for the holiday. 'Keep the sun on your right-hand side' – that didn't sound like her. His phone still had no signal, and searching for one was running down the battery, especially as he hadn't charged it. He really did wonder how they would get back. Relying on just the sun to know you were going in the opposite direction was surely too simple. What's more, they weren't going in a straight line. They were constantly zigzagging through the jungle of tangled vegetation. Low branches blocked their way and they had to keep ducking underneath them, while bushes and branches clung to them like hands, desperate to stop them coming through. They could only really see the path in the sections where the grass was less tall. The sun was sometimes behind them as the path meandered, disappearing behind the trees and then re-emerging in a gap in front of them. Franck remembered what the owner of the bistro had said about the tracks around here; they were totally overgrown. Here, nature had won the battle. As well as the branches that blocked their way, the ground was strewn with dead wood, thorny bushes and creepers, making it difficult to walk. He understood why nobody came here for motocross: you would only be able to get through this treacherous maze on foot.

Lise moved effortlessly, sailing past the obstacles. She had no trouble with the walk, but Franck was finding it harder and harder to keep up. He was assessing his fitness as he went: he clearly didn't do enough exercise. She walked ahead without stopping even once, not at all bothered by the heat and apparently enjoying herself, while he was out of breath and dripping with sweat. But he told himself that was hardly surprising given how uneven the terrain was and how hard it was to keep his footing. With every step he slipped on stones and his shoes slid over roots or dry ground. He thought about the load on his back weighing him down, the picnic and the bottles of water, plus the two foam mats and box of watercolours. Sometimes Lise got way ahead, by twenty, thirty, fifty metres. When she realised she had gone too far, she stopped to admire the scenery and quietly waited for Franck to catch up with her, asking him with an uncertain smile, 'Sure you're OK?'

'Yes. All good!'

Nonetheless, he was annoyed that he was getting tired so quickly. Was he just too sedentary, going from lunch to a meeting, to a seat on the TGV or an aeroplane? The worrying realisation that he was no longer in good shape, not even capable of a half-hour hike in the woods, struck him. His pride did not allow him to ask Lise if they could take a break, yet he was out of breath and it was stiflingly hot. He felt somehow powerless. If he had to run or fight for himself one day, if he was pursued by some unknown danger and needed to get away, he would be out of breath after a hundred metres and at the mercy of the predator . . . Thinking back to his emails, he was suddenly aware that he was easy prey, an ageing male who would be caught by the first predator that came along. The image of Liem and Travis as greedy hunters came to mind. If they were really coming after him, would he be able to fight back? If they tried to force him to give up his entire library for a deal with Netflix or Amazon, would he be able to stop them? He remembered what a handler on a shoot had told him: 'When you're confronted with a wolf, you have to think like a wolf.' That's what he had to do, or their energy and youth would get the better of him. He couldn't carry on being the wise, self-assured fifty-something, a veteran bolstered by past successes. Past successes were useless in a world where you needed to be constantly reinventing yourself, throwing yourself back in, challenging yourself . . .

'Franck, are you OK?'

'Yes, damn it, I'm OK . . . Everything's fine, Lise, everything's fine.'

Until now he had opted to trust Liem and Travis, but that had given them the impression he was pliable, harmless and resting on his laurels. Appearing harmless had been his mistake. How could he see off their suspect plans, how could he confront them if he didn't show that he was just as tenacious and willing to attack? The toughest prey is the one that fights back.

Every ten metres, he feared they would come face to face with the wolf dog or the animals from the other evening. He said nothing to Lise, but he was keenly aware that they were entering enemy territory, being watched or tracked. He was not enjoying the trip. He and Lise were like two pet cats that had been released into the jungle for the first time. On the other hand, the walk was inducing a kind of concentration, a mental focus. Lise was no longer talking. She was probably nearing enlightenment, whilst he was mainly aware of his shortness of breath and the anger building inside him. Lise was savouring the moment, the landscape lifting her into a meditative weightlessness, as he was getting more and more tense. At the foot of the hill, Franck looked nostalgically up at the house right at the top, that cosy sanctuary with its shady ground floor, its thick breeze-block walls that kept it cool, and those tall trees surrounding it like a little island. From a distance, the house was simple but unusual, perfectly balanced atop its hill. Looking at it like this, he found he was almost falling in love with the house, built in such a strange place. Who would build a house so far away from anything else? What kind of person could have decided to settle there, and why? They had a good view of it from below. The top of the hill was covered in those large trees, a mass of vegetation like an oasis, with the water tank at its centre. The steep slope that led down from it was grassy and the house proudly presided over the surrounding countryside. They had closed the shutters when they left to stop the heat from coming in, and the car was parked on the other side. From here, the house looked abandoned.

After an hour of walking, Franck could go no further. The straps of his backpack were digging into his shoulders and it was becoming unbearable, yet the further they went, the more he felt grateful to Lise. Thanks to her, he was getting the measure of his vulnerability. He found a shady spot on the right, a sort of alcove surrounded by rocks, a haven of flat ground. It would be the ideal place to eat and have a rest. But Lise was already further ahead, and she signalled for him to continue. She was planning to tear down the second hill in order to tackle the third one, as she was sure that the third was higher than all the others. They would have an impressive view from up there, and they would be able to see the *igue*.

He joined her, propelling himself down the new slope. Lise was far ahead but was no longer worried about it. He had always relied on his wife, who guided him without even being aware of it. He was no longer sure what direction they were going in, but he liked the idea of leaving it to her, trusting her. She was tearing ahead like an antelope that couldn't be stopped and would carry on running even after it had shaken off its hunters, an incredibly light and free antelope.

There was no doubt that they were getting lost. The route was so winding that Franck was sure of it. The sun was behind them now, when it had been in front of them two minutes before. When they got to the third hill, the path disappeared under the tough plants that covered everything. Here, wilderness reigned supreme. It was a snarl of holm oaks and thorny bushes, a tangle of branches weaving themselves into a prickly, impenetrable scrubland. His phone still had some battery left but no signal. When he opened his compass app, he realised it only worked with an internet connection: it wasn't a real, self-sufficient compass. The north point changed every second.

There's a level of exhaustion where the body carries on automatically, sleepwalking to the rhythm of your breath, but the mind is in a hypnotised state. Franck stared at Lise's pink trainers in the distance, trying hard to stay focused on them. Many images went through his head. There, with his eyes full of sweat, he remembered that it was Lise who had assuaged his doubts when Liem and Travis had come to dinner a year ago. He hadn't had a good feeling about them, but Lise had said: 'Go on, go for it; they're good guys. They're young, they'll give you a fresh take on things. I'm sure you'll work well together . . .'

'Oh, come on, what have I got in common with a couple of guys who watch films on their phones?'

'Exactly. They'll give you a different perspective on things. You can make good films that are not necessarily good art, don't you think?'

'I can't believe you're saying that!'

In the end, it was Lise who had convinced him to join forces with them, simply telling him to stop being so distrustful all the time. Just as it was Lise who had told him not to fear the luminescent eyes staring at them in the dark, the animal watching them from the edge of the woods.

He stopped halfway up the hill, hands on his hips, mouth hanging open, and put down the bag with the straps that were cutting into him. Lise was still climbing up ahead and didn't even turn around; she was nearly at the top. Perhaps she was still emptying her mind, switching off as if meditating. There was so much sweat on his face he couldn't see any more, and it stung his eyes, as if he were drowning in the ocean. He wiped it away with his T-shirt, and when he looked up, he couldn't see her any more. With the sun in his eyes, he couldn't even see the path in front of him. There was no longer a path, it was just a tangle of brambles and branches that seemed to pull at his feet. It was turning into a nightmare. He picked up his bag and started walking again but didn't know where to go, so he headed for the top, the crest, where Lise must have started her descent. Either she was enjoying the feeling of being unstoppable, or she was simply trying to scare him. To lose him. That's what he thought when he reached the top of the third hill and still couldn't see her. And yet he could see everything from up there; he felt as if he was on top of the world. Franck turned around, letting the whole panorama sweep over him. The little house seemed very far away now, lost in its surroundings. It was the only house on the 360-degree horizon, in a land where past and present merged. It was a timeless scene, unchanged for centuries, with nothing to suggest what time or era it was, and it was only the three small clouds drifting in the sky that seemed to connect it to the world. There were rows of hills as far as the eye could see, the same view endlessly repeated, with no sign of civilisation, not even the cables of a power line or the rising smoke from a power plant or bonfire. 'In the middle of the Black Triangle': he remembered the expression he had come across on the internet. Lise had wanted them to get lost, and she had succeeded.

There were too many trees and bushes to clearly see what was going on below, but in front of him was what looked like a great limestone crater, an abyss, an immense depression in the ground, as if a section of earth had one day collapsed and sunk a hundred metres. Lise had gone into the great mass of shadowy green, walking into the pit with no hesitation. She probably wanted to see if there was any water inside, as the area must have been full of springs. Franck didn't have the strength to carry on. He had already drunk three-quarters of his water. He needed to recover. He sat on a strange drystone mound, a sort of tumulus that could have dated back to the Romans. Lise felt at home in this no man's land, while he was struggling to let go of his life, of his worries. Even there, soaked in sweat and with his shirt open to the waist, he was still a film producer. And yet, up in these secluded hills, without a phone, where the only things that mattered were drinking, finding shade and recuperating, he was finally approaching a more natural state. Suddenly, he heard Lise calling up to him urgently from the very bottom. He couldn't see her, but he could hear her.

'Quick, quick, come and see!'

'Lise, what's going on?'

'Come and see!'

He started making his way down, cursing as he went – his knees, God, his knees hurt! It wasn't even just a slope any more, it was a steep rock face that he kept slipping down, and it looked like a long way to the bottom. He had to cling on to branches and let himself fall, thinking how difficult it would be to climb back up later. As he got closer to the bottom, the flora became thicker, cooler and more humid. It was indeed an *igue*, and he was about to disappear into a kind of enormous pit covered in vegetation. The plants were as dense as a mangrove forest; there was moss all along the branches, a beautiful, thick, topaz-green moss, and a whole network of creepers and climbing plants, lush plants that looked almost tropical. He let himself be carried down into the cool atmosphere, stumbling, then sliding on his backside. Lise was still talking at the bottom, but Franck couldn't see her through the thick vegetation. She must have found a spring, or a lake. Every now and then he saw a glimmer of light or a flash from below; he could make out the sky up above and a rock face opposite like a Pyrenean cirque. Franck completely tumbled down the last twenty metres, grazing his thighs and forearms on the ground. He found Lise at the bottom in the middle of an enormous pergola with golden bars flecked with rust, a great cage made up of arches more than four metres high that resembled a large rotunda or giant birdcage. How strange that the only sign of civilisation round about was this cage, a circus cage at the bottom of a jungly *igue*.

'Lise, you're crazy coming all the way down here! D'you know how hard it'll be to get back up?'

'But look at this – I'm sure no one's been here for centuries!'

At that moment, the bushes right at the bottom began to stir. Something was moving in there and coming towards them. A human would never have been strong enough to get through the thickets, and it sounded more like an animal. They could see the tops of the box trees moving as the animal got closer. They looked at each other without saying a word. Franck thought about the noises he had heard on the first evening. He instinctively grabbed Lise by the arm and stepped back into the cage, protected by the bars. When an animal charges, it rushes straight ahead, and it doesn't care if you know it's coming. Once it's started, it's already too late.

May 1915

At night cats' eyes shine like the lightning bolt of Zeus. Foxes' eyes glow with an acid orange light, hares' eyes show red and, in the moonlight, deer's eyes look blue. In the wild, any eyes that shine in the night are hunting or fleeing and they might belong to lions, tigers, wolves or lynxes. Every night in the hills animals' eyes gleam in the white glow of the moon which ensures that even the wild boar can see clearly. The blue-green eyes of the dogs watch over the hunting fauna, all noticing and avoiding each other. There are millions of animal eyes, rendered phosphorescent by the tapetum lucidum, all able to see in the dark so that they can find their prey.

Once winter was over, the villagers wondered if the German let his wild cats go at nightfall. The hillside looked as if it were on fire there were so many luminescent eyes. You could not tell what animals they belonged to but you could see the eyes from your window. Now that the first spring days were warming up, everyone slept with their windows open, so the lions could be heard even in the middle of the night, their sudden roaring startling the villagers from sleep. As well as those whom the lions awakened there were the women who could not get to sleep, those who found the peace of a lonely bed unsettling. Where previously desire might have prevented sleep, since the beginning of the war in Orcières everyone had been worried and exhausted, and bodies no longer touched. Now bodies worked in the day and rested at night far apart from each other. After sowing had come the planting of potatoes, tending the garden, and preparing the sheep to go up to the summer pasture. Even more than in winter, in spring the lifting, dragging, pulling and carrying went on all day, so even though the weather was better now, bodies were overcome with fatigue.

At night, those awoken by roars sat bolt upright in bed. It was only the children who enjoyed that. To them, the low growls provided night-time entertainment; the roars rolling down from the rocks gave the darkness a feeling of mystery. On those nights, the kids played a sort of hide-and-seek. Their bedrooms became like bivouacs or hidden encampments in a wild jungle and the growling of the predators prompted dreams of daring. But when the windows had to be open at night, as they looked up past the houses, sometimes some of them were frightened. The slightest stirring of the leaves or movement of the curtains made them think they saw the back of a lion, or a tiger, or God knows what animal . . . And they imagined they could feel the rough tongues of the felines licking their feet and they started to howl and call their mothers. La Bûche heard none of this. Years of banging his hammer on the anvil had damaged his hearing. But when others told of their fear, he vowed in one way or another to put an end to it, in the hope of winning Joséphine's favour.

Fernand's nights were haunted by his fear of the post. He was afraid of hearing that one or other of the men had died and having to go and tell the family and it kept him awake. In a way he almost welcomed the screams of the wild cats, because they reminded him of the excitement that life could have brought him. Hearing the beasts, he saw himself as strong and nimble, picturing himself as a daring lion tamer shining under the lights of the ring, conquering terror and playing on the fears of his audience. Since the beginning of the war, he had felt that everyone was looking to him as mayor. They all knew he was the one who would relay the bad news brought by the gendarmes and the *préfet*. Like mayors all across the country, he found himself thrust into the limelight. He was expected to know everything, as if he could do something about the war. Everyone was avidly waiting for the information he received, and sometimes suspected him of keeping things from them. People dreaded hearing from him that their husband or son, father or brother had been killed, and they hoped that, like an oracle, he would one day announce that the war was over and France had won, in the same way that he had suddenly announced that the war had started. The fears of his citizens seemed as hard to contain as wild cats, so, to the mayor, the lion tamer who lived on the mountain was the embodiment of all that he wasn't, someone detached, confident and strong. The lion tamer was the model of the man he dreamed of being, a man who was free, an adventurer dominating an exotic and disturbing world. Without seeking him out, he was determined to make friends, always willing to chat to him when he came down to the village. Not least for the physical pleasure of looking at him, seeing how his muscles showed in his immense body, how they sprang to life with his smallest gesture and danced over his body like an armful of snakes. The man's body fascinated him.

After a restless night with a full moon and heart-rending growling, Fernand, like the children, was well pleased. Before getting up he stretched fully, feeling as though the foot he no longer had was there again, stretching too. He inhaled deeply, his arms spread wide. With the presence of the lions, he felt invigorated; the appetite for life that sustained him before he lost his foot under a plough had returned. He rediscovered the sensation of strength he used to wake up to, stretching and feeling all his muscles, equal to anything, whether it was harnessing the oxen or wielding the axe, using the scythe or embracing someone. As he listened to the lions he was reminded of the impression the lion tamer had made the first time he met him.

That day the gladiator had stood in the door of his office in the town hall, blocking out the light with his bulk. Fernand had been reading war papers and, when he looked up and saw the man, he was instantly fascinated by the athletic figure and by the jolts of the wild cats shaking the covered wagons outside, cages covered with wooden panels. He looked at the fellow and was immediately jealous of his strength. The lion tamer was bigger than anyone else in or around the village; all the men left here were old or infirm and only the women were fit and healthy. When the man asked permission to settle in the hills, promising to buy animals and even to pay money to acquire land, Fernand immediately thought of the winegrower's house, which everyone avoided, that hell where ten sheep had fallen from the rocks. No one would live there now, everyone who had lived there before having lost everything including the land and their lives. The idea of living up there was terrible and no one in the village would ever wish it on anyone, even a German. Quite the opposite. In a sense, it suited the mayor that the lion tamer and his wild beasts should live on Mont d'Orcières, if only to see if such a superior being, the braggart with his lions, would be able to thwart death and see off misfortune. The mountain brought bad luck – everyone here was convinced of that – but perhaps the lion tamer presented an opportunity to see if the curse could be lifted.

That day, Fernand had invited the lion tamer to lunch. The three large red-and-gold caravans were parked in the shade, two of them containing the immense cages with the closed shutters. You couldn't see the wild cats, but their carnal odour hung in the air and you could feel the powerful shaking of the caravans. The lion tamer was accompanied by his two circus hands – Italians – who had preferred to stay in their truck. They had bread and pâté to eat and they were happy with that. The next day they were returning to Italy.

The man's strong, gentle voice came from deep within him. His tone changed often but he spoke calmly. Fernand made an effort to understand. Although he spoke good French, he had that spiky, dry accent. For two hours the mayor listened to him, hypnotised by his presence, and by the feline odour that emanated from his tanned neck, a neck like a girder; you could support a house with that neck. Everything about him was fascinating, right up to the way the man made his chair creak every time he moved a little. The chair was like an allegory, subdued or rather tamed. The mayor was mesmerised by the power of the lion tamer and his complete authority over his animals, which he probably exercised over everything.

It wasn't just that Fernand was captivated by the man, he also told himself that the villagers would be reassured to know that there were lions up there. Being watched over by this colossus and his colony of wild animals would be like having holy protection. Perhaps the wild cats would instil in the villagers some of their irresistible force, in the same way that it is sufficient to breathe the air of forests to become as strong as oak oneself. The lion tamer did not care about the supposed curse on the hill; his only aim was to find somewhere remote to protect his beasts from the fury of the world. His mission in the war was to save his wild cats, to keep his eight large animals alive.

Then came that night in May when the lions roared more than usual, a balmy night when the Big Dipper dominated Camelopardus, when Cepheus under the Pole Star sat beside Draco. That night all the stars that could shine were on show in a cosmic display not usually seen by man. It was almost two o'clock, Jupiter was in Sagittarius and it was no doubt the unusual luminosity that agitated the lions. They began to roar like never before, as if they had escaped and were howling in excitement at their new-found freedom. Joséphine, who was far from asleep, did not move, attentive to the groans which affected her intimately. The roars, which did not scare her in the least, sent sweet, savage tremors through her, as though she were bewitched by the calls of the wild cats up above. Even though he was no longer there, the doctor could not doubt how the lions were affecting her. A man gets close to a woman when he understands her, making the journey from egoism to comprehension. The ghost of the doctor saw everything about the body of his wife; even in death he stood by her. This woman who moved alone in her bed, with her firm body longing to be touched, her curves visible even in the shadows, her wide hips and her narrow waist; even in death he set her free. He was well aware that a woman like her, a woman so exciting and full of life, would not be satisfied with compliments alone. Yet, the things beyond words he knew she wanted, he did not do to her, even when he was still alive. And if he was prepared to forgive his wife everything, even the solitary love she gave herself up to in the night, never could he have imagined that one day she would find herself dreaming of lions snorting up on the rocks. Even in life, he would not have imagined that one day she would be aroused by the roars which to her spoke of embraces, that her body would long for strong hands to hold her round the waist, the hands of a lion tamer, as greedy as the animals above.

Joséphine rose and briskly closed the window, shutting out the animals that highlighted her failings. She got back into bed, relieved not to be betraying the man who was no more. She must not listen to those savage feline growls any more. At night she would have to block her ears and drink extract of lime to help her sleep. Tomorrow she would make sure that valerian and orange blossom would deliver a slumber where dreams were pious. She was aware that everyone thought she should give herself over to the contemplation that mourning demands. A widow, that was all she was to everyone here, and they thought she should conform to the role. In the country, mourning was taken very seriously, more so than in towns, and since she did not want to dress in black as it was, she wished to avoid running the risk of being harshly judged. All desire was impossible during mourning, but she did feel desire, and the stronger it became because it was forbidden, the more imperative it was to extinguish it.

August 2017

Lise and Franck knew the high rusted bars of the large round cage would protect them from the big dog that was barking furiously, ready to bite. The worst thing was the way it stared at them, howling unrelentingly. They hadn't been scared of it before, but now, seeing it yowl with such fury, its blood-red gums foaming with drool, they were worried it might attack. They kept away from the bars but the dog could easily have slipped in through the opening. Yet it remained on the other side of the cage, as if something was stopping it from coming in. Franck had a hunch. He took Lise's arm and told her to follow him. They quietly bent down and crept along the curve of the circular cage towards the opening, and the dog calmed down. Once they got outside the immense birdcage, they carefully stood up again. The dog was still staring fiercely at them, but then it relaxed and came towards them. It became so mellow that it rubbed itself up against them, wagging its tail and offering its side for them to stroke. It was calm and affectionate again. Lise stroked its soft coat, crouching down to put her arms around its neck, as you might do with a friend or a child after a fit of rage. Franck was happy that they had found the dog again, especially there, at the bottom of a pit where he felt so out of place. He could tell that the animal was the master of a world that he and Lise knew nothing about. He wanted to find out why it had barked like that, so he stepped back towards the cage, bent down and pretended to go back inside. The dog immediately stiffened and got to its feet so abruptly that it knocked Lise to the ground, then it started barking again and rushed at Franck, ready to bite him. Franck moved away from the cage, and the dog eased off again. It didn't want them to go near the cage or inside it or even to touch it.

'Hey, dog, what happened with the cage, eh, and what's it doing here?'

'You know, Franck, we should give it a name.'

'Maybe it doesn't have one.'

'Exactly.'

Lise started to lay the picnic out on a rock a little way off. Meanwhile, Franck inspected the round cage that was more than fifteen metres long and four metres high. This metal hemisphere must have been here for years and probably couldn't be taken apart any more as the rivets were now welded together by rust. He didn't dare go inside because of the dog, but there were two wooden barrels right in the middle. From where he was standing, he couldn't tell if there was anything inside them.

It looked like one of the domes at the Jardin des Plantes, a cage in a zoo, or the stage for an animal tamer's circus act. Two holm oaks had grown inside, or maybe the cage had been built around the trees. There was a sort of hollow in the ground despite all the plants, a basin of clay with a bit of water inside. It could have been a spring, or a puddle of rain. Maybe water couldn't evaporate here, at the bottom of a gully shrouded in shadow. The trough of the valley was in complete darkness and it was a nice temperature, almost cool. The cage looked like a set where everything had been carefully considered, but he didn't understand what for, or why the dog was guarding it.

'You know, Lise, that's the thing that was shining on Google Earth, the bars in the sun . . . Disappointed?'

'Not at all. The metal arches among the green, the creepers everywhere, the trees underneath . . . It will make a good subject. Not in watercolour, in oil . . .'

'That's good then! Good.'

202

'Why do you think it goes crazy when you go inside?'

'Lise, I still can't talk to animals.'

'But I saw you trying earlier.'

'Well, it doesn't work.'

'There must be something in those barrels.'

'What do you mean – gold?'

'Don't be stupid. It's just weird that it gets so angry when you go near the cage.'

They hungrily devoured their picnic of bread and pre-prepared salads. The dog again seemed disappointed by what they were eating, but it stayed close to them. Lise got out the big sheets of drawing paper and the box of watercolours while Franck decided to go and explore the surroundings, looking for a spring or river, or any kind of watering hole. He didn't take his bag or anything else, not even his phone. The dog seemed unsure whether to follow him or to remain with Lise, but in the end it chose to go with Franck. It stayed by his side, keeping so close that it was almost pressed against his legs, as if it were trying to show it was there and offer its support. Franck was moved by the dog's sudden display of affection. It was watching his every move and trying to get in front of him now – in fact, it was starting to lead the way, as if it had sensed where they needed to go. It was touching. Franck felt connected to this animal by an inexplicable friendship. It had impressed him, and he admired everything about it: its freedom, its independence, and, in particular, the way it had wandered into their lives. The dog had adopted them – perhaps now more than ever, seeking them out in the remotest part of this wild area. Maybe it thought they were lost, or maybe it wanted to rescue them and help them find their way back to the house. It was a comforting presence.

The dog turned around every twenty seconds, seeking its master's approval, even though its master was simply following it. They just needed to get to the lowest point to find water, but it was difficult to get through the brambles, thorny bushes and exuberant climbing plants.

The dog suddenly started sniffing at the ground, and then went off to the left and over to the dense undergrowth at the foot of the rock face, a high limestone cliff that was the steepest side of the *igue*. There was some sort of stone shelter that the animal disappeared into, hardly visible because it was covered in vegetation. Franck walked up to it. It was a small building about a metre and a half high, a dry stone structure with a domed roof of jumbled tiles. Although it was dark, he could tell there was a deep pit where the ground should have been. It was a spring. An abandoned spring. Franck pulled the ivy and brambles out of the way. The plants were strong, but he managed to create an opening so he could get inside. The dog had already gone two metres down and was unconvincingly lapping the stagnant water. There was a little spurt of water gushing out far below the surface, dainty bubbles rising from the depths of the earth. The dog turned round and looked at Franck, as if telling him not to do the same, advising him not to drink this water. Looking at the shelter smothered in ivy and brambles, Franck thought about the script he was reading, though he wasn't really interested in the story. It took place in the near future, when mankind had disappeared and only five astronauts had been able to return to Earth from Mars after years of thinking about it. After ten years without humans, nature had taken over. He had learnt one thing at least from quickly scanning it: it only took a few years for cities to be completely reclaimed by vegetation. Tree roots would soon begin to attack the foundations of buildings, and concrete towers themselves would suffer from not being looked after or cleaned; the salt in the air would start to corrode the cement and loosen the stones of every building. Everything would collapse if it wasn't looked after, and the Earth would soon look like this place, abandoned and wild . . .

Franck went towards the water and dipped his feet in as a gesture of gratitude to the dog for leading him here. The water was freezing but it felt great; it came halfway up his calves, and the shock of the cold immediately tempered the heat that was making his veins bulge and his feet swell. There was a sort of stone basin at the back of the shelter, a reservoir with water gently lapping the edges. Franck perched on the side, and the simple act of sitting in the shade of the arch with his feet in the cool water felt just as good as diving into a swimming pool. He was enveloped in the humid air; rarely had he experienced such peace of mind. The dog was still drinking distractedly. From time to time it looked outside, as if afraid that somebody might disturb them, or perhaps it thought Lise was going to join them and was watching out for her. Franck closed his eyes. He was getting close to the state of bliss that Lise must feel when she meditated, sitting in her yoga position. Time stood still for him. Then a noise shattered the serenity – nothing more than the buzzing of a hornet that had followed them into the shelter and was filling it with the coarse sound of its wings. Franck didn't like bugs. He was always scared of being stung; whether it was a wasp, a bee, or anything else, all flying insects made him panic. He was afraid he would swell up if he was stung, just like his brother had when they were children and they'd had to take him to hospital. He swatted the hornet with his hand, but it came back to circle above his head. It wouldn't go away. The dog understood what was going on; ears pricked up, it followed the bug with its eyes, watching it spiral above.

Franck said playfully: 'Go on, get it . . . Go, catch!'

The dog obeyed him once again. It devoted itself completely to the task at hand and caught the insect in one quick, precise gulp, chewing it carefully to kill it, and then went back into the water and dropped the insect on the stone, just next to Franck's hand. Astounded by this gesture, Franck thanked the dog, as he would thank any human who had done him a favour. But the dog looked him in the eye as if wanting to tell him something; it even let out a few little yaps that sounded almost like speech. Franck picked up the insect, briefly wondering if he should pretend to eat it. Maybe the dog, transformed by its hunting instinct, only wanted to satisfy the demands of a master and retrieve game for him; in its mind, every animal was prey. Franck held the hornet in the palm of his hand; the dog was staring at him expectantly. Franck decided to put the hornet in his shorts pocket in an attempt to please the dog, but then it started barking, and the sound bounced back under the stone cupola and rang out in an ear-splitting echo. Franck took the hornet out of his pocket and made a show of putting it in his mouth, before pretending to eagerly chew it. At this, the dog was visibly satisfied, and it eased off and went back outside. Franck was just as relieved as he was overwhelmed, as enchanted as he was frightened. He realised two things. One, you could fool this dog – as observant as it was, the animal still had some gullibility that you could take advantage of. But secondly and more importantly, he realised that the dog expected something from him, and whatever it was, it had nothing to do with playing together.

May 1915

That morning the village awoke earlier than usual. No one wanted to miss the big parade, which was always treated with the utmost solemnity. It was a ceremony not to honour the sun, or any god, but to celebrate the departure of two hundred sheep, ten cows, two donkeys and three dogs. More than ever this year, the animals were the centre of attention. As well as keeping an eye on the weather since the previous evening, the women had been up at dawn inspecting the animals' feet to check for wounds and scratches. They had to make sure that all the ewes would be fit enough to survive the hours of walking, especially as it would be hot. At about seven o'clock all the sheep had been taken out of the barns and assembled in front of the church and town hall. Fernand had given his speech about the merit of the journey and other things; the priest who had come specially for the occasion blessed everyone, the sheep as well as those accompanying them, the dogs as well as the shepherd. He assured them of his protection against storms and wolves, promising that the pasture would be abundant that year and peaceful thanks jointly to St John the Baptist and to the dogs. Of course the men weren't there, but the sunshine and good humour of the occasion cheered everyone and the women began to sing.

That year ten cows had been added to the flock of sheep. It would not be easy for the shepherd, but there was too little hay in the barns, and it had not rained since winter, so they had decided to send the cows which gave no milk up to the summer pasture. Up there, the grass was plentiful; the ewes and cows would be able to eat their fill during the day, so that at night they would sleep instead of continuing to graze. And well-fed ewes that sleep well are always easier to watch over. People were pleased to think that the cows would be up on the other side of the hill, well sheltered. And this year they were going to take the animals higher than usual, towards the meadows where there were no roads and no gendarmes, so at least they could be sure that no one would go and inspect them, no one would ask for them to be counted, and they would not be requisitioned.

The pastures were on the other side of the meadows of Mont d'Orcières. The fact that they had to pass close to the wild cats added a little danger to the journey. All summer the sheep and cows would graze about three hours' walk away from the lions, a long way certainly, but the villagers knew that every night they would be worried. All summer long they would fear for the sheep and cows, first because the war was spreading, and secondly because since winter the wolves had returned. That was why, that year, Le Simple would be backed up by three dogs. No one dared admit it, but three dogs seemed a meagre insurance against wolves and lions. And although the shepherd was not as incapable as he seemed, he had never taken cows that far away. So that year he was also provided with two shepherd's rifles, just in case. With three dogs and two rifles, he should manage. And Le Simple had a talent for knowing which route to take and for feeling the wind, knowing that there are two things sheep hate – being on their own and being in the wind. He took them where there were at least five hundred hectares of pasture, little shady woods, plenty to feed his animals and to protect them all from forest fires.

Twice a week, someone would go up to see that he was all right. Joséphine offered to do it because she had a horse, and the excursion would do her good. Over the years, Le Simple had become a sort of farmhand, a servant available to everyone. Cheerful and reliable, he had been born to a woman from around Pasturat, near the river, who had been ashamed of her pregnancy. At first she had been able to hide it, and then she had hidden the baby himself and left him in a thicket on the riverbank down in the village. It had been like finding Moses that day, but there would be no Egyptian princess to adopt him and he would not later seek to become the leader of a people. No one had exactly decided to take charge of him, so he was passed from family to family while he was growing up and until he could be useful. Everyone acted as if they cared about the boy, so as not to appear heartless, and to demonstrate their faith in front of the priest. The boy had grown up without anyone to pay attention to his speech or to any part of his upbringing. By the time he was ten, they had all decided that he was, if not feeble-minded, at least different, and habitually predisposed always to say yes, but that was just the product of the way he had been raised. However, since the war, Le Simple had become precious to them, because now he was a man he was strong and hardy, he was very good with animals and he was an expert farmer. Le Simple was someone that the folly of nations had made into an exceptional person, a humble person who had become invaluable and irreplaceable.

Because of the priest's sermons – wasted words for not much effect – the animals did not begin their journey until nearly nine o'clock. It would take three hours to reach the pasture, if they went at a good pace. Some women and children were going with the sheep, and some of the old people too, at least for the first couple of kilometres because after that, the path became steeper and steeper. To reach the hills, you first had to climb Mont d'Orcières, and from there branch off to go due east. As they climbed they wondered how the animals would behave as they approached the summit. They were worried the sheep would take fright at the smell of the wild cats, because ewes have an acute sense of smell, and always react to an unknown scent. They fear smells they have not encountered before, and they would definitely never have smelt the emanations of lions and tigers. Fortunately there was no wind, but the women were worried about what would happen as they reached the top of the mountain, and prayed they would be able to head quickly in the direction of the high pastures that stretched away towards the granite slopes of the Massif Central.

They also did not know how the wild cats would react as they caught the scent of all those sheep and cows coming towards them. The scent might drive them wild; they might even break the bars of their cages. Everyone could picture the eight monsters making for the flock, raging like foxes descending on a henhouse, killing ten times more hens than they would actually be able to eat. Animals often do that: dogs go in for that kind of excessive killing and so do wolves when they come across a lot of livestock. The men were doing the very same at that moment, lobbing grenades into trenches filled with soldiers, and men were not the only species to behave like brutes.

As they approached the top of Mont d'Orcières, the sheep became more and more nervous, but the cows remained docile, not sensing any danger. The smell of lions did not register with Limousin cattle as something to be afraid of. They were calm ruminants, accustomed to meeting danger with insouciance.

Standing upright in their cages, the lions had sniffed the incredible procession that was coming towards them, the riot of living flesh that was approaching across the dry grass. The lions and tigers kept their heads up, their snouts extended, as if a prairie fire were raining down on them all the animals of creation. In the delicious-smelling wafts, they could make out flesh heated under hide, juicy, supple muscle, and then pink, liquid blood alongside the slightly musky scent of ageing sheep. They also recognised the scent of women and children and, as the crowning touch, from the cows there was the aroma of dried cow dung which buffaloes smell of when they're frightened. The eight wild cats felt all the best flavours of the earth were converging on them; a rising tide of meat was on offer and they were enjoying the explosion of scents. They were excited at the thought of plunging their snouts deeply into flesh which they would rip apart to enhance the odour, of tearing off whole chunks of their prey, their chops dripping with blood. The lion tamer picked up the agitation of his animals and went over to the cages. A man's sense of smell is nothing like a lion's so he didn't immediately understand and went to take a look over the edge of the cliff. And there they all were below, climbing the twisting path.

He turned back towards his lions. He had never seen them so wrought up. They were normally calm in the late morning. He wanted to get them out of the big display cage and put them all into their separate ones, but they would not listen to his orders. They did not even see him this morning. Their gazes were fixed far beyond him; he no longer existed for them. Wolfgang knew they would not calm down; quite the opposite: tremors shook their bodies, their tails were upright, and their muscles strained with growing excitement. They paced nervously up and down in a sort of symmetrical dance, the choreography of famished beasts. Faced with this, the artist took over from the tamer. Because the perfectly synchronised quadrille made a fascinating dance, Wolfgang imagined the feverish music of Richard Strauss or Beethoven played by a little circus orchestra. It would make a beautiful spectacle in a lit circus ring, but he would never be able to reproduce such an act as he would never be able to get the eight of them to coordinate their movements in perfect symmetry. So he would be the only one to witness the most beautiful performance of his lions, and he wasn't even in the cage with them. Behind him he now heard cowbells getting nearer, and then the sound of dozens of animals climbing up towards them, and that was when he understood that the idiots had not turned right; they had chosen to come up higher to cut across by the valley probably. But that would gain them, what, twenty minutes? And then they would have to go down the gentle slope and then climb up the next one.

The villagers and their animals passed less than twenty metres from the cages. Le Simple led the way, pulling his donkey, which was so overloaded its back was bowing. About twenty women and children followed with the flock, all walking with their heads down to avoid looking in the direction of the lions and tigers, suspecting that they were being watched. At the top of the hill, the two worlds met, one devouring the other with its eyes. Only the three dogs stopped to study the large cats from afar. They sensed they should not go near. The lions, for their part, feared nothing and nobody; they knew they were the strongest, yet in these circumstances they were powerless. Of all the animals in creation, they knew themselves to be dominant, with no rival as strong as they were, but they would never have the chance to prove it.

Seeing the flock in an endless line at the edge of his land made the lion tamer angry, as agitated as his big cats, which he feared would now be upset for a long time. They would be uncontrollable and wild for weeks. The stream of ewes and cows passing under their noses was provoking unusual fury, a rage that would, if he were not careful, lead them to bite the bars, or bite each other, and would never leave them.

This morning the lions had learnt that their habitat was a place where herbivores passed through, that the hills that surrounded them were inhabited by docile flocks which dared to parade right there in front of their eyes. All they had to do now was wait for them to pass by again.

Once they had that idea in their heads, the tamer would have lost all his power over them. They would think: If there is so much small game here, what use is this master who deprives us of all the prey right here under our noses? To get to the wonderful flocks all they would need to do was stop respecting the cages. Instead of waiting for the miserly huntsman to provide for them, they would no longer submit to the authority which kept them locked up and they would have thousands of chances to escape the vigilance of this lion tamer who continued to make them rehearse in return for such meagre recompense. That was the defiance that he could read in his wild cats; he knew that from now on they would do nothing but watch out for the processions of herbivores. The large flock had turned off to the east and was straggling down the slope. Once at the bottom they would start up the little path on the hill opposite. They were going in the direction of the Auvergne; up there the plateaux were not made of the same soil and the land was fertile, as opposed to the limestone that ruined the roots here.

An hour later, the lions were still pacing round in circles in the big cage. Wolfgang wanted to make them rehearse to keep them occupied, but did not feel he should get too close to them. They were not listening to him. He was afraid they would attack him. He had hidden the sheep from them and now they would not trust him. They might even decide to kill him. He did not know what vision of horror would be unleashed if his wild cats no longer obeyed him. When wild cats deny the power of their master, they rebel. They would try to escape, but if they succeeded, they would make this their territory; they would rush down into the valley and find the farms with all that they contained – pigs, chickens, rabbits, women and children. The old people would barely count as prey. The men not being there and the women not bearing arms would mean that the lions would be masters of everything. The lion tamer understood that he would have to be much more vigilant now, that he would have to take great care not to be killed. He had to stay alive so that all the people down below could stay alive too.

To reaffirm his power, that evening he doubled the rations. He would have to feed them generously for several days, bringing them no less than twenty kilos of flesh each. He would feed them so that their stomachs were distended; he would stuff them full until they forgot about the sheep and cows. From this evening onwards, there would have to be plenty of raw meat and the trap would have to provide ten times as much food, otherwise he would be eaten.

August 2017

By now they really had taken ownership of the place. Franck could feel it in the seamless way everything was coming together in the house. Lise had found her bearings and they had each, naturally, developed their own habits. There's always a moment when you start to feel at home in the house or room you're renting.

That evening was perfect, the music pleasant. The setting sun suffused the sky with red, promising rain tomorrow – or was it a sign that it would be a nice day? Franck couldn't remember. The old Telefunken radio was playing smooth jazz. You still couldn't change the station or the frequency, but every time Lise or Franck turned it back on, the radio would be playing music that went perfectly with the atmosphere. It was a bit like the radio was deciding for itself what was appropriate, as the random selection of music always seemed to fit the moment. The device was old, but the sound was good; you just had to make sure not to move the big collapsible aerial or it would crackle.

At the end of the afternoon, the dog had helped them get back from their walk. It led the way and they just followed, which was lucky as they hadn't really remembered the route – around here, everything looked the same. In the end they had spent over four hours in the green pit, the verdant sanctuary near the spring. They had even taken a dip in the pool of gently bubbling cool water, and they had stayed a long time sheltering from the heat, taking the waters, under the dog's watchful eye. The animal would growl every time it saw Lise or Franck put their face near the surface of the water, but only in a protective way. Lise asked what its name could be, and they came up with a game. They played for a good while and tried out all the names that came to mind, from Lassie to Rex, Médor to Bulle, from Baikal to Samba, Biscuit to Ulysses, from Ascott to Brutus, Kali, Tara, Roxy . . . At every new suggestion, they would look at the dog as they called it by that name. The animal usually didn't react; it just looked uninterested but didn't stand up. Sometimes it didn't even seem to hear them. None of the names were right. Trying out all the combinations of syllables until they found the right one would take for ever. The dog had perhaps never been given a name. To put an end to it, Franck and Lise decided to try to think of a suitable name each. If they came up with the same one, they would call it that. But if they came up with two different ones, they would each use the one they had chosen and see which name the animal responded to best. If necessary, they would keep both. Franck had chosen Alpha, the name of his company. Lise had gone for Bambi, because the dog always came from the forest, because it was at home there, and like the deer in the book, it seemed to bring drama with it. Bambi didn't suit the dog at all, but it made it seem softer.

They packed up their things and stood there watching the dog, which had already set off, helping them find a more human-friendly route that was less steep than the way they had come down. It guided them around the outside of the *igue* along a wide path, which meant they could get back up without having to do any serious climbing. When they got to the top, they had no idea where they were or what direction the house was, but the animal was already ahead of them. They just followed.

After such a long walk Lise and Franck were starving by evening. When they had eaten and cleared the table, Franck lounged in postprandial contentment on an old wooden chair that he tilted backwards. Legs resting on the stone bench, he watched the dog, which was still sitting under the big tree, not moving. All through dinner they had offered it morsels of food. But nothing seemed to interest it. Nothing was right. It had barely deigned to sniff at the bits of bread that Franck had thrown after dipping them in the dressing from the tomato salad. Even then, it would lick them but wouldn't eat them. Lise was taking advantage of the summer break to eliminate dairy from her diet and give up all animal protein, so there was nothing in the house that would appeal to a meat eater. Franck wondered what the dog could actually eat. Could a dog decide for itself what it ate and be sure of finding it? He didn't know. Nowadays dogs just ate dry biscuits – at least, all the dogs he had seen; even the dogs he had filmed with. Dogs that had to be terrifying according to the script and had played their bloodthirsty part on camera only ate the multicoloured biscuits their handlers gave them after shooting. There was nothing wild about that. Alpha really didn't seem bothered by hunger. He remained calm and a little weary, his head resting on his front paws, which were crossed in front of him. Maybe the long walk had tired him out as well.

'Alpha . . . Alpha.'

Hearing Franck call him, the dog raised his head a little, without much conviction.

'Bambi . . . Bambi.'

That name didn't work any better. Franck reflected on Lise's decision to call him Bambi because of the landscape, the untamed countryside that surrounded them. It was probably true that the dog was an orphan who had lost his mother or master and been left to fend for itself, eventually becoming wild again. He had chosen the name Alpha after his company, but it was also the name of the main character in the futuristic script he was reading, one of the ones that Liem and Travis had sent him. He didn't like the script in which, yet again, he detected the influence of the fantasy world of video games, but the fact that the hero was called Alpha made him look more favourably on the text. He generally had no interest in science fiction films, apart from *Blade Runner* or *Metropolis*, *Brazil* or *2001:*

A Space Odyssey, and a few others, like *Soylent Green* or *Planet of the Apes* . . . In fact, now that he thought about it, there were actually quite a few sci-fi films that fascinated him, but he would never invest in that kind of project as a producer. It would no doubt be another source of conflict with Liem and Travis.

In the bathroom, the style of the music changed. For a while it had only been playing classical music, but it suddenly switched to country. A female singer with a mournful voice over a banjo melody gave a Western feel to the sun setting over the hills. Finding himself in this environment, alone in this wild landscape, Franck could easily imagine himself producing a Western, but one set in the countryside, perhaps even right here, though the stone house wouldn't really go with it. He looked around and he wondered who had lived here. What kind of person could have decided to live so far away from everyone else, in such a remote area? They must have had a spirit of adventure and done work that didn't involve interacting with people.

He would never get the funding for a European Western. Anyway, Westerns didn't make money any more, not even in the US. Unless it was a minimalist Western, with just a few characters, some panoramic shots of deep, isolated countryside, and with that particular kind of light, like *Days of Heaven*, a whole film shot in the red glow of sunset. Just then he noticed something stirring at the very bottom of the long meadow in front of him. He could see the grass shaking with jerky little movements. Franck lifted his head for a better view, without getting up from his chair. There was a creature all the way over by the trees, a small animal about a hundred and fifty metres away that he could barely see; it must have been a rabbit hopping from place to place, or a hare – he couldn't tell the difference. The dog was still half asleep, eyes closed, but he sensed that Franck had spotted something; he pricked up his ears and looked at Franck, again waiting for an order. Franck tried not to return his gaze, for fear of influencing him. But he couldn't help himself, probably because of the country music, which was becoming less and less melancholy. Franck felt the hunting instinct take hold of him, and he wanted to unleash something in this peaceful setting. He wanted to set off some wild chain of events to see if he really had any power over the environment around him. He suddenly wanted action, vigorous action, and he wanted to act the cowboy, one of the tough cowboys who are in control of their surroundings and are part of the cycle of life, deciding on the fate of animals as well as humans.

'Alpha! What's that over there? Eh? What's over there?'

The dog leapt up, already hungry for action, but what exactly? Strangely, dogs always know that they should look in the direction the finger is pointing. Alpha located the hare to the west; he stood still, not moving, nose in the air, trying to work out where he was. He stayed like this, tense as a loaded weapon ready to go off; they exchanged a quick glance, and then Franck simply said, 'Get it!' The dog immediately bolted off in the direction of the hare, and the hare, which sensed the predator coming at it from far away, bolted in turn and scampered off towards the woods. Hares can run twice as fast as dogs, but dogs never give up, even if it means running ten times as far on an absurdly steep slope. Franck regretted his decision, especially when he saw Alpha race to the end of the field, not even stopping at the bushes but noisily ploughing straight through them. He tore through the box trees and brambles at the edge of the woods, which plunged down steeply about fifty metres later, turning into a cliff that overhung the old village of Orcières. Franck was angry with himself for having set the two animals off on this fatal course. He couldn't believe how crazy the dog was, launching himself at full speed down the slope through the undergrowth, with the rock face at the end, at risk of tumbling the whole way down the rock. Yet he was fascinated by his irrepressible energy. What would the dog bring him back this time? A bumblebee? A cone from a cypress tree? Or the hare?

Behind him, the radio had started playing 'Saravá', a frenzied piece by Baden Powell. He recognised it straight away: it was a perfect match for the intensity and confusion of the jungle, for the danger always lurking in wild places, where nature is teeming with peril. Franck walked across the field towards the woods, wanting to know if the dog would continue chasing its prey further down the hill, if it would carry on running after its prize, or if the two of them had thrown themselves into the void . . . Maybe the dog was looking for a master – either way, he wanted to please Franck, showing an unrelenting willingness to sacrifice himself for him and obeying the orders that he only reluctantly gave. But, now, he had to stop the dog, he had to prevent him from killing the animal, and so Franck went further into the woods, leaving behind the deadly percussion and demonic rhythms of the music that was pulsing through the air. From afar, all he could hear was the distant drumming of the next piece. Perhaps the dog wanted to involve him in a sort of initiation, like the Masai ritual where each newcomer kills a lion with his bare hands and eats it to give him strength and courage and admit him into the world of 'men'. Maybe the dog wanted to bring him the hare as an offering, delivering it in person for him to eat. He was horrified by the idea of Alpha coming back with a dead animal, a hare torn to shreds and dangling from his mouth. He was appalled just thinking about it. He would never be able to pick up the corpse of a bloody animal, still warm and damp from the slobber of its panting murderer, and besides, what would he do with the hare? He would put it straight in the bin, because spending a night thinking about the cadaver in the kitchen downstairs was unbearable. And yet that was what the dog was going to do, he could feel it. Alpha was going to bring him the rabbit, hoping he would skin it, cook it and eat it. Franck finally understood that that was how the game worked between them; the dog hunted so he could dedicate what he caught to Franck, out of respect.

When Lise got out of her third shower of the day, she saw Franck moving around right at the bottom of the field. He seemed to be looking intently at the undergrowth and calling 'Alpha'. But the dog didn't come. She was amused by the scene. Franck turned around and hurriedly came back up the field towards the house.

'Something wrong?'

'Yes, Lise, I think . . . Well, I think I've done something stupid.'

'Oh? What have you done?'

Franck walked up to Lise and took her in his arms.

'No, nothing. Nothing. Nothing.'

They held each other tight, like two people reunited on a train platform after months of separation. Here in this primitive place, they were rediscovering the strength of their bond; they knew that they loved each other even though they didn't say it any more, that they loved each other in such a way that they didn't even need to tell each other or think about it. The final stage of harmony and bliss between two people is perhaps when love becomes so natural that it no longer needs to be spoken of out loud. Franck desperately held his wife against him, hugging the woman who had brought him all this way to lose himself in a lost world, a world that was simple and complete; to lose himself and then to find himself again. Maybe all you needed in life was a house surrounded by hills. As soon as you start expecting something else from life, you always want more, and it never ends. His sudden tenderness was as much out of gratitude as fear. He was afraid of finding some forbidden happiness, of falling for the illusion of going back to his roots where he was free from the rest of the world and its obligations, from his job, his partners, his bankers . . . It would be a truly cruel kind of happiness that made him believe he was free, just like that, able to leave behind the life he had made, suddenly released from every tie, and above it all.

The next piece on the radio was film music. A man was speaking in Catalan, but because of his poor microphone and the fact that his voice was breaking up, you couldn't understand anything he was saying. The poor quality of the recording made it all harder. Then the voice got quieter and was replaced with another film score, from Sakamoto's *Merry Christmas, Mr Lawrence*.

The sun had just gone down and daylight had almost completely disappeared. It was the time of day when you might think about switching on a light, but Franck and Lise didn't move. He was still holding her in his arms, turning his back on the meadow with his eyes closed. It was Lise who saw Bambi come back into view in the distance, sturdy, strong Bambi coming back out of those deadly woods. She couldn't decide whether he was more dog or wolf, but he jumped slowly and wearily over the last bushes, visibly worn out by his race through the brambles. Lise didn't say anything, but watched the dog coming back up the meadow towards them, not running and in no hurry, with the sheepish air of someone who is not proud of themselves. Franck squeezed her tighter against him.

'Lise, what's in his mouth?'

'What?'

'The hare . . . did he get it . . .?'

'Franck, what are you talking about?'

Franck turned around, relieved to find that the dog didn't have the little animal in his jaws; it looked like he hadn't caught it. The dog came quietly closer and positioned himself near them, shaking his head like someone who is annoyed with himself. It was at that point, both disheartened and exhilarated, that Franck realised he had made a real ally, a firm, unfailing ally; and now he would be able to get this dog to do anything, but the deal needed to be sealed with a real reward.

Lise bent down to stroke the big, sullen animal, and she could feel he was hot under his soft, rough coat, but the stubborn dog remained despondent. Lise spoke to him tenderly and reassuringly and cuddled him like an exhausted runner, but the poor dog only had eyes for Franck. He looked right at him as if expecting forgiveness, and more importantly, the promise of doing it again. Yes, Franck could sense that Alpha was counting on him to play again the next day, but with a different target, something that wasn't a hare this time, nor a ball or cypress cone. Yes, next time he had to aim for something much bigger, something more valuable and incriminating, a much more dignified game animal. Why not a deer or a wild boar, a stag, or a man? Why not . . . ?

May 1915

That morning as she saddled her horse Joséphine was troubled. There was no reason why she shouldn't go up there, but she felt guilty about it. However, should anyone see her going up that side of the mountain, if anyone down below saw her disappearing behind the junipers and climbing up towards Mont d'Orcières, they would assume that she was going to visit Le Simple in the pastures. In a sense that was true. It was just that she had a hope that she held on to as tightly as the reins of her horse, that she would meet that man again. No one doubted that it was out of the sheer goodness of her heart that she had already taken provisions up to the shepherd three times in the last fortnight, bringing him bread and fresh milk. As the ewes were delicate and their feet were always bumping against ruts and thorns, Joséphine would take a pot of copper sulphate and some Vaseline to treat their wounds. She was certain that every time she examined their feet she would find cuts. Joséphine knew how to look after ewes. Her parents owned land in Bergerac and, unlike her sisters, she had spent a lot of time on the smallholdings, because she loved all animals, not just her horse. Back then she saw the world as a large book made up of exciting scenarios, each of which had a role for her, whether in the flower-filled rooms of the parental home, or in the farms on the estate.

It was particularly audacious of her to venture onto the mountain because her horse baulked at climbing that path. At some points the slope was almost vertical, and the stony ground spat stones at the poor horse whose journey was made harder by having someone on his back, light as she was. In spite of this, Joséphine pushed the animal onwards without dismounting; today she wanted to pick up the pace; she didn't want to waste time on this beautiful afternoon which she had free. Today she wanted to use her freedom to pursue her plan of losing her way.

Again the wild cats smelt them coming from afar, the horse and the horsewoman. For two weeks, they had been restless. The excitement produced by the sheep passing had given way to a profound resentment that would not dissipate. In order to try to reassert his authority, Wolfgang had poached at least ten wild boar and three deer, but despite his best efforts to get them fresh meat, the lions had not softened. They were not happy in captivity any more; they could not stand it. They could not forget the smell of the hundredweight of legs of lamb and sides of beef; they kept thinking of the tons of meat they could have had. For two weeks the eight beasts had their mouths open and were short of breath. Their jaws were clenched, a sign that they could smell that the prey was still in the vicinity. From time to time, the wind carried particles of new flesh to them, wafts which upset the coherence of the group and agitated them all. Not since the beginning of time had lions had such an abundance of smells in their area, never had they sniffed a herd nearby without being able to get to them. Smelling them without being able to see them was agony. Beyond the bars that penned them there was not just holm oaks and scrub, but also dense woods of which lions have a horror, because trees and bushy scrub hinder their path and obstruct the way. When lions hunt they need to run through flat, open savannah. More than ever they cursed those trees, those bars and that man. For two weeks, everything had been making them mad.

When she reached the top, rather than taking the path to the east, Joséphine looked over towards the cages. She kept her distance but from where she was she could see them all. She was profoundly moved by their growls, a sign that they were agitated. She was a bit frightened. It was the first time she had come up this far, into that man's territory. Usually she turned off at the crossroads just below the summit.

Advancing slightly, she discovered the little building, the much-discussed winegrower's house that everyone said was under a magic spell. It was a simple, modest house, but splendid in its isolation. It nestled proudly on its hill, a house that did not seem to fit the man who lived there with his imposing beasts.

By coming this far she thought her mere presence would be enough to set things off, that it was enough for her to set onto his land for the lion tamer to welcome her or turn away from her. No matter: she would take the slightest gesture or acknowledgement from the man as an act of love. Even if he pushed her away, the sensation, although fleeting and disappointing, would be more invigorating than a life spent beside a dead body, a husband now even more absent in death.

The absence of humanity weighed heavily on the place; it was too hot for the big cats to be in the display cage, and the growling of the eight felines hiding in their house, in the shade of the two big red-and-gold caravans parked under the oak trees, made the atmosphere rather eerie. Because of the blinding light, Joséphine could not see the animals clearly now, but she could make out their bulky shapes, and she felt their presence all around. The meat-eating monsters made silken but terrifying noises. The large round cage at the back was empty. Joséphine recognised it; it was the one he had had at the circus, the one in which he performed his acts. There was a dismantled cage nearby, the extension gates flat on the ground. When she saw that, she wondered if one day he would join a circus again, if life, including the performances of these captive lions, would start up again as if nothing had happened.

She found it strange that he was not there. It would have been improper to call him – besides how would she address him? She couldn't call him Wolfgang – perhaps Monsieur. Or she could just call, 'Anyone there?' She went closer to the house; it was as scary as going up to the lions. She was astonished to find window boxes of bellflowers and gardenias at the windows for she knew how much delicate care it took to make those flowers grow. She leant forward to sniff them; the smell of gardenias was as complex as any of the best perfumes, a perfume so subtle and gentle that it was like a personal statement. The shutters were folded over the window, a little open, to create a draught. Through the small gap she could tell that the house was in darkness; it seemed that no one was there. Even so it would be rude to knock on the shutter.

Embarrassed to be looking inside, she turned to go over to the cages. She was walking full in the sun, but as she got closer she started to see the animals huddled in the shade more clearly. As her eyes got used to the gloom, the eight massive shapes revealed themselves gradually until they were perfectly clear. Standing back, she took a good look at the magnificent, terrifying beasts, which stared back at her, indifferent and disdainful. They were all at the back of the cage, as if protecting themselves from the sun. She was amazed to find herself there, in a landscape she knew well, countryside that she had been coming to her whole life, but standing opposite eight totally out-of-place felines. She went a little closer. The old male, a thickset animal with an abundant mane, occasionally threw her a glance. He would appear to look at her, but immediately closed his eyes to conceal it. He would close his eyes for a second before opening them again on something else. Then his immense eyes, rimmed in black, would turn back towards her, staring over her shoulder, not even granting her the favour of looking her in the face. These lions and tigers were like enormous cats, gigantic soft toys that she wanted to stroke because, lying down, they looked languid, and the flashes of violence they displayed were softened. Joséphine went even closer, fatally attracted, thinking she detected in them a liking for her or, at least, a tolerance. Already they had stopped growling and roaring; they recognised that she was an ally. So she went still closer. She was almost within reach of the bars now. Standing barely a metre away, she was gripped by the desire to slip her hand through the bars, to finally touch these frightening toys. She had never seen them so close, and so calm. She thought she heard a sort of growl from one or other of them, more like a tender purring, so she went right up close and put her hand on the cage, but Théo, the big male, let out such a ferocious breath that she recoiled. She thought they were intrigued by her presence, whereas in fact they were brooding on the cold anger that had been gnawing at them for the past two weeks, the frustration of not being able to hunt real prey. Although separated from them by the bars, Joséphine was frightened again, aware that they could inflict death on her at any moment. But, feeling them so close, these eight unctuous wild cats, these eight big teddy bears, she had a sudden desire to fling herself amongst them. They were the wild cats of the man she had there within reach, and to get close to them, to almost be able to touch them, was as exciting as getting close to him.

The lions and tigers were all still disdainful except for Léa, the largest female, who slowly rose and nonchalantly turned a little and stood in the centre of the cage, motionless and calm. Then suddenly, in one bound, she flung herself at the bars. The noise of the attack was incredibly loud. She opened her mouth wide before launching herself on her hind legs, her body taut and arched. Although the bars stopped her, she prolonged the attack by spraying a stream of slobber over Joséphine, her mouth twisted in a desire to bite. Then she let out ferocious growls and dropped her head, her back legs spread, as if warning Joséphine not to approach. Joséphine dared not move. She was petrified by the display of anger and could neither breathe nor retreat. The growls had pierced her like a blade, her heart was still pounding and she struggled to get her breath back. Then Léa began to stiffen again, spitting with her eyes closed, her face contorted in a hideous rage, her tail down.

Rather than an act of temper, Joséphine detected disappointment. She took three steps back in an act not just of retreat, but of vexation at the knowledge that she was excluded from all this, and the certainty that she had no place here. This whole world was pushing her away, the wild cats as well as the man. All that had seemed to her the highest ecstasy suddenly seemed as dangerous as it was forbidden, and it also seemed unbearable. In a sharp return to reality, she now perceived that sometimes gardenias smelt like sweat, that the wild cats were nothing more than ineffectual carnivores that would be dead one day, that she was a widow, that the sun was burning hot and that love caused suffering.

She mounted her horse, which she had tied up a little way off, and left, annoyed, bitter and hurt as we are when we become aware that the world cares nothing for our feelings. She was dismayed to realise that her life awaited her elsewhere, down below, where there was no passion and no one to desire; there was only fear and work, and the anguish of a country engaged in an endless war. She was cross with herself for having believed there could be something for her here, for believing in passion, in the mad embrace that would blot out the world, and even that she might find love. When in fact all that awaited her was an existence that did not even try to promise anything, an existence that did not even offer her real pain. Nothing is harder to swallow than the realisation that one will never be loved again. To be rejected by the lions and not even to have seen the man was worse than coming back to reality. Here everything despised her. She almost went back down the path, almost forgot that she needed to continue east, almost forgot about the shepherd.

Behind the closed shutter, his body hurting from having stayed still so long, sickened by the smell of the gardenias, he saw her leaving and turning to the east and understood that she was going to visit the sheep. He saw her fine head and blonde chignon shining through the trees before she disappeared. He had been aware of that woman since the very first day, in the village. From the very first, he had sensed that she was offering him her eyes, her skin, her body, but he was afraid of having an affair, after the last one. He was afraid of adding desire to the complications of the existence he was now trapped in; he was too afraid that the lions themselves, the lions more than the tigers, would be offended if he had an affair. The lions would smell her on him straight away. They would pick up the fragrance of the woman's milky skin mixed with his own sweat, and jealousy would drive them wild.

He sighed as he got up carefully, his joints painful from being bent double for so long. He opened the shutters to get some fresh air, although it was even hotter outside than in. He felt distress at having to live alone. A house on top of a hill expresses more eloquently than anything else the shape of solitude. Solitude is a mistake, but he knew the perils of getting close to anyone in the village, especially a woman, and more especially that woman. That woman, he would have to be mad to want her, to take the risk of loving her. Wolfgang swore never to think of her again.

Well away from the house, the lions hiding in the shade were no longer stirring. The incident was over. But Léa, Bianca and Zhan had not sat down again; females are not as lazy as males, especially when it's hot. That afternoon there was no wind; the air did not carry the scent of the flock of sheep, but that woman and her horse had been there right in front of them, and they had added her to their memories of prey. They had not forgotten about the sheep; they knew they were there, behind, three hills away. Wild cats never give up; they would never forget that the sheep were nearby; one way or another, one day they would break their bonds, one day they would escape their chains. Lions, far more than man, never give up on their desires.

August 2017

Franck woke up the next day feeling the need for civilisation again. He wanted to see people, get a coffee and inhale its aroma, and feel a crowd around him. He missed the commotion of the city, the ever-changing murmur of other people's conversations, and passers-by, and cars, that constant flurry that serves as a distraction from the void. He sat down once more right at the back of the Paradou bistro. He felt grounded again, enjoying his spot far enough away from the rest of the customers that he felt peaceful, but surrounded by the reassuring buzz of human activity.

Since they had been at Mont d'Orcières, he had been doing something completely new. For the first time, he was experiencing the strange sensation of living in a house a long way from anything else, lost in both space and time. Thanks to the gîte, he was discovering that solitude could be rewarding, and that it was possible to find fulfilment away from others. All through the year he was around people, yet he was alone when it came to making decisions, alone when it came to his associates and alone when it came to his financial partners and the people circling, always asking him about his accounts.

Franck was acutely aware of all this as he turned on his phone to find eight messages and a torrent of emails from Liem and Travis. He dreaded the messages, but opened them one by one to see how their offensive was going. He could tell they were testing him just by skimming through their proposals; they were trying to get him to give in and be a good dog while they showed him who was boss. It wasn't just a collaboration with Netflix. Their idea was to sell them shares, so Netflix would own a part of Alpha Productions. Not content with handing over his library, they were prepared to hand over control as well. As he looked at the attached documents, Franck realised that this time they were going ahead without him. They were intending to sign a broadcasting contract with an exclusivity clause, but he knew from experience that once the fox is in the henhouse you'll never get it out. As he looked through the new clauses, he wondered whether he was dealing with two evil geniuses, or two reckless idiots. He had underestimated them from the beginning. He had let himself be swayed by their youth and vigour, which he assumed brought a fresh approach, drive and knowledge about new technology – all the things that he now found annoying.

He was used to reading contractual documents, but these seemed convoluted and bizarrely translated from English by a software programme, with expressions that were incomprehensible. The new clauses were covered in coloured highlighter on the PDF document. He was lost. Rather than trying to make sense of it all, he called them. As he had feared, the conversation went badly from the start. Liem and Travis always insisted on putting the phone on loudspeaker, so he never knew who had just spoken because their two voices constantly overlapped. Franck never liked these noisy telephone conversations, but especially not now that it was two against one in the middle of a café. Every time he talked business with them, he felt as helpless as he would if a smartphone salesman were explaining new apps to him that he would never use. This time Liem and Travis were aggressive and full of confidence. They said it was important to think long-term and get ahead of the market and make the most of the new European directives that would soon be voted on in Brussels, protectionist measures that from 2019 would force the tech giants to reinvest fifteen per cent of the revenue they made in France into local production companies.

He had a feeling that Liem and Travis were trying to confuse him with these vague possibilities. Draft bills don't always see the light of day, especially in Brussels, and especially when it involves going against Big Tech. But his partners were confident that they needed to act quickly, swearing that Netflix and Amazon would have to invest in France and diversify their catalogue by at least twenty per cent with local works. In other words, all the American tech giants would be forced to produce in France, and they would soon need French professionals to take on these local productions, if only to meet the quotas. That was the big opportunity. He should move quickly, positioning himself as the executive producer everyone needed, especially as the bosses of most French production companies were on holiday.

'We need to make a move, Franck; we're gonna overtake them all.'

'God, you're naïve! Remember that Big Tech, like all large companies, always think they're above the law, always; they'll get round the rules one way or another, and believing they're trustworthy would be the bloody stupidest thing to do.'

Franck could sense they had an ulterior motive. What Liem and Travis weren't saying was that they eventually wanted to produce series. They were only interested in short formats, not feature films; for them, cinema was part of a romantic, completely outdated perception of the profession; in the future, people would watch films on tablets and mobile phones, but not in cinemas . . . Franck refused to believe the battle had been lost. Above all, he didn't want Netflix or Amazon to get shares and buy into the company – he had never needed them to make films before. He knew Liem and Travis wouldn't stop twisting his arm about renegotiating their partnership agreement and so suddenly he tossed out a proposal that had come to him in a flash of inspiration that surprised even him. He spoke with the confidence of someone who had been thinking about it for months.

'All right, OK, we can do that, but on one condition: you give me a budget of five million to make the film I want to make.'

'No, Franck, we can't do that. The three of us work together now, so no personal projects, not for you or any of us.'

'Five million a year.'

'Look, you need to come back to Paris so we can talk about this calmly.'

'Talk? We can do that just fine on the phone; we're doing it now.'

'But we can never reach you . . . No, we really need to see each other face to face to sign, and, come on, you're not really going to spend three weeks in that hole!'

'I'm doing very well in this hole, as you call it. Very well indeed. I don't think it would do either of you any harm to take a step back—'

'A step back? You shouldn't step too far back, you know, especially not now. Careful, Franck, taking a step back means going backwards.'

'No, it means seeing things more clearly.'

With all the irony he could muster, Liem retorted: 'Hang on, you're not trying to make us believe that you can see things clearly stuck in the middle of nowhere . . .'

'Well, I have a clearer idea than you about the films I want to make.'

Travis went on, in the scornful tone Franck had already noticed he was capable of: 'Get with the programme, Franck. The brain is like an iPhone; you have to install the updates.'

'The kind of cinema I like making will still be made in a hundred years.'

For the second time, Travis launched into his tirade: 'Releasing films in the cinema is too risky. One day you'll have to think digital, Franck. Can't you see, these days everyone is glued to their phones from the day they're born?'

'No.'

'Trust me, if you had kids, you'd get it.'

He had already played that card in person three months ago. The killer remark. Franck hadn't thought he'd do it again. It was either sheer nastiness, or it was thoughtlessness. Franck took it like a punch to the jaw, rendering him speechless. But, again, he did not react.

Never before had anyone thrown in his face the idea that not having children was a defect, that not having children was shameful and excluded you from civilisation, from the future of the world, that it excluded you from the cycle of life. These two idiots were denying him his right to understand anything at all.

Rather than carrying on talking, Franck told them he would call back tomorrow. Tomorrow he would let them know what day he was planning to come back to Paris. They would get their meeting, and he would sign. He said goodbye to them without anger or bitterness, but this time something inside him had snapped. Two minutes after hanging up, he realised he couldn't work with the two young fathers who were continually making digs, saying he knew nothing about the world today because he didn't have children, implying that they were the future because they were young, they were modern, they were parents. Deep down, he had always been aware of a gulf, a divide between himself and the world of those with children. He had a gnawing sense of guilt about it, as if not reproducing were a disgrace, a form of sabotage. He and Lise hadn't had children. It was a long story, but they hadn't been able to – it was too many stories in fact; they didn't have to justify themselves. But as he sat in a café far away from everything, the last cutting words rammed home all his failures and disappointments, as if a lifetime's bad luck and disillusionment had suddenly caught up with him.

Franck looked at the phone in front of him. He was already annoyed with himself for not reacting, for not having come up with a suitable retort for Travis, or Liem – after all, he didn't even know for certain which one had said it. Yet there was nothing he could have said. In life there are things like this that you just have to take, truths that people tactlessly throw in your face to weaken or break you, but that are nonetheless true. He ordered another double espresso and the waiter brought it straight away. He drank it down in one go, without sugar, causing his heart to pound and great beads of sweat to form. For some reason, he had a vision of the dog yesterday evening, when

234

he had taken off after the hare at full speed, as if he were listening to him. He really should start thinking of the huge, loyal dog as an ally – a real ally, unlike his partners. A faithful ally who would stand by him and maybe even help him come up with a plan, some kind of revenge involving a trap, turning the two hunters into sweet prey.

PART III

August 2017

Coming out of the café, Franck was startled by the light, surprised to find himself in Limogne. He had had six coffees without realising it and spent almost an hour with the phone pressed against his ear – the right-hand side of his face was still warm. As the conversation had gone on, his anger had gradually welled up and reached a climax at the final jibe.

After that hour in the bistro, talking to his partners with his eyes closed so that he could almost imagine he was sitting opposite them in the office on Rue de l'Arbre-Sec in Paris, now here he was in full sunlight, as if he had just returned from some dark planet to find it was midsummer. The disjunction was stupefying. He walked aimlessly, ending up in the main square. The market was here again today, but it was smaller this time, with fewer vendors and fewer customers. He walked towards the stalls in the shade, feeling as though he were visiting a set before filming had started; everything seemed unreal and yet very concrete at the same time.

He was still angry with himself for not coming up with a biting retort to show that he wasn't at all bothered. Often you only think of something to say afterwards, when it's too late. But he must not let those two jerks get to him. He needed to regain control and throw them off balance with some kind of threat, though he didn't know what yet. He had to force them out of their comfort zone, even if it meant getting them to come here, to this spot that had become his territory in just a few days. The idea quickly took shape in his mind: he would entice them here, somehow trap them and make them pay for their arrogance and plotting. He thought back to the dog savagely pursuing the hare and had a sudden vision of the dog going after them, simply because he had given the order . . . He was so on edge that he was trembling. The caffeine was making his head pound and he was sweating all over, so he moved into the shade of the stalls.

He immediately noticed how quiet it was, with none of the bustle of Sunday. It was cooler in the shade. Franck tried to stop thinking about his partners, but he couldn't prevent the image of Alpha coming back to him, Alpha chasing them and forcing their spiel back down their throats, making them sign new amendments, new clauses to their detriment . . . He focused on the fruit and vegetables arranged on the bright stalls. The tomatoes on the vegetable stall caught his eye. Misshapen, their skin didn't have the sheen of plastic-wrapped supermarket fruit and they glowed with vitality. The potatoes next to them were earthy, caked in centuries-old mud; the lettuces were bursting with life; the tips of the stacked carrots pointed at him; the courgette flowers were lined up like yellow-stained paintbrushes; and at the front were all sorts of fruits separated into crates, unprocessed, probably freshly plucked from the tree. Yet he was still most fascinated by the great red stand on the other side, the butcher's stall and the crimson tarpaulin that reflected the light. The sun beat down on it, making everything more vivid, reminding Franck of red velvet theatre curtains. A huge leg of cured ham took centre stage, an enormous thigh presiding over the rest of the meat and charcuterie. In that light, it was fascinating. The ham was fastened to a wooden stand almost a metre in length, and pinned at both ends. The whole leg in all its glory was held in place by a vice for everyone to see, hideous and yet somehow touching. For a moment, Franck saw himself as the ham, trapped there, sadistically sliced and carved up by his partners.

The most disturbing thing was the butcher standing behind the device, cutting off slices with a long knife, even though there were no customers at the stall. It must have been for an order, or to put on display. The giant in his red-stained white coat was leaning over the leg of ham as if worried it would escape, holding the blade flat and slowly sliding it into the flesh. There was something delectable about the movement. Franck thought of Alpha and how good it would feel to take a few slices back for him, so the dog could join them when they were eating instead of just watching. Then at least he would have a real reason to stay with them. It would be a way of getting closer to him, of forming a bond. The dog had the right attitude: in this life, you had to be determined, ready to charge at your prey without mercy and grab your enemy by the throat.

Franck went up to the stall and said something he hadn't said for ten years.

'I'll have some ham, yes, that one, ten thin slices. Actually, not too thin.'

The butcher shot him a stern look, like a tobacconist eyeing a six-year-old kid.

'Thin or not?'

'Not too thin.'

Franck looked around, as if worried he was being observed. Then with automatic generosity, the butcher held out the slice he had just cut, a strip of dark-red meat that hung from his knife.

'Try it first, then you can tell me if you want your slices fine or not.'

Franck took the bit of ham as if it was an insect he had been told to eat. He didn't dare say that it wasn't for him, that it was a gift, but he came up with a perfect excuse in the nick of time.

'No, really, I've just had coffee; I've still got a sweet taste in my mouth.'

The butcher looked him in the eye, then brought the knife to his mouth and gulped the meat down in one go, devouring it with his eyes closed and savouring the taste as delicately as he would a sugared rose petal. He chewed it for a long time, no doubt exaggerating his enjoyment of it. Not knowing quite what to say, Franck looked at the other things on the stall. He was confronted with relics of a bygone world, like an ethnologist trapped at some savage feast in the middle of the jungle. In some ways, by not eating meat, he was no longer part of this old world. But by not having children, he wasn't part of the coming world either. Everything was mixed up in his head, and the memory of what that dried meat must taste like came back to him remarkably clearly.

'So, how much do you want?'

'I don't know. Actually, I don't think I want it any any more.'

'You know what, I'll cut you ten thin slices and give it to you for free.'

'No, really—'

'I won't take no for an answer, I don't have any customers this morning anyway. Then you can tell me if you like it and you can come back on Sunday. OK?'

Franck didn't dare refuse. He thought about the dog and the pact that this would seal between them. The butcher began to carve the leg again as precisely as if he were whittling wood. Franck looked upon the repulsive sight like an anthropologist. Fifteen years ago, he had tried to co-produce a docudrama about Claude Lévi-Strauss. There would have been plenty of exotic settings to work with here. What he remembered of the project was fragments of script and stories of primitive harmony, of a time when man and beast spoke the same language and ate one another. Nowadays children were still given cuddly toys that they couldn't stop chewing and hugging, as if they were animals themselves. He had never even held a baby and he knew that.

The butcher still hadn't finished carving. Watching the blade glide into the thigh made Franck very uncomfortable. He looked up at the medals nailed to a wooden board, trophies that had been won in competitions, alongside a row of framed certificates. He thought about his own office in Paris and the prizes from relatively prestigious festivals. A good fifteen of his films had won awards, and just as many had been nominated for several prizes.

'Impressive, all these medals. Bravo . . .'

'The Famille Bardasse, butchers for six generations. We've been feeding local people for more than a century. The kids around here get their muscles from us.'

'You can get muscle from other things too . . .'

'Oh really? From beetroot and lettuce? No, you need to eat muscle to make muscle. That's what nature intended.'

'Maybe.'

'For centuries, we've fed the men in these parts by butchering animals. Our meat has nurtured the living. That's quite something, don't you think?'

Franck's expression was set in a grimace. He didn't know what to say without pointing out that it was truly archaic for modern man to eat animals, but he didn't want to start a lengthy debate.

'I'm telling you, the Bardasse family even fed lions!'

'Oh really, in Africa?'

'No, here. There were lions around here in my great-grandfather's time, and the old man used to give them the fifth quarter – in those days butchers bought the animals alive, you know, and killed them themselves. Well, I say old man, but he wasn't actually old at the time.'

'What's the fifth quarter?'

'All the bits humans don't eat.'

Franck looked at him suspiciously, annoyed at being told tall tales. The man was clearly making fun of him, taking an easy opportunity to tease the tourist with his stories. As a Parisian, Franck couldn't stand the provincial habit of treating newcomers like fools. The world had been against him all day, what with Liem and Travis, and now he responded in the way he hadn't managed earlier.

'Why are you telling me all this crap? Do you take me for an idiot? Is that it – you think I'm an idiot?'

The butcher drew back, knife in hand, genuinely taken aback by Franck's annoyance.

'Whoa there! Easy now.'

'Sorry, I've had too much coffee. I thought you were making fun of me.'

'No, I'm telling you it's true! There used to be a guy who raised wild animals in the hills, and then one day he was eaten by his lions. His wife wanted to carry on feeding them after he died. Staying with the lions kept her close to the man they'd eaten, and if that's not love . . .'

'Is this some kind of legend?'

'Yes, it's a legend, but it's true. Anyway, one of the Bardasses fed the lions after this guy died.'

Franck remained bewildered.

'You clearly don't believe me . . . You don't eat meat, do you?'

'Why do you say that?'

'Because it's obvious.'

The story stirred something in Franck. He thought back to the cage deep in the gully, wondering if it might be linked to what the butcher was saying. The house he was living in had perhaps been home to the woman and the man, and the wild beasts. The butcher carried on telling him terrible things. He was clearly exaggerating his stories about the lions, claiming that, one night, a guy who was jealous of the lion tamer had set the wild beasts free. He opened the cages and the animals descended upon the village and ate everything – sheep, horses and men too. He pictured the peaceful house on the hill, where these horrors had occurred. He had grown to like the place. The butcher held out the dense parcel of meat, a package he had just made up with his big hands. The red of the paper was the same bright red as the stall, a pure, glorious red. Franck weighed the parcel in his palm. It had been years since he had picked up a piece of meat or held it in his hand, or even touched an animal that wasn't alive. It was a powerful sensation, and yet it wasn't repulsive.

'But before he died, how did the tamer feed them?'

'Ah, he had a special way of feeding his lions.'

'What was it?'

'I can't say!'

'Why?'

'Because they're still poaching up there. But he had a way, believe me. He used to catch everything: wild boar, deer; he even got lynxes and wolves.'

Franck got out his wallet to pay.

'No, no, I said it was a gift.'

There was a good three hundred grams in the package. Franck pictured Lise's face on finding the red parcel from the butcher in his basket, and then imagined the great cage in the *igue* yesterday with Liem and Travis locked up inside it, guarded by lions . . . The butcher held out his business card.

'Take it, you never know!'

'You never know what?'

'When you'll have wild animals to feed!'

Franck took the card and looked at the guy as coldly as he could.

He went back to the car, feeling guilty and embarrassed – not from having the flesh of a dead animal in his hand, but from rediscovering the ancestral pride of the hunter, the prehistoric way of life that he felt himself being drawn into: he felt himself becoming a hunter again.

High up in the hills and far from everything, the house had forced him into radical isolation but it also gave him an overview of his own life, of himself in some ways. From up there, he could see where the enemy was coming from. He knew he was connected to the house in some way to the house, as if the building and the dog had been trying to tell him something about himself all along. The place had a feeling of serenity and immense tranquility about it, even though it was in the middle of savage countryside that could be filled with violence. The endless wooded hills looked so peaceful, but the dog had made Franck aware of the rivalries being constantly fought out in their midst; the blackbirds, the jays and the tits themselves were only singing to keep others away. All the animals in this no man's land were eyeing one another closely, always trying to work out which one was going to eat the other.

He drove along with all the windows open, watching the bars on his phone disappear one by one. With every bend he got deeper into a place that was free from all constraint, completely wild. He slowly returned to the hills, not listening to any music, but looking at the now familiar landscape in which he almost felt at home as if he had just performed some sort of ritual acceptance. He now knew the land was not neutral: he was following in the footsteps of the woman, the man and the lions, if they had really existed. He felt strangely linked to these characters that time had forgotten, beings from a different century. Their history was still somehow hanging in the air, in memories that people were trying to silence or forget. He thought of Lise. She was perhaps still asleep in the wide-open house, the doors and windows as he had left them. The dog would probably be there already, waiting for him in the shade of the oak tree. Everything was waiting for him there: the living and the rest.

May 1915

Since the beginning of the war women had worked hard to keep things going but yields had fallen by half, mainly because the equipment was too old and heavy and because they had no fertiliser any more, no arsenic or sulphur, nothing to help things grow. The chemical industry now only serviced the war effort, so in Orcières the women had to bend double to pull out bindweed and couch grass with their bare hands. For a year they had been weeding using nothing but their own strength. Without any draught animals or fertiliser, the ground was a hundred times more difficult to work, and their hands grew calloused and their arms as hard as steel. Chemical products were used to make toxic gas that drove the men from their trenches and then killed them in the open air. All industrial efforts were geared to making more cannons and firearms; day and night the assembly lines worked to churn out brand-new aeroplanes and tanks, so there was no prospect of them starting to manufacture spades or ploughs again soon, still less fertiliser or scythes. In any case, there was no money to pay for any of that. Since the departure of the men, the land was more depleted and the nights more lonely. The spring days might have been beautiful, but there was no chance to sit down in the shade of the walnut trees or draw fresh water from the well. The only advantage of the punishing work was that it kept the women from thinking too much, or waiting for post that never came, or dreaming of leave for their menfolk in the event that they did not get killed.

Since the end of winter, Joséphine had been helping on the farms, even in the fields. She had not wanted a commemorative mass for her husband, nor even a wake. As the death had not been marked, the villagers were unsure how to behave towards Joséphine. A death without a burial seemed insubstantial and abstract, more of an absence than a death. So Joséphine spent exhausting days in the fields of others and they understood that she wanted to be something other than just a widow, From then on, as well as helping them write letters and look after the children, she donned clogs that were too big for her to go weeding, harrowing, hoeing. She wore farm clothes and took on all sorts of chores, which left her wrung out and dulled, as if she had taken wine that was too strong. Unlike the others, she welcomed the fatigue that allowed her not to think of her husband, nor of the lover who would not offer himself to her, nor of her fierce desire which remained unfulfilled. There was no need for her to commune with God to experience the bitter thought of sin.

She was always the first to offer herself for work and was often up at dawn operating the plough. As she only weighed forty-eight kilos she had to push very hard on the handles to engage the plough in the soil. When the ploughshare stuck on a stone or a thick rut, a jolt as if from the depths of the earth lifted her like a wave – it was exhilarating and the more the ploughshare dug into the silt the higher it lifted her. Using her muscles fired her up; she could feel the blood pounding in her temples, making the labour pleasurable. Her blade responded to her desires; all she had to do was apply her whole weight.

When she was in the fields with the other women – whether it was Gisèle, Fernande or Léone, with their children always about them – when they were all bent double concentrating on their task, Joséphine felt ashamed to be thinking of the lion tamer. So she worked harder to banish him from her thoughts, bracing herself to dig the plough into the earth, but all that happened was that she was reminded of the strong grip of those hands round her waist, on her breasts. The harder she worked, the more she felt how wonderful it would be to give herself to the gladiator.

What she had seen of the lions had only increased her longing.

Everything in the man's vicinity recalled the carnal act, even the groaning of the wild cats, their silken roars and the sighs emanating from their huge bodies. Every time she heard them, she trembled all over, and imagined herself up there, devouring and being devoured.

When she went home at the end of the day, fatigue was a satisfaction; she returned as exhausted and sweaty as after a night of love. In the evenings everyone went home to feed the children and look after the old people; it was as if a whole new day began after work. But Joséphine, alone in her big house, dined off nothing but a little bread and some cheese. She bathed for a long time and brushed her hair, which she had under a scarf in the morning; she became a woman again. Then, rather than stay at home reading, she went out for a long walk. She walked without seeing the path, in perfect darkness. As she passed near the houses, she sometimes saw through a window a group of women and old people sitting in a circle around a candle – there was no paraffin for lamps. When she saw those gatherings she knew they were rereading the latest letter received from the front, from Fernande's husband or Léone's brother, Simone's son or someone's fiancé. Letters which gave less news than they wanted, where the men gave them instructions and warnings, as if the land could not be tended without them; letters sometimes about nothing at all, but which were upsetting because of the circumstances. Joséphine did not want to take part in these intimate gatherings, but she guessed what they were like. Reading the letters they had all received forged a bond between the villagers. They resolved that from now on they would tell each other everything, and reassure those who were worried. As close as Joséphine felt to the collective of women in the fields during the day, in the evenings she felt distant from them. After walking all the way round the village she would return by the path along the river. Night was her world; she hid her desires there, and her despair. Her footsteps made a faint noise on the dry path; she was very aware of being overlooked by the mountain, which added its shadow to the darkness. She had always been attractive to men;

every time she went to Limogne or Villefranche she was surprised by the look in men's eyes, for without doing anything she charmed them, with that same charm that no doubt magicians used to make doves disappear. But there were no more men left to admire her now.

She no longer knew where she was going in this world or what to hope for from love. Would it provide self-abnegation or would it make her feel more completely herself? In a world full of hazards, a world where no one had the strength to hope any more, she was certain of only one thing, and that was that two men were waiting for her up there, one man in heaven and the other close to the clouds, or perhaps it was the other way round. And whilst a widow had to forbid herself to go up there, a free woman could ask herself the question. Had it not been for the calls of the wild cats, she would perhaps have succeeded in blocking out thoughts of the man, but every evening when the noise started up, and despite her fear, she could not help feeling they were tender calls, rather than warnings.

August 2017

Lise had been disconcerted by the package of ham on the table since they started eating, especially as Franck had unwrapped it next to his plate. She felt disgusted just looking at the mass of white-trimmed red meat. Franck kept telling her that it was in honour of the dog, a gesture of gratitude to their constant companion and nothing more. The animal came every day and was turning into a guest in his own right, quietly becoming a part of their holiday and a kind of friend. Showing him some attention and giving him something to eat was really the least they could do.

'Franck, dogs don't eat at the table. At least, we shouldn't get him into the habit of it.'

'It makes me happy, Lise. Making him happy makes me happy. And the poor thing really has to eat; he's always there watching us when we're eating. It's annoying . . .'

'For you?'

'No, for him.'

'Don't worry, dogs like that can find everything they need by themselves. You told me the valley's full of deer and wild boar at night. I think he'll be all right.'

'D'you really think he could kill a wild boar or a deer just like that, all by himself?'

'Franck, have you seen his jaws? Have you seen his mouth, his paws – the size of those paws? Sometimes he scares me. Sometimes, I really can't tell if he's growling or if he's happy. In fact, I think we should report him.'

'Report him? Who to? Anyway, he doesn't have a collar.'

'Exactly, that's what's weird.'

'Come on, Lise, if you think it's normal that there are wild boar, deer, rabbits and all sorts of creatures roaming in the wild, why are you surprised that there's a dog too? Why shouldn't a dog be wild as well? Wild dogs must surely exist; in Russia there are hundreds of thousands of them. And, anyway, maybe he's not a dog.'

'What is he then?'

'A wolf!'

Alpha stayed at Franck's side, sitting on his hind legs, waiting; he obviously knew they were talking about him, but, more importantly, he had obviously sensed that there was meat on the table for once. This made things much more interesting for him. Franck shot him a glance. He knew that a new connection was being forged between them, a bond that was even more tangible because it was connected to food. Lise was open-minded and did not like to criticise other people for their actions or choices. So she didn't really take offence at seeing Franck peel a slice of ham off the pile and hold it above the dog's nose. The dog remained calm, almost sceptical, fascinated by the incredible piece of meat in front of him. Franck slowly lowered the slice and the dog didn't react at all; he remained just as calm as before and didn't jump for it. When the ham came close enough, he snapped it up with a swift flick of his jaws, then sat back down to chew it carefully. It was obviously important to him; he seemed to treat it with the same dignity as a religious offering. Lise had made a pasta salad with courgette, peppers and herbs, and she served the two of them. Franck wanted to see what would happen if he added some bits of ham to his plate; it was it would almost be breaking the rules, but it was tempting. He took another slice and placed it on his salad. Lise watched him, stopping herself from saying anything. She clearly couldn't believe it. Franck cut his ham into small pieces, then mixed them into the pasta. He was surprised to find that he didn't feel at all disgusted or guilty. It was an appetising combination.

'Lise, honestly, the guy was talking to me and carving slices straight off the ham. Normally it would've put me off but this time it looked so good . . .'

'What are you expecting me to say? It's not banned.'

'I know, I know, it's barbaric, but it's just so tempting.'

He took a mouthful of meaty salad and instantly remembered the sensation of really chewing something, when your teeth have to work to break down a piece of meat. He reacquainted himself with the distinctive way your jaw tightens when you bite into a substance that is just like your own mouth, flesh that is the same as your tongue, your gums, and your entire body. Closing his eyes, Franck gave himself up fully to this form of timeless savagery, as if he were reconnecting with the cycle of life, the food chain in which everything is food for something else. Right now, buried in the hills, he was directly involved in the cruelty that surrounded him; he was part of the same animal kingdom as the dog, the hawk circling in the sky, the deer hiding in the valleys and the chirruping cicadas. Eating the meat felt like a dizzying sacrilege.

'So?'

Lise was looking at Franck as if he was a kid smoking his first cigarette. He was still for a moment, unable to reply, but as he prepared to swallow, his mouth turned to stone.

'No . . .' He spat out the soft, dense morsel that he had been compacting in his mouth. 'I can't do it!'

Lise laughed, buoyed up by a profound sense of relief. Franck put the bits of ham to one side and ate the pasta salad. Lise didn't have much of an appetite because of the heat and only ate half a plateful. Then she went to get the peaches and the crate of little goat's cheeses that Franck had bought, as he was fond of them. But, first, she wanted to splash some water on her face. It was so warm that even eating made you hot.

Franck found himself alone with the animal again. The dog was standing upright, tense and almost stationary, watching Franck uncomprehendingly, or perhaps selfishly waiting for him to offer him another slice. He knew there was plenty of ham on the table and didn't understand why Franck wasn't giving him any more of it. Looking Franck straight in the eye, he took a step backwards, staring at him aggressively as if he wanted to say something, and then he barked three times, ferocious barks that rang out across the landscape, three loud outbursts like gunshots before the most complete silence. Franck gazed out over countryside that was suddenly muted. It was as if all the unseen animals – that hawk, those jays and cicadas; the wild boar, deer, rabbits and thrushes – as if all potential quarry were breathing a unanimous sigh of relief, celebrating the fact that one more human was opting out of the Great Chain of Being to rejoin the society of repenters seeking absolution. That must be how animals see things: every human being who stops eating meat is hoping to exonerate themselves from the evil they have done to their fellow creatures. Becoming vegetarian was a way for humans to keep themselves to themselves and survive without animals. In the silence, Franck thought he could detect universal approval from the wildlife around him, from all the animals that were observing him and had thought he was about to have a change of heart and rejoin them in the cycle of death. Humans and dogs had separated when they stopped eating the same food. Before dog food and biscuits, they used to eat the same flesh, the same meat. Humans would eat the chicken breast and thighs and dogs would finish the carcass; humans would cook the game and dogs would eat the offal. Now, humans and dogs eat completely different things.

The dog was still tensed, fixing Franck with a harsh stare. But instead of looking away, Franck held the animal's gaze. He quickly sensed the dog was close to yowling or barking as he clenched his jaw and drew back his lower lip, to the point that Franck feared he might bite or attack him. In the eyes of the wolf dog he saw the kind of carnivorous frenzy that makes wolves fight over the corpse of the wild boar they have just killed, that voraciousness of wolves, which will bite and rip each other apart, even as they are destroying the body of their prey. Franck reached out and dropped three slices of ham on the ground for Alpha and the dog calmed down. He lay down to lick them thoroughly, before swallowing them one by one.

Lise came back with her sarong knotted and damp. She brought the crate of Cabécou, the peaches and a large jug of icy water. She asked Franck if there had been many people in town that morning, completely oblivious to what had just happened with the dog and the rest of the wildlife. From Franck's evasive response, she instinctively knew he had been talking to Liem and Travis again.

'How're you getting on?'

'With what?'

'With Liem and Travis.'

The question completely dumbfounded Franck. It seemed wrong to start worrying about that kind of thing here and now. Returning to the house, coming back to this landscape had been like freeing himself from his life, his problems and the idea that he even had a life somewhere else, or a job, partners and plans. Living here was like entering some kind of carefree time warp, thanks to the sea of green hills that surrounded them and the cicadas everywhere. It called for total disconnection. On this land, at least, nothing could touch him: he couldn't be contacted by phone, email, tweet or anything else. He was out of reach.

'You know, Franck, I understand if you don't want to talk about it.'

'I don't have anything to hide, Lise. My mind is just on other things.'

'What are you planning to do with them?'

It was a light-hearted question. She thought he was strong and still in control of everything, still the solid producer who would somehow always get what he wanted. Franck didn't want to reveal his doubts. He didn't want to tell her that he no longer knew how to handle them, or that he was being manipulated by two kids who were forcing him into negotiations and would eventually take over. More importantly, they had made that horrible jibe for which he truly hated them. For that, they had become enemies.

'I don't know, Lise. Not yet. They're asking for too much. But I won't let them push me around.'

'Oh, has it got that bad?'

'We'll eventually find a middle ground, but it won't be easy.'

Lise was surprised to see her husband so defeated; she wasn't used to seeing him like this. She collected the empty salad bowl, cheese and peaches on a tray, since the wasps were buzzing around them. Though it was really the ham they wanted – the open package of meat was driving them crazy.

'No, leave the ham; I'm going to give him some more. He'll finish it.'

'All right. I'll make iced coffee, but let's have it inside. It's too hot out here.'

'If you like, Lise.'

Franck watched her walk back towards the house. He felt as if he'd always lived there in the depths of the countryside, disconnected from everything and attached to nothing. He didn't want to think about Liem and Travis again, not now. Now, he just wanted to take a nap under the big oak tree, immerse himself in the wilderness all around, and then go for a long walk around the gullies back to the cage. He didn't even know where he'd left his phone. Probably in his trousers, or in the car. He just had to stop thinking, especially about the two arseholes who were pushing him around like lions ganging up on a wildebeest. Just thinking about the phone call filled him with rage. The dog was still staring at him. He again pictured wolves devouring each other over their victim's corpse. He stroked Alpha, who nodded his head approvingly. His coat was thick but soft.

Once again he felt intuitively that he needed to form an alliance with the big dog, who he was sure would do anything for him. They just needed to seal the agreement. Franck took another slice of ham and dangled it above the dog's mouth. The animal again grabbed it in one swift movement, perhaps a little less nervously than before, as if accepting the authority of his master. Franck watched him chewing it with relish. Then he took another slice, but brought it to his own mouth this time and ate it. He chewed it at length, taking great delight in drawing the juice out of its fatty, salty texture and strong natural flavour. He enjoyed the way the salt made his mouth water. He was waiting for the dog to react, but there was no sign of animosity. Instead, the dog came up to him and put his head on his thigh, as if demonstrating that he was on his side. Franck stroked the animal's strong neck; trust had been established between them. Suddenly, for no real reason, Liem and Travis didn't seem so bad any more; suddenly he felt less alone and better armed against them. He now knew that he had an ally, and he just had to get the bastards to go somewhere they knew nothing about, somewhere they would never win. They would be the losers; yes, he would get them to sign a new, radically different contract, a new deal that would make them the victims. They would be the losers, not him.

He would call them the next morning and tell them he was ready to sign. He would agree to their terms and open the company to new investors – but they would have to sign as quickly as possible. It would be best for them to meet him here, so they could put their names to the new agreements and stop talking about it. He knew they would show up. It would be quite a journey: six hours by train, and then he could pick them up at the station in Gourdon or Souillac. At a pinch, they could spend the night in Orcières and leave the next day, amendments signed, and it would all be over. Franck just needed to add the clauses he'd been thinking about for a while. He would draw up the changes tomorrow morning at Sören's, the illustrator who lived on the old farm, print six copies and then wait for them to sign.

Alpha's head was still on Franck's knee. The dog looked him straight in the eye, as if giving his approval. Franck gazed at the landscape, at the centre of which he and the dog stood, trying to picture the lions that had once lived there, reigning over everything. In a way he felt ready to follow their lead and summon a bit of that violence he needed to defend himself – and, more importantly, to attack. The dog was encouraging him to do it, better than any person could.

May 1915

For five years, Joséphine had lived in her husband's wake. Their lives were regulated by consultations and home visits and their conversations were about his patients. Without the doctor, she was not sure if her life had any meaning. To be a widow at thirty in a village in the middle of nowhere was to be condemned to solitude, especially in a time of war, and when they had had no children. She felt the need to help in the fields so as not to be alone all the time. But every evening, she was alone, and despair set in, a despair that worsened as the war spread throughout Europe and to Africa, in the air as well as on the ground. It was said that now bombs were falling on towns and cities as well as over the trenches, that lethal weapons dropped from zeppelins and from aeroplanes, and it was possible that one day the world would disappear in one gigantic explosion. At the rate men were dying there would soon be none left. In a small community, all the husbands and sons were losing their lives to fulfil history's destiny, which meant that a woman of thirty who found herself widowed would not remarry and without children she would not even receive a pension.

Each battle, each new day of combat, obliterated couples; every day there were more black dresses, thousands of them. From every point of view, love was being lost. Joséphine was aware of the perils of being a woman living on her own. If only because, in the space of a few months, she saw what she had become in the eyes of others: an old maid . . . 'Old maid'; the term seemed to define her, fitting her like a made-to-measure garment. For the rest of her days, that was all she would be, an old maid, unless she broke with convention and denied love the right to desert her.

As well as being an old maid she was also a war widow, a term dreaded throughout the countryside, with its attendant dignity and grief. Joséphine knew she was condemned to loneliness and despair, but she still could not face going back to live with her parents in Bergerac.

In the atmosphere of perpetual tragedy, in a world where everyone was frightened, some nights were worse than others. Even the optimistic lost hope and every time there was news from the front it was more catastrophic than the time before. The lions' roars were like an echo of the bad news. For a month they had been howling with no let-up; it was becoming a background noise, like the war itself, the mood music to the great drama. No one knew why the lions now roared from morning until night; maybe the lion tamer was no longer feeding them. The dogs no longer dared bark in reply, crushed by the sheer volume of the noise. The mayor wanted to know why they were behaving this way, so he went up to see the Hun to find out the real reason. He knew it was something to do with the summer pasture.

Ever since the lions and tigers had seen the procession of sheep, since they had discovered that the sheep were grazing on the plateaux and not on the lower pasture where they had been the previous summer, they sniffed the scent of new flesh all day long. The wind wafted the odour of sheep and cows towards them and stirred up their instincts. Down in the village, people were starting to fear that the noise would attract the gendarmes, or that one day one of the lions would escape, make for the village and eat them all.

Couderc reminded them of the law of nature that decreed that males howled to mark their territory and scare their prey. 'Every male is driven by that instinct, to be master of his area and push rivals away. In the savannah these howls can be heard miles away, whereas, here, rest assured that the roars are muffled by the hills and the woods.'

'But who's to say that one day they won't give the Hun the slip? He's only one man on his own; he won't be able to fight eight wild cats . . .'

Everyone prayed that Le Simple up there on the pastures could not hear the roaring devils, otherwise the sheep would take fright. Sheep panic at the slightest thing. And since the supply of meat had dried up, since the army was requisitioning everything, even one ewe was worth its weight in gold. The flock was their treasure, up until now a well-hidden treasure; no one must know about them and, if one day the authorities should take it into their heads to ask questions about the sheep, they would have to be told that they weren't there any more, that they had all panicked and thrown themselves from the top of the cliff. If the worst came to the worst, they could say they had been eaten by wolves, or they could blame the Hun and say they had been eaten by the lions. Whatever happened, the sheep must not be requisitioned.

'They've stolen our men; they're not going to take our sheep. Our sheep are not going to feed soldiers to give them strength to go and get killed . . .'

While everything was so grave, Joséphine felt ashamed of her feelings. Her troubles were nothing compared to the tragedies of the world. She was not so badly off, after all. She withdrew into her suffering, trying her best to be discreet, even though, unlike the others, she welcomed the roaring. She was the only one who waited for them at night, because the growling carried to her on the hot evening air made her quiver with anticipation. The roars did not frighten her but pulsed through her veins. The growling called to her from a world cleansed of fear and sin, a tempting world of savagery, verging on the impure. She must free herself from this, or she would go mad, or someone would discover her secret; they would suspect an attraction or an affair.

When the doctor had been alive, Joséphine had been a person of standing, but now that she helped in the fields, she was viewed as an equal, an ally upon whom the villagers relied. Because of the insane taxes it was no longer worthwhile to farm the large plots, so the women concentrated on fruit and vegetables. At least they could be sure of selling what they did not need. It was, however, very labour-intensive and was making them ill. Butter, cheese and milk were all so heavily taxed that you could not sell them since no one in the towns would have had enough money to buy them. All this meant that more than ever the sheep were essential: they grazed on the pastures for free. Every farm also had a pig for emergency rations, giving beautiful ham the colour of leather. Seeing them hanging from the rafters was reassuring for the future. Times might be hard, but at least they had some supplies.

Joséphine ate little for lunch – just an apple, and a little bread without any cheese, which she brought in a basket that she left on the edge of the field. No one knew what she ate for her evening meal. One or other of them would ask her home for supper, but as she always refused, they insisted on offering her food to take with her; that was how they noticed that she did not eat like the rest of them. Although widowhood did not decree that she should not eat meat, Joséphine always refused cuts of ham or *pot-au-feu*; she never wanted any meat. She probably spurned company because she did not eat like everyone else.

So it was all the more surprising that during the day they saw her working with all her might in the fields. She spent hours bent over the plough, and yet she ate practically nothing. People thought that she was ill. Someone who does not eat meat, who works hard but does not want to replenish their strength, is someone who does not want to live. Unless she took her strength from somewhere else. Seeing her grasp the plough handles with both hands, watching her press down with all her weight so that the ploughshare dug into the ground, they saw she was strong, but it must come from something other than meals.

The old people were annoyed that she did not eat meat and refused the precious animals they were so careful not to declare. Here, families had fought for generations for the right to eat meat. In the country, it takes time to overcome the old ways and the privileges passed down through the centuries said that only landowners had the right to red meat. Not so long ago only they could eat the tender meat of calves and lambs. Farmers had to make do with pigs, muddy animals that lived on scraps. They were allowed to eat bacon, but no other delicacies.

In not eating meat, it was as though Joséphine were denying the concession they had won. When she was asked about it she pretended that it was to keep her skin white, and that digesting meat tired the brain. She was mad to think that, but people respected her point of view. Anyway, it was getting hotter and they all found themselves eating less meat. With stoves no longer lit, everyone cooked less. At the evening meal they had bread soaked in milk; it was refreshing; the children loved it and it was known as dog soup. The old people would have preferred to eat meat, but now that they had lost their canines, and, like cattle, were left with only a few bottom teeth, they could no longer chew it. They hated becoming herbivores like cattle, when in their youth they had strong molars and canines as sharp as wolves. Ageing meant turning from a young wolf into a ruminant. So to see Joséphine rejecting meat did not sit well with them. Humans had teeth to masticate with, jaws to tear flesh to pieces and crush it vigorously, like cats or dogs. No doubt this woman preferred not to think of herself as an animal. She thought she was better than the rest of them. Now that she was a widow she didn't eat like everyone else any more, rejecting all the beautiful livestock they were so proud of. The old people became more and more suspicious of Joséphine.

August 2017

Lise set up her easel on the bedroom balcony. It was an excellent vantage point from which to paint the landscape, with the three trees in the foreground, the long slope descending all the way to the valley, and the hill in front of her, and many beyond, extending the panorama as far as the eye could see. She was in her element in the countryside, where nobody could watch her. She couldn't stand the gaze of an audience any more and the sickening feeling of being under scrutiny, especially in the theatre. On some evenings, thinking about all the rows of eyes made her anxious, knowing that she wasn't really herself in front of them, as if by performing she no longer existed.

The canvas needed at least four layers of perspective. She took up the challenge, feeling a little daunted by the blank canvas and the countryside she wanted to paint. She first had to capture the blue of the sky, and then add the green of the hills. When she thought about it, she noticed that the green had become less bright since they arrived, the trees apparently suffering from the interminable heat. She would have to use the late-afternoon light to work out the shades, since the sun now overpowered everything.

The most interesting parts of the scene were the two pine trees and the hundred-year-old oak in the foreground, with the stone hut right in the middle, a shelter probably once used for keeping animals – rabbits or hens, or tools perhaps. Since the beginning of the afternoon the sun had crept behind the dense foliage of the oak tree, so Lise could paint on the balcony without even needing an umbrella. She was lost in shadow, hidden at the heart of an ocean of light. Franck had been asleep downstairs for over an hour, but she could tell he had just woken up. The shutter squealed as it opened again, and then, having barely moved for an hour, the dog sat up and started stretching and yapping, and ran around barking. He could probably see Franck moving in the living room as he prepared to go outside.

Lise could see everything from her lookout, concealed under her natural sunshade. Franck came into view just below the balcony. He was in the sun, wearing shorts and walking purposefully towards the old shed. The dog was following, easily keeping pace. She almost called out but stopped herself, deciding to leave him in peace and watch as she diluted the blue and the white with water. Franck tried to open the decrepit old wooden door of the shed. The latch was stuck and wouldn't give, no matter how hard he tried to force it. Lise wondered what he wanted to do in there, and why he wanted to investigate it in this heat. After fiddling with the handle, the door finally opened with a long creak. Franck paused. He had a look inside, but the blinding sunshine prevented him from seeing anything in the shadows. He eventually went in. The dog stayed behind, looking at Franck without much conviction. He sat down and watched from a distance, visibly confused and aware that he was not needed. Lise kept an eye on them as she washed the freshly mixed blue colour over the canvas – the dog sitting outside the shed and Franck bustling around inside, apparently moving things around. It was a picture of country life and a painting in itself. She thought about what their lives would have been like if they had been farmers there fifty or so years ago, when people lived in the area, imagining that they were the first occupants of the house and spent their days working in the sun, or in the cold. They would have had to look after their crops, animals and land: a life of constant labour, the opposite of the present afternoon. She put down her paintbrush. She was going to sketch it with a fine pencil first. She wanted to include every detail of the trees, the hut, and the hills in the background. The light was coming from the right, and she looked at the canvas, thinking about how the scene would look in two or three hours when the sun was lower. It was hot and the paint dried quickly. But she didn't mind.

As she studied the view, she wondered whether the trees had been there back then, the walnut and oaks in particular, whether the hills had looked the same and which crops had been grown here. The worn patterns of leaves and grapes carved in the stone door lintels suggested that there had been grapevines once, probably before the phylloxera outbreak, but what happened after that? Who lived there in the thirties, or the fifties, or even before? She didn't have the faintest idea, but it was important that she know. She was trying to soak up the atmosphere of the place. When you stay in a hotel room – the coldest, most impersonal type of accommodation – you never think about who occupied it before you; in fact, you really don't want to know. But when you're renting a house, especially an old, isolated one, and you're trying to paint it, you delve into time without realising. It's an intimate process that takes you back to the forgotten existences that once filled the house with life. Lise wanted to know everything about the people who had lived in the house before them, the bodies that had slept there and loved there. She was sure that she was the first to paint and daydream about it so vividly, that nobody else had ever chosen to depict that landscape, asking themselves questions about the spirit of the place but also about everybody who had lived there . . . The paint on her brush had dried.

Franck was still fumbling around in the old shed; she could hear him moving things about. It sounded like he was rifling through all sorts of things, though she didn't know what he could be looking for – a bicycle maybe, or tools. Perhaps she should follow his lead and explore every inch of the house, trying to get the objects to reveal their secrets. The attic was the only place she had been curious about. The little wooden staircase that went up to it was not promising and the room itself was full of old, forgotten furniture, a jumble of items including two iron beds and an ancient coffee grinder, but no books, although, strangely enough, there were three whips, long cords of braided leather hanging on the wall like trophies. She hadn't gone into the old barn by the water tank; she didn't even know if they had the key. There were many things she hadn't yet discovered, but there was one thing she was sure of: the house was being let for the first time. She could feel it. There was the mattress that was too new and a bit hard, with its label and plastic wrapping, and then the cutlery that was too old, as well as the glasses and plates – the tableware was far too worn to still be in regular use. Lots of things in the house weren't quite right: the toilets for a start, with the strange noises the pipes made when the water was running slowly through them, and the circular sockets that didn't work. If the house had been rented before, people would surely have complained. Having such low pressure in the ancient shower was impractical, not to mention the tin stains on the bathroom mirror, which meant you had to bend down to see yourself, and there were a thousand other details that would have been fixed if there had been complaints or comments on the internet. The old furniture and clapped-out cupboards were the biggest nuisance – the drawers that had to be forced open, as well as the wardrobes that kept their secrets locked inside and the furniture that threatened to collapse at any minute. All the evidence suggested that the house hadn't been occupied for years and had rarely been opened up or aired out. When she found the advert three months ago, Lise had known instinctively – though she said nothing to Franck – that nobody had rented the property before them, nor lived there for ages. The novelty of it had drawn her in.

Franck finally came back out of the shed, doubled over and covered in dust. The dog stepped backwards as if an alien had just appeared out of nowhere. Franck had draped an old rope over his shoulder, a thick, coarse lead-rope or tether. Lise leant back so he couldn't see her. She wanted to carry on watching him. Still, she was relieved that he had found something to do; she had been so worried that he would crack after two days and beg her to spend the rest of the holiday in a hotel or at the beach – anywhere but here. Franck was so used to comfort that she had had trouble picturing him in a remote house in the hills. It had been fine in the end. Nonetheless, she had absolutely no idea what he wanted to do with the rope. She would normally have called out from the balcony, even if it startled him, to ask what he was planning to do with it. But she didn't want to disturb him or get in the way of whatever it was he was up to. After all, he could do what he pleased with the rope. But a terrible thought crossed her mind: might people have hanged themselves here before? Maybe the reason the house felt so mysterious was because its occupants had killed themselves, leaving behind no successors, no family or children, a bit like herself and Franck. Franck went back into the shed to get another rope that looked quite thick. He threw one over each shoulder like the straps of a big bag. She was intrigued but stopped herself asking him any questions. They had operated like this all the time they had been living together, giving each other space and being careful not to pry. Franck never commented on what she was painting; he only encouraged her. He encouraged her in everything she did but, first and foremost, as an artist; when she attempted to direct a film for instance, or when she told him she wanted to stop acting and devote herself to painting instead. Rather than telling her she was mad and should carry on acting, or making her feel guilty, he simply asked if she preferred oil or gouache.

She had loved him for more than twenty years precisely because of his thoughtfulness. Franck had only ever supported her, just as he did everybody else – scriptwriters, actors, technicians and directors. On principle, he always encouraged them. Perhaps the most important quality in a producer is being able to support and strengthen others, taking the strain off them.

Franck was back in the house. Lise could hear him on the ground floor and the dog was standing ready to make a move, watching Franck as if waiting for him to announce the plan.

'Lise?' Franck called up to her.

She answered him, pretending to be surprised.

'I'm going for a wander.'

'No problem!'

With that, she saw him go back outside. He hadn't realised that she was on the balcony; he must have thought she was in the bedroom or attic. He didn't even turn around as he was leaving. This time he had his backpack with him, and the two ropes wrapped around his shoulders. He walked briskly and began going down the slope towards the hills.

Lise watched him for a while. Then she returned to her canvas. She needed to paint the oak tree last, straight after the shed with the door that Franck had left ajar, somewhat ruining the painting she had in mind. The shed wasn't at all the same with the door open. Yet it was pretty, and in a way it gave it some life. She knew that she was completely alone now, and relished the feeling as if it were an achievement. Apart from a few quiet, scattered cicadas, there was complete silence. But it didn't panic her; instead she welcomed it like a fifth element. It was nothing like the forced silence you get just before filming a scene, an agreed silence where everybody is quiet at once, nor the dizzying silence of the theatre. No, it was a primal, elementary silence, a silence she got better at every time she meditated. Franck and the dog were gone; she could see them getting further away, at the foot of the hill one minute and then in the woods, and she was no longer worried about what they were going to do with the rope. She was close to utter peace.

June 1915

In Orcières, it wasn't what they heard about the war that affected people most, it was what they no longer heard. The silence of departed men was haunting, a constant reminder of their absence. Since time immemorial there had always been men here tilling the land; their voices could be heard all through the day, and not to hear them calling from one plot of land to another was more heartbreaking than the racket had been disturbing. There at the bottom of the *causses*, nestled between the hills and the chalky cliffs, the shouts of the men shepherding the animals in the morning no longer rang out. They could not be heard talking to the oxen so that they would stand quietly to be harnessed. There was no more ranting as the men guided the draught animals, nor swearing, and none of the everyday words that accompanied work and the hunt. When the men had still been there, they spent their lives outside, moving about, yelling and laughing. The women didn't see them much but they knew they were there. Now all that was left of them was the silence that reigned all over, a silence that was rent by the cries of the lions; it was worse than death. Even the dogs no longer barked.

Up there in the trenches the men were no doubt shouting, but for different reasons and much too far away to be heard in Orcières. The villagers imagined the front like a giant inferno, a furnace that could never be satisfied, a ceaseless volcano of flame and lava. Sometimes, when reading the news or listening to the mayor telling them about things that were not in the newspapers, the women wanted to believe that things were going to settle down, that the war was like a great fire that would soon run out of fuel, and that suddenly all the hate that had grown up between nations would collapse in on itself. Sometimes the papers would announce that the army was going to demobilise soldiers over the age of forty-six, and those who had more than four children. At least those men would be coming home, although here that would only amount to a few men, no more than three. But that relaxation of the rules never took place. Each time the inferno just kept going, the furnace kept roaring and demanding more and more men, always more soldiers. It was now the summer of 1915 and none of the soldiers here had had any leave. Without the noise of the men, only birdsong and cicadas could be heard in the fields, other than the roaring of the lions which went in waves, but always reminded everyone that fear was never far away.

The women prayed that their husbands and sons would return. And yet they were worried about what they would say when they did return. How would they react when they realised that the farms and mills had continued to function without them? Perhaps they would take it badly, perhaps they would find thousands of things to criticise. They might say that the Taillis plot had been sown too sparsely, or that the hay was piled too high, or that the fencing round the cows was not high enough, or that the riverbanks had been destroyed by coypus. If they came back they would only see what was wrong. Because, after all, the land had always been theirs and they had their own way of doing things. Perhaps it would be difficult when they returned. Some women began to worry about it. They feared that when the men came back, nothing would be the same as before, that they wouldn't recognise their husbands. And the men might be annoyed that life had continued to roll on without them, and be for ever offended. In the countryside women had just extracted from the earth a terrible confession – that the harvest could be done without men. In farms and factories, mills and fields, everywhere, life had gone on without them.

In towns, it seemed women had the right to join their spouses in rest billets, even if only for a few hours, but there was no question of country folk doing the same. There would have been too many papers to fill out and it was too far to travel. Besides, in the village, women didn't have a second to themselves, between the farmyard and the fields, the kids and the old people, the kitchen and the laundry – how could they waste hours and hours to go and hold their husbands in their arms, travel for days just for a kiss? It would have made no sense. It was proof that the towns were a whole different world, another version of humanity. Here, for love, as for everything else, you had to make do without men.

But knowing that the world kept turning in the men's absence was no small matter. The women worried that it was sacrilege to be able to live without them, and some, instead of being proud of their work, felt a terrible guilt. So much so that when they learnt that the ewes were disappearing from the pasture above, that every week there were two or three fewer, instead of immediately blaming wolves or the wild cats, the women thought it might be their punishment, retribution for their new-found emancipation. Discovering the disappearance of the sheep, their first intuition was to tell themselves that, had the men been there, nothing so calamitous could have happened. The men would have known what to do to stop the loss of the sheep.

The number of missing ewes rose quite quickly. First there were five, then ten, then, tragically the week after, nearly twenty had gone missing. Everyone in the village started to panic, and because everything tends to get worse when panic sets in, at that rate there would be no sheep left at all when it was time to bring them down again.

It was thanks to Joséphine that everyone knew of the disaster. Every week when she took Le Simple his bread and terrines she always inspected the animals one by one, checking their hooves. Every time she did the count there were two or three fewer.

Fernand and Couderc were both the arbiters of reason. They were both well informed and capable of rationalising situations without immediately jumping to the worst conclusion. Their first thought was that it was wolves, except that no carcasses were ever found in the pasture, nor any other evidence of their activity. Then they thought of theft, but no intruder or poacher could have gone up there, still less come down again, without Le Simple or his dogs noticing. Only the priest seemed to know the truth, even though he was not from here, and only came once a week for Mass, and did not really know anything about the village. But he was certain that this was God taking his dues. According to him every wound had a purpose, and the sacrifice of men – men who must, incidentally, be honoured with incessant prayer, for living without them could lead the women into sin – as of beasts, was the price to be paid for peace returning one day. Moreover, the villagers should be willing to make any sacrifice necessary, because all pain and loss was another reason to be chosen by God. He proved this by quoting from his old gilt-edged bible at the pulpit: 'Exodus chapter 20, verse 24: "You are to make for Me an altar of earth, and sacrifice on it your burnt offerings and peace offerings, your sheep and goats and cattle. In every place where I cause My name to be remembered, I will come to you and bless you."' The priest said that true pain was not suffering, but the failure to accept it.

They were wary of the priest, or at least they feared being punished if they did not believe him. And what he said made sense: God was taking the sheep because they had not wept enough for the men. But his God was greedy, because after a month the sheep continued to disappear, although there were no carcasses, no bones and no vultures flying over the pasture. God was taking the animals in the same way that the nation had taken their men from them. Everyone prayed hard, but that changed nothing; the sheep still disappeared and the lions still roared. It felt as if the curse sent down by Mont d'Orcières was stronger than their prayers to God, and was engulfing the whole village.

August 2017

Franck focused on the sound of his feet trampling the dry grass as he went down the hill. They made a sharp noise, a bit like a scythe. It was steep and he had to tread firmly to stop momentum carrying him forward. The dog was walking right beside him. His tongue was hanging out as if he were thirsty, though they had only been walking for five minutes. The symphony of sounds was hypnotic. Besides the sound of Alpha's panting and his shoes beating against the grass, the buzz of the cicadas was all around. Yet there was not even the faintest echo of civilisation, not one engine, chainsaw or car, nor a plane. Franck took a break in the shade of the holm oaks at the foot of the hill. The forest unfurled in front of them, its dark mass covering the hillside. The dog was staring at him as he always did, fixing him with a look of assent. Franck stared straight back at him, thinking about the previous night.

Around two in the morning, he had gone downstairs with his laptop. He sat at the old table outside in complete darkness to make the amendments to the contract. Hundreds of tiny insects flew into the backlit screen when he opened the computer, an entire miniature world. He spent two hours going back over the PDF documents, adding one clause that meant he could keep an eye on shareholders, one giving him free rein over feature films and one allowing him to set up a line of credit for his own purposes. In short, he was making sure he could produce a film every two years, one he would have total control over and be able to budget for without his partners' consent. The dog stayed with him the whole time, sometimes sitting, sometimes lying down. Franck was comforted by his presence and felt that the animal supported his bold plan. Lise was asleep upstairs. They had turned the lights out much earlier because of the mosquitoes. The computer screen was the only thing emitting light for thousands of hectares. At that moment, the nature of the bond that had existed between man and dog since the dawn of time became apparent to him; there in the pitch dark, he understood why they had always been allies. If the dog hadn't been there, the slightest noise would have made him jump and the slightest rustle in the distance startled him. Hectares of wild, untamed woods stretched into infinity, producing creaking and rustling sounds, and suspicious noises that made you panic about what or who might have caused them. Without the dog, the noises would have troubled him. Alpha had become his lookout, closely watching what was going on around them. He was taking care of him.

Franck took a large swig of water before he started climbing the second hill, hitching the ropes back up onto his shoulders. He couldn't believe he had been so bold as to come up with such a plan, though he wasn't completely sure he was ruthless enough to go through with it. Once more, the look on the dog's face spurred him on, a look in which he saw the iron will of an animal used to hunting, biting and killing. As much as it comforted him, it was full of violence. It told him that sometimes it was necessary not merely to defend oneself, but also to attack.

It was getting cooler under the trees. Franck climbed between the tightly packed oaks, no longer even trying to find the winding path that had now almost vanished. His sights were set on the summit. With every step came the sharp snapping sound of old branches breaking, and twigs clawed at him on all sides, clinging to him and whipping through the air as they sprang back again. He felt he was entering a completely different world that demanded stamina, strength and endurance, where he just had to concentrate on avoiding the brambles and rocks and getting past the traps along the way. The slope was difficult and steep, but at least it was in the shade.

Lise left the balcony to make herself an iced tea. She didn't want to disturb the silence, but she turned on the radio for some background noise. This time, it was strangely set to reggae. The selection of tracks wasn't entirely random; a certain type of music played for fifteen to twenty minutes – the next one could just as well be jazz or classical, country, rap, or even Léo Ferré. She was surprised by how hot it was as she went back upstairs. She looked at the hills she was about to paint, moved by the knowledge that Franck was walking through the trees at that very moment. Her husband was integrated into the scene she was planning to paint, but he couldn't be seen, and no one would even know he was there. She couldn't spot him anywhere in the mass of green. He would probably get to the top of the hill opposite soon and then go down the other side, always hidden by trees. She didn't understand why he had set out in the heat; it was almost forty degrees. No doubt he wanted to go back to where the big cage was, with the spring just next to it. She knew it had made an impression on him, but it was still strange that he wanted to go back again the very next day, especially when it was so hot.

Half an hour later, Franck was going down the second hill. When he got to the bottom of the gully, he sat on a tree stump in the shade and drank the rest of his water in one gulp, not even pausing for breath. But the dog wanted to carry on, and immediately set off again, going even deeper into the valley. The humidity and constant shade had transformed the soil and made the vegetation lush and plentiful; there were thick creepers and sweet chestnut trees with knobbly trunks, trees that must have been very old, frozen in time with their sap slowly flowing. It gave them a ghostly aura. When he came across a pile of old treated pine sleepers, he realised it was the remains of a railway that had probably been closed for decades. It was damp inside the cathedral of plants, the foliage rising in flying buttresses more than thirty metres high. Franck felt as if he were at a distant latitude. It was probably ten degrees cooler here than in the south-facing areas; the valley must face directly north. He thought about the tropical forest in Guyana where they had shot fifteen years ago, and about the other film in Serbia, a German co-production about two prisoners escaping from a gulag. The valley had a similar feel, recalling the stifling stickiness of the forest canopy in Guyana where all sorts of animals would be moving above you and you had to watch out for snakes . . . The trees here weren't as tall or as wide, and of course there weren't any capuchin monkeys or vampire bats, but he could make out a small animal right at the top of the branches, a squirrel that wasn't moving, surprised at being disturbed and trying to decide whether to run away or not.

Franck didn't move. He could hear the dog coming back from his exploration of the bushes; he must have found a spring or puddle of water because he was soaked, looking thoroughly refreshed with his head glistening. Seeing him so alert and excited, Franck knew he wanted them to set off again straight away. Movement and action were all he wanted. At times, the dog seemed to be truly at home in the wild, especially lost in the woods like this. In this environment, he was in control and became the master. He looked at Franck as he always did when he was waiting for him to move or get back up again, but Franck wanted to relax a bit longer and enjoy the coolness. The squirrel above them still wasn't moving; either it wasn't frightened or it was too terrified to stir. Franck was watching it from below, and the dog understood perfectly. The animals around here were continually observing one another; they were always on the alert, either because they feared the other or were hunting it. The forest is a place of combat. Peace seems to reign, but when you stop for a moment, you become aware of an entire kingdom of vigilant creatures around you, you can sense thousands of ears listening out and eyes keeping a close watch; the tension is palpable. Perhaps the deer were observing him at the bottom of the gully and the wild boar were hiding, or the foxes were patiently waiting for him to leave, because, in every human, these animals could smell only one thing: a hunter.

The dog's gaze was fixed on the squirrel. Franck knew it would only take one word, not even an order, for the dog to rush headlong at this tree and do everything he could to try to catch the rodent up there, just as he would do with any other game animal. Say the word and he would go after it. He was almost waiting for the order to throw himself at the little creature. Franck feared that the dog would get caught up in the game again, that he would start barking like mad and try to climb the tree to catch the squirrel, breaking its neck in one swift bite. A bird settled on top of a tree to its left. It was a jay, one of those big birds that occasionally let out a terrible noise, an exotic-sounding alarm call that cuts through the silence and, as you approach, other birds echo their cry, warning each other that there's someone there. The jays are at home in the forest; it's their territory, and they'll betray the presence of any human.

'Go, fetch!'

The dog started moving frantically at the bottom of the big tree, mortified by the complete impossibility of climbing it, infuriated that he couldn't honour the command.

'Come on, catch it!'

Franck was testing out his new-found authority. The dog was weak in the face of an order he couldn't carry out and started barking while staring at the top of the tree. The jay didn't move, not afraid in the slightest. Franck was at the heart of a savage triangle, halfway between the predator and the prey, and yet aware that he was more on the side of the predator than its quarry, because he could decide which went after the other. He was discovering that he had a power over life or death that made him a part of the animal kingdom in his own right. The squirrel had disappeared, but the jay stood up to the dog and squawked even louder. In the middle of this pagan ceremony of barking and birdcall came a noise, far in the distance.

Franck thought he could hear the drone of an engine, a big one, probably a lorry, a hoarse-sounding vehicle that was making its way through the hills with some difficulty. It seemed to be coming from the other side, from where the cage was. The dog carried on barking. Franck ordered him to hush but he didn't stop, becoming more and more agitated at the sight of the scornful bird.

'Be quiet!'

Franck raised his voice and looked at the dog sternly, stopping him in his tracks. He didn't bark or even move, but he pricked up an ear. The jay took off spontaneously and the squirrel was no longer anywhere to be seen, but the sound of the engine was getting louder. Franck got up and started walking. He wanted to scale the slope in front of him and do it quickly. With superhuman effort, he flew up the hill. He would never have believed he could climb that fast, but he had to get up to the top of the *igue* to see who else had decided to explore the cage on this boiling-hot afternoon, and what kind of vehicle could even get to it.

July 1915

Since the dawn of time people had relied on sheep to provide wool to keep them warm, and meat to feed them. Sheep were the animals which fulfilled all their needs, and especially the Bizets, plump and healthy and never troubled by mange, hardy beasts that could be kept almost all year round without hay. So the disappearance of so many of them was like a leak in a boat that was drifting out to sea. Powerless to stop it, the women felt as if they were sliding into the abyss a little more every day. The men, the sheep, all these beings swallowed by the night, were a sign that the world was abandoning them. Not only did they feel guilty for going on living without the men, but, worse, they sometimes had thoughts of the flesh without really thinking about their husbands. They could not help the sin of feeling desire deep within them, and at night they sometimes rubbed themselves against the sheets. Little by little, they became convinced that they were living in sin, without the assent of God. The fever that flowed in their blood was a poison that took over their bodies. Yet all those hours spent working, embracing the plough, their breasts pressed against the iron handles, all that expended energy flooded them with fatigue, as lovemaking did. Every evening they stopped work as if being released from the arms of a lover. But if their toil helped to quell their longings, it in no way fulfilled the need to be caressed.

Twenty ewes lost in one month: the endless debate about the shepherd went on. In the countryside it was often thought better to have the sheep watched over by a woman rather than a man. As the saying went, 'What makes a good shepherd? A shepherdess.' To watch over animals outdoors all day long took care and consideration, and above all the ability to sense the onset of illness or fear in the animals, to detect the smallest wound or dangerous chill in the air. To make sure that Le Simple was really up to it Fernand and Couderc decided to go up again themselves. Towards midday, the mayor once more harnessed up the rickety old carriage, and he and Couderc got in, taking care to put up the hood. It was the schoolmaster's idea to take eight paraffin lamps with them, so that Le Simple could have light at night. 'If it's wolves that are stealing from us, it will stop them coming. Wolves don't like dancing flames. Flaming torches are even used by Masai shepherds to scare off lions.' Despite the midday heat they climbed right up to the summer pastures with bread and cheese for Le Simple. For the dogs they had brought dead chickens and giblets they had crammed into a barrel; it stank but that didn't matter, they had to get to the bottom of the mystery. It took them two hours to reach the flock. When Le Simple saw them, he thought the end of summer had already come and that it was time to go back down again. His joy was short-lived.

The mayor and schoolmaster inspected the pasture. There was no trace of blood, and not even the smallest piece of carcass, no remains and no guts. Nothing could be found, not even any wool caught on the thistles. They searched in the nearby woods, watched by the jays at the top of the trees and by crows which, like good birds of prey, were on the lookout for signs of a sacrifice or an orgy. Only the birds knew what was going on up there.

At the end of the afternoon, Fernand and Couderc set off back down to the village. It was even trickier to get down with the cabriolet than it had been to come up. From the seat, the two men saw the horse trapped between the two shafts of the cart, the weight of which pushed the horse downwards. The brake rubbed against the worn-out wheel and when they saw that the horse couldn't go on they decided to stop at the lion tamer's house to give the brave animal a drink before tackling the end of the slope. But the horse baulked. The scent of the lions was so strong in its nostrils that it refused to turn off towards the little house. So they had to continue down towards the village with the thirsty horse and the burnt-out brake.

The next day the mayor called an assembly so that they could report back. There was nowhere indoors big enough to hold them all, not even the mairie, and the women refused to go into the church, because Christ on the cross stared down at them; wherever they stood, he was always looking at them, as if he could turn his head. So they gathered under the plane trees in the square. Everyone was eager to speak, but no one wanted to incriminate Le Simple. But if he had nothing to do with the thefts then who had? Fernand and Couderc let them all have their say, knowing that everyone already assumed who was to blame.

'If it was the German stealing the ewes, Le Simple would have seen him,' said the mayor. The grave look on the schoolmaster's face signalled his agreement.

'Le Simple has seen him!' retorted Léone, from La Brasse farm. 'But he doesn't dare say anything because he's frightened. It's understandable that he's frightened of a man with lions . . .'

'I'm sure it's his lions eating them. I hear them at night.'

'But what about the dogs?' asked the mayor.

'Dogs against a lion tamer! They probably don't even dare bark; they're probably as gentle as kittens with him!'

'Maybe it's the lions themselves that go; they escape from their cages at night and make for the flock . . .'

Someone else piped up that they were sure that one night, between nightmares, they had heard barking and even the squealing of a sheep being eaten alive.

'From down here? I'd be surprised . . .'

'If the wind's blowing this way you can hear . . .'

'I'm telling you, he lets his wild cats out at night. You can see shadows up there; you can see him driving them to the flock with his big whip, like he does in the cage. It's obvious; he puts his lions before our sheep; he couldn't care less about our sheep.'

'We have to give him up to the gendarmes; we have to turn the Hun in, before he eats us all.'

'Yes, turn him in!'

'Wait!'

Joséphine did not normally speak up, and certainly never gave her opinion. But, this time, she got up on the stone bench beneath the trees, because her voice was quiet. Without preamble she admitted that she had already been up there and seen the famous cages; she was the only one who had seen them up close, and it was quite obvious the wild cats never got out of them, except to go from their individual enclosures to the big display cage, a cage that was wide and tall, wider than a circus tent, where the lion tamer made them go in the afternoon to practise their circus tricks. The lions were never free to wander around and go out at night as people were saying.

Before she started helping in the fields, everyone had thought that Joséphine was a delicate woman accustomed to fine lace, with cotton flounces that suited the flourishes of her hands. She was the only one who ever thought of wearing perfume or had time to think about what she wore, and always smelt disconcertingly of jasmine. For years she had been regarded as a happy person entirely devoted to helping her husband, someone who was comfortably off and just happened to be beautiful, a creature of the drawing room absolutely not concerned with the toils of the land and the animals. And she wasn't from here, but from Bergerac, from upper Périgord. However, since they had seen her working the plough with all her might, they had recognised her qualities. Standing on her bench, Joséphine commanded all their attention. Her head brushed against the lowest leaves of the plane tree, so that from time to time she tossed a twig from her, as you would a stray lock of hair, in a gesture both elegant and casual, that no one else from here would have known how to make. A narrow band of light fell on her chest, the luminosity rendering her blouse see-through, and you could just about make out her breasts, caressed by the July heat, unaware of their impact, as the rest of her body was covered up in faded cotton.

They listened to her but they were not convinced that she was right that the lion tamer was innocent. They knew she would never speak badly of anyone; she never pointed the finger at people, and had always been respectful and defended anyone who was blamed for anything. The villagers revered Joséphine, all the more so because she was, to this day, the only one to have lost her husband in the war. The doctor was still the only official death in the village and Joséphine was respected in the same way as a house that has been struck by lightning. They were grateful to her for taking the blow so that they did not have to, because lightning only ever strikes once, and they hoped that next time death struck it would be elsewhere, far from here, not in Orcières, because Joséphine had already paid their dues. Although Joséphine was the only one of them to have suffered tragedy, she did not show the slightest sign of weakness or despair. Since she had known of her husband's death her dedication had continued undiminished and she had sacrificed herself as nobly as he had done. And so, eventually, they decided to believe her. If she said the lion tamer had nothing to do with the thefts, they must accept that.

Throughout the meeting a man had been standing at the back, looking at everyone in disdain. At the age of fifty, La Bûche had never had a wife. He was rather ugly, but, worse, he drank like a fish to counteract the heat of his forge. He discerned something other than love of humanity behind Joséphine's defence of the lion tamer. He had understood from the beginning why she had always insisted that the German should be allowed to remain up there and that he must not be denounced. He had seen her going up the mountain several times. He had seen her starting up the track on her horse and continuing on the left-hand path towards the top rather than turning right towards the pastures and Le Simple. It obviously wasn't the lions that she was going to visit up there, especially as, once, he had seen her on her way back down looking dishevelled. La Bûche was too old to fight in the war, but he was not too old to be jealous. Jealousy was the only feeling he could really indulge in. Jealousy was all he would ever be able to feel in relation to women, and to this woman in particular. He knew better than anyone what jealousy could lead someone to do. A hundred times the idea of getting rid of the German had entered his drink-addled mind. A hundred times he had already stabbed the lion tamer; a hundred times he had climbed the road that led from the village to murder him; a hundred times his virtual ascents had exorcised Joséphine's attraction to the German. Except that, each of the hundred times, he had come up against the image of those immense wild beasts he heard roaring. A hundred times his desire to smash his rival had foundered on the terror he felt for the wild cats. Without the lions, La Bûche would already have quenched his hatred long ago. Without those lions, he would not have been frightened of the German. But there they were, mighty beasts pacing in circles, contained only by too-thin bars. In his mind, the lions were a large part of the attraction Joséphine felt for the lion tamer. La Bûche was the only man on earth to be in love with a woman who was more interested in lions; he was the only man to be jealous of lions.

He was so consumed by anger that he barely heard Joséphine explaining her idea. She was offering to replace Le Simple. For one month she would go up and be the shepherd. She was prepared to devote herself to taking care of the ewes; at least that way they would see if they continued to disappear. And it would liberate Le Simple. He could come back down to the village and help in the fields; the hay mower had broken and they needed his strength here, especially as the harvest would soon be upon them.

The women exchanged looks, and, without having to say anything, they all had the same thought. Since it had been established that Joséphine attracted misfortune, that she was a magnet for lightning, if she were up there she would act as a lightning conductor. Since it was she that misfortune sought, once she was up there, the rest of them down below would be safe.

They knew that Joséphine was reliable and that she would know what to do to prevent the sheep from disappearing. Everyone agreed to the idea, except for La Bûche whose jealousy was now even more intense. If Joséphine went up there, she wouldn't even have to hide the fact that she was going to be with the lion tamer. In his view, the only reason Joséphine was offering to look after the sheep was so that she could be with him without anyone seeing or knowing. But the worst thing was that if she lived up there, she would quickly understand what sort of predators were preying on the ewes, the beautiful Joséphine being much cleverer than the simple shepherd. She would soon work out what the shadowy figures poaching the sheep were.

Franck had been listening to them moving around at the bottom of the *igue* for ten minutes. There were two men doing something near the cage. He had gone as far as he could on the spur in order to see what was going on, the dog right by his side. He stayed hidden, feeling almost like a soldier in enemy territory, hardly daring to raise his head above the scree for fear they might see him from below. Through the bushes he could see the men bustling about without speaking; they looked focused and in a hurry. He carefully parted the branches for a better view and spotted a gun hanging from the door of the vehicle, just hanging there as if it were unremarkable. The 4×4 itself was the one he had seen in Limogne the day before, the one that belonged to the hunters, but the big dog cages were no longer on the pickup, and in their place were two barrels and equipment that the men were unloading. Franck couldn't see everything through the branches, especially since there was a tree on the right that obscured his vision. He had no idea what they were up to. He just had time to see the younger guy take three large, apparently heavy, translucent blocks off the pickup truck and carry them into the cage. They looked like enormous ice cubes from a distance, giant blocks with a cord through the middle. He thought they might have something to do with the spring, or they might be salt licks. Perhaps they were planning to shut animals up in there, or making preparations to lure wildlife into some kind of trap. Franck kept an eye on Alpha, who was still calm but refused to sit down. He was worried he might move or start barking and betray their presence, but Alpha was surprisingly obedient, listening and doing as Franck asked – or at least, obeying his silent instruction to stay still at all costs.

Franck had no desire to see the men again, or talk to them. He didn't want them to know that he had found the cage. Nobody must know he had been there, because he needed the cage now. He had a plan to use it. These guys might screw it all up; the fact that other people came to the bottom of this isolated ravine could compromise everything.

He couldn't care less about whatever they were plotting. The hunters shouldn't be there anyway; it wasn't their land. Franck had no idea how large the grounds of the rental house were. If the men were up to something on his property, he would be perfectly within his rights to turn them out.

Alpha didn't seem to be enjoying the game of hide-and-seek very much. He had obviously had enough, and was starting to wag his tail and shake his head so much that Franck had to pull him towards him and tell him to keep calm.

The older man had sensed movement just above. He quickly grabbed the rifle from the car door, positioned it and took aim. The younger guy put the bucket of earthworms he had just picked up back on the pickup, went over to the old man and forced him to lower his weapon.

'Don't be an idiot, Maurice, no sense in shooting over there.'

'It's wild boar, I swear.'

They stayed still and waited, listening for the faintest rustling sound. They both knew that wild boar never came out by day and you didn't usually hear them. Yet they had heard something.

Franck had got down as low as possible and could no longer see them, but the bastards obviously thought he was a wild boar in hiding. He needed to stop moving. But then he might be shot at. The dog was staring at him, again waiting for an order, a word, and Franck pushed his head to make him lie down, which prompted more noise.

The men below – who had grown up in these woods and spent their whole lives here – had been right about something moving up above, but it wasn't like anything they knew. They said nothing, but both were thinking it might be a lynx, or a wolf; they had been making a comeback for a few years and this area of untamed forest was the perfect place for them to hide. What a coup it would be, to shoot a wolf.

The dog shattered the silence by starting to bark. He looked at Franck intently, barking as if ordering him to get up too.

Maurice turned to Julien, shocked that a dog could wait silently, concealing itself as if hunting game, and then suddenly start barking.

'A dog? What the hell . . . ?'

Alpha ran to the end of the spur and stood there for the men below to see. Franck had no choice but to come out from behind the bushes, aware that the dog had gone out to protect him, sacrificing himself in a way. Maybe that was the animal's intention, especially as, with a weapon involved, the game could quickly turn dangerous. The men recognised Franck. But they didn't recognise the big dog running down the cliff towards them. They stared at him as if he were some strange beast. Franck was further behind, feeling sheepish. He tried to get rid of the ropes slung across his shoulders, but they were too tight and he felt restricted by them as he hurtled down the cliff face with the bitter taste of surrender in his mouth.

He should really be asking *them* what they were up to; they were the intruders. He tried to persuade himself to stand up to them. He had to. When he got to the bottom, they looked at one another; he didn't know whether to shake hands or not. The men didn't move, the older guy still holding the gun with the barrel pointing down.

Franck sensed that they were a little uncomfortable. They were obviously in their element, but maybe not on their own land.

'What are you doing here?'

'What are *you* doing here?'

'What are you doing with those ropes?'

'This is my property, isn't it? I'm renting it, it's my land.'

At that, the older man lost his temper, and he raised his gun and pointed it at Franck.

'It's nobody's property, understand? Nobody's . . .'

Julien grabbed the weapon and pulled it unceremoniously from the old man's hands. The dog began to bark and instinctively rushed at the young guy who was now holding the weapon, baring his teeth, ready to bite.

'Control your dog, damn it!'

'Alpha, heel, heel . . .'

Franck had to throw himself at the dog, who had already got the bottom of the guy's jeans in his mouth. The guy lost his balance, still holding the loaded gun.

'Control your dog or I'll shoot it!'

Franck grabbed the dog by the scruff of his neck and pulled him towards him, gripping him so tightly that it might have hurt him, but the dog calmed down and didn't even react. The four of them remained where they were.

'Look, guys, I'm not trying to make trouble.'

Julien picked himself up, inspecting the hem of his trousers and found that Alpha had torn them badly.

'Shit, what's with this dog?'

Franck didn't dare say it was his, especially since it wasn't true and, at the end of the day, the dog was free, he was wild. Now Franck felt like the aggressor, even though the men were armed and could easily have turned their weapon on him. Alpha had just flipped the balance of power. Franck thought he might owe them an apology, or an explanation at least.

'Don't worry, I don't care about your hunting. I'm not going to ask you about it, I assure you.'

'Just as well,' replied the old man. 'Just because you're renting that place doesn't mean you've got any rights. The woods are ours. These ten thousand hectares are ours, get it?'

'Look, I don't give a shit about whose land it is. I just need the cage for a few days, that's all.'

The two men looked at each other, then turned to face the cage. The younger guy realised he had left an empty bucket inside. He went back over to the cage, ducked to get inside, picked up the bucket and inspected the two tree trunks, running his hand over the black tar he had painted on the oaks in the middle. Then he came back out and walked over to Franck, watching the dog the whole time.

'Yeah? What d'you need it for?'

'That's my business.'

Julien cast an eye over Alpha, who was still staring fiercely at him.

'Your dog's strange; he uses his eyes more than his nose. There's wolf in him; he's some kind of cross.'

The old man broke open his rifle and removed the two bullets. Offering his expert opinion, he said, 'It's probably crossed with a Saarloos. The Braquier kids up in Saint-Clair used to breed them with German shepherds for fun.'

'What are you hunting with that?'

'That's none of your concern.'

The men collected their things. The older one got into the passenger seat but the younger man went over to Franck, taking his wallet out of his back pocket.

'Let's forget about what just happened.'

'Agreed.'

Julien held out a small business card. 'Take it, just in case.'

'What's this?'

'Our number, for tracking wounded quarry. You never know, your hunt might take a turn for the worse.'

July 1915

After three days living up there, Joséphine felt a sense of liberation. She was free of her burdensome life in the village, free of the obsessive fear of gendarmes they all lived with every day. In the countryside the gendarmes had become harbingers of doom, and every day people trembled at the thought of having anything to do with them.

It was a huge change for Joséphine to live in the simple drystone hut. There were no creature comforts here, but in the basic one-room structure, with a door on one side and a little window on the other, she felt as if she were floating above the world. Finding herself in the middle of the summer pastures, she felt as if she had left the war behind and broken her connection with the village where the spectre of death hung over everything. She had never lived in such a state of destitution, with nothing more than a stone sink and an oil lamp. The hard bed was only slightly softened by a little woollen mattress, but despite it all she had never felt so free. In the middle of the grassy hills she felt alive, with nothing to guide her but the sun and the colours of summer, as if nothing of her life before had ever existed.

However steep the hills were, the grass in the meadows was abundant and lush. The sheep grazed all day long and in the evening returned sated and round, almost drunk, and it was easy to pen them for the night. Once they were assembled as close as possible to the hut, they slept all night without requiring anything from her. When sheep are on land that is less satisfying and there is not enough to eat, they go on grazing after sundown, sometimes all through the night.

They scatter and don't sleep and the shepherd has trouble keeping an eye on them all. That was why Joséphine always gathered the sheep at the end of the day and penned them in to protect them from wolves or wandering dogs. The three Beaucerons stayed awake standing guard. They were dependable, and Joséphine could go to sleep without worrying.

In leaving the village, Joséphine had left behind the fears of the villagers and no longer had to witness the effect of the letters that the women had been receiving for some time, which they read together in the evenings and which spoke of shelling, of cries, of endless exhaustion and wounds. She even managed to forget the English articles Couderc had read to her, and only to her, to save the others from visions of the apocalypse. As she walked amongst the ewes during the day, Joséphine's gaze wandered over the sea of peaceful hills, even though she knew that in the north, eight hundred kilometres from here, scenes of horror were playing out in front of terrified civilians. Joséphine also knew that at that very moment, in the villages near the front, women and children had to endure squads of German cavalry charging down on huge black horses, spurring on their excited mounts, which dragged behind them strange packages attached by straps. These were the bodies of French soldiers. Whilst here, in the hills, everything seemed so tranquil, over there, mad cavalry were galloping with their trophies into the centre of villages, making for the main square where they would parade as if they were a circus attraction. The corpses attached to their horses scraped along the ground, throwing up dust. The officers' game was to draw their sabres and slice one of the heads of the vanquished in two, so that the parts twirled merrily as if on a roundabout . . .

Now that she had some distance from Orcières, she understood that the reason Couderc had read her all those reports was that he thought that hearing of such horrors would make the death of her husband less painful. Dr Manouvrier was not the only victim of the war, and in the scheme of barbarity, in a sense, he had been spared.

But Joséphine was not consoled and had felt nothing but profound disgust for humanity.

At least up here in these meadows, she was no longer a war widow or an old maid; here she felt herself and nothing else, without anyone to stare at her or condemn her. She discovered how rare and wonderful it was to exist just for herself and not to have anyone looking at her. In the hut, she slept well and was at peace. There were strange noises at night but they were never worrying. Of course, she heard all sorts of things going on outside; sometimes she even felt a field mouse scrabbling under her bed, and whereas down below the tiniest spider would have sent her leaping from her bed, here in the middle of the vast meadows in the middle of nowhere, she was afraid of nothing and nothing attacked her.

On the fifth morning, Joséphine woke to bright sunlight. As every day, she splashed water on her face then opened her door wide to drink in the fresh air. The sheep in the pen were still asleep and everything appeared calm. But she suddenly saw that the three dogs had stood up and were all looking in the same direction, a sign that something was approaching. At first she thought it must be a lost dog, or a wolf; she even thought of the lions. Perhaps it was true that the lion tamer let them out, and that he guided them here, or they made their own way here. At least now she would know for certain. She pushed the door to without closing it completely. Through the gap she could not see or hear anything, but all it would take was one ewe jumping up for them all immediately to do the same and, from one moment to the next, the peaceful flock would be in chaos. Luckily the flock were all still penned, so they could not escape and run off who knew where. The dogs were nervous, whining but not barking yet. Joséphine positioned herself so that she could see down the left-hand path, and then she noticed the lion tamer coming out of the wood on his horse. He was obviously trying not to be seen, or at any rate, he was staying in shadow. He tied his horse up to a tree and, rather than crossing the meadow to come to the hut, he seemed to be walking past it, keeping to the edge of the wood as if he were trying to hide. So he was the one stealing the ewes, after she had defended him to the whole village. The juniper bushes made a screen and she lost sight of him when he walked behind them. He knew what he was doing, because the dogs did not howl, probably because he was facing into the wind. Unless he exercised some kind of control over them; maybe even from this distance he was able to subdue them, as he did all animals, control them and bringing them to heel. Or maybe the dogs already knew him and he had already tamed them. In the little house there was only one window at the back and there were no openings giving onto the junipers. If she wanted to see better, she would have to venture out. But she wanted to see what he was up to without revealing herself. So she stayed quite still by the door, her gaze fixed on the tiny opening, waiting to see where he would pop out, and how he would succeed in stealing the animals.

Her heart thudding, she was sure she would be able to surprise him but, in the event, it was she who jumped, because he appeared right there a few centimetres from her door. She had not heard him coming. He stared at her, saying nothing. She froze, then saw his face break into a wide smile. This man, this time, had come to her. After travelling for kilometres he had taken the last enormous step that brought him right inside the house. He had set off before dawn to be here at daybreak, and without a word he hugged her tightly to him. She had been thinking he had come to take the sheep, but it was she he took in his arms. He held her as feverishly as a tiger with an antelope, and it was with the same eagerness that he breathed in the scent of her hair. They found themselves there, together, elated; it was so unexpected and Joséphine was so overcome that she was robbed of breath. As she buried her face in the man's neck, holding him as if she would have liked to disappear into him, she realised that he must have seen her already several days ago, that he must have been watching her. It was crazy how quickly bodies could change.

She felt like a dry, forgotten river suddenly flooded by a storm, passing in a second from total aridity to great energy. Time stood still. The ewes were still enclosed. Not being able to spread out over the tempting meadow, they started to eat where they were. Nights here were so fresh that the grass became saturated with dew and in the morning it stood tall and green, blooming like the new day.

Wolfgang forgot everything; he forgot his precautions about perfume and that this evening his lions would not understand why he smelt of jasmine; he forgot that Joséphine was the wife of a man who was not long dead in combat. But as their hearts beat fast, melting into one another, it was Joséphine who was holding him close, to expel all thought and dislodge the protective hand of her husband, who, although dead, tried to keep hold of her . . . The penned ewes were restless and disturbed the dogs; all the animals wanted to get to the pastures that were being denied them this morning. The flock, tightly packed in their enclosure, wanted to frolic and run across the fields, whilst behind the door Joséphine and Wolfgang were passionately embracing.

She offered herself, this early morning, to a man already covered in sweat, as the dogs on the other side of the fencing started barking at the sheep which would not stay still. It drove the dogs mad to see the sheep behaving like that but they could not reach them to control them, and the more the dogs barked the more agitated the sheep became. Neither Joséphine nor Wolfgang paid any attention to the furious chorus. The bleating sheep enraged the dogs, which were now barking in the direction of the house. The lions over on the other slopes must have begun to roar. They couldn't be heard from here as they were too far away, but the sheep stirring and knocking into each other would be spreading droplets of sweat on the wind which the lions would scent. They would be able to smell the bleating flock getting heated as they tormented the dogs. And down in the village that morning, the lions could be heard louder than ever; people shivered in fear at the incessant roaring. By making love on top of the world, Wolfgang and Joséphine electrified the wildlife, shattered the peace of the morning, and drove the women to swearing.

Once the wildlife had calmed down, Joséphine and Wolfgang improvised breakfast on the little table set up outside. At the farmhouse in the village it was not done to eat outside; there might be an arbour to enjoy the fresh air in, but to eat bareheaded in the sun was not allowed. Besides coffee, there was only bread and cheese, with a few unripe figs. It was not much. All sorts of insects danced around them. Bees, hornets and wasps created a an insistent gentle buzzing. Joséphine had set the ewes free and they had all gone down to the bottom of the little valley, accompanied by the dogs. They were grazing on the hillside, clearly visible from up here. Wolfgang watched the animals. The bond between the three dogs and the sheep was touching. He thought of his wild cats, which he had left well shaded in the cages at the back, because it would be hot today. Knowing that Joséphine would not refuse him, he had planned to spend part of the day here. The relationship had been forged long ago. Seen from here, the land stretched away to infinity. The hills around them were sharply outlined, but in the distance you could have seen as far as the Massif Central, while to the south you could imagine the Pyrenees, or else all those distant mountains were actually clouds, the cumulus of the beautiful weather. Since they had made love, it was if their bodies were continuing a conversation; they spoke little; they were two beings at peace, looking out over all others.

'Why did you come and live up here?'

'Ewes were disappearing. In the village they thought you were stealing them for the lions.'

'My lions have enough to eat. I have enough to feed the whole village.'

'I believe you. I would just like to know what kind of animals are taking them from us – perhaps it's wolves.'

'It's not wolves.'

'How do you know?'

297

'Look around at these hills. Millions of years ago, this land was at the bottom of the ocean. All these trees and meadows are growing on the remains of life at the bottom of the sea. When the sea retreated, the hills found fresh air, so plants grew, then animals appeared; some evolved into man. At the time wolves and men were equal, hunting the same prey on the same land, in the same forests. Then they began to organise, wolves in packs and men in groups, and were for a time allies in coordinating hunting. Still now, wolves and men are the same, except that when a wolf steals an animal it's obvious; a wolf never thinks of hiding its crime.'

'Why do you say that?'

'If a ewe disappears without trace, it has not been killed by an animal.'

August 2017

Franck went to pick Liem and Travis up from the station in Souillac. He could tell they were on the defensive as they walked along the platform towards him. They had taken the seven o'clock train from Gare d'Austerlitz and were exhausted after six hours of travel. They couldn't believe it had taken such a long time. They kept saying that it took as long to get to the Lot as it would have taken to get to New York, as if it were some great achievement.

'And it's not over yet, guys. You'll see, there's still a good hour to go . . .'

'You're joking. Are you trying to kill us or something?'

Franck glanced at Travis in the rear-view mirror and smiled.

'You won't regret it when you get there, you'll see. And it's worth it for a signature, right? You wanted to do things quickly and soon it'll be done! We'll sign and everything will be sorted.'

'Franck, we're just signing the amendments, not a contract.'

'That remains to be seen . . .'

'What do you mean?'

'Nothing, just that a signature is always a formal agreement.'

Travis tried to catch Franck's eye in the rear-view mirror; he was keeping an open mind but he found Franck's high spirits a little suspicious.

'By the way, did you bring your walking boots?'

Liem lifted his leg to show Franck the blue Meindls he was so proud of. He was always boasting about the trek he had done when he was twenty. Not exactly a round-the-world trip, he had walked from Paris to the Urals, having originally planned to make it to Beijing. It was something he was quite proud of, but his complacence was always slightly tempered by a note of defeat. Franck knew Liem was the weaker of the two and would probably be the first to crack. Travis, though he had never attempted any kind of major expedition, was probably in very good shape because he ran every day and had been boxing since childhood, and he had one of those cocky, unflinching gazes.

They started out on the main road that was known as the 'old road to Paris'. From there, Franck turned off to the left onto a much smaller B-road. He hadn't had any trouble finding the signs for Souillac when he was driving to the station earlier, but now he was relying on his instincts, using the sun and aiming for the south. There weren't many signs apart from the small blue ones for local places, where there usually weren't even any houses. He was going quite fast, but the Audi was so smooth that it felt as if they were flying over the potholes and verges. Franck was driving as if he knew the route perfectly, when in fact he was just waiting for the sign for Limogne. Once he got there, he would know how to get back to Mont d'Orcières. He refused to use the GPS because there was no fun in that, and he didn't want Liem and Travis to work out where they were or find out the exact address, especially as there wasn't one. He didn't want them just to feel lost, he wanted them to *be* lost.

'Listen, I'll level with you. Do you know why I asked you to come?'

'To sign!'

'Yes, but not just for that.'

'I don't know – do you want us to do a team-building thing, a hike through the forest to bring everyone together, is that it?'

'No, I asked you to come because I didn't want to go back to Paris. I've already agreed to your terms; I wasn't going to come running to you like a good doggie.'

'But, Franck, the terms work for all of us! Trust us, we're doing it for the company; we've got to be the first ones in France to team up with Netflix; we'll pull the rug out from under everyone else.'

'We're not going through this again now. But it's fine; don't worry, I'll sign.'

Franck wavered when he got to a junction without any signs. There were three options, but he used the sun like Lise had said and took the right-hand turn, and he recognised the Limogne road five kilometres later. The right turn took him directly south.

'Hey, Franck, is this a joke? Isn't there any signal here?'

'It depends, Travis, not everywhere. In some places there's no signal at all. None at all . . .'

Franck could see him in the rear-view mirror. He hadn't taken his eyes off his phone for quarter of an hour and was looking increasingly worried.

When they arrived at the access road, Franck purposely turned sharply onto it and drove aggressively up the slope to shake them up a bit.

'Bloody hell, where are you taking us? To some kind of hole?'

'Well, no, you can see we're going up . . . It's the opposite of a hole.'

Once they got to the top, Liem and Travis glanced at the view, and were impressed by the spectacular panorama despite themselves. They soon noticed the tall dog running behind the car. Franck was driving slowly along the track over the crest and the dog was trying to see what was inside the car; who Franck had brought back.

'So you've got a dog then?'

'Yes.'

When they got out of the car, the dog came up to Franck and greeted him excitedly, visibly delighted to see him. But he quickly got Liem and Travis's scent, sniffing their shoes and calves. Neither of them seemed particularly comfortable with the dog.

'Can we stroke him?'

'You'll have to ask him.'

The large animal's inscrutable expression did nothing to reassure them. However, Franck could tell they were genuinely happy to see Lise again as they kissed one another, and in the natural way they behaved around her. Watching them hug her warmly, he thought of two children reunited with their mother. He quickly did a calculation. He realised it was possible, however crazy it might seem, that he and Lise could be the parents of those morons. He despised them even more because of it, though it moved him too. He again admired Lise's poise and her openness in welcoming them, her way of being there for other people. She helped them get their two large bags out of the boot – one each, as if they were planning to stay for a fortnight, the idiots. Lise invited them to sit down and make themselves comfortable. Then, at exactly the same time, they looked at their phones and noticed the same thing.

'Hey, there really isn't any reception!'

'No, not here.'

'Hang on, haven't you got Wi-Fi either?'

'Don't worry, I'll take you somewhere you can go online.'

For them this was worse than being told there wasn't any water. They looked at Franck with a mixture of anger and incomprehension. They were annoyed with him, as if it were his fault.

Lise came back with a jug of cold water with some flowers steeping in it.

'It needs to infuse first. In the meantime, come with me and I'll show you your room.'

She took them up to the room just under the roof, a strange space that was as much an attic as a bedroom. She had managed to sort out some sleeping arrangements, using the two old beds that were up there and putting her yoga mats on top. Franck didn't know how she she had managed it. She could do anything. She could have turned a cellar into a palace, a picnic into a banquet, a fleeting instant into a moment of grace. He could hear her talking to them, full of genuine kindness and generosity, and he thought to himself that she was truly the best part of him. He couldn't remember which artist had said 'My wife' in response to the question 'What is the best thing about you?' In this instance he wanted to believe it because if Lise represented the best of him, he could be his worst self and not feel bad about it; he would be as hard, cruel and violent as possible.

Lise showed them the upstairs rooms and the balcony. Alpha stayed with Franck. He seemed to be waiting for an instruction or an order so he would know what to make of the two newcomers. Were they wild boar or squirrels? Was he supposed to be good and gentle if they decided to stroke him, not barking, and behaving like a pet? Or should he growl if they held their hand out to him, frighten them and treat them like wild boar?

Franck had noticed how carefully Alpha had sniffed them when they got out of the car. The dog had gathered lots of information and taken it in, without them even realising, and would already have been able to find them anywhere in the hills, in the forest. With their scent, he could either hunt them down or rescue them. The dog's head was resting on his knee and Franck felt closer to him than ever before. He drank a large glass of the infusion Lise had made by immersing various plants in the big jug of water. He looked at the little posy undulating in the glass pitcher; it was like a flowering tea. With the dog at his side, Franck was reminded of the fundamental ambiguity of life. It wasn't about being the good guy or the bad guy, just as business wasn't about submitting or attacking; it was a question of balancing two opposing sides. That duality is inherent in every animal. The sweet cat that purrs when you stroke it becomes a pitiless murderer of field mice once it's outside. Just as you can sometimes catch a flash of anger in the sleepy poses of wild beasts at the circus, and the submissive paws they put on their tamers' backs can take the head off a buffalo. Many hidden instincts lie dormant in even the most affectionate animals; legs ready to run, jaws ready to grip prey and teeth ready to tear it to pieces.

Liem and Travis came back down from their room, followed by Lise. They seemed more mellow since she had shown them around. Franck noticed that they were suddenly relaxed and revived, friendly and alert. They were smiling. They walked over to the outside table where Franck sat. Lise told them she'd made another cold drink with herbs, herbs she had picked in the meadow and left to infuse. She had been trying out all sorts of odd things since they arrived, and Franck was always slightly worried that one of the plants might turn out to be poisonous.

Travis glanced at the dog sitting at Franck's feet, while Liem, evidently more interested in animals, went up to him but couldn't decide whether to bend down or not. He didn't dare stroke him.

'Can I?'

'Have a go and you'll see.'

'Your dog is strange, it's like a wolf.'

'He's a bit of both.'

'When did you get a dog?'

'It was the dog who adopted me.'

As for Travis, he couldn't get over the house and its setting, 'You were right, Franck; this place is insane. There's something about it, I don't know what, but something.'

'Maybe it's because we're going to sign the contract here,' replied Franck, casually returning to the reason for their visit.

'You know what, I completely forgot to bring the champagne. Have you got any here?'

'Don't worry about it, guys, we have time, we have all the time in the world.'

July 1915

Ever since Joséphine had been living up on the pastures, life had seemed free of all expectation and fear. Time was now her friend. She felt sustained by the land around her and also by the thought that she would see the man again and love him without constraint. Love is not rational; it's an irresistible madness. This man for her was Ulysses returned from his voyage, Noah liberated from his pact with God; he was the freest man on earth. However, love is never simple, and although it was true that they were both all alone in the world, lost in their kingdom of infinite possibilities, it was also true that Wolfgang lived on the other side of the hills and to reach him there was no direct road or path. It would take nearly two hours on horseback, and she might get lost or injured.

It was a perfect day. Since morning the sun had dominated the sky, without a cloud in sight. The ewes, which had been grazing since daybreak, were already sated by midday so, when the sun reached its zenith, they had felt the heat coming and returned to shelter under the trees. Now they idled at the edge of the forest in the shade and would not be moving from there. Nearby was the little stream which filled the drinking trough with delicious fresh water. The sheep would definitely be staying where they were until sunset. The dogs, also in the shade, were calm and vigilant. Peace reigned.

Joséphine could count on several hours to herself, so she saddled her horse and hurried him along the intermittent paths. In spite of the heat, she made him gallop as soon as the path was visible. The animal did not like galloping as the sun beat down; she could feel he was nervous and hot between her legs, his coat already covered in foamy sweat, a sign that he was baulking, but she drove him on even where it was wooded. The more she advanced the more their way seemed to be barred by branches, and every thorn appeared to want to catch at her, but she refused to see this as a sign. Yet as she approached the lion tamer's property, a guilty premonition seized her and did hold her back. After all, she did not know the man very well. And, worse, he was a threat and a danger, first because he was German, a deserter admittedly, but still an enemy, and secondly because he was a man hard-hearted enough to live all alone on this accursed plot and ferocious enough to subjugate and tame wild animals. Then she thought of all the women toiling down in the valley, bent double in the sun, and very quickly she dismissed any guilty thoughts.

Rather than going over the crest of the hill, Joséphine wanted to stay in the shade and went down towards the ravine. The horse was baulking more than ever and refused to go into the wood down the slope; he kept slipping on the parched earth. Joséphine was a good rider; she knew how to steer carefully between obstacles, but the pitch was steep, and even though the horse occasionally spread his legs wider he sometimes almost lost his balance, the muscles in his shoulders spasming. So she dismounted. At least there was shade under the trees. She told herself that the animal could recover there where it was cool. The descent was still getting steeper – this short cut had been a mistake. But she was sure there was a path up to Mont d'Orcières somewhere on this route, even though she could not yet see it.

Suddenly she heard the noise of metal striking metal, from her left, even though Wolfgang's house must have been over on the right, beyond the second hill on the west side. The metallic sounds were definitely coming from the left, from the other side of the hill just above her. She continued down, picking her way carefully through the tightly packed oak trees and holly bushes until she found herself on a little spur looking over at a ravine with a sheer face. The sounds were coming from the bottom of the *igue*. Who else but him could be making such a racket? She tried to go forward but the gaps in the rock were too narrow and the descent too steep for the horse. She tied him to a tree and went on alone through the brambles. Down below Wolfgang heard something coming and picked up his stake, thinking a deer had strayed or a young boar been attracted by the tar. But then, above, he caught glimpses of the familiar pale-coloured dress, and he realised who was coming down towards him. She held on to the tree trunks as momentum propelled her forward, but she stumbled over the last few metres and when she reached him, her arms and legs and even her face scratched all over by the brambles, she literally fell into his arms. He wiped the drops of blood from her cheek, and the time should have been ripe for them to kiss and hold each other as though they hadn't seen each other for months. But Joséphine felt trapped at the bottom of the *igue*; suddenly she felt lost, almost panicked. She was trembling like the muscles of her horse earlier, but rather than snuggle up in the arms of the lion tamer, she mainly wanted to know what he was doing there.

'Don't worry, it's the old travel cage. I brought it down last winter and I just wanted to make it bigger.'

'Why would you put the lions so far away?'

'It's not for the lions.'

Wolfgang was annoyed that Joséphine had seen the cage. He would have preferred to be the only one to know about it. He especially did not want anyone in the village to know; however, now that Joséphine was there, he had no choice but to explain the trap, his method of using grain to attract animals, how the wine casks he had found in the abandoned house had holes pierced in them and were filled with grain that the boar came to eat. Then he showed her the Norwegian tar he had painted onto the base of the trees, and the seedlings for the yellow worm. Joséphine did not grasp exactly how it worked, but she understood this was how he trapped wild animals and used the cage to hold them. Since the start of the war, the hills had been awash with prey, and he had found a way to tame them. He could catch as many animals as he wanted in his zoo trap, and he would never run out of food for his wild cats.

'So you can tell everyone in the village that you can have as much meat as you want and more; tell them that and then they won't suspect you of stealing their sheep . . .'

But Wolfgang did not want anyone to know how he managed to catch so many animals without firing a rifle. Otherwise, sooner or later children or old people would try to make traps like his, but they would do it badly, and very quickly the livestock would run out and everything would be ruined.

'Joséphine, what you see here must be a secret.'

'Between us, everything is secret.'

He had installed the old cage at the bottom of the *igue* all by himself. It had taken a herculean effort to transport all the parts here and assemble them in this chasm in the middle of nowhere – the old cage was thirteen and a half metres long and nearly four metres high. This karstic well was a kind of lost territory, an ecosystem never exploited by man, never cultivated. Perhaps in the Stone Age people had lived here, but any plant or tree here now had come from him. There had never been any cultivation or sowing here, no fertiliser or tree-cutting. Since the dawn of time nature had done its best by itself. It was a world apart here, and boar and deer were attracted into the cage by the bait and the tar. Animals came in and found water, and grain in the casks. It was like heaven for the boar which kept coming, sometimes several at a time. Wolfgang used the dog to keep them in – the German shepherd never let his guard down even when faced with tusked boar. Then when Wolfgang, watching from the top of the *igue*, saw that the food cage was well filled, he pulled the cord and the door closed.

'I used to have a small trap, but now I'm making it bigger. You see – it's bigger than a circus tent!'

Joséphine took him in her arms, but she felt uneasy. It was because of the wood at the bottom of the *igue*. Down here it was fresh, almost cold. The sun could not penetrate the tree canopy and the light here was like a November morning. The vegetation was unsettling and strange. Then there was that tall cage, and the bars on the ground that he was going to erect, and all the heavy tools in the wagon; everything here spoke of death, certain death for so many animals to come . . . She did not want to stay here, and anyway she had to go back up to reassure the horse she had left at the top, and to return to her hut. Suddenly, everything was frightening, and she felt the same sense of loss and emptiness from her life before, before the war, before death, before these bars and cages, before the sheep and wild cats, before the animals that disappeared and had to be watched, before all this . . .

Wolfgang went with her. They climbed up a slope that was less steep, a gap where the rock had collapsed. They walked on broken stones which almost made a path. Once they were at the top, since Joséphine's horse was on the other side, they went round on a path overlooking the *igue*, which gaped like the crater of a diabolical volcano, a volcano boiling with leaves to the centre of which animals scurried, attracted by the odour of tar, unwitting prey throwing itself into the wolf's mouth.

Wolfgang suggested that Joséphine stay with him for the night, but she had to get back to the ewes. What she did not say was that she also wanted to get back to her hut opening onto the meadows. They were not sorry to part this time, certain that they would see each other soon.

When Joséphine left the wood, she found the bright summer light where she had abandoned it, there on the narrow path leading to liberty. She made the journey back without hurrying the horse. She simply let him go at his own rhythm. In the distance she could see that the ewes were still in the shade. They had not moved. A few had got up to graze again, but the heat had not lessened. Joséphine went into the hut where the air was cool. She could not believe how delighted she was to be back in her humble abode, as if the simplicity of the surroundings helped her to think clearly. But then she noticed a pot placed at the foot of the stone sink, a pot that had not been there all the time she had lived here. There were four blue notes tucked under the pot, twenty francs in all. When she raised the lid, she immediately recognised the smell of slow-cooked *sauté d'agneau*. But she especially recognised the earthenware receptacle. It was the kind one of the butchers in Limogne had always cooked his terrines in. She rushed out to count the ewes, but her haste upset the sheep. Seeing their shepherd dashing towards them, they began to run about in all directions, making it hard for Joséphine to count them. It took her a while but she succeeded and clearly two ewes had gone.

Le Simple must have been selling them for some time, one by one, or two by two. Maybe he was trying to make money, or maybe he didn't dare refuse the butcher, who bribed him with banknotes. Joséphine was panicked at her discovery because she could not accuse Le Simple. If she denounced him she would feel she was the one committing a crime. She couldn't do it. But if she said nothing she would be complicit, and in spite of her presence, in spite of all her vigilance and care, two ewes had just disappeared. There was nothing she could do about it. And as she looked around the inviolate meadow and at these plateaux deserted by everyone, she said to herself that the world was mad. There was evil in everything. Wherever she went, even here, even deep in nature, far away from everyone, she was trapped by malevolence and strange alliances.

August 2017

It was the dog that led the way. The three men walked in single file behind him, zigzagging through the trees. After just ten minutes of ascent with the sun hot on the back of their necks, they were out of breath and had stopped talking. Alpha was moving fast, and Franck was reassured by his determination. The animal seemed to understand the plan and was taking them exactly where Franck wanted him to. He had been watching the way the dog behaved around Liem and Travis ever since they arrived; the animal must have sensed his distrust.

Alpha was guiding the group, expertly leading them down the best paths. He had realised they were going back to the *igue* and that, once there, he would have to help Franck by inspiring in him the touch of ferocity he lacked to stand his ground, perhaps even teaching him how to bite.

Liem and Travis wanted to take a break at the crest of the first hill. They had been sure they would get a signal at the top, and now they were frustrated. Their Sports Tracker apps were useless as the GPS didn't work, and their phone batteries were already dying from constantly searching for some reception. With so many elements out of their control, they felt their sporting endeavours were meaningless.

Franck walked over to them.

'Set them up for a hike, did you?' he said, sarcastically.

'Yeah, step count, gradient, heart rate . . . Everything you need to monitor yourself.'

'Your legs will tell you how far you've walked; you don't need an app!'

Travis couldn't resist a little dig. 'You know, Franck, if you're trying to prove you're still in shape, it's OK, we get it.'

'That's not it. I'm not trying to prove anything, but it's good to meet face to face, in the open air, don't you think?'

'And this spot you've found, you're sure it's worth it?'

'It certainly is. I want to show you, it's an insane place, as you would say – a four-metre-high tiger cage at the bottom of an *igue*; it's like you're in the Venezuelan jungle.'

'And there's a signal at this place?'

'Don't worry . . .'

They started walking again, downhill this time. Again, the slope was incredibly treacherous, but they were keeping up with the dog as if scared they might lose him. The stony ground gave way under their feet and brambles scratched their legs as they followed him; branches hit them in the face, and they stumbled over buried roots. Their calves hurt. The dog carried on, occasionally looking behind to check they were still there. Liem didn't trust him, fearing that he was leading them back in time, trying to get them lost in some ageless, wild land where time had stood still.

Franck was bringing up the rear and now could see them from above. He was amused by how hard they were trying to follow an animal. He thought back to his two years of hell with two successive flops, and the way the people around him had reacted. They had all turned their backs on him for several months. It had been as humiliating as it was infuriating. It's hard to watch others losing interest in you; it's not exactly that they pity you, more that they worry that failure is contagious. He thought about the shifty looks he had got at festivals and parties, and the former distributors and partners who had stopped answering the phone or suddenly had other projects with other people.

He had met Liem and Travis at Cannes. At first, he thought it was a godsend; they were so energetic, and they knew so much about new technology and video games – 3D war games that were impeccably designed. They said they had considered their options and wanted to get into the film industry; they seemed to have lots of ideas. In a sense, they were newcomers and he was a bit washed up, which helped them get along, especially as Cannes is so fickle. Like all festivals, there is a feeling of overwhelming euphoria at Cannes: everyone is beautiful and triumphant, all plans are promises, and everyone says yes to everyone, but once the festival finishes you never hear from them again. They had produced two short films 'for fun', but they swore their experience in digital would help get Alpha Productions back in the game; they were used to the multimillion-euro investment plans of video game production. When Franck met them, he had been convinced he needed new blood and help to relaunch his company. He believed they were genuine and only later realised they couldn't care less about films and were actually planning to use his library to lure in the tech giants. Obviously their only ambition was to get into sponsored series and bank on the internet . . . His foot caught on a root and he almost fell. His lace had come undone and he bent down to tie it.

'You're getting old, mate. You don't want to see that things have changed!'

'What?'

'Nothing, nothing, Franck. I was just asking if you're OK . . .'

'Yeah, I'm fine.'

'Hey, when we get to the bottom, are we gonna have to go up another hill?'

'Yes, we have to go up one more hill and back down again, and then we'll be there.'

Franck stood back up again but his head started to spin; blood was beating in his temples and he didn't know if it was from heat or anger. He was soaked in sweat and could feel acid rising in his throat. Ever since he'd started eating meat again, he'd been getting heartburn and a slightly acidic aftertaste from digesting the flesh of another animal; flesh that was the same as his own. Eating meat was like eating the body of an enemy or prey. Actually, he would have liked to devour those two. He really hated them.

The dog didn't even pause when he got to the second gully and headed straight for the final ascent. Good Lord – he thought about what heartburn must be like for dogs, or even more for wild animals, the big carnivores that only ate raw meat, and lions that didn't eat any vegetables. God, their stomachs must burn with acid, enzymes and frenzied protein. Their minds must be ablaze with aggression and violence, because now he was sure of it: eating meat made you greedy and grasping, and it was that greed that helped you win, made you want to fight, conquer the world and destroy your opponent. In wartime men are encouraged to destroy the enemy, or kill them at least, kill all of them . . . He wanted to declare war on the guys walking in front of him and destroy them – yes, destroy them. He thought to himself, 'They're here because they think I'm going to sign; sheer greed has driven them all this way. They've travelled seven hours and are willing to walk in forty-degree heat because they think they can manipulate me into signing their contract.' But now, he was the one manipulating them – or, rather, the dog was. They were walking without the slightest idea of what was in store for them.

As he looked at the men, flanked on one side by him and on the other by the dog, like prisoners being escorted, he could feel his animal side reawakening. In the middle of these woods he felt he was part of the environment, could feel himself becoming one with the wild countryside. He too was becoming wild again, just like the woods, rocks and paths that nobody had ever trodden, paths used only by the wild boar that came down to the soft soil and watering holes at night; wild boar that fought for survival like their fellow mammals and always followed the same route, wearing the ground away to create tracks that resembled human paths. It had been a long time since there were any humans in the area. Apart from the three of them, there was not a living soul there. And there were fewer and fewer hunters to explore the remote parts and stray from the beaten paths. The younger generations didn't go hunting there any more, having moved far away and left the farms behind, and the older generations couldn't tackle the steep hills. Deep in the valleys of the hills, nature had become wild once more and the animals were dancing.

Lise had gone up to the balcony. She was planning to do a fifty-by-sixty-centimetre painting. She wanted the light to be coming from the left, so she needed magenta and yellow at the bottom of the canvas, with light blue above it for the sky. She would have to put the bright sun-drenched light in the foreground first, with a softer light for the background. The only problem was that the sun was scorching hot and the paint might dry. She made some sky blue to test it out, but she needed more white to make the pure shade she could see in front of her for the bottom layer. She was starting to sketch when she suddenly heard barking in the distance – yes, just there, on the other side of the hills, a series of quick, deep, rough barks that didn't sound like a dog. But what other animal barks? She didn't know. She thought about Franck and the hike he had been so keen to do with his partners, even though it was more than thirty-six degrees and he might get lost, sunburnt, fall, or even have a stroke. She had never seen him as tense or serious as he had been when they left.

The barking started again, louder this time, but coming from even further away. She had promised herself that she wouldn't give in to fear, or worry about anything ever again, nor would she allow herself to be affected by life's various disappointments and failures. Though she sometimes noticed that fate had not been kind to her, she did her best to live in the moment, like now, appreciating how lucky she was to be able to paint in this remote spot, to be alone, to look around and quite simply to breathe. Of course meditation is good, but it's like a wall that always sends you back to yourself. On the other hand, painting for hours is a very real kind of meditation and at the end you have something to show for it. As she stood on the balcony of this house amid an ocean of hills, she realised that a house is a sort of living organism that feeds on the space around it. First it receives water, then it collects it in gutters and transfers it into a tank or pipes; in winter it feeds off the wood in the forest for heating, consuming entire trees year after year, as well as the fruit and vegetables growing around it. A house is a body that claims everything around it: rainwater, heat, sun, flowers, fruit. A house swallows everything up . . . At that point, Lise noticed the black cable that led to the house, coming from the wooden post next to it. It must be the electric wire. If it was a telephone wire, she would cut it . . .

Her obsessive fear of the telephone also stemmed from the fact that one day it had stopped ringing. People had stopped calling after her illness, and the phone had turned into a deadly, accusatory reminder of that. It had been quite the opposite before, when she had been fed up hearing it constantly ringing or vibrating. Then one day it fell silent. At least she was uncontactable here, happily unaware whether anyone was calling her or not. She felt a slight anxiety though as she heard barking again, coming from far in the distance this time. Were they being attacked by stray dogs or wolves? Did wolves bark like that?

They had almost finished the final ascent, taking them to the high ground above the *igue*. The strange barking returned. Franck wondered if it was coming from behind them, near the house. The worst thing about it was that the cries didn't sound like anything, apart from perhaps a stray dog or a jackal, or a lynx even.

'What's that?'

'Wolves! No, I'm joking. I've no idea – foxes maybe.'

'Oh yeah, because foxes bark . . .'

'Anything is possible around here. There were even lions once.'

'Jesus, what are you trying to do? Freak us out?'

'I promise you, there are loads of animals around here. It's normal, it's just nature, it's nothing to worry about.'

Franck was used to his surroundings and nothing would have surprised him. It didn't matter whether the noise was coming from foxes, polecats or wolves; he couldn't truly say he would recognise any of their cries. The dog was the only one there who knew that the barking sounds were coming from deer alerting others to a threat. He stopped for just a moment. For now, they were of no interest to him.

Liem and Travis paused when they got to the top. They glanced at their phones, and Liem put his finger on his throat to take his pulse.

'What is it?' asked Travis.

'A hundred and sixty,' replied Liem, proudly.

'Not bad. The hamstrings are fine, but we'll really feel it in our calves when we start our descent.'

'You're not even going to look down?' Franck gestured towards the panorama, or at least what you could see of it through the trees. Liem and Travis hadn't realised that they were at the very top of a chasm, looking out over the thick vegetation of a sort of limestone crater. They could see the glimmer of the metal cage at the bottom through the greenery. The sun was beating directly down on the *igue*, giving the metal an unexpected brilliance.

'Now that, that is insane . . . I know you, Franck. You must have something in mind if you're showing us this. Is it a set?'

'No, it's for you. It's not for anything, it's just so you enjoy the walk . . .'

There was still a good five minutes to go, five minutes of trying not to go tumbling down. Franck already knew Liem and Travis would go inside the cage; it was too tempting. They would willingly go and stand in the middle, the only place where you could see the sky at all; they would want to look at the huge barrels and the pool up close. They would walk straight into the lion's den. He just had to hope the dog would understand that he had to keep them inside, and then he would close the metal gate and secure it with the ropes. They would laugh at first, and then they would stop laughing. They would tell him to stop fooling around. He would make sure that Alpha knew he had to stop them untying the ropes through the bars, and then he would leave them there all night to think, with the dog guarding their prison. Franck knew they wouldn't sign the new amendments straight away, not without reading them at any rate, and then they would need at least one night, or maybe two, before giving in and begging him to set them free. He wouldn't release them until he had their signatures.

Their view of the giant birdcage among the trees was getting better and better as they walked.

'Franck, this place is incredible . . .'

Franck slowed down and let them get closer to the cage, keeping a good thirty metres behind them. He was watching from above as they ducked under the entrance and then went into the cage. It was perfect. They looked like two figurines trapped inside a snow globe; you just had to close it and shake it to make the snowflakes fall. He'd got them. Alpha seemed to be seeking his approval; he knew it too. They'd got them.

The dog stood outside the cage, tense and panting. He looked at Franck, who was almost at the bottom, waiting for an order. But who was giving the orders, Franck or the dog? What would take over, the wolf part in the human, or the human part in the dog?

July 1915

Wolves hunt at speed, ambushing flocks that move slowly. They often wait for fog to spring out at the terrified animals and chase them or throw them into the air, their forty-two sharpened teeth visible in their gaping mouths, forty-two blades ready to rip open the animals' throats, spilling their blood. Unlike men, animals have to fight to live. And they have to do it continually, in order to eat or guard their territory; even birds spend their life on alert. Blackbirds sing in the morning not to brighten the sky but to warn off possible rivals. Joséphine lived in peace, the peace of the hills, yet all around her animals were killing each other to feed themselves. For many of them violence was the essential element of their existence. Boar ate broods of pheasants when there weren't enough acorns; foxes slaughtered chickens when there weren't enough hares; hares ate worms and midges. As for the buzzards and kites wheeling about the sky all day long, they swooped on mice and the mice fed on caterpillars. Even wild cats end up being devoured by cowardly hyenas that wait for them to die before attacking.

In this scheme all man does is add to the cruelty, particularly in periods of war when restrictions and shortages are conducive to wild hunting and poaching. Caught in between the battle lines, soldiers allowed themselves this kind of mischief. Behind their lines some had ambitious hunting plans, in complete contravention of the law, but driven by extreme hunger. Some infantrymen threw grenades into the rivers to stir up the fish, others who were further from the front practised battue hunting. Hunting was forbidden in areas of armed confrontation, but officers turned a blind eye. No one would have tolerated it if officers who sent their men off to be killed by the enemy had sanctioned a soldier for killing a dog or a trout.

War is a carnival of terror, a purveyor of atrocities and sorrow; it treats men like animals. But here on the green *causse*, since there were no men to hunt, the war gave respite to the prey. And so wild animals proliferated. Boar, deer, foxes and wolves all profited from the absence of men and reclaimed the territory. In this great realignment of free land, it was only the lion tamer who continued to hunt. At the bottom of his *igue* he trapped animals to feed his beasts. Joséphine, in her role as guardian of the high meadows, felt completely detached from the war. Seen from up there, what the men were going through seemed like a faraway hell, and the women at the bottom of the hill must be sinking ever deeper into despair.

Around the hut, the hills were gentle and the animals easy to manage. It was not like in the mountains where the slopes were steep and you had to keep a close eye on the ewes. They must not be taken to steep slopes in case they slipped and fell. Here the hills undulated and the meadows were lush; the sheep slept on the flat. Every morning Joséphine rose at dawn. The sun stayed behind the mountains to the east for a little then slowly came out and woke the world as the birds began to sing, day returning like rosiness to cheeks. Joséphine was there, an attentive observer. There was always a fox that had lingered to catch field mice before returning to the woods as the buzzards and kites positioned themselves on posts or in trees, perching on anything they thought high enough to give them a good view of any movement in the grass. The boar and deer, so active at night, now slunk away into the shadows. People said that the wolves had returned but Joséphine had not seen any. And she could not hear the lions from here either. Now all she could hear of the lion tamer when he was not with her was his voice inside her head, that voice speaking its imperfect French. She kept his words and their shared intimacy for her evenings and for her nights; he never left her.

Spending her days in a state of original destitution, she felt as if she had gone back to the dawn of time. She did not even try to work out whether it was fear or selfishness, or perhaps generosity, that had brought her here. It didn't matter. For the last two months life had recovered a semblance of enjoyment. Wolfgang came every other day. He never stayed more than a few hours, because he was afraid of leaving his wild cats unattended. But for the few hours he was there, they forgot everything; they loved each other, without even thinking of any future.

Joséphine enjoyed her humble paradise of forgotten hills, until one day a man, a new man, destroyed everything. Man, that creation of God who bribes and squanders, who makes it his work to sully and to ruin. Even without cause for malice, jealousy, frustration or anger, man, by his very presence, can destroy everything.

That evening, Wolfgang had gone up to the meadows. Before he left, he fed his lions copiously so that they would stay calm. He planned to stay the night with Joséphine to experience the joy of waking up beside her in the morning. He had slept on his own for years now, and the thought of spending the night with a woman filled him with wonder. He was actually a little scared. He knew that he was taking a risk with his wild cats, not because he was leaving them on their own, well locked up but without supervision, but because the next day they would smell the scent of his adventure and would be annoyed that he had abandoned them. He knew already that, one way or another, they would make their jealousy manifest; he would definitely have to be careful when he opened the cage to feed them, but it was a risk worth taking. He would ignore the risk so that he could indulge his only comfort, which was spend one whole evening and one whole night with Joséphine.

They made love even before penning in the sheep, deep in the meadow, as the sun was setting. Their meal was frugal, but their appetites were elsewhere. They talked and talked; they talked to each other as they never had before, sitting on the stone bench in front of the house. The air was cool after a day of too-hot sun, and it was soothing after the great heat. Unusually for her, Joséphine opened up to him. In the village, she would say little, never confided in anyone and instead listened to the troubles of others. For years she had listened to the ills of her husband's patients who poured out their feelings to her before going in to see him. For years it had been as if no one accorded her the right to her own sadness or pain. What's more, she was surprised to find herself talking to Wolfgang about her husband. She never did that. She told Wolfgang that she had come up to live in the meadows because she could not bear the doctor's house any more. Since her husband's death, since she had proof that he was no longer alive, she had had a terrible realisation, a sort of revelation, that secretly there was only one thing that could one day validate her.

'Joséphine, what are you trying to say?'

'No, Wolfgang, I can't tell you. But it's a question that only you can provide an answer to.'

She put her head on Wolfgang's shoulder. She could see the ewes in the distance, replete, but continuing gently to graze. The sun had sunk behind the hill.

It was dreadful that she could not tell Wolfgang exactly what she meant, even though he was right there, and even though she felt certain she loved him. But she could not tell him that her husband had always told her it was because of her that they could not have children, that it came from her, and because he was an honest doctor, loyal and frank, and she had always trusted him, she had believed him about that too; she had always believed it. Except that since his death, she had told herself that possibly it was not true, possibly it was he who was unfertile, sterile, and not her. She was sure that when he was at the front dicing with death, he must have thought about that all the time. She was sure the thought had haunted him day and night until his death, that it had driven him mad, the thought that one day she would fall pregnant, if he did not return from war, and then she would discover that he had lied to her for all those years. It was horrible to think about.

So that the evening would not be overshadowed by melancholy thoughts, she took Wolfgang by the hand and led him towards the hut, where it was now hotter than outside. They undressed, forgetting the ewes scattered across the western flank.

The world was at war, but here there was peace and the air was mild; the sheep grazed in tranquillity in the boundless meadows, never hungry. Inside, they did not light the little oil lamp. The door was wide open and a little of the glorious atmosphere outside came in; the moon had come out, and now was a time just for them. There under the night sky, far from the troubles of mankind, Joséphine and Wolfgang gave themselves up to the simple pleasure of forgetting everything.

August 2017

Franck put down his cup, feeling a sense of wonder and complete harmony with the countryside around him. This morning he really believed he was part of it. The hills and the blue sky were waiting just for him. He and Lise were eating breakfast outside. He stood up and walked over to the house, coming back a few moments later with a thick red parcel from the butcher that he put on the table with the bread and jars of marmalade, to his wife's astonishment. He odd new behaviour, took a slice of ham and held it out in front of him like an offering to the hills, as if he were symbolically dedicating it to the dog at the bottom of the *igue*, the canine partner working for him. Then he brought it towards him, smelt it and stuffed it in his mouth. It was so large that he had to push it in with his fingers, before chewing it hard and relishing the flavour. Lise was watching him, no longer surprised by this new odd new behaviour but wondering how he could eat it.

'You know, Lise, it wasn't actually them who wanted to play Robinson Crusoe yesterday.'

'What do you mean? You told me they wanted to stay and sleep under the stars . . .'

'Yeah, that's true, but actually I kind of forced them to. I left them in the cage.'

'What are you saying?'

'I left them in the cage on purpose, with the dog standing guard . . .'

'You mean you trapped them? How could you do that?'

'Lise, do you know what they were going to do to me?'

'But, Franck! You've left two men in a cage for a whole night? How could you?'

'Hang on, I'm not the one keeping them there. I'm right here.'

He stood up and spread his arms wide, taking a deep breath as if drinking in the entire scene: the beautiful rolling hills and the sky, and the big clouds appearing in the east, like mounds of whipped egg white that seemed to float slowly towards them.

'Lise, this is what's keeping them there. The countryside, the woods, the wild animals, the dog . . . It's all this, not me.'

He walked back over to Lise, indicating the panorama as if offering it to her, as if she were seeing it for the first time.

'Look at that, look at those enormous clouds coming towards us – it's for us, just for us. You were right, Lise, it feels great to reconnect with nature, and you know what? I think I'll stay a bit longer – I mean, once all this is over and done with . . . We could rent this house for the year – the hills, the woods, nobody comes here anyway. It's a good idea, right?'

Lise looked at him as if he were drunk or mad, or had suddenly been struck by a strange illness, and was now delirious. Franck sat down opposite her.

'Let me explain, Lise. The terms I'm getting them to sign mean I'll be free, free to make the films I want to make, a feature film every two years, with a guaranteed minimum budget of five million . . . And you know what, I want to make a film here . . . Yes. Here. The story? No idea, but I like the landscape; I want to use it . . . I'm sure this house has plenty of stories, we just need to look for them . . . And the ruins down there, the village that was abandoned overnight, I can tell it's full of stories, I can tell it's a goldmine . . .'

Lise held her cup of tea in front of her face; she didn't know what to say. She watched him get up and walk back to the house. He picked up his bag and walking boots from the doorway, put them on and pulled the laces tight. She could see him from where she was sitting. Then he walked over to the car and got some stapled sheets of paper out of the boot, holding up three A4 documents for her to see.

'I left them the contracts to read yesterday, but I'll take duplicates just in case; they probably got them all dirty last night. And I think it's going to rain before evening . . .'

'Oh, you can predict the weather now?'

'You'll see, Lise, you'll see. I feel as if I can identify with nature.'

He was so determined that Lise didn't want to disagree. She had always been able to tell how strong someone else's resolution was. And yet, when he came over to kiss her before he left, she couldn't help speaking her mind.

'Still, it's quite something to leave two boys outside for a whole night. You know, you're in danger of having—'

'Having what?'

'Well, I don't know, kidnapped them?'

'But, Lise, you saw what they wanted me to do! They wanted to bring me down!'

'Human beings speak to one another; we talk things over.'

'But they're not human beings, they're jackals; they're behaving like jackals, finding an injured animal and taking advantage of it, stealing my library so it'll be easier to get rid of me afterwards, taking twenty-five years of work away from me. All this just to get those bastards from Netflix! Can't you see, if we let them push us around, they'll use their millions to squeeze everyone else out. We had to face tycoons in the past, fat, sweaty American producers, but this is a thousand times worse. These are huge corporations attacking us. These digital giants are monsters, they're got no limits, and to top it off, they don't pay taxes.'

'But they're just two people, two kids!'

'Lise, I think I've got a problem with the new generation. We can't let them walk all over us, believe me, we can't . . .'

Franck went down the hill. The grass and soil were drier than ever. In some ways, Liem and Travis had been lucky; it could have rained last night and drenched them. For that matter, the fat cumulus clouds were still getting bigger, moving slowly for the moment but heralding what was to come: those angry black clouds that grow as the air warms up and often culminate in a thunderstorm.

He had no trouble finding his way, using the sun and the paths he had taken before, and above all trusting a sort of instinct that was leading him back to the dog. He tackled the two hills with an ease that surprised even him. He wasn't out of breath like last time; he was already acclimatising and his body was getting stronger.

When he got to the top of the third hill, he stood on a spur and looked out over the *igue*. He could make out the metal of the cage among the trees, right at the bottom. The clouds had moved closer so the sun was no longer glinting off the steel; the storm was on its way. There was a dull rumbling in the distance, like muffled cannon shots, as if the far-off sky were a battlefield. It must have been beating down on the Massif Central in the east, and Franck knew the thunder and hail would be heading towards them. He couldn't leave Liem and Travis in the cage; it was dangerous. Unless he used the fury of the elements to panic them even more, to frighten them and make them realise that lightning would strike if they didn't sign, attracted by the metal bars . . .

Franck knew the dog would become restless when he saw him, staying where he was but showing how pleased he was to see him. Liem and Travis would undoubtedly be sitting in the centre of the cage. They would be waiting, stubborn and upset. Franck carried on going down, the view of the bottom of the *igue* through the branches becoming clearer. He could see the interior of the cage and the barrels knocked to the ground, but he couldn't see the men or the dog, and, even more strangely, he couldn't hear a sound. He tore down the slope at top speed, panicking at the thought they might have got away. Yet how could they have got out of the cage, let alone have lost the dog, and where could they go?

But they had managed it. The door hadn't been forced or even opened, and the ropes were still secure and tightly knotted, so they must have escaped by hauling themselves four metres to the top of the cage. There was no one and nothing there any more. Apart from the contracts, which had been thrown on the ground, three bundles of paper, still not signed. Franck picked them up and stuffed them in his pocket.

Then he called the dog; he whistled; he made his name echo off the sides of the great limestone crater.

'Alpha . . . Alpha . . .! Al-pha . . .!'

He was seized by a feeling of total powerlessness that made his legs buckle. He sat down on a tree trunk and scratched his head, massaging it with his hands. Finding the hunters' business card was the only thing he could think of: 'Tracking injured quarry, battues, finding lost dogs,' it read.

But he needed to climb all the way back to the top to get a signal; the hunters had told him there was some reception up towards the east, the same direction the storm was coming from. He set out on the path the hunters had come down the other day in their 4×4.

The thunder was becoming more and more insistent, rumbling closer and closer. The slope wasn't as steep on this side, but it was long, and he walked for a long time. The rain began to fall harder and harder. He was worn out. He still couldn't get a signal. He felt as if he really was sinking into the wild countryside, plunging so deep into it that he would never be able to get out, unless perhaps the trees were closing in on him. The eastern side was higher up than the others. When he got to the top of the *igue*, the horizon opened out in front of him and he could see all the way to the Mounts of Cantal. The clouds were no longer white and fluffy but black, and heavy with mineral dust. The torrent rushed towards him; there was a howling wind and pouring rain. Franck got his phone out of his bag. He had one bar; one miraculous bar probably brought back to life by the electric fields. He rang the number and the man on the other end picked up immediately.

'Yes?'

'I . . . I need you.'

'Who is it?'

'It's me. You gave me your card the other day, for tracking.'

'You've lost the dog?'

'Yes, but it's not just the dog.'

'Oh really? What are you hunting?'

'Look, can you meet me at the top of the *igue* straight away?'

'All right.'

He hung up and the rain got even heavier. It quickly turned into hail, which pelted the trees so hard it sounded like machine-gun fire. At that point he panicked. Everything was catching up with him at once: fear, the thunderstorm, his anger at the bastards' escape, and worry that something might have happened to the dog.

The men offered him a rag when they arrived, a kind of old tea towel, and Franck dried himself with the dubious cloth. He was drenched. There were two cages on the back of the pickup with the two big dogs inside. They were the ones he had seen the other day, but now they were twisting and turning, either excited by the prospect of the mission or on edge because of the storm.

'Right, what are you looking for?'

'Men. Two of them.'

Maurice and Julien looked at each other, suspicious and disbelieving.

'Sorry, we don't do that kind of thing.'

'Oh, come on, we've all got our little schemes; you've got yours with the cage, and I've got mine. You think yours are more noble than mine?'

'Do you have a piece of clothing?'

'What kind of clothing?'

'Something that belongs to them, something with their scent, so the dogs can track them.'

Franck didn't have even a handkerchief or a sock. Then he

thought of the contracts. He got out the copies he had left with them yesterday.

'Take these. I'm sure their fingers will have been all over them. They held them; probably even sweated on them . . .'

'That'll work.'

July 1915

When Joséphine left the village La Bûche could not stand the thought of her living up there. Not just because he was attracted to her, but because he used to spy on her every summer. He would quite openly watch her when she went to bathe on her own in the river or the Lauzès pond. Everyone knew what La Bûche was like, that he enjoyed eyeing up women, but everyone took a benevolent view and did not want to believe that he meant any harm. Women did not like to be stared at and he ogled them for pleasure, but people found it sad rather than dangerous. He was not only the blacksmith but also the farrier. As was often the case when faced with bad behaviour, people in the village said that he would not hurt a fly, although, like everyone, he killed flies.

No one took La Bûche's behaviour seriously – he was single and jealous, that was all. For La Bûche, not having the doctor's wife to look at was worse than being rejected. And he did not need to go up to the meadows to know that the lion tamer was in love with Joséphine. And he was sure they made love. They must have felt free to do what they liked in the hills in the beautiful weather; they must spend hours having each other and touching each other. They were together now for ever and that idea drove La Bûche mad. It was the war that had made it possible for them to love each other and it was the war that provided them with protection. Without the war they would never have found each other; their love would never have existed.

This disgusted La Bûche. Especially as he had a status to defend. He had always been regarded by everyone in the village as the strong

331

man. He was basically a farrier and on top of that a blacksmith; he was a force of nature, a force to be reckoned with, because, first of all, he was constantly near fire, and his forge, which belched out steam all the time, and also because blacksmiths spend their days swinging their heavy hammers. In normal times, the monstrous clanging of hammer on anvil could be heard from one end of the village to the other. But since the animals had been sent to war and there was no more coal, La Bûche no longer fired up the forge or produced anything. He was reduced to repairing tools all over the area, because many were breaking, 'because the women don't know how to use them,' he said – everything was the women's fault. More than ever he had the arrogance of those men who think they're above everything, better than other men, and, obviously, better than women. Since the men had gone off to war, he considered himself the only proper man in the village; but the lion tamer challenged that position, and his arrival had immediately annoyed La Bûche.

Rivalry between men will never end, even when there are only two men left on earth. Now that La Bûche knew that the doctor would not be returning, he felt that it was his job to protect Joséphine. He thought he had rights over her. He was deluded enough to think that she desired him, that all she wanted was him. Every evening he made a tour of the village, casting a suspicious eye up at the mountain in the fading light. He could not hear the lions – because of his years hammering against his anvil, he was completely deaf in his right ear. But there was nothing wrong with his sight and it seemed to him that this evening the mountain was more prominent than ever, that its shadow was more dominant than usual; he felt as if it were coming down on him like the prow of a sinking ship. There was a feverish atmosphere this evening; dusk formed the sky into an alcove where everything seemed sensual. That evening he felt it: Joséphine was in the arms of the other man; they were making love at this very moment in the black skies above him. Yes, at that very moment they were up there, the two of them, entwined in the darkness, making love in the vicinity of the lions, and it had to stop! It was this evening that he would have to surprise them, this evening he would punish them. So he waited until everyone had gone to bed, and all the candles had been blown out, before leaving the village and going up the mountain by the rough path.

He walked with the aid of a pitchfork that he held the wrong way round, using the handle like a walking stick, knowing that once he got up there, he would have quite another use for the implement. He would use it to push back the lions and tigers should they try to get near him. He was sure he would be able to hold them off if they came at him when he opened the cages. Because that was what he intended to do. While the lovers were sleeping or making love on the first floor of the house, he would unlock the cages so that the wild cats escaped. Once free, the famished beasts would rush at the house and throw themselves at the lovers to devour them. Or they would scatter into the countryside and wake everyone up, spreading panic all over the region. Then there would be widespread and long-lasting fear because no one would know how to hunt lions. The lion tamer would be held responsible for the fear and carnage. One way or another, he would make the lion tamer disappear. Either he would end up eaten by his own beasts this evening or he would be hounded out tomorrow as the scourge of the region. Either way, he would be gone.

But once he opened the cages nothing went as planned. La Bûche tried to haul himself on top of the bars and push the lions out so that they would go to the house, but they did not move. The lions and tigers, astonished by their sudden freedom to choose wherever they wanted to go, did nothing. At first they just stayed where they were, not bothering to sniff the house or the road. They growled a bit, pretending to bite each other, opening their mouths wide and cuffing each other, either playfully or because they were arguing about what to do. La Bûche hoped that the noise would bring out the German and Joséphine, but neither appeared; it was as if they weren't there.

Then, without La Bûche understanding what was happening, he saw the wild cats raise their heads and sniff the air. They had picked up the slight wind which had just got up in the east, and the next minute they slipped out of the cages as if they had been summoned, heading due east towards the meadows where the ewes were.

August 2017

Deer have rapid heartbeats, which means they can run off and escape in just a few leaps, but they get worn out if they have to run for a long time. Just as lions weighing two hundred and fifty kilos can run at over eighty kilometres an hour, yet only for short distances. There is great variation among human beings: some people can run for miles, while others are exhausted after the slightest exertion. None of them have any chance of catching up with a dog, because dogs never stop running.

The Rhodesian ridgeback and the Hanover hound were racing ahead of the Land Rover, and you could see the sheen of their coats through the dirty windscreen. They were leading the way, relentlessly following the trail. And yet twenty minutes later they still hadn't found Liem and Travis, nor had they managed to trace Alpha.

'They must have walked fast, your two. It's hard in this rain, but they've managed it . . .'

Franck said nothing. The three of them were squashed into the front seats. A vague sense of guilt came over him. Now that he was involved in a manhunt, he was taking stock of what he had done and the situation he had put himself in, especially as the strangers driving him were now witnesses, and perhaps even accomplices, in what amounted to false imprisonment.

He was comforted by the fact that the poachers had no qualms about what they were doing and were going about the hunt as if it were completely normal. They didn't even have to play along. As accomplished hunters, they were happy to track game that had got away as they always did, except that, this time, they couldn't possibly finish the animal off at the end of the chase, let alone shoot it. They just needed to track it down and bring it back. It seemed simple to them, normal even, but Franck was worried stiff and remained silent. Julien was at the wheel, doing his best not to lose the dogs, which were speeding along the rutted paths. The driving rain was too much for the old windscreen wipers, which were struggling to sweep it away. It was hard to see anything through the dirty windscreen.

'If the dogs don't find your guys in the next kilometre, I reckon they'll have gone towards Crégols,' said Julien, keeping his hands firmly on the wheel to stop the car jolting too much. 'But if they go that way, they're going to come a cropper.'

'What?'

'The cliff,' replied Maurice, never one to talk much.

'Which cliff?'

'The cliff of one hundred sheep,' Julien explained. 'A steep hillside over a hundred metres high, above the river. They'll be trapped because it's a dead end. And they definitely won't be able to jump over it.'

They could make out some sort of bulky shape in the distance through the misty windscreen, something wide, dark and glistening, a strange creature that the dogs stopped to sniff. As well as the rain, condensation kept forming on the dirty window.

'What the hell is that?'

Franck couldn't work it out at first, but the two men quickly realised that the enormous conical form standing in the middle of the track, the sinister phantom, was simply a penitent wearing a raincape that covered him from head to toe and puffed up with each gust of wind. He was leading a mule that was also wrapped in a flapping tarpaulin.

'Don't worry, it's a pilgrim . . . Perfect timing, actually.'

They stopped the car. Julien rolled down the window to talk to the man.

'Well, St Christopher, are you lost?'

The two men enjoyed their sarcasm; they probably thought the idea of taking a mule from Conques to Santiago de Compostela was ridiculous.

The man looked out from under his dripping hood. He clearly knew where he was going, indicating a map in a clear plastic bag, a map that was now soaked. The dogs were still sniffing him as if making sure their prey wasn't hiding under the tarpaulin.

'Tell me, pilgrim, did you by any chance see two guys and a dog this morning?'

'No, I haven't seen anyone since yesterday.'

'Did you walk along the cliff?'

'No . . . Actually, I'm keeping away from it.'

Julien whistled to call the dogs back, waved at the man and started the truck again. Franck turned around to look at the odd pairing of mule and pilgrim, dripping wet underneath all the plastic.

'Idiots. If they didn't follow the Grande Randonnée, they'll be heading straight for the cliff.'

'So?'

'So, we have to track them down before they jump,' Maurice blurted out. 'No, I'm joking.'

Franck was finding it harder and harder to hide his unease in the company of these two determined, methodical men, especially since they had started asking questions.

'Are you chasing them for those contracts?'

'Partly, yes.'

'You wanted them to sign them, is that it?'

'Yes.'

Franck had only been on safari once, a photographic safari in Kenya at that, a picnic compared to hunting two men in the rain with blood-tracking dogs following their trail. He had produced this kind of scene several times in films, but now he was part of a real manhunt. He focused on Alpha. After all, he wanted to find Alpha too.

'And the dog? Why do you think he left?'

'Your dog is doing his job; he's following them. I bet you we'll see him before them.'

'I don't understand – he should've held them back when they got out of the cage; he should've . . . I don't know, attacked them.'

'You mean you wanted him to harm them!'

'No, just keep them there.'

'If you didn't give him the order to attack them, he wouldn't do it. He wouldn't do it of his own accord.'

Franck tried to stoke up his feelings of hatred by concentrating on his two bastard colleagues taking advantage of his rough patch to hand his library over to Netflix or Amazon. At least by cornering them with three dogs and two guns, he would give them a taste of the violence that had made them all their money – the stupid, ultraviolent games in which the aim was always to kill as many targets as possible, to shoot anything that moved in order to gain points. When he saw them again, he would throw it in their faces: 'So, guys, you're obsessed with violence – war games, hunting games, the hyper-realist gameplays that made your reputation and made you a living . . . Well, here you go, you're right inside one now. Not so funny when it's for real, eh?'

The track got narrower, turning into little more than a footpath between two drystone walls. And then Alpha appeared, standing right in the middle of the path in the rain. The other dogs caught up with him, sniffed him and then returned to their quest, while Alpha stayed where he was, watching the 4×4 come towards him as if he had been waiting for it.

Julien cut the engine and went out into the pouring rain. He whistled twice. Franck got out too and Alpha rushed towards him, head lowered, and rubbed up against his legs.

'See, your dog's done his job. I'd better get mine back or they'll give your boys a bit of a fright.'

Julien whistled again and the two dogs turned around, their coats drenched and their faces grim. It was now a mixture of rain and hail that hammered down on the truck.

Julien and Franck got back in the Land Rover. Suddenly, the sound of hailstones pummelling metal was all you could hear. Maurice got out a pack of tobacco and rolled two cigarettes with his fat, dry fingers. He offered one to Franck, who declined.

'OK, so we're not going yet?'

'We'll wait for it to let up a bit, because it's gonna get heavy. Look at the dogs – you can tell it's going to get worse.'

Julien got the dogs to climb into the truck. They looked nervous and had their heads lowered, signs indicating an imminent storm The three dogs struggled to squeeze inside, two of them taking up the floor space by pressing themselves up against the men's legs, and Alpha sliding behind the seats, next to the guns.

'Anyway, don't stress. Your guys have got to be over there. See, there's a gap at the end that looks like a path, except there's nothing there but a kind of cave above a sheer drop. They must be sheltering there.'

'What if they get away?'

'They can't go right and they can't go left. This is their only way out, unless they jump . . . But hurl themselves a hundred metres into the water? They won't do it.'

The poachers drew on their fat cigarettes, coughing up dirty brown smoke that hung in the air like a cloud. Franck sat between them, and he asked Julien to open the window a little, but a shower of rain came flying in. Then the clouds following the river got even darker, shot through with lightning. The three of them watched the spectacle, spellbound and fatalistic, at the mercy of the elements, while the dogs looked like they were trying to disappear into the ground.

'You know the house you're renting . . . Well, you're kind of repeating the story.'

'What story?'

'The hundred sheep.'

'What do you mean?'

'An animal tamer lived there once, a real one, with lions. I mean a hundred years ago. Ask Maurice – the shepherdess was sort of related to his great-grandmother.'

And then Maurice, who never said a word, probably inspired by the raging skies, told him about how his great-grandfather, the one with the lions, had gone to meet the shepherdess one evening. She lived in a hut at the end of the fields on the left, at the top of the meadows. It was during the war and nobody knew about them, except one man in the village. One jealous man.

July 1915

Heads forward, ears flattened, the lions and tigers followed the path through the hills. They were tracking the scent of the lion tamer and the wonderful aroma of the far-off flock. For weeks now they had caught the whiff of fresh flesh, for weeks they had dreamed of hunting and stalking the ewes. Tonight they were – running into the wind straight to the ewes. They knew their prey was too far away and the wind was blowing in the wrong direction for the ewes to sense that the lions and tigers were approaching. But still, they moved stealthily, without either crouching down or creeping along and sped up to cross exposed parts of the route. But once the ewes were in sight, they started to run. They had never run as fast before. Born into captivity, they had no experience of stampeding or stalking prey. They were guided instead by instinct towards the flock on the pasture.

The eight wild cats stayed together. Théo led the way and the others followed him in single file through the velvety night. La Bûche remained near the house, panicking at the thought that the big cats were roaming free. He didn't know whether they were still nearby, right by the house or whether they were by now far away. He dared not stir, seeing movement in every bush, terrified that at any moment a giant beast ready to eat him would spring out. He trembled at the thought. He didn't even have the guts to return to the village, fearing he would be pounced on by the pack. Although the lions were streaming towards the meadows.

It was their first experience of freedom and they were determined to enjoy a glorious hunt; from now on there would be no more cages for them, no more war, nothing except the sea of ewes whose scent was growing stronger the closer they went.

Wolfgang and Joséphine were lying on the bed, naked in their peaceful world. When she saw the red terracotta pot under the sink Joséphine was once more struck by the sourness of human nature.

'Do you know the butcher in Limogne?'

'A little. At first he used to give me bones and offal, but now he sells everything for top prices, bones and even intestines . . .'

'You know, I think he was the one stealing the ewes and giving Le Simple money so that he wouldn't say anything. I haven't seen him, but I have the proof.'

'That doesn't surprise me. When food is short, men become more savage than animals. Lions don't kill each other to eat, but men will.'

They were silent after that, thinking it over. They lay beside each other in perfect harmony, escaping far from the world as their bodies touched. In the background there was the gentle jingling of the ewes' bells; this evening they were staying awake, nibbling on wild thyme and clover although they were no longer hungry. They were gathering their strength as most of them would lamb in the autumn. Joséphine could tell from the noises that they were widely dispersed; they would have to gather them together and lead them to the enclosure while there was still moonlight. How good the summer night felt.

Suddenly there was a commotion. It began with the bells starting to ring louder as if the ewes were running, as if they had suddenly decided to scamper off. Very quickly the noise swelled like a wave; now all the bells were ringing wildly at the necks of the galloping animals. In the midst of this curious noise, Wolfgang thought he recognised a roaring sound, and then he was certain of it. They both got up and went out to the front of the house. In the dim light of the waning moon they saw all the sheep careening directly east and bunching together. Wolfgang immediately understood what was happening and went back into the hut to get his rifle.

In a second their idyllic Eden had become the most terrifying nightmare. It was as if a bomb had gone off. Wolfgang knew that his eight wild animals were here ready to attack the ewes. He knew he had no choice but to kill the lions and tigers. If he did not, after decimating the ewes, they would go on down to the valley and start on the women, the men and maybe even the children. The eight agitated felines continued to push the ewes towards the cliff, ripping them open one by one as they passed, determined to kill the entire flock, like wolves and foxes drunk on death, and overcome by their own folly, starting to kill everything before eating it. So Wolfgang fired, which terrified the fleeing ewes even more and propelled them ever faster to the gully that led to the cliff.

The rain had eased off and the air was cool after the hail. In the end, the hunters had smoked three more cigarettes. Franck hadn't had a single one, yet his head was spinning from the smoke and the stories and he was in a daze, like a child giddy from too many bedtime stories. He was moved that he could finally put lives, if not faces, to the house. And if there are places that mould you, places that are associated with your childhood and shape you in their image, then there are others you discover later in life, when you're older, that change you. Franck could feel a common history linking him to two people he had only just discovered, two people he would never meet but who had lived within the same walls, two strangers whose first names and fates he now knew. He felt close to them for the simple reason that they had known the same landscapes as him and Lise, the same silences in the morning and evening, the same land. They were proof that when it comes down to it, peace is not possible in this world, and there is no such thing as a peaceful life. Half the sheep had thrown themselves off the cliff, Wolfgang had been forced to kill his lions, and the tigers had been lost. They must have been killed by other people, unless they were still on the run in the minds of some, as lost legends.

'There are even some people who say they went down to the village the next day and ate everyone, and that's why the village was burnt down. But that's all bullshit; I think it was the opposite. I think the farmers around here ate the beasts.'

'And the tamer? Did he stay here for the rest of the war?'

'Yes, they both stayed up there. They bred sheep to build up the flock again, and the tamer took apart the cage near his house and built one in the *igue*, the one that's still there now. He used to catch loads of deer and wild boar with it, and he fed the whole village until the war ended.'

'And then?'

'Then they went to America. He didn't have his beasts any more, so Wolfgang went to Barnum; the circuses there were spectacular. They had a daughter, Iris, and they always talked about this house as if it were, I don't know, paradise on earth. Joséphine sold her house in the village, and she used the money to buy the house on the hill and all the surrounding land, over a hundred and twenty hectares of it. They used to go there from time to time in the fifties, and their grandchildren sometimes spent summers there afterwards. Anyway, their descendants are scattered all over the world, and they've been letting the house go for the last twenty years. In fact, Iris is the one who wants people to stay there; otherwise it will fall into ruin. Now she's almost a hundred, and her children have decided to make some money from it.'

'And would they sell it?'

'Nobody would buy around here any more – it's too isolated.'

'Yes, but selling it would be good for all of them . . .'

'Why, do you want to buy it?'

The dogs had got out of the car a while ago and were watching the three men from the other side of the windscreen, pawing the ground as if waiting for action.

'Right, are we going to get them to sign your contracts?'

'No, I'll go on my own.'

'Whatever you want . . . But take the dogs.'

'All right.'

'If they get too aggressive, just say "stop" or "heel", but you have to be firm. They'll back off straight away.'

Franck got out of the car holding the three rolled-up copies of the contract, gripping them tightly like a stick. The restless dogs realised it was finally time to find the prey they had been tracking for two hours, the prey that was hiding just hundreds of metres from there. Franck set out on the path and the dogs went on ahead, staying close to him. The path was now more of a narrow gully between two walls, a corridor covered with box trees and small maple trees. As he walked along it, he thought about the sheep that had thrown themselves off a hundred years ago. He imagined that the dogs running ahead of him were wolves or lions, animals intent on hunting down their prey, and now he was just like them. He was the one filling two kids with terror. They came to a gap in the bushes and the two dogs stopped, while Alpha came back towards him, waiting for an order. Franck carried on, and he finally spotted them in the distance, walking towards him. They hadn't jumped; they looked worn out and were shivering; they were drenched, but mostly they were terrified of the two dogs that were coming towards them growling.

'Control your dogs, for God's sake!' they shouted at Franck.

They were at the end of their tether. Their phones must have got wet and they couldn't have had any battery left, yet they were holding them like kids who wouldn't let go of their security blankets.

Alpha turned and stared at Franck. He decided there was enough hatred in his eyes and charged at Liem and Travis, clearly prepared to catch them like hares. The other dogs followed his lead and they all rushed at the two men.

'Stop . . . Stop!'

Franck ran in front of the dogs to restrain them but they wouldn't stop; they wanted a fight and carried on barking as if they had just cornered a wild boar. They believed they had to keep their quarry at bay until they heard shots or the blows of the hunting spear. But all they could see was Franck, waving the contracts at his two partners.

'OK, OK, calm down. We'll sign, we'll sign . . .'

'You've read it?'

'Yes! We'll sign, we'll sign, no problem . . .'

'Really? Just like that, you're going to sign because three dogs are threatening you? I can't believe that you can bear to admit that *animals* have got the better of you.'

The dogs were barking aggressively, getting as close to Liem and Travis as possible, looking as if they couldn't control themselves any longer and were determined to bite.

'Hold your dogs back, damn it!'

'Remember your dirty scheme to trap me? Well, now you're the ones who are trapped!'

'OK, if that's what you think, but call your dogs off!'

Franck ordered the dogs to stop barking with a click of his fingers. Strangely enough they sat down, still twisting and squirming, but sitting down. Franck unrolled the contracts, smoothed them down, and then he paused. Instead of giving them to his partners, he held them to his chest and ripped them up.

Liem and Travis watched him, stunned, then immediately began to panic again.

'What are you doing?'

'It's fine. I've seen what I wanted to see.'

'Seen what?'

'Fear. I wanted to see it in your faces. I wanted to see that imploring look in your Bambi eyes when you saw the wild animals, and now I've seen it, I'm happy. You guys can go to war, you can fight with your banks, with Netflix and whoever else. Go for it, but I'm warning you, once you start a fight it will never end, especially when you don't know the rules. It never ends.'

'You're the one who'll be in trouble.'

'Why? Are you going to bring charges? If you do that, I'll destroy you; I'll destroy you in front of the whole industry, directors, actors, co-producers – I know all of them. The film industry is still run by human beings, something you haven't quite figured out.'

'So what do you want then?'

'I want you to stay away from me.'

'Come on, Franck, you didn't need to do all this just for that. We could have talked.'

'I know what you were trying to do.'

'No, I promise you, you didn't.'

'You want me out of the picture. You wanted to be free to make your precious series and your precious *content*, and now you can. I'm going, I'm out of the picture. You can have the film rights and I'll take the money.'

'Are you serious, Franck? Come on, don't talk crap, we need you. We've never really done film production; we don't know anything.'

'Look me in the eye and tell me it's not the rights you're after.'

He could tell they no longer had the guts to lie.

'So?'

'Yes,' said Liem, finally. 'The library is important; it might even be a deciding factor.'

'In the last contract, weren't you trying to make me artistic adviser or something?'

'Basically.'

'Well, fine, that's OK with me. As long as I can make a feature film every two years, and the whole company is at my disposal whenever I need it. I couldn't work with you guys anyway. I don't want to be part of an eternal power struggle – because that's what you guys enjoy, that's what you're expecting. It might seem like the power balance has been forgotten but it always crops up, between three partners, between a boss and his employees, even between two stakeholders. Rivalry is the lifeblood that spurs us on; every achievement comes from some conflict or competition, but competition is brutal. And I don't want that any more. I just want to take a step back, get some distance. And I think I've found the perfect place.'

EPILOGUE

The dogs had tracked down their prey and forced it out of hiding, like the good hunters they were. Then the poachers took the quarry back to the house on Mont d'Orcières, where Liem and Travis got cleaned up. After that Franck took them to the station. Lise was not surprised when he came back and reiterated his idea of settling and working here, living at a slower pace. Though it is impossible to live away from everyone and everything, since there is no place in the world where you can be truly isolated, there are at least some oases of calm amid the commotion.

Alpha was not certain he had accomplished what was expected of him. Humans could be difficult to read. Sometimes they hunted in packs, but sometimes they turned against one another, just like wolves and lions. There was something inside Alpha that set him apart from his ancestor, the wolf, and that was his need to rely on a being whom he did not so much serve as support, and from whom in return he received a kind of assurance, a shelter, a bowl always filled with fresh water, and an understanding that was not far off friendship. But what he did retain from his ancestors was the knowledge that he must not go into houses. So Alpha stayed outside all night. He slept in front of the house, near the door, quiet but with one ear pricked, as if he wanted to provide a sort of peace of mind. As if promising himself to watch over them like a faithful ally, without even knowing that the very next day they would finally decide to call him Bambi.